JAYNE ANN KRENTZ

Midnight Jewels

WARNER BOOKS

A Time Warner Company

WARNER BOOKS EDITION

Cover design by Diane Luger
Cover photograph by Alexa Garbarino

Warner Books, Inc.
1271 Avenue of the Americas
New York, NY 10020

Visit our Web site at
http://warnerbooks.com

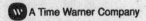 A Time Warner Company

Printed in the United States of America

First Printing: November, 1987
Reissued: August, 1992

15   14

THE QUALITIES THAT MAKE
JAYNE ANN KRENTZ A BESTSELLING
AUTHOR ... MAKE HER ROMANCES
UNIQUE, IRRESISTIBLE AND JUST
PLAIN WONDERFUL TO READ

Midnight Jewels

"FIVE STARS! Like all of the best novelists, Jayne
Ann Krentz slowly reveals layers of characterization
blended with the finest details of suspense to turn
Croft and Mercy into a heroic couple
par excellence."
—*Affaire de Coeur*

"THIS PRICELESS GEM OF A BOOK will be a
lasting treasure to be enjoyed over and over
again. . . . No other author writes with such
complete symmetry of plot and characterization.
Every detail, every phase is exquisitely orchestrated
to produce an incredible harmony that reverberates
in the soul as it sets ablaze a fierce sensuality to
scorch the heart of every reader."
—*Romantic Times*

"A GREAT AUTHOR!"
—*West Coast Review of Books*

Also by Jayne Ann Krentz

Sweet Starfire
Crystal Flame
A Coral Kiss

Chapter
ONE

The advertisement on the last page of the bookseller's catalog was small and discreet. Only a knowledgeable collector of rare books would know that the volume offered for sale was a unique example of eighteenth century erotica.

FOR SALE: Burleigh's Valley of Secret Jewels. *First edition, 1795. Plates. Exc. cond. Contact Mercy Pennington, Pennington's Second Chance Bookshop, Ignatius Cove, Washington. (206) 555-1297.*

Croft Falconer had already spent a great deal of time studying those tiny four lines but he read the ad once more as if he might somehow find a clue to the remarkable fact of the book's appearance after so many years.

Croft ignored the phone number offered. He didn't have a phone at his house on the coast, just as he didn't have a television, radio or microwave. And, while he could have driven into town to use a pay phone, he knew that effort would be futile.

He would have to see the book himself to be sure if it was the right one and he wanted to see this Mercy Pennington in person. He had to find out who she was, how much she knew and how she had acquired the volume.

The only thing he was certain of at this point was the most disturbing fact of all: The book should not exist.

Valley should have been destroyed along with everything else in the fire that had swept through Egan Graves' island fortress three years before. Croft had witnessed that fire firsthand. He had felt its hellish heat, seen the all-consuming flames and heard the shattering screams of its victims.

How could something that should have been eaten by those flames resurface in an insignificant bookseller's catalog? The existence of the book opened a gaping hole in a case Croft thought he had closed for all time. If the book had survived the fire, then Croft had to face another possibility: Its owner, Egan Graves, might have also escaped and survived.

And that meant Croft had failed.

The ad for *Valley* raised questions that had to be answered. It indicated a trail that had to be followed.

And that trail began with a Miss Mercy Pennington of Ignatius Cove, Washington.

Croft gazed at the dawn-lit Pacific outside his study window and wondered about Miss Mercy Pennington. Before he could come to any conclusions the Rottweiler whined softly behind him. Croft glanced at the heavily built dog. The animal gazed back expectantly.

"You're right, it's time to run," Croft said. "Let's go down to the beach. It's a cinch I'm not going to get any meditation done this morning."

The dog silently accepted the response and padded to the door.

If anyone were to ask him about his affinity for the Rottweiler, Croft would have said simply that he was one of those people who got along well with dogs. In truth, he had much in common with the creature who paced at his heels. The ancient, wild, hunting instincts still ran in the veins of the Rottweiler, even though the animal generally behaved with the good manners acceptable to the civilized world. But under the right provocation, the facade of politeness in both man and dog could vanish in an instant, leaving bare the predator underneath.

Croft slid aside the shoji screen panel and stepped out into the hall. The room on the opposite side of the tiled corridor beckoned. He looked into it, feeling the pull of its stark simplicity. The bleached wood floor, the woven mat and the elegantly austere flower arrangement in the low black ceramic bowl all promised a haven. Croft's period of quiet morning contemplation was as much a part of his daily life as running and the demanding workouts that kept his exceptional martial arts skills well honed.

Croft's rituals were important to him. All of them, from his morning meditation to the cup of perfectly brewed tea he would enjoy later, were part and parcel of his carefully organized, neatly self-contained world. He did not like to forego even the slightest of his chosen routines.

But he had little hope this morning of stilling his mind to the point where he could slip into a meditative trance. Too many questions were swirling in his head; too many dangerous possibilities were materializing.

The morning run would have to do, he decided. He went out through the back door of his beach front cottage, the Rottweiler at his heels.

Croft was wearing only a pair of jeans, and if there had been a woman watching she would have found the subtle shift and glide of his shoulder muscles fascinating. A healthy, trained and controlled power radiated from the man.

But there was no one to see the easy masculine grace with which Croft moved. Croft had never brought a woman to his isolated home on the Oregon coast.

Five minutes later man and dog were loping easily across the glistening sand at the water's edge. The light and energy of a new day filled the air and Croft and the dog drank in the essence of both as they covered the ground toward the distant point of land at the end of the beach.

As his body fell into a strong, easy rhythm, Croft found his mind wandering to the one totally unknown and unpredictable piece in this new puzzle—Miss Mercy Pennington.

Mercy eyed the huge stack of romance novels and mysteries that had just been plunked down on the counter near the cash register. She tried to keep all hint of mercenary satisfaction out of her eyes as she smiled at the woman on the other side of the counter. Christina Seaton was an excellent customer. She could be counted on for a minimum purchase of twenty paperbacks a month. Mercy experienced a pleasant tingle of anticipation whenever Christina came through the door of Pennington's Second Chance. She told herself that only another small business person could fully understand the nature of her fondness for this particular client.

"Will that be all today, Christina?"

Christina grinned. At thirty she was a couple of years older than Mercy and had a freshly scrubbed attractiveness that perfectly suited her designer jeans, loose knit sweater and expensive loafers. "Are you kidding? My kids will have to go without shoes this month as it is."

Mercy laughed. Very few children in Ignatius Cove were in danger of going without shoes or anything else their little hearts desired. The small town north of Seattle was an enclave of prosperous, upwardly mobile types, most of whom worked in the city but preferred to raise their families in a small town environment. Ignatius Cove had the best of both worlds. They were close enough to Seattle to enjoy its urban benefits, but they had all the fun and advantages of living in a self-consciously quaint village at the water's edge.

Mercy had been well aware of the distinctive qualities of Ignatius Cove from the moment she had discovered it. When she had begun searching for a place to open a bookstore two years before she had known exactly what she wanted: a community of the affluent and educated, potential book buyers who had the cash to indulge their interests. Ignatius Cove fit the bill perfectly.

Mercy didn't attempt to compete head on with the one other bookstore in town which specialized in newly released hardcover bestsellers and art books. Instead, she had gone for the thriving secondhand market, supplementing her large, well organized stock with popular, new paperback releases.

The mix had proven satisfyingly profitable. By the end of the first year Pennington's Second Chance had earned enough to ensure its survival. By the end of the second year of business, the shop was well established with a solid customer base. Mercy measured her success by the fact that she was now removing the corks instead of unscrewing the caps of the wine bottles she opened at home.

"Dorrie says you're finally going to take a vacation next week," Christina observed as Mercy rang up her purchases. "It's about time."

Mercy smiled and her slightly tilted green eyes lit with pleasure. Automatically she lifted a hand to push an errant tendril of golden brown hair back behind her ear. "Part business and part vacation. I'm very excited about it. I came across an interesting old book in a box of junk I bought at the flea market last month. Turned out it had some value. I advertised it in a little antiquarian booksellers' catalog and within a few days a man in Colorado phoned to say he wanted to buy it. I'm going to deliver it to him next week while I'm on vacation."

"You're going to take it to Colorado yourself? Isn't that service above and beyond the call of duty? Why can't you just mail it to the man?"

"He wants it hand delivered. He told me he doesn't trust the mail and this book is very important to his collection. He's been looking for it for some time, I gather. At any rate, he considers my trip expenses to Denver part of the purchase price of the book. He says he prefers not to travel."

"He's paying your way?"

Mercy nodded as she finished totalling the sale. "He said I was to fly first class, but of course I won't. He's being generous enough as it is. I'll fly to Denver and rent a car to drive to his place in the mountains. I get the feeling it's quite a remote location. He's invited me to stay at his place for a couple of days. After that I'll take a leisurely trip through the Rockies and end up back in Denver. I'll fly home from there."

"Hmm. This sounds interesting. Young or old?"

"Who?"

"Your customer," Christina said impatiently. "Is he young or old?"

"Oh." Mercy wrinkled her nose slightly, thinking. "To tell you the truth, I'm not sure. He sounds very charming on the phone. Has a great voice. Cultured, if you know what I mean, but I can't tell how old he is for certain. Maybe somewhere in his forties."

"A little old for you, but not too far beyond the realm of possibility. A woman has to be flexible these days."

Mercy smiled. "Whatever his age, he's definitely not too old to spend a fortune on a book. He had the money wired into my account yesterday."

Christina burst out laughing. "You're too young to let money replace romance in your life."

"Don't you believe it. Running a small business ages a person in a hurry. The money he paid for *Valley* is going to pay the rent on this shop for several months. What's more, he hinted he might be talked into throwing in a couple of books from his private collection as part of the purchase price. I could turn around and advertise them the same way I did the first one. I'd actually be dealing for real in antiquarian books. That's the classy end of the used book business."

"I can see it now." Christina narrowed her eyes as if seeing a glowing sign in the distance. "Mercy Pennington, dealer in rare books."

"Has a nice ring to it, doesn't it?" Mercy acknowledged happily. "First editions, private printings, beautiful eighteenth century bindings, copper plate illustrations. Definitely high class."

"Does that mean I'll have to start shopping somewhere else for my romances and mysteries?"

Mercy laughed. "Not for quite a while. It takes a great deal of money and a lot of time to get into the rare book business in a big way. Even if everything goes well with the sale of this book I found I'm going to be selling paperbacks for a long time to come. The rare book business will be a sideline. For a lot of dealers it never gets beyond that point."

"Well, good luck to you. And enjoy the trip to Colorado. Is Dorrie going to handle the shop for you while you're gone?"

Mercy nodded. "I think she's looking forward to being in charge for a full week. I've never left her alone here for longer than a couple of hours." Actually, that was an understatement. Dorrie Jeffers was positively elated at the prospect of running Pennington's Second Chance by herself. After several months of part-time work, she was eager for the opportunity.

"That's exactly why you need this vacation. You treat this place as if it were your first born. You're much too devoted to it. You need to get away from it for a while." Christina took the paper sack full of books from the counter and turned to leave. "Have a great trip and drive carefully. Those roads in the Rockies are something else."

"I'll be careful."

"And take a good look at your customer. Do yourself a favor. Try to see him as something more than a means of launching your new career in the rare book business. You never know. He might be a sexy recluse just waiting for the right woman to come along and take him out of the mountains."

"Somehow I doubt that. Why are you always so eager to see me married, Christina? Haven't you been reading those studies that show that single women are happier than married women?"

Christina grinned. "Us married types can't stand to see you single types so happy and prosperous and independent. Ruins the image of marriage. Besides, misery loves company. Take care, Mercy. I'll see you when you get back." When she opened the door the little bell overhead tinkled merrily.

Mercy waited until the bell was silent and then walked around the counter to finish straightening some shelves at the back of the shop. The place was empty and it was almost time to close for the day. She started thinking about dinner.

There was a package of buckwheat pasta in the cupboard at home. And she was almost certain there was still some pesto sauce in the freezer. There was also a bottle of zinfandel resting in the wire wine rack in the corner of her kitchen. The long summer evening stretched out before her and it was, after all, Friday. Friday was always deserving of some sort of celebration, even though she would be opening the shop again the next morning. Six-day work weeks were normal for small business entrepreneurs. After two years of working them, Mercy was accustomed to the hours.

When she left for Colorado on Monday morning she would be taking her first real vacation in two years.

Not everyone would count the trip as a vacation, Mercy reflected wryly. After all, it was definitely a business venture. But she was as excited as if she were about to embark on a cruise. The sale of *Valley of Secret Jewels* was a milestone in her new career as a bookseller. A whole new world was opening up to her. If she played her cards right, she would actually be entering the rarified atmosphere of antiquarian book dealership. Ignatius Cove had been good to her.

Life had changed a lot in the past two years, Mercy thought with satisfaction. Exactly two years earlier she had been learning how appalling her judgment in men was. She'd been busy canceling wedding plans and quitting her job in a public library. Now she was far more cautious with men, happily single and successfully established in a new career.

Mercy's thoughts returned again to dinner as she stretched on tiptoe to reach a book high on the shelf. Her fingers closed around the volume when she suddenly had the strange feeling that she was being watched. The sensation was unnerving, especially since the bell over the door had not rung as it was designed to when anyone entered the shop. She knew with a sudden, sure instinct that she was no longer alone. Mercy went very still.

"I'm looking for Mercy Pennington."

Mercy yelped and spun around. A man stood at the end of the long aisle of books. Her first impression was of darkness...unsettling, overwhelming darkness. Her shop had been invaded by a midnight phantom, a lean, somber ghost with hair the color of a raven's wing. He wore black chino trousers, low cut black boots and a black twill shirt that was open at the throat. Even the sound of his voice

invoked the night and all its mysteries. The echo of her own
name was as deep and dark as the bottom of the sea.

Only his eyes offered a sense of light. They were a
strange shade of hazel set in a bronzed face. The intelligence
in his gaze was coupled with a strangely detached quality
that was disturbing. Mercy looked into his eyes and wondered how any man could achieve such a degree of deep,
remote calm.

She wondered what it would take to put ripples into the
quiet seas of such eyes. Some primitive, feminine part of her
longed to discover the secret. For a tempting instant Mercy
found herself wanting to slap the man or kiss him to see if
she could jar that remote expression.

Mercy was shocked when she realized that her reaction
was a direct response to her attraction to this stranger, which
had sprung into life without any warning. Never in her life
had she met a man who had instantly awakened such a violent sense of awareness within her. The feeling was so strong
and unsettling she clutched the nearest shelf for support.

She imagined he must be in his mid-thirties, perhaps
older. His face was fierce angles and planes; high cheekbones, a rock hard jaw, an arrogant nose. No softness anywhere. But he stood in front of her with a poised, almost
erotic grace that seemed to assault her senses.

His mouth was a firm, unyielding line. That mouth should
have promised a total lack of emotion, but for some reason
Mercy got just the opposite impression. She saw the potential for emotion there, saw too that it was under a rigid self-
control. The problem was she couldn't begin to tell if it was
passion or violence that lurked beneath the surface of his
cooly set mouth.

Any emotion this man chose to focus on a woman would
be overwhelming, Mercy thought. She shook off the paralyzing awareness.

"I'm Mercy Pennington. You startled me. I didn't hear

you come in." She took a firm grip on her shaken nerves. "The bell over the door must be broken."

The man glanced back toward the door. "It's not broken."

"But it always rings when the door opens."

He shrugged. "It didn't this time." He dismissed the matter completely. The mystery of the non-ringing bell was obviously not a mystery to him. "If you're Mercy Pennington, then you have a book for sale. I would like to examine it, and if it's the one I want I'll meet your price, whatever you're asking."

"A book?" Her mind went blank. Something about this man was totally disorienting. He was asking her about a book, but she had the oddest sensation they should be talking about far more personal, more important matters. A flickering feeling of communication went through her. It was as if she already knew him on some level, though she didn't even know his name. "I've got hundreds of books for sale."

"Burleigh's *Valley of Secret Jewels*. I've come a long way for it."

He made it sound as though he'd come from the outer reaches of Hades. "Oh, *that* book." Relieved that this whole thing was going to be over very quickly, Mercy rushed on with the news. "I'm sorry, I've already sold it." She smiled brightly. "It's unfortunate that you had to drive out of your way for nothing."

His hazel eyes narrowed. "When did you sell it?"

"A couple of days ago. A man in Colorado phoned and said he'd take it sight unseen."

"Has he picked it up yet?"

"Well, no, as a matter of fact, but—"

"I'll top his offer."

Mercy was nonplussed. "I couldn't sell it out from under him. That would be unethical. He's already paid me for *Valley* and I've promised to deliver it to him."

"You would find it . . . unethical to sell to a higher bidder?"

"That's right," Mercy said quickly, not liking the new, even more intense interest he was displaying. She sought for a way to break the strange spell that seemed to be engulfing her. "Now, if you'll excuse me, I have a few more things to do before I close this evening. It's already after five." She deliberately moved down the aisle toward him, hoping he would take the hint and get out of her way and leave the shop. The fact that she was alone with him was making her nervous.

This was not the sort of man one wanted to encounter in a dark bookshop aisle or a dark alley, Mercy decided firmly. But she had no sooner finished phrasing the silent warning to herself than her mind leaped to the image of a dark bedroom. Impatiently she brushed aside the evocative mental picture of meeting this man in such dangerous surroundings.

He didn't move as she moved bravely down the aisle. He stood at the end of the narrow corridor watching her. His stance was both relaxed and balanced. Somehow his very stillness was as alarming as anything else about him. Less than two paces away Mercy was forced to halt. Her hands tightened around a couple of books she had picked up to reshelve as she began to seriously wonder just how dangerous he was. Ingatius Cove had very little crime, but an isolated shopkeeper at the end of a working day was always a vulnerable target.

"I said, will you please excuse me?" She put as much force as possible into the superficially polite query. Somewhere she had read one had to be confident and controlled when dealing with situations such as this. There was always the hope that one could bluff one's way out of danger. She mustn't lose her nerve. "You're in my way."

"I would like to see the book."

"It's not here."

"Where is it?" he asked with a patience that was unnerving because there was absolutely no indication of how long it would last.

Mercy swallowed. "I've got it at home. I didn't want to take a chance on anything happening to it here. It's rather valuable."

He stared at her for a minute, his hazel eyes pinning her. Then he nodded once, apparently coming to a decision. "All right. I'll go to your place. How far is it?"

Mercy hesitated, trying to figure out the safest course of action. "Not far. Walking distance." Once they were out on the street she would have a chance of calling attention to her situation, if she indeed was in a situation. Outside there were cars and pedestrians and other shopkeepers closing up for the night. She would feel much safer. "If you care to wait outside, I'll just be a minute."

He nodded again, that single, economical movement of his head, and then turned, walked to the end of the aisle and disappeared.

Mercy stared after him, holding her breath as she waited for the bell to sound, indicating he had actually left the shop. She couldn't believe it was going to be this easy after all. The part of her that was convinced she was in jeopardy was still sending bursts of fight or flight signals through her nerves. But another part of her was perversely disappointed to see the stranger leave. She had never met a man who had such an instantaneous effect on her senses. It was a strangely beguiling, if perilous experience.

The bell didn't tinkle and she didn't hear the door open or close, but Mercy knew she was alone in the shop. Cautiously she walked to the end of the aisle and glanced out the window.

The dark stranger was out on the sidewalk, lounging easily against the fender of a black Porsche. His gaze was centered on the shop door as he waited for Mercy to emerge.

His brand of patience was that of a hunter waiting for its quarry.

Mercy sucked in her breath and set down the books she'd been holding. She darted toward the door, reaching for the dead bolt. Once she had him locked out she could either slip out the back way or call the police.

As if he had read her mind, the man moved, reaching the door before she did. The knob turned, the door slid open just far enough to admit the toe of his boot, and Mercy knew she had lost the short race. The bell overhead tinkled this time, which was absurdly reassuring for some reason. That shot of confidence united with the adrenaline in her blood to make Mercy abruptly angry.

"If you don't mind," she snapped, shoving the door against his foot, "this is my shop and I would like to lock up for the night. Get out of here."

He stared down at her assessingly. "You're afraid of me, aren't you?"

"Let's just say you aren't the sort of customer I like to encourage."

"It's all right, Mercy Pennington, you have nothing to fear from me. I just want to see the book. I won't hurt you."

Mercy opened her mouth to tell him that under the circumstances he could hardly expect her to believe that, but when she met his eyes the protest died in her throat.

For some groundless, totally illogical reason she *did* believe him. Somehow, she realized, she would know if she were truly in danger from him. The information would be there in his gleaming hazel eyes. At the moment she was safe. Mercy didn't know how she could be so certain of that, but she was. The strange sensation of having communicated with this man on a subliminal level went through her again, providing reassurance even as it raised odd questions.

Tense seconds ticked past as her gaze locked with his. Neither of them moved. There would be no harm in simply showing him her precious copy of *Valley*, Mercy thought suddenly. Her hand fell away from the door.

"I'll get my purse," she muttered and turned back toward the counter. He stepped out onto the sidewalk as she moved away from him. It was the lack of music from the bell rather than the sound of it that warned her he was gone again.

When she emerged onto the sidewalk a moment later and closed the door firmly behind her, the bell chimed as brightly as ever. Her unusual customer spoke as she turned the key in the lock.

"Doesn't that damn bell annoy you?"

She glanced at him in surprise. "It lets me know when someone's entering or leaving the shop. It's not an annoyance, it's a warning."

"I would find it a definite nuisance. It's unnecessary. The sound it makes isn't even very pleasing. And there are other ways of knowing someone's around."

She had known he was around even though the bell hadn't rung when he had entered the shop the first time, Mercy reflected. She frowned. Then she dropped her keys into her red leather shoulder bag, letting them jangle as she did so. The small action was deliberate. She just knew that he would never jangle a set of keys. They would slide silently into his pocket.

"What I would like to know," Mercy announced with a touch of aggression as she set a brisk pace down the street, "is why that bell didn't make any noise when you were entering or leaving."

"I told you," he said, moving silently along beside her, "I don't like the sound it makes."

Mercy glanced at him sharply but he wasn't paying any attention. He was examining the deliberately quaint, tree-lined, unmistakably prosperous street. Most of the boutiques and shops were closed for the day. The storefronts were elegantly rustic, the goods in the windows discreet and expensive. The few cars that were still parked at the curb tended to fall into the BMW-Volvo-Mercedes category. The people on the sidewalk were casually dressed in polo shirts with little animals embroidered on them, designer shorts and name brand sport shoes. They looked sleek and healthy.

"I don't believe we've been properly introduced," Mercy pointed out.

"My name is Croft Falconer."

"Where are you from, Mr. Falconer?"

"Call me Croft or Falconer if you prefer, but skip the mister. I'm from Oregon."

"I see. Then you really haven't come such a long way for *Valley* after all, have you? Oregon is just a three- or four-hour drive."

"Not all distances are measured in terms of miles."

She couldn't quite decide how to respond to such a cryptic comment so Mercy decided to change the subject. She was aware that she was no longer afraid of him, but she was very definitely feeling wary of the man. He didn't fit into any category of male she could identify and label. That fact was as intriguing as it was unsettling. "What about your car? Are you sure you want to leave it here on the street?"

"It should be reasonably safe for a while, don't you think? Ignatius Cove doesn't look like the sort of place where gangs start stripping cars on the main street five minutes after the sun sets."

"Well, no, but—"

"Don't worry about the car, Mercy."

"I won't," she assured him tartly. "After all, it's yours, not mine."

Mercy led the way for two blocks, past the small plaza and fountain at the end of the street, and then turned left, away from the view of the cove, to climb the hill toward her apartment. By the time she reached the end of the rather steep street, she was breathing a little heavily, as usual. The walk home was definitely something of a workout. As she stopped in front of her apartment building she was well aware that Croft's breathing hadn't altered. The knowledge irritated her. The man must have *some* weakness, she rationalized.

"What is your field of interest, Croft?" she asked as she dug the keys back out of her purse.

He gave her a quizzical look. "My field of interest?"

"Your book collection," she said impatiently as she walked up the single flight of stairs that led to her second-story apartment. "You've come all this way to see *Valley*, so you must be a collector. What's your chief area of interest?"

He smiled for the first time. It wasn't much of a smile, just a faint lifting of the corners of his firm mouth. Mercy got the impression he didn't have a lot of experience in smiling. But it was a genuine smile and she was rather pleased with herself for having drawn it from him.

"You mean you want to know why I'm trying to obtain *Valley of Secret Jewels*?" he asked in mild amusement.

Mercy gave a small cough to clear her throat and opened her front door. "Well, it is a rather unusual specimen."

"It's erotica, pure and simple," he stated flatly. "Some of the best ever written."

"Yes." Mercy wasn't quite certain what else to say. Uneasily she remembered her earlier image of meeting Croft in a darkened bedroom. Talk about erotica. Deliberately she made herself ask the logical question. "Is that what you collect? Erotica?"

"No, Mercy. My interests lie in another direction."

"Which direction?" She turned just inside her doorway to face him, aware that she was feeling nervous again. She quickly tried to analyze her reactions and came to the conclusion that, while she wasn't physically afraid of him, she simply couldn't shake the dangerous frisson of sensual awareness he seemed to evoke in her.

She reminded herself that ghosts, even the ones that weren't actually threatening, always sent chills down the spine.

"I suppose you could say that my main field of interest is the philosophy of violence."

He walked through the door and closed it behind him before Mercy could assimilate the meaning of his words. She stepped back, automatically giving him room. Her eyes widened.

"Violence?" she whispered.

"I'm something of an expert on the subject."

Chapter
TWO

She took the news well, Croft decided. It pleased him that she wasn't the kind to scream and have hysterics. Of course, he could have been more subtle. But he was still annoyed at the way she had tried to lock him out of her shop earlier, so he couldn't resist the chance to shock her.

The fact that she had managed to draw such a response from him at all surprised him. Normally he did not allow himself to act on the basis of such minor emotional prods. He was accustomed to people acting uncomfortable in his presence. Sometimes they had good reason to feel that way.

Mercy was still edging backward, probably heading for the kitchen where there was undoubtedly a back door. She was watching him alertly, waiting for him to pounce, but her eyes held a staunch challenge. She was no coward.

"What exactly do you mean by saying you're an expert in violence, Mr. Falconer?"

Croft sighed and shoved his hands into his pockets. People were always reassured when a potential aggressor kept

19

his hands out of sight. "I own three schools of self-defense. Two in California, one in Portland, Oregon."

She blinked and relaxed slightly. "You mean you're an expert in judo or karate?"

"Something like that," he answered vaguely. "The method I teach is my own. It's based on some ancient martial art techniques that most of the western world isn't very familiar with."

She smiled suddenly, clearly relieved to be given a logical explanation. "That's fascinating. I guess it explains it."

"Explains what?"

"The way you move. The way you seem to sort of, well, float. It's very disconcerting." She gave up trying to explain. "Never mind. I'll get *Valley*. I've got it in a box in the kitchen closet. Remember, you're welcome to look at it since you've come all this way, but it's definitely not for sale." She dropped her purse onto the sofa, turned and went into the kitchen.

Croft stared after her, aware that he wouldn't have minded more time with that smile. He liked the way it lit her eyes. She had very nice eyes. They were a green shade that mirrored her emotions with compelling clarity. It was like looking through a piece of translucent jade. In the short time he had known her he had seen everything from curiosity to fear in that gaze. He found himself wondering how Mercy's eyes would reflect passion.

Croft shook his head, a little startled by the direction of his thoughts. He was there on business, and when he was working he never allowed anything, especially sex, to distract him.

Still, Croft acknowledged with his usual blunt honesty, he couldn't deny that Mercy Pennington interested him. It wasn't because she was exotically beautiful. He decided the earlier analogy to jade was appropriate for the rest of her.

Jade was a subtle stone that rewarded only the careful observer.

One had to study jade and get to know it thoroughly before one could properly appreciate it. The way it reflected light, its inner strengths and shadows, the way it warmed to the touch were all quiet manifestations of its character that were not obvious to the casual eye.

But Croft had learned long ago to look carefully at that which interested him. And Mercy, for some reason, perhaps because of her connection with the book, definitely interested him.

He guessed she was in her late twenties. She wasn't tall, probably only about five foot five. A good seven or eight inches less than himself. Her hair reminded him of the tawny sections of his rottweiler's black and tan coat. It was a rich, warm shade of brown that made him want to put out his hand and stroke her. He wondered in silent amusement how Mercy would feel about being compared to his dog.

Her hair was caught up in a neat little twist at the moment. Croft guessed it would fall below her shoulders if a man were to remove the pins that anchored the silky strands. As it was it revealed the delicate nape of her neck, a soft, vulnerable curve that reminded him of a flower stem. He realized he was finding the sight sensual and provocative. His body stirred and Croft grew annoyed. He had learned to master himself over the years and it was disturbing to discover that this green-eyed slip of a woman could jar that sense of self-control.

Her face was a collection of well-defined, reasonably attractive features. Wide eyes, faintly almond shaped, tilted up at the corners. Her nose was pert, mouth soft, lower lip slightly fuller than the upper.

The rest of her was even softer looking than her mouth. She was wearing a variation of the Ignatius Cove uniform, khaki slacks and a close fitting green cotton polo shirt. But the shirt didn't have an animal on the left breast and the slacks didn't have a designer logo. Her loafers were scuffed and pleasantly aged.

Croft paused to think about that left breast. Both it and its companion were on the small side, but there was a satisfying fullness that appealed. It was not his nature to be attracted to the overblown look. As in everything else, it was subtlety that caught his attention.

The khaki slacks fit well over her gently rounded hips. He could imagine cupping those well shaped buttocks in his hands, lifting her up until he could cradle her intimately against his thighs.

"Damn," he muttered.

"Something wrong?" Mercy called from the kitchen. A cupboard door slammed.

"No." There was no way he could explain what was wrong. He didn't understand it himself. Better to deny it altogether. He heard her footsteps on the kitchen tile and realized she was returning with the book.

It was the book he was there to study, not Mercy Pennington. He would do well to remember that. Normally he didn't have to caution himself about getting distracted. He seldom if ever got distracted unless he chose to be.

He glanced around the apartment as he waited for her to appear in the doorway, unconsciously picking up further clues about Mercy. The place was filled with color and a certain amount of casual clutter. She obviously favored bright, vivid hues. There was no mauve, pale mint green or baby blue in the compact, well lit room.

The sofa was lemon yellow, accented with turquoise throw pillows. The lamps were high tech in design, deep orange with all sorts of kinky twists and turns. The bookcase was also orange, finished in a shiny lacquer that added sparkle to the room. There was more sparkle from the mirrors on the wall behind the sofa that picked up the tiny scrap of cove view. The carpet was a strong slate gray and the walls were stark white.

The pictures on the walls caught Croft's attention. There were dozens of them, all watercolors, all done by the same hand and all showing a terrible technique and a total lack of understanding of the medium. There were pictures of the cove as seen from the tiny balcony of the apartment, pictures of sunsets on the water, pictures of sailboats, pictures of the islands lying offshore.

The colors of sky and water had been laid on with a heavy hand. A lot of purple and cobalt blue. The sails on the boats were far too bright. The islands were thick green blobs on the horizon instead of misty, half-seen visions. The sunsets were the same orange as the bookcase in the living room. Whatever delicacy of line or subtle color that might have been achieved had been ruined at the start by a brush that had obviously been wielded by an assertive, poorly trained, although clearly enthusiastic hand.

Croft was startled to find himself oddly charmed by the cheerful watercolors on the walls. Normally such lack of restraint would not appeal to him. At the same time he felt an urge to take the painter by the nape of her neck, lead her to the paper and show her how watercolors should be done.

He knew without asking that the pictures had been painted by Mercy Pennington.

The one other purely ornamental feature in the living room was a brilliantly hued wooden screen. It was in three parts and stood six feet high. This was a professional, not an amateurish creation. The panels were painted with a stunningly exotic tropical motif, all lush green leaves, turquoise sky, brilliant flowers and vivid orange fruit that must have come directly from the artist's head. It didn't look like any fruit Croft had ever seen. All in all, the scene was one of primal innocence, a tropical paradise, an unreal, too vivid dream.

But in the center panel a sleek, golden-eyed leopard crouched. It was an intruder, a lethal visitor that was not truly a part of its surroundings. It was a creature from another, far more sinister world and it brought a threat to paradise and innocence. It dominated the environment in which it found itself, faintly disdainful of the soft, bright beauty surrounding it. The expression in the leopard's gaze was remote and superior, arrogant and detached. It was as if the leopard knew another kind of reality and preferred that other, more natural habitat. But there was a longing in those great, golden eyes, too, a silent, secret wish to be part of the lush, sweet brightness that was all around.

The impossibility of the leopard ever being accepted in paradise was what made Croft turn away from the panel painting. For its own peace of mind, the creature of the night had better continue to enjoy its separate, more dangerous reality.

Croft finished his examination of Mercy's living room just as she walked in with an old, leather bound book in her hand. "Did you buy your furniture to match the screen or did you buy the screen to match the furniture?" he asked out of curiosity.

She grinned, her eyes bright with appreciative laughter. "I bought the screen and then had to get new furniture to go with it. Not the most efficient way to furnish a place."

"No, but there's a certain logic to it," he admitted.

"I take it you don't approve of my taste?"

He thought about that, turning the question over in his mind while she raised her eyebrows. "It suits you," he finally said, satisfied with the decision.

"Gee, thanks. I think. I'll bet I can guess how your house is furnished. Very bare, with no unnecessary bits and pieces hanging around to clutter up the place, hmm? Maybe the austere, Japanese style with shoji screens, wooden floors, a couple of elegantly stark pieces of furniture? That would go nicely with your line of work and suit your image."

He was taken aback by the easy, off-the-cuff guess. It was far too accurate. The fact that she had read his tastes so easily was mildly alarming. Lucky guess, he decided. "How did you know?"

"We all have our gifts," she said pointedly, clearly delighted with her own perception. Her eyes were alight with the small pleasure. It was obvious she was warming rapidly to him, becoming increasingly relaxed in his presence. "Some of us can keep door bells from ringing. Others are good at taking wild guesses about strangers' homes. Actually, it wasn't all that hard. There's something about you that makes me think of austerity and total self-reliance. I'd hate to know your politics. I don't see you as the liberal type. Are you one of those crazy survivalists who lives out in the Oregon woods and collects high powered rifles and small tanks?"

He couldn't tell if she were teasing him or not, and that was disconcerting. "What do you think?"

She sighed. "I think that, whatever else you are, you're not crazy. You're far too self-controlled to be nutso the way those survivalists are."

"I've managed to survive so far," he said carefully. "But I'm not interested in guns. They're too impersonal. And I don't own a tank, large or small."

"Just a Porsche."

She nodded as if that explained something else. He was about to demand just what the car explained when she forestalled him by holding out the volume in her hand. "Here's the book. Maybe it won't be the copy you want, after all. Then you won't have to feel bad about missing out on it."

"There are only a handful of copies in existence. As far as I know all of them are in the hands of European collectors.

I'm almost certain this is the book I want. That's why I drove up here from Oregon this morning."

"I'll bet you never do much of anything unless you're absolutely certain you've got all the answers first," Mercy grumbled.

He looked up from the title page of *Valley of Secret Jewels* and saw the flare of deep feminine awareness in her eyes. The knowledge that she was attracted to him made his mouth curve very slightly in satisfaction. "I've found it pays to have answers before I take action, especially when it comes to dealing with people. There's an old saying about knowing your enemy. I believe in it."

She smiled a little too brightly. "Got a lot of enemies?"

"No. I'm as selective about my enemies as I am about my friends." He checked the roman numeral publication date of the book in his hand, turning the old, yellowed pages with care.

"How about your lovers? Are you just as selective about them?"

The question amazed him. He would never have thought Mercy Pennington bold enough to ask such a thing. Croft raised his eyes slowly from the page he was studying, aware from the slightly higher note on which she'd ended the query that she was already regretting her rashness. Then he saw the embarrassment in her gaze. He knew she would have given anything to call back the words. Unwittingly she had just revealed a great deal about herself. He could use what he was learning about her.

"A man has to be far more careful about his choice of lover than he does about his choice of either friend or enemy. Friends and enemies are well defined. You always know where you stand with them unless you're stupid. But lovers aren't as easy to know and understand. They can go either way, can't they? Become friend or enemy. And who can tell the difference until it's too late?"

The embarrassment and chagrin he saw in her green eyes were very revealing. So was the light wash of color in her cheeks. A suitable punishment for her recklessness, he decided. She was sincerely wishing she hadn't allowed herself to be goaded into the question in the first place.

That was the thing about impulsiveness. It contained the seeds of its own retribution. He had a hunch Mercy Pennington had suffered before for her own brand of rashness. She knew the consequences but sometimes she couldn't help herself. She was the kind of woman who would let her emotions sway her logic. In a tight situation she would follow her instincts, and those instincts would be tied to whatever emotional bonds she had established. If she had children she would be as protective as a lioness.

If she had a lover, she would be fiercely, passionately loyal unless she felt she had been betrayed. Then she would be dangerous.

Croft smiled slightly, satisfied he understood Mercy's fundamental qualities. He went back to examining the volume in his hand. He turned a few pages until he found a beautifully drawn black and white plate of a man and woman making love. "This is the volume I want. It's an original."

"Of course it's an original. Did you think I was trying to pass off a reproduction?" Mercy was obviously miffed.

"It's possible you might have made a mistake," he said placatingly.

"Well, I didn't. I described the book very carefully to Mr. Gladstone and he said he could tell from my answers over the phone that it was an original. He was very pleased and didn't doubt me for a minute."

"Mr. Gladstone?"

"The man from Colorado who's buying it."

"You'll have to tell me more about Mr. Gladstone." Croft turned to another plate. This one was a lovingly rendered detail of a voluptuous woman reclining on her back while being artfully pleasured by a man who was kneeling between her legs.

Mercy stepped forward to peer down at the plate. "I don't have to tell you anything about Mr. Gladstone. I have an obligation to protect my clients. Besides," she added in a rush of honesty, "I don't know much about him. I do hope you're not going to stand there and drool over the pictures. The saliva stains might lower the value of the book."

"I try to save my drooling for the real thing."

"That's not exactly a compelling image," she retorted crossly. "Have you read *Valley?*"

"No. This is the first time I've actually seen it. Until now I only knew of it. I had a reason to learn about it three years ago."

"What reason?"

"It was part of a very valuable collection. I was interested in the man who owned it. I wanted to learn as much as I could about his book collection, and in the process I learned something about this particular book. You have to admit *Valley* is rather, uh, distinctive."

"Why were you so interested in that particular book collection?" she demanded. "Did you want to acquire part of it?"

"No. I wanted to know as much as possible about the owner. The kind of books a man collects can tell you a great deal about him."

There was a short, intense silence. "Yes," Mercy finally agreed. Her eyes were wide and serious. "A person's book collection could tell you much about him."

"Or her." Croft closed *Valley* carefully. "Have you read this book, Mercy?"

"If I had I wouldn't stand here and admit it. Not to you at any rate."

"Why not to me?" he asked curiously.

"You're a stranger, for heaven's sake. And that book is

nothing short of erotica. An uncharitable soul might even call it porn."

"And you aren't about to admit to a stranger that you read that sort of thing?"

She gave him a mockingly smug smile. "Any examination I may have made of *Valley* was done purely to establish its identity and verify its provenance and authenticity. I'm an ex-librarian, you know. I was taught to examine books from an objective, professional viewpoint."

"Of course." He knew he was smiling faintly again and that Mercy was the cause. "I have great respect for professionalism of any kind."

"Good. Have you finished with *Valley?*"

"No. I told you, I want it."

Irritation replaced the taunting expression in her eyes. "Well, you can't have it. I've told you, the book has already been sold. I'm not going to sell it out from under my client."

"When does he take possession?"

"Tuesday."

"Gladstone is coming to Ignatius Cove to pick it up?" This might turn out to be easier than he had first thought.

She shook her head impatiently. "No, I'm going to deliver it to him. May I please have the book back if you're finished with it?"

He continued to hold it in his right hand. "You're going to deliver it? In person?"

"That's right."

"How?" He saw her flinch slightly in surprise and realized his voice had contained far too much command. For an instant the soft flicker of awareness in her eyes was dimmed with caution.

"I'm taking a few days off to fly to Colorado. I'll be renting a car in Denver and driving to Mr. Gladstone's home. I don't see what business this is of yours."

"No, you wouldn't understand. Where does Gladstone live?"

"He has a place in the mountains, he said. He didn't give me directions over the phone. Much too complicated apparently. There will be a map waiting when I pick up the car in Denver." She made a sudden grab for the book he was holding.

Croft had seen her telegraph the move with her eyes and rather lazily moved *Valley* out of reach. He didn't move it far, just a couple of inches. Enough to ensure her curving fingers missed their target. Mercy's growing irritation now bordered on anger. Her hand fell to her side as she regarded him with smoldering annoyance. Her head came up with proud challenge.

"Are you going to abuse my hospitality by stealing *Valley?*"

He sighed, reluctantly handing the book to her. "No, I'm not here to steal it. But I'm growing very curious about your client."

She shrugged, snatching the volume from his grasp and hugging it possessively. "Well, maybe you can convince him to resell *Valley* to you. Once Mr. Gladstone has the book, he can do anything he wants with it. I, however, am under an obligation to deliver it to him."

"Do you always fulfill your obligations, Mercy?"

"I try," she replied stiffly.

"So do I," he heard himself say softly, his gaze never leaving hers. "That's why I'm here. We have something in common, Mercy Pennington."

She shook her head in denial, but she couldn't hide the flash of reluctant curiosity in her eyes. "I doubt it."

"Give it a chance." He kept his tone low and persuasive, watching her intently. Croft was certain now that the expression in the depths of her green eyes was more than mere feminine awareness. She saw him as a man who, while he might yet prove dangerous, was also proving fascinating. She was just impetuous enough to act on the shining allure of such an unusual possibility.

Her streak of rashness would work in his favor, Croft decided. With some careful coaxing she could be made to ignore the warning bells of her common sense and respond, instead, to the pull of a very basic sexual attraction. He had already proven himself adept at silencing warning bells.

That the attraction existed and that it existed on both sides, Croft didn't bother to deny to himself. He accepted the fact that he found Mercy Pennington sexually intriguing with the same matter-of-fact attitude with which he accepted hunger or cold. If necessary he could ignore all three. But he didn't have to ignore Mercy. For her sake, in fact, it would be better if he didn't. She was proving to be a stubborn little thing, and in this case her recalcitrance might prove dangerous.

There were too many unknowns at the moment. He needed to find answers quickly and Mercy Pennington was the shortest route to those answers. That meant he had to find the shortest route to Mercy Pennington, and that looked as if it would be via the sensual awareness that was flaring to life between the two of them.

"Dinner," he said succinctly.

She frowned, still clutching *Valley*. "What about it?"

He smiled again. "I'd like to take you to dinner. It's the least I can do under the circumstances."

"That's not necessary."

"It would be my pleasure."

"Don't you have to get back to Oregon?"

"Not this evening. I'm staying at an inn here in town tonight."

"Oh."

He gave her a few seconds to absorb that and then pushed gently. "Do you have other plans?"

"No. Tomorrow is a workday. I have to get up early."

Croft nodded. "I'll have you home early. I give you my word."

She looked at him with an odd curiosity, as though she were searching for something in him. It wasn't the first time she'd studied him in such a manner. There had been those few moments back in her shop when he had told her she was safe with him.

She had had the same strange curiosity in her eyes then. It had been followed by a clear acceptance of his words. That expression of acceptance was in her eyes again now. She probably didn't even realize the full implications, but Croft did. She trusted him on some basic, feminine level, whether she knew it or not.

He liked that. And he could use it.

"I was going to have dinner here this evening," Mercy said finally, as if feeling her way through a mine field. "I bought some buckwheat pasta. I planned to open a bottle of zinfandel I've been saving. After all, it's Friday."

"Fine." Croft nodded equably.

She blinked warily. "I beg your pardon?"

"I said that sounds fine. I like buckwheat pasta and I like zinfandel."

Mercy stared at him. She looked as though she didn't know whether to laugh or scream in outrage.

Croft smiled to himself. Mercy was quickly falling right into the palm of his hand.

Twenty minutes later Mercy still couldn't decide whether to laugh or scream. She ceased rinsing broccoli, picked up her wineglass and leaned back against the counter to take a sip. Her guest, whom she had decided fell into the uninvited category, was straddling one of the diamond shaped, black wire mesh kitchen chairs, his arms resting easily along the back. He held his own wineglass lightly cradled in his hand.

The rich, deep, near purple color of the zinfandel looked right clasped within those strong fingers. It was another example of darkness suiting him, Mercy decided.

Whatever else could be said about the man, he didn't appear to have a drinking problem. He was savoring his wine, but he sipped with great restraint. Mercy had a hunch Croft Falconer did everything with restraint. She wondered if that applied to making love and decided it probably did. He might be very skillful at it, but he would also be very much in control. It was hard to envision this man surrendering to any kind of strong emotion.

She still wasn't quite certain how she had come to let him stay for dinner, but she had the distinct impression there had been a certain inevitability about the situation from the start. She was too aware of him, too intrigued by him, too curious about him for her own good and she knew it. But he was there and she was the one who had let him stay.

"How long have you owned the schools of self-defense?" she made herself ask casually. Mercy had been doing her best for the past twenty minutes to keep all conversation light and superficial. She wanted the time to think about and evaluate him as well as her own unfamiliar reactions.

"I opened the first one nearly three years ago. The second one a year after that and the third six months ago."

"Where did you pick up the expertise?"

"I've studied. And traveled."

"Do you do a lot of traveling in your, uh, field?" she pressed.

"No, not anymore, except when I visit my schools to teach special courses or give demonstrations."

"Who teaches the regular classes?"

"Friends. Former students. They handle the day to day management of the schools."

"Leaving you free to sit by the shore and twiddle your thumbs in Oregon?" She smiled.

"You could say that."

"Nice work if you can get it," she declared with humorous envy. "Beats my routine."

His mouth lifted at the edge. "You said you were an ex-librarian. When did you go into business for yourself?"

"A couple of years ago." She set down her glass and went back to work on the broccoli. She didn't particularly want to encourage the discussion in that direction.

As if he sensed her desire not to talk about it, Croft deliberately focused on the one direction Mercy didn't wish to go. "What made you decide to open a bookstore?"

"It's only natural for a librarian to be interested in trying to sell the product she's been loaning out for years, isn't it? I see bookselling as the mercenary side of librarianship."

"Are you from Washington?"

Mercy shook her head, beginning to worry that he wasn't going to let the subject drop. "California."

"Why didn't you open your bookshop down there?"

"I looked around for several months before choosing a location. I like Washington, I like Ignatius Cove and I thought it could support the kind of store I wanted to run." She was very busy with the broccoli now, cutting the florets, running them under cold water again and stacking them neatly in the perforated steamer pan.

There was a short silence. "Why did you leave California?" he asked.

Mercy stifled a groan. "I told you. I did a lot of looking and decided business odds were better up here."

"I think there was more to it than just a business decision. For you to pull up stakes and move to another state there must have been some other reason involved. You're not the kind of woman who would move easily. You forge ties and put down roots."

She whirled around, startled by his cool deduction. "Why on earth do you say that?"

He took a sip from his glass and contemplated her flaring eyes. "Was it a man?"

She closed her teeth with a small snap and wondered how one got rid of a dinner guest before dinner. "That," she informed him, "is none of your business, is it?"

"It was a man." He inclined his head once, as if satisfied. Then he took another swallow of wine. "Were you running away from him?"

His casual invasion of her privacy infuriated Mercy. She slammed the lid on the steamer. "No, I was not running away from him. I was engaged to him. When the engagement ended, I decided I wanted a fresh start somewhere else."

"Why did the engagement end? Did he cheat on you?"

Her fingers were trembling, Mercy realized as she ran water for the pasta into a kettle. She focused her attention on the small task. "I don't know. If he did, I wasn't aware of it. That wasn't the reason the engagement ended."

"It would take a lot for you to walk out on a man."

"That may not be saying much about my intelligence."

"So what happened?"

"Are you always this rude?"

"It's my nature. I like to understand what I'm dealing with."

"The only thing you're dealing with tonight is a free meal. That shouldn't require much understanding."

"The hell it doesn't. You know as well as I do that there's no such thing as a free lunch. There's always a reckoning."

She couldn't decide if he was laughing at her or not. Mercy didn't dare turn around to find out. "Feel free to walk out the door before you find yourself in too deep."

"I'm already in too deep. But don't worry, I think I'm willing to pay the price. What happened in California, Mercy?"

He was too much. But when she shot him a quick glance

over her shoulder, she found her irritation evaporating. Instead of a mocking or prying inquisitiveness she instead saw in his eyes an intense, almost physical awareness. She experienced an overwhelming desire to explain everything to him. She had never talked about this particular part of her past with anyone, but now she wanted Croft to understand what had happened. "Remember what you said earlier about how difficult it was to choose a lover because one never knew for certain if one was choosing a friend or an enemy?"

"I remember."

"Well, my fiance turned out to be an enemy. He used me to try to defraud my aunt and uncle, who happen to be quite comfortably established due to some excellent investments they made several years ago in California real estate. I found out what was happening just in time, broke off the engagement and told my relatives what was going on. It was an extremely unpleasant situation. Unfortunately, there was no way to prove anything. When it was all over, I'm sure Aaron just cut his losses and went on to his next victim. The only satisfaction I got out of it was reporting the whole thing to the authorities. At least they can keep an eye on him now. Maybe if he tries another scheme they'll catch him."

"Not sufficient revenge for you, though, hmm?"

She could feel his gaze on her as she turned up the heat under the kettle of water. "No, frankly, it wasn't. I would have liked to have done something a great deal more permanent to Aaron Sanders."

"Because he tried to defraud your aunt and uncle?"

"No, because he used me to do it." She wiped her hands on a kitchen towel and collected her frazzled emotions. Damned if she would allow this man to spend the rest of the evening unnerving her. It had been a serious mistake to invite him to dinner.

But, then, she hadn't exactly invited him, Mercy reminded herself wryly. Somehow she'd been quietly coerced into doing it.

Croft's eyes met hers. His gaze was disconcertingly serious. "I understand how you feel. But I think in your case it's better things ended where they did. Once you'd taken the next step in revenge, which would have been violence, there would have been no easy way to modify the end result. It might have consumed you as well as him. Once violence has been initiated, forces are set in motion that can't always be controlled. A new Circle is formed and must be completed."

She stared at him. "A Circle?"

He nodded. "A subset within the structure of universal reality that must be completed if it isn't to shatter and cause problems in other areas."

"What on earth are you talking about?" she demanded. "What is this Circle business?"

"A concept."

"Your own?"

He shrugged. "In the same way that my style in the world of martial arts is my own. We're all responsible for shaping the concepts we use to deal with the world."

Mercy hesitated, trying to understand. "This concept of a Circle is your personal philosophy, then?"

"You could call it that."

"Tell me about it," she insisted. She had forgotten her previous irritation, uncomfortableness and even her sexual awareness of her guest. She had lost all self-consciousness and now just wanted to know everything she could about Croft Falconer.

He paused, as if searching for simple answers to a complex question. When he looked up again his eyes were gleaming. "It has to do with a way of knowing. A way of understanding. A way of living. You're right. It's my philosophy of life. I've learned that in order to maintain an equilibrium in my world it is first necessary to keep all the Circles of reality closed."

"I don't think I understand."

"It's not necessary that you do. Maybe someday I'll explain it further."

"But not tonight?"

"No, not tonight. Just take my word for it. You were wise not to push your desire for revenge into the Circle of violence. You're not trained to handle it."

She caught her breath at the certainty in his voice. His gaze held a knowing quality that almost frightened her, an expression that said he understood all too well what he was talking about. He had more than a casual knowledge of the potential of physical violence; his was a deep, unequivocal understanding and acceptance of that harsh reality. He had said his field of interest was the philosophy of violence, and Mercy suddenly believed him.

"Did you know," Croft continued easily, as if she weren't staring at him with an expression that suggested he was really from Mars, "that a strong sexual attraction has something in common with violence?" He got to his feet with a lazy grace and walked toward her. Mercy stood rooted to the spot, unable to move or look away from his gleaming gaze. He reached out and slowly, deliberately stroked her cheek. "Once certain initial steps are taken, it's very difficult to control either force. A new Circle is begun."

With a shuddering effort of will, Mercy regained a measure of poise. "Well, then," she announced as she turned back to the stove, "we shall just have to make certain the initial steps aren't taken, won't we?"

Chapter
THREE

By the time dinner was over, Mercy felt as if the leopard painted on the screen in the living room had come to life and padded silently into her kitchen. He was there, a visitor from another reality. There was danger, she realized, but her overwhelming feeling was simply of being enthralled by this new and fascinating creature.

The fact that he was aware of her fascination and willing to let her pursue it both troubled and excited her.

Croft Falconer was a man she would very much like to know better. Part of the attraction was physical. Mercy was too realistic to try and deny something so powerful. He had touched her senses in a variety of ways, stirring everything from the fine hair on the nape of her neck to the adrenaline in her blood.

Admittedly, she had not been physically involved with a man for a long time. There had been no one since the fiasco of her engagement. Aaron Sanders, her fiancé, had provided her first and only experience with sex. The few times she had been to bed with him had left her frankly wondering what all the fuss was about.

But the two years of being without a lover didn't account for her intense feelings this evening. She had certainly met enough men on casual dates during the past few months. None of those dates had ended in bed, nor had Mercy wished they had.

Sex had never been an overwhelming force in her life, never been anything she couldn't easily control. It was true she had had a rather old-fashioned upbringing, but that didn't account entirely for her limited experience. The truth was, she had been quite comfortable for the past two years, just as she had been comfortable, if curious, during the years before she had met Aaron. There had been no sense of desperation or compulsive need to find a mate. In fact, Mercy had begun to wonder if perhaps she simply wasn't endowed with all the hormones that seemed to drive other people in her age group.

For the first time she no longer doubted that she had received the full complement of female hormones and instincts.

The sensual attraction was thick in the atmosphere around the glass topped dinner table. It was disconcerting and she was very much afraid Croft had been right when he claimed that this kind of thing might have something in common with violence. Both could prove uncontrollable. It was a revelation for Mercy.

Still, she was a strong-willed woman who had been through a lot since the day she had discovered the appalling manner in which Aaron Sanders had tried to use her. Mercy had enough self-confidence to know she could handle a strong physical attraction, even if it was something new and fascinating in her life. It should have been possible to view Croft as she would an exotic piece of art: Compelling, tantalizing, intriguing, but definitely out of reach in terms of price. She could admire such art, even desire it, but she could walk away from it with a sigh and a shrug.

Unfortunately, her feelings for Croft Falconer were not merely a question of attraction. The very remoteness of the man drew her to him in a way she couldn't explain. The self-contained quality about him spoke of a unique kind of aloneness. She wondered if that state of isolation ever slipped over the border into a state of genuine loneliness. Surely at the edges the line between those two states was very thin.

Or perhaps, like the leopard on the screen or a ghost from another dimension, Croft Falconer did not need or want to share his world with anyone else.

Mercy sensed the strength and pride and power that made up Croft's nature and realized that a part of her responded with a sense of respect. This man was rock solid all the way through.

Mercy chatted easily during dinner, guiding the conversation into safe channels. She told her guest about her shop, about living in Ignatius Cove, and asked him questions about the business aspects of running his self-defense schools in two different states. He talked easily, politely, and with civilized grace, but he said very little that Mercy could grab hold of to analyze and examine in detail.

All the while she was silently looking for answers to questions she wasn't yet sure how to put into words. She felt driven to learn as much as possible about Croft, and his reluctance to talk about himself only increased her need to learn his secrets.

She wondered about his past, about the kind of life he had led that had made him choose a career in the world of martial arts. She would have expected an American involved in such a physical business to come across as either a highly competitive, professional athlete or a super macho, thick-brained gorilla.

Croft clearly did not treat his career as a sport. He did not have the mentality of a jock. And although he was quietly, supremely sure of himself, she couldn't write him off as a muscle bound gorilla. There was too much thoughtful, analytical intelligence behind his golden gaze, too much evidence that he had done a great deal of critical self-evaluation. His self-assurance rose from the fact that he knew himself well and accepted that which he knew. She sensed instinctively that he had evolved an all-encompassing lifestyle. It had its own rules and scale of right and wrong, both of which probably operated somewhat independently of society's norms. The important thing was that he would always abide by his own rules.

The philosophy of violence, the study of it, was apparently a way of life to him. A tiny, warning shiver went through Mercy as she wondered if perhaps Croft were equally knowledgeable about the actual practice of violence. Studying the martial arts was one thing, but in truth most karate and judo experts never used their skills outside a gym. She did not want to believe Croft had firsthand experience of his subject.

But what else could have given his hazel eyes such a dark, fathomless quality?

Mercy pushed aside her doubts until the meal was over. At that point she found herself faced with finding a subtle but firm way of terminating the strange evening. She told herself she had indulged her growing fascination with this man long enough for that night.

"You'll be on your way back to Oregon bright and early tomorrow, I imagine," she said with a calm she wasn't feeling as she poured two tiny snifters of brandy. They had moved back into the living room. It seemed to Mercy that the painted cat on the screen was watching his counterpart with complacent interest.

"No." Croft spoke with a calm that was far more genuine than Mercy's. "I don't think so. I owe you a meal."

She smiled involuntarily. "Afraid of being in my debt?"

"I like to keep the Circle closed."

"So you've said."

"This is a debt I will take pleasure in repaying." He smiled, set down the brandy glass and got to his feet. When she looked at him he reached down to pull her up beside him.

Mercy was unprepared for the small shock that gripped her when his fingers closed around her wrist. She was even more unsettled by the gentleness of his touch. The power in him was under exquisite control. A woman would always be aware of the strength in this man, she thought, but she would never fear it. Yet even as she was stunned by the realization of him, he was releasing her.

"Croft?"

"Dinner tomorrow evening?" He stood very close but made no effort to take her into his arms.

Good grief, surely that wasn't what she wanted. Not so soon at any rate. She needed time. Once again she heard a distant chime, the faintest of warning bells. But the bells fell silent as she looked into Croft's eyes. The reckless need to know him more thoroughly overtook Mercy.

"Dinner," she repeated. She heard the acceptance in her own voice. "I'll look forward to it," she added impulsively.

"So will I."

He moved to the door and she followed. When she opened and held it for him, he stepped over the threshold and then turned to face her. Standing just outside her apartment he seemed to be a part of the night's shifting shadows. Something told Mercy she might be safer if she kept him outside her door. Croft regarded her silently for a long moment and then he lifted his hand.

Mercy's fingers tightened on the wood of the door. Part of

her belatedly urged her to step back out of reach, but she couldn't move. His fingertips touched the nape of her neck, gliding softly. It was the lightest of caresses and Mercy forgot all about wanting to dodge those questing fingers. Instead she was almost overcome with the desire to turn her face into the palm of his hand to kiss him.

She was afraid the longing showed in her eyes when she looked up and saw the recognition and flare of masculine satisfaction in his hazel gaze. His fingertips moved once more across the nape of her neck, stirring the fine hair that grew there. Mercy shivered.

Croft removed his hand. "I've been wanting to do that all evening. Good night, Mercy."

"Good night, Croft." She could barely speak.

He turned away, vanishing into the darkness before she even got the door closed. She sank thoughtfully back against the wood panel and worried briefly about him walking all the way down the hill to his car at night. Ignatius Cove was a safe little town, but still. . . .

Then she shook her head at the ridiculousness of worrying about Croft Falconer. If she was going to waste time worrying about anyone, it should probably be herself.

Croft waited for Saturday to pass with a restless impatience that was almost alarming. He wasn't accustomed to this kind of simmering uneasiness. Inevitably in his life there was a time for waiting and a time for action. Each reinforced the other, fitting together with a symmetry that kept the Circle closed. But this period of waiting was different. It was not the kind that presaged violence, yet it contained some of the same elements. There was the familiar, acute sense of awareness and the feeling of intense physical readiness. The difference was that he didn't seem to be able to channel or control his impatience the way he normally would.

It was because this time he was waiting for the woman, Mercy Pennington. Waiting to discover her completely. Waiting to claim her.

At dawn he found a secluded spot on the beach below the inn and tried to slide into his morning meditative trance. The results were fragmented at best. The running afterward went better, but it didn't do much to stem the tide of urgency that was building in him.

He told himself to slow down mentally and let the course of events work its inevitable way to the ultimate conclusion. He knew what he was doing. He could control the end result. After all, he had seen the wonder and the wanting in her last night.

His fingers curled briefly in a small flare of desire as he remembered the feel of her. Touching the nape of her neck had let him know what it would be like to touch the rest of her. He doubted if she even realized just how much he had learned with that single caress. She would be soft, sensitive, vulnerable, and graceful in bed.

He wondered what she was thinking today at work. He knew she was still wary of him. He deliberately hadn't done much to counter that and he knew why. He couldn't tell her everything, but he found himself wanting to be as honest with her as possible.

Croft thought of the man who had used Mercy so badly in California and winced as he walked back up the beach to the inn for breakfast. Mercy would not be quick to forgive another man whom she perceived as a user and a liar.

But he had his priorities, Croft reminded himself. The book was the key and Mercy had possession of the book. Furthermore, she was not about to give it up. Nor was there any way to simply take it from her. She would know instantly what had happened and who had done it. No, Croft decided. He and Mercy were bound together for a while whether she liked it or not. He couldn't let her out of his

sight until he had followed the trail of the book and found
the answers he needed.

But he was honest enough to admit that he had other reasons for not wanting to let go of Mercy. Reasons that had
nothing to do with closing a Circle of justice and violence.

The image of fire blazed fiercely in his mind as Croft took
the steps to the inn two at a time. An early summer sun
warmed him, but in his mind flames leaped into a midnight
sky and screams echoed in the warm night air.

Croft's mood had not improved by the time he sat down
for breakfast in the dining room, where he discovered he
would have to make do with a tea bag and tepid cup of hot
water.

As usual when he encountered such annoyances in a restaurant he didn't bother to tip. He was not unaware of the
dirty look the waitress gave him when he left, but he wasn't
bothered by it.

The second evening with Croft began smoothly enough,
Mercy reflected later. She had been filled with a deep, exciting sense of anticipation all day. That sense of anticipation
flowered into happiness when he picked her up in the
Porsche and drove her to an excellent fish restaurant a short
distance from town.

She relaxed and watched him drive, taking pleasure in his
skill. He handled the car with a quiet, efficient competence.
His reflexes were apparently excellent. The sense of self-
control he radiated could be reassuring at times, she decided.

At other times it was a damned nuisance. Croft had the
ability to put up brick walls or simply walk away from sub-
jects and questions he didn't want to discuss. Mercy encountered that stubborn resistance whenever she began to
gently probe his past. It didn't take her long to decide she
didn't want to ruin the evening by forcing issues Croft didn't

want to have forced. She seriously questioned whether any-one could force a discussion on Croft Falconer.

She was halfway through her salmon when he startled her by stating calmly, "I think I'll go with you to Colorado."

"You *what?*"

"You heard me. I think I'll go with you to meet Glad-stone."

She was horrified. "But you can't."

"Why not?"

"Because you weren't invited. Gladstone's invitation was for me alone. I got the impression on the phone that he values his privacy. I'm sure he wouldn't take kindly to hav-ing another guest foisted on him, especially one who's after the same book he wants."

"Don't tell him I'm after it. Let him think I'm your lover and you just brought me along on vacation."

"Well, you're not my lover, and even if you were there would be no reason to bring you along. This is a business trip, at least the first three days are going to be devoted to business. I'm hoping it will be the start of a new direction in my career, in fact. The last thing I want to do is muck up my reputation as a professional, reliable antiquarian book dealer. Successful, reputable business people do not allow their per-sonal lives to get tangled up in their work."

"You haven't got a reputation as an antiquarian book dealer," he pointed out patiently. "This is your first sale."

"It's a beginning!"

"You don't mind beginning this prestigious new career by dealing a piece of pornography?"

Mercy took offense at that. "In case you aren't aware of it, we in the trade refer to such items as Burleigh's *Valley* as curiosa."

"It's curious stuff all right. Most people, if they're honest, have a certain curiosity about that kind of curiosa from the age of five on up. Forget that side of things. Even if you were an established dealer, no one would question your choice of a traveling companion."

"Why are you so insistent on meeting Gladstone?"

He smiled challengingly. "Business reasons."

"You want that damn book for your own collection."

He shrugged negligently. "Is that such a crime? I'm a collector. Collectors will go to great lengths to get what they want. Remember that, Mercy."

"Is that a threat?"

"Of course not, just a piece of advice. I never make threats."

"Ha."

"It's true." He looked surprised that she should question the statement. "Threats are a waste of everyone's time. They leave room for doubt. They encourage an opponent to test your willpower or your strength."

"I can see you've given the subject a great deal of thought," she remarked acidly.

"There's another reason besides my interest in *Valley* that I would like to go to Colorado with you."

"What's that?"

"I'd like to have the extra time with you."

Now she really was alarmed. "I'm not sure I particularly want to be lumped in with your book collecting project." She went back to her salmon with a vengeance.

"Mercy."

She looked up warily. "Yes?"

"I'm being as honest with you as I can be. I want the book. Barring that, I want to meet Gladstone. But I also want you."

"Are you hoping for two out of three?"

"You're upset."

"Damn right."

He sat quietly for a moment and then nodded as if coming

to some decision. "All right. We'll drop the subject for now."

"Does that mean the evening is over?" she asked bluntly.

"What do you think?"

"Around you," Mercy admitted with a sigh, "I'm never sure what to think."

"If it's any consolation to you, I sometimes experience the same problem around you."

"I don't believe you. You always think you know what you're doing." She waved a fork at him. "That's a bad habit, Croft. It can lead to all sorts of problems."

"Is that right?" He didn't seem worried, merely amused.

"You better believe it." It wasn't much, but she did get a small amount of satisfaction out of having had the last word on the subject.

Croft didn't take her home until after midnight. Nor did he linger on her doorstep. But just as she decided he was going to leave without anything more than a polite good night, he touched her as he had the night before. The white, scoop-necked knit dress she was wearing left her throat and the hollows of her shoulders bare and vulnerable. This time his fingers traced the faintest of patterns against her skin. Involuntarily Mercy trembled.

The caress seemed somehow more intimate than the one the previous evening. How ridiculous, she thought wildly. By any standard the light touch should have been classified as casual, almost impersonal.

Yet when she felt the gentle tremor that went through her senses and looked up into Croft's eyes she experienced a disorienting sensation of having just had a glimpse into her own future. It was almost as though she had read his mind. He wanted her. Mercy knew that with a woman's absolute certainty.

But she knew it with something more than a woman's intuition. She felt Croft's desire with a new sense of awareness that was unfamiliar. It was almost as if she really *had* read his mind.

She didn't know whether to turn and flee or throw herself into his arms.

He turned and descended the stairs before she could decide how to handle the eerie, tantalizing sensation.

It wasn't until she was sliding between the sheets of her bed that night that she realized he had made no mention of seeing her the next day. Sunday was her day off.

She ought to spend it packing for the trip to Colorado, Mercy told herself firmly. She didn't need to spend it traipsing around with a man she didn't fully understand. She wasn't at all sure she wanted to understand Croft, anyway.

Somehow she didn't think it would be safe to do so.

She lay awake in bed for quite some time, studying the night darkened ceiling. Her thoughts drifted from Croft to the valuable book that was temporarily housed in her kitchen cupboard. Her mind and body were wide awake and she was feeling restless. The evening had ended on a note that had jangled her nerve endings the same way the shop door bell chimed its warning.

There was an unfamiliar, oddly uncomfortable sense of physical awareness rippling through her. When she realized its source she was wryly shocked. She wasn't given to lying in bed at night aching for the touch of a man.

Her normal bedtime thoughts usually revolved around sales receipts, book orders, accounting bills and business taxes. It had been two years since she had lain in bed and seriously thought about a man. And two years ago thoughts of her fiance certainly hadn't done *this* to her body. This strange ache between her thighs was unsettling.

A glass of milk might give her senses the distraction they needed.

She got out of bed, wandered into the kitchen and opened the refrigerator. Light spilled out into the dark room. She peered inside and realized she had forgotten to buy a fresh carton of milk. Scratch that idea.

As she started to close the refrigerator door, the shaft of light swept over the kitchen closet door and she remembered *Valley*. Mercy recalled Croft holding the book in his powerful, sensitive hands, turning the old pages with great care.

Before she could give herself time to think about it, Mercy closed the refrigerator door, switched on the overhead light and went to the closet.

Valley of Secret Jewels was where she had left it, snuggled innocently into its protective box. The worn leather binding gleamed dully in the kitchen light. It wasn't just age that had given the leather that burnished patina, she knew. *Valley* had been through a number of eager hands, and not all of those hands had belonged to respectable book collectors of the twentieth century. In the late seventeen hundreds and well into the eighteen hundreds, *Valley* had undoubtedly been frequently read for its original intended purpose, which was, of course, outright titillation. Such usage could prove extremely wearing on a book.

But, Mercy reminded herself, she was a book dealer with a legitimate interest in antiquarian treasures. She wasn't the type to mar the cover of *Valley* with sweaty hands. Her interest in the volume was purely professional. After all, the book was worth a couple of thousand dollars and represented the start of a new direction in her career.

She lifted it out of its box and carried it into the bedroom to study for a while before sleep claimed her.

Mercy rose early the next morning, padding into the shower with her eyes only half open. It was a luxury to be able to take her time waking up. Six days a week she made herself bounce out of bed and scurry through an efficient, organized routine of showering, dressing and eating breakfast. On the seventh day she wandered far more slowly through the same routine.

It was as she dawdled over her second cup of coffee that she allowed herself to think about Croft Falconer.

There was, of course, a very good possibility he had given up trying to get her to introduce him to Erasmus Gladstone and had left for Oregon.

On the other hand, he had said he would be going with her to Colorado, and while Mercy had no intention of letting him accompany her to the mountains she was convinced he wouldn't give up so easily.

He had said he wanted the time with her as much as he wanted to meet Gladstone.

Maybe he had lied.

Mercy was packed for the trip to Colorado by ten o'clock. She was considering a quick visit to Pennington's Second Chance to check that everything was ready for Dorrie to take charge on Monday when she glanced out her front window and realized what a perfect scene was captured within the confines of her small scrap of view.

The cove was filled with colorful sailboats skimming a glistening sea. The sky was a perfect blue and there was a sun-drenched perfection to the cliffs above the cove. The rooftops below her window that tumbled down the hillside toward the water were awash with light. Her painting instructor would be thrilled by such an opportunity.

Mercy knew she was never going to get a better chance to capture the scene. Perhaps immersing herself in her watercolors would help take her mind off Croft Falconer. Quickly she set about dragging her paint box and easel outside onto the small deck.

Half an hour later, when she saw the black Porsche ease into the parking lot, Mercy acknowledged that she had been half right. This was, indeed, the perfect chance to capture the view with watercolors, but the project hadn't done much to take her mind off Croft. She realized as she stared down, watching eagerly as he climbed out of the car, that on some level she had been waiting for him.

He looked up with that riveting gaze as he closed the Porsche door. "Good morning, Mercy."

"Hello, Croft." She had to stop herself from adding that she thought he would never get there. Ridiculous to be so excited. Deliberately she made herself put down her paintbrush, get to her feet and walk over to the railing. She leaned against it, watching him climb the steps to her apartment. He was a fascinating foil for the warm summer light, a creature of the night roaming at ease during the day. Croft was wearing jeans and a dark, short-sleeved shirt that left his sinewy arms bare. The jeans were close fitting, riding low on his lean hips. The open collar of the shirt emphasized the strong column of his neck. The darkness of his hair caught the sunlight and absorbed it.

When he reached the deck he paused, his eyes going from her to the unfinished scene on the easel. "So I was right. You're the source of all the paintings on your walls."

"I'm taking lessons. As you can see, I've got a few things to learn."

He nodded, not denying it. "Yes, you have."

Mercy wrinkled her nose. "You could at least tell me I've caught a unique interpretation of the scene or that I've got obvious talent," she informed him.

He gave her a questioning look, as if to be certain she was teasing him. Then he apparently decided she was. "You've caught a unique interpretation of the scene."

"What about obvious talent?"

He hesitated and then said carefully, "If you've got any obvious talent, I'm afraid it's buried under all those layers of paint."

Mercy held up her hand, laughing ruefully. "Forget it.

You're not much good with the social compliment, are you?"

"I can produce one if that's what you want."

"Somehow it just wouldn't sound sincere now." She tilted her head, studying him curiously. "What are you doing here today, Croft? I thought you'd gone back to Oregon."

"Why would you think that? I told you, I'm going to Colorado with you."

"You've got a one-track mind," she said with a small groan.

He shook his head immediately. "No. Everything is interrelated. Understanding the whole makes it possible to understand the part. I try to focus my mind, but it's not the same as being single-tracked. There's a difference."

She threw up her hands in mock protest. "Enough. It's too nice a day to argue about your brains or lack thereof."

"How about driving into Seattle instead?" he suggested easily.

Her eyes widened. "Seattle?"

"We can have lunch there. Maybe walk through some of the galleries in Pioneer Square or take a ferry ride. How does that sound?"

"It sounds wonderful," Mercy said instantly. "Just give me a minute to put this stuff indoors." She turned and swooped down on the paints, easel and the unfinished watercolor scene, gathering them up and hustling them into the living room. Five minutes later she brushed her hands on her jean clad thighs. "I'm ready."

"Just like that?" he asked.

"You want me to take another half hour to get ready?"

He grinned and there was an unexpectedly exciting, thoroughly wicked attraction in his rare laughter. "I'm not going to question my luck. Let's go."

They spent the afternoon as tourists, arguing over the merits of paintings in the galleries, eating a sidewalk picnic lunch on the Seattle waterfront and browsing through some downtown bookstores that were open on Sundays. They skipped the ferry ride on the grounds that the afternoon was rapidly slipping away and they didn't want to spend a lot of time sitting and sampling the view through a window. Every minute seemed somehow very important. They ate dinner at a popular pier restaurant and drove back to Ignatius Cove as the late summer sun began to set.

The afternoon jaunt to Seattle represented the first time Mercy had actually relaxed around Croft. She savored the feeling, hugging it to her during the drive back. But by the time he had parked the Porsche in the lot below her apartment, a niggling sense of doubt had risen to ask if she hadn't been *meant* to relax.

In the morning she would be on her way to Colorado and Croft had told her more than once he intended to accompany her.

She climbed out of the Porsche with a return of the uncertain feeling that had been pleasantly absent for the past several hours. As she closed the door of the car she looked at Croft over the low roof of the Porsche. He stared back at her, waiting.

"I'm still not going to invite you to go with me to Colorado, you know," she said with what she hoped was a casual firmness.

"The evening's not over," he pointed out, not bothering to sound casual at all. "I thought I'd come in for brandy."

"Did you?" Her pulse throbbed in her throat.

He didn't say anything else. He simply took her hand as she walked around the car and started up the stairs. She probably ought to halt him at her door, Mercy thought.

But she knew she wasn't going to do that.

At the door he took the key from her without a word and turned it smoothly in the lock as if he had every right. Mercy took a deep breath and stepped inside her apartment, flipping the light switch on the wall. Across the room the unfinished watercolor scene confronted them. Croft's eyes went to it.

"I'll get the brandy," Mercy said softly. She hurried into the kitchen. Perhaps it wouldn't be totally impossible to take him with her to Colorado. She was only going to spend two nights with Gladstone. If her client objected too strongly to her bringing along a guest she and Croft could always stay at a motel. If she could convince Croft not to embarrass her by making his desire to own *Valley* too apparent, then maybe . . . just maybe. . . .

A week in the Colorado mountains with Croft Falconer stretched out before her, tantalizing her unmercifully.

She shouldn't do it. It was a bad idea. She barely knew Croft and she didn't want to embarrass herself in front of her client. Besides, although she believed him when he said he wanted her, there was no doubt that he was equally interested in that damn book. Mercy didn't want to play second fiddle to a piece of eighteenth century pornography.

There were so many excellent reasons for not letting Croft accompany her.

He was still studying the watercolor scene when Mercy returned to the living room with the two glasses of brandy in her hand. He glanced at her assessingly as she moved to stand beside him. He looked as though he were choosing his words carefully.

"I should warn you, I don't take criticism well," Mercy told him, handing him his brandy.

"You're taking the wrong approach with your painting," he said very seriously.

"It's just practice for my art class." She glanced idly down at the scene on the easel. "Seemed like a nice day to catch the view. Do you paint?"

"I've studied watercolors."

She sipped her drink. "That surprises me."

"Does it? I found them very," he paused, "satisfying."

"Why?" she asked with sudden interest.

"Because on the surface the medium is very transparent. Very straightforward and obvious. There aren't multiple layers of paint to get in the way of the viewer, just a clean wash of color. Watercolor painting lets the artist create an impression with light. What could be clearer than light?"

Mercy shook her head. "You said watercolor painting is that way on the surface. But I don't think it would have held your interest if there had been nothing more to it."

"You're right. The transparent quality is fascinatingly complex when you study it. It reveals so much with so little. And that's where you're going wrong in your painting, Mercy. You're trying to put too much detail in your work. You're using a technique that depends on light as though it were pen and ink or oils."

"Oddly enough, I didn't let you in here tonight to give me a lesson in painting."

His mouth edged up at the corner. "No? Then why did you invite me in this evening?"

She shied away from the blunt question, not wanting to admit the answer to herself, let alone to him. "Perhaps as a polite thank you for the pleasant day you gave me?"

He considered that and then discarded it as an unacceptable reason. "Not good enough. There is a place for polite responses, but this isn't it."

"Croft—"

"Watch." He interrupted her to lean down and pick up a brush. He dampened the fine bristles in the little dish of water and stroked it across a pot of yellow. Then he combined the yellow with a touch of blue, creating a delicate green.

Mercy watched. She couldn't help herself. He was thinning the paint out far too much for her taste, she decided. But then he drew the brush across the paper in a swift, sure stroke and she realized in amazement that he had just laid down the perfect shade of the sky at sunset over the cove. She would never have thought to use green to render that color and she would never have used such a restrained wash of paint to do the job. The result delighted her.

"Beautiful," she whispered, entranced.

He set down the brush. "I think," he said slowly, "that making love to you would be like painting with watercolors."

Mercy went very still.

Croft put his hand around the nape of her neck, using his thumb to lift her chin. His eyes were almost golden. "All color and light."

His mouth came down on hers before Mercy could even think of moving.

Chapter
FOUR

Mercy felt her responses leaping to life the instant he touched her. The sensation was wildly disorienting, unlike anything she had ever experienced in her life. His touch was, she thought fleetingly, exactly as she had dreamed it would be, a riot of color for her senses.

The snifter in her hand trembled and then it was gone as Croft removed it from her fingers without lifting his mouth from hers. When both of his hands closed around her she caught her breath. His warmth and strength reached out to capture her and pull her into a glittering trap. All the fascination, the physical awareness and the deep, underlying compulsion to know Croft that had been unsettling her for the past two days swamped her now.

She knew he was aware of her reaction. It made her feel vulnerable, and for a moment some of her wariness returned to initiate a losing struggle against the inevitable. Croft's hands tightened on her.

"You want me," he said, his mouth brushing her own.

"I've seen it in your eyes. You can't hide it from me. Your eyes are as clear as a watercolor to me. And I want you. I'll be careful with you. You have no reason to fear me, Mercy. I've told you before, you're safe with me. You know that, don't you?"

Once again she believed him, just as she had the first time he had told her she would be safe with him. Mercy relaxed in his hold, leaning into the captivating heat of his body. The pressure against her mouth was deep and persuasive and undeniable. When his thumb touched the corner of her lips and urged a response, she moaned softly. She opened her mouth to him and braced herself for the invasion of his tongue.

It was subtle when it came, not a storming of her defenses, but a careful, coaxing foray that left her shivering. It was only as he slowly filled her mouth, tasting her intimately, that she began to realize just how thorough his ultimate possession would be. This kiss was a sample, she knew, a probing exploration and a claiming that was only a forerunner of what was to follow.

When he reluctantly broke free of her mouth and began to trail questing, tormenting little kisses along the line of her jaw and up to her earlobe Mercy sighed in wonder. Her arms wound around his neck. The hard, muscled contours of his shoulders compelled her touch. She pressed her nails delicately into the fabric of his shirt, finding the resilient flesh beneath the garment.

"I was wrong," Croft muttered against her skin. "There's more than light and color in you. There's strength. Beautiful, subtle, feminine strength. We're going to find something very special together, you and I."

"Perhaps in time," she whispered, closing her eyes against the exquisite feel of his teeth on her earlobe.

"Tonight," he corrected.

She didn't argue. She was already beyond arguing. This was what she wanted. He knew it and she could finally acknowledge it. It was happening much too fast. She knew far too little about him. But never in her life had she needed and wanted a man the way she wanted Croft Falconer. Denying herself tonight would have been to deny a possibility that until now she hadn't even dreamed existed. She couldn't leave that unknown unexplored.

"Are you still a little afraid of me?" he asked. His hands slid down her back, forcing her gently against the length of him. When his palms reached her rounded buttocks he cupped her and lifted her up into the heat of his thighs.

"Yes. No. I don't know." It didn't matter, Mercy realized. Whatever fear existed was submerged beneath the flaring desire. And the desire was mutual. She could feel the rigid shape of him pushing against the fabric of his jeans.

"How can you be afraid of me when you can tell so easily how much I want you?" His voice was a husky groan as he pressed her even more intimately against him.

"Oh, Croft."

Mercy buried her face in the curve of Croft's shoulder, inhaling the raw, primitive scent of him.

"I want to see you come alive under my hands the way a watercolor scene does on paper." Croft shifted, turning her slowly in his arms until she was standing with her back against him. When she struggled slightly, not understanding, he whispered, "Don't fight me, sweetheart. Open your eyes."

Mercy did so and found herself staring at their reflected images in the mirror in front of her. She was almost shocked at her own languid, heavy-lidded gaze. She could see the desire in herself and it startled her. This was what Croft was seeing, this open invitation, this combination of sensual pleading and feminine command. The sight of herself might have embarrassed her beyond recovery if it hadn't been for the other image in the mirror. This second reflection showed the hard-edged arousal in Croft's face. His golden eyes glittered with it.

He watched her expression as he caged her within the circle of his arms and began undressing her. Slowly and deliberately his fingers moved down the front of her tailored shirt. When all the buttons were undone he eased the garment off her shoulders and tossed it casually aside. Then he put his lips into her hair, his eyes still meeting hers in the mirror as he cupped her breasts in his hands.

Mercy was aware of a wave of delicious weakness going through her. She stared into the mirror, fascinated by the sight of herself encircled in Croft's bronzed arms. Her gently rounded breasts nestled in his hands, the nipples peeking over the edges. Even as she watched he lightly grazed his thumbs across the rosy peaks, drawing them to full attention.

She clutched at his arms, feeling so sensitized that she feared the next caress.

"Please," she managed, "I don't . . . It feels so strange."

"You're very sensitive. I knew you would be. Are you afraid it's going to hurt when I do this?" Croft circled each dark aureole with the edge of his thumbs. He watched her face in the mirror with a relentless intensity.

Mercy gasped as her nipples puckered into even tighter peaks. The feeling was almost unbearable, an ache and a longing and a sizzling sensitivity. Her lashes lowered until her eyes were almost closed. She said with total honesty, "I'm not sure what to expect with you."

"Sometimes there is a very fine line between pleasure and pain."

"Do you always know the difference?"

"Yes. Always."

She believed him and knew she should find the knowledge terrifying, but it was exhilarating. He was a man who was at home with violence. Perhaps he was not adverse to crossing the invisible barriers between pleasure and pain when he was aroused. Instead of caution, however, Mercy was suddenly filled with supreme trust. Croft did know the difference and he would never cross the line. She could give herself to him in perfect safety. With him she could learn the thrills and pleasures that lurked at the farthest edges of sensation without fearing the fall that would take her over the edge.

This man would always protect her. She could trust him. Once again her eyes met his in the mirror and this time she smiled at him.

It was a slow, sensuous, utterly female smile of invitation and longing and ancient promise that came from the depths of her being and radiated in her eyes. There was a warm flush to her skin that started just above her breasts and lightly colored everything in its path all the way to her cheeks. She knew from the look in Croft's eyes that he was vitally aware of her glowing excitement. His body was tightening in reaction and he muttered thick, dark words of encouragement into her hair.

Her fingers still clung to his forearms but she offered no resistance when he released her breasts and let his hands glide to her waist. There was a faint metallic rasp as he unsnapped her jeans and slid the zipper down. Mercy could feel the shift of muscle and sinew in his arms as he began to push the jeans over her hips. She was very conscious of the hard pressure of his manhood straining against his own denims. He had pushed himself close into the small of her back where she could feel him very distinctly. He was big, she thought. Solid and heavy and totally male.

"Do you have any idea how sexy you are? I could look at you for a long time, sweet Mercy. You're full of soft, round curves and hollows waiting to be explored. All kinds of shadow and light."

Mercy heard the words, but she didn't see his face because she had closed her eyes again when he shoved the jeans down her thighs. She could feel her panties going with the denim and knew that if she lifted her lashes she would see herself completely naked in the mirror.

Her natural inhibitions rose suddenly to assault her. "I don't want to be the only one standing here in front of a mirror without any clothes on," she whispered in protest.

He laughed softly, the sound dark and sensual in her ear as he leaned forward to kiss her shoulder. "Then undress me."

With a small cry she turned in his arms and opened her eyes to meet the lambent flames in his gaze. Something she saw there both provoked and excited her. "I want to touch you."

"I need to feel you touching me."

She unbuttoned his shirt, having to concentrate on the small task because her fingers were trembling. Croft didn't make matters easier for her. He kept murmuring sensual promises and dropping light, unbelievably tantalizing kisses on her temple and behind her ear. His fingers played havoc with the sensitive nape of her neck as she fumbled with his garments. Never had she realized just how sensitive that part of her body was.

Croft shrugged impatiently out of the shirt when she had it undone and then he pulled her close again. When her breasts were lightly crushed against his chest he looked into the mirror behind her and smiled. Slowly he stroked his hands down her back to the curve of her bare hips. When he let his fingertips slide along the edge of the small cleft that separated her soft buttocks, Mercy caught her breath.

"*Croft.*"

But he ignored her. His touch went lower, tracing a sensual path until he found the damp, feminine heat that told him all he needed to know about her state of readiness. As he drew his fingers through the gathering dew between her legs Mercy splayed her hands across his broad chest. Her head tipped back and a small cry was caught in her throat. She sank her nails through the crisp, curling hair and into his skin just above his flat male nipples.

When she heard his sharp intake of breath she became conscious of what she was doing. Anxiously she looked up at him. "I didn't mean to hurt you."

He laughed silently down at her. "You couldn't possibly hurt me. But you could easily drive me out of my mind."

She smiled back at him, reassured. Then, with a boldness that was new to her and that she quickly discovered she enjoyed, Mercy unfastened and unzipped his jeans. The heavy shaft of his manhood spilled out into her hand, filling her fingers and thrusting far beyond to brush against her stomach. The hard, blunt shape of him was as unyielding as steel but its tip was covered in the softest of velvet. The contrast was enthralling. Mercy cradled him in her hand and stroked him gently, wonderingly.

"You're rather like a painting, yourself," she said. "There is a great deal more to you than first meets the eye. More than I expected." Much more, she added silently. He seemed massive, filling her fingers and pulsing with life and energy. She wondered if they were going to fit together as well as he seemed to think. She licked her lower lip and said carefully, "You're very large, Croft."

Croft slipped one hand down between their bodies, raking through the soft thatch of hair at the juncture of her legs. Then, without any preamble he eased one finger just inside her hot, moist channel.

"Oh!" Mercy's body clenched around his invading finger and she staggered a little, releasing her intimate hold to clutch his arms for support.

"And you're very small," he murmured gently. "Silky smooth. We're going to fit perfectly. I can't wait to get inside you and feel you around me. This isn't going quite the way I had planned. You're so ready for me. I thought I could draw it all out a little longer. I wanted to take the time to do it right."

"The way you're going about it doesn't seem wrong, believe me." She swayed against him, her body filled with an unbelievable urgency.

"You don't understand," he muttered. "But this isn't the time to try to explain. Look at us, Mercy. Take a look in the mirror and see how right you are for me."

He moved, turning them both sideways to the reflective glass and Mercy glanced to her right, half afraid of what she might see. The sight of her slender body pressed against Croft, his hands possessively gripping the rounded globes of her derriere was disconcerting, even though she had been expecting it. She drew a deep breath, unable to take her eyes off the scene in the mirror.

"What is it, Mercy?" Croft eased one muscular leg between her thighs, forcing her to part her legs. "Don't we look good together? Don't you like what you see? We're creating a watercolor in that mirror." He caressed her hip, moving his palm upward until it rested alongside her breast. The contrast between his bronzed fingers and her white breast was very erotic. His dark head bent over her tawny one made an equally sensual contrast. His leg tangled between hers was a bold invasion of her softness. "Sunlight and shadow."

She pulled her gaze away from the hypnotic scene in the mirror. Her fingers sank into his shoulders as she looked up at him. The dark, husky sound of his voice was a seduction in itself. She felt very open and vulnerable as he moved his thigh gently back and forth between her legs. His muscled leg was hard and hairy and enticing, sliding up along the delicate skin of her inner thigh. She knew she was dampening him with her uncontrollable response; knew, too, that he was highly aroused by it.

Mercy didn't understand how he could be as aroused as

she was and still so much in control. Something was wrong with the situation.

"Croft, you're very aware of what you're doing, aren't you?" she whispered, searching his narrowed gaze. He was with her every inch of the way, she thought, but there was a difference. She felt dazed and disoriented by her body's reactions, but she sensed that Croft was still completely in command of himself. It would probably take a great deal to shake that control, much more than the expectation of one night with a woman who melted like warm honey in his arms. The knowledge hurt a little, briefly disrupting the sweet web of passion that was weaving itself around them.

"Hush, Mercy," he breathed, leaning down to lightly taste the skin of her bare shoulder. "Don't cloud the moment with logic. This isn't the time for logic and reason. This is a time to feel. Just let your body respond to me. Look at the lady in the mirror. She's not afraid. She's feeling free and wild and alive. She's not going to ruin tonight with questions that can't be answered."

Before Mercy could gather her glimmering thoughts to pursue those unanswerable questions, Croft was easing her down onto the carpet in front of the mirror. The last of the unexpected, unbidden wariness within her evaporated.

Out of the corner of her eye Mercy saw the woman in the glass clinging to the man above her as he lowered himself down to cover her body with his own. When that other woman cried out and arched upward, offering her breasts to her lover's hungry mouth, Mercy was stunned by the degree of her uninhibited response. Her hair, *my hair* Mercy reminded herself in a desperate effort to maintain a distinction between image and reality, fanned out on the slate gray carpet. The man in the mirror shoved his fingers into the thick, tawny mass as he carefully set his teeth to one hard nipple.

Simultaneously Mercy felt the sensual, twisting tug as her own lover laced his hands through her hair. She sucked in her breath in wild pleasure as Croft's teeth teased the peaks of her breasts. The woman in the mirror raised her knee and in the same instant Mercy felt the hard, muscled contour of Croft's buttocks on the inside of her own leg.

She was vividly aware of the waiting, pulsing masculine flesh poised between her thighs and knew the woman in the mirror was strung out on the same tight wire of anticipation.

"Now." Mercy's voice was almost soundless, but the feminine plea in it vibrated through the air. "Please, now, Croft."

The woman in the mirror lifted her hips in wanton, aching invitation. Mercy felt the curling silk of the hair between her legs brush against the rough, crisp nest that surrounded Croft's jutting shaft. Croft groaned, the wordless sound hoarse and rasping in Mercy's ear.

"I've waited long enough," he said through clenched teeth as he settled himself more intimately between her legs. "Too long. Years. Maybe forever."

Mercy didn't understand what he meant, but she wasn't in a mood to ask any more questions. He was there at the core of her body, pushing into her slowly, as if he intended to savor every centimeter of possession. And then, as if some part of her knew how thorough and undeniable that possession would be, Mercy tensed.

The woman in the mirror dug her nails into her lover's shoulders in sudden, silent protest as Croft forged carefully into Mercy's tight body. Mercy felt the taut, stretching sensation that hovered on the brink of pain and held her breath, unaware of how deeply her nails were scoring Croft's skin. Some of the delicious ache that had been driving her faded abruptly. Her senses focused on the reality of what was happening and she went taut with a sudden fear.

"Relax," Croft ordered gently. He held himself still with an obvious effort. He was only part way into her. He rested on his elbows, waiting for her body to ease a little around him. "You're fighting it. There's no rush. We've got all night. Don't fight me or yourself." His fingers brushed tangled strands of hair back from her face as he gazed intently down into her eyes.

Mercy could feel his muscles tighten as he fought sucessfully to hold himself in check. "You're so damned controlled," she gasped. It was a stupid protest, but it was the one that flared within her as she stared up at him.

"If I weren't, I might hurt you tonight. You're very tense, very tight. You must still be a little afraid of me, I think. Is it me or is it because you've been so long without a man?"

"Maybe I'm nervous because you're too sure of yourself, too much in charge of your own body." She moved her head in restless dissatisfaction and disappointment. "I won't be able to relax and let go until *you* do," she concluded rashly. "Stop it. Stop everything. This has gone too far."

Something fierce lit his eyes for an instant. "You know I want you."

"You want to seduce me. There's a difference."

"You're an expert?"

"I'm not a complete fool. Don't you dare laugh at me."

"No," he breathed tightly, "you're not a fool. But you're letting yourself get fragmented by a hundred different fears. You'll tear yourself apart tonight if I let you."

"You're the one who's tearing me apart. Literally."

"You know that's not true. I've told you, you're safe with me."

"I don't believe you." She was grabbing at straws and realized it. She didn't know what it was she hoped to accomplish. Mercy was aware only of a desperate need to provoke him out of his contained, controlled desire. She wanted him as wild as he had made her. She needed to know he was as caught up in the wonder and excitement of the moment as she was. "Do you hear me, Croft? I don't believe you. I hardly know you. How can I possibly know what passes for honor with you? How can I trust you? A woman would be an idiot to put herself in the hands of a man who admits he's an expert on violence. I don't believe you anymore. I don't trust you."

She felt the change in him immediately. Mercy was elated by the abrupt, trembling tension that suddenly gripped him. But when she saw the new brilliance in his eyes she feared for a moment she might have gone too far.

"Damn it, you don't have any choice except to believe me." Croft's voice was suddenly raw. "You're going to belong to me."

"Am I?" She was taunting him and knew that in the morning she would be appalled by her own recklessness.

He wrapped his hands in her hair, chaining her. "Admit it," he breathed fiercely. "Admit you want me. Say it."

She caught her breath and then gave him the truth, unable to deny it. "I want you."

"Tell me you trust me. Tell me you were lying when you said you didn't believe you could trust me."

She sighed and surrendered to the rest of the truth. Her limited self-control was gone already. She didn't have his power or his strength of will. And she wanted him so desperately. "I trust you."

"Thank God you don't know how to lie to me." His hands seized her shoulders and his mouth closed over hers with a savage eroticism that threatened to swamp Mercy. The muscles of his hips bunched as he drove himself slowly, inevitably forward.

She felt him move within her, surging completely into her with an impact that took away her breath. Her body adjusted eagerly to his. There was no pain, only an unbelievably taut, filled sensation. Then she forgot about the woman in the mirror, forgot about everything except the sensual wonder of having Croft inside her.

"Oh, my God, Croft." She clung to him, wrapping her

legs around him in a desperate effort to hold him as deeply as possible within her.

"Sweet Mercy," he muttered. It was an oath and a prayer and a hoarse shout of triumph.

Croft held her as tightly as she held him. His fingers were clenched deeply into her soft flesh. Mercy gave herself up to the enthralling excitement, aware of her body tightening in a new and totally different way as Croft plunged into her and then withdrew in a rhythm of mounting tension.

Mercy felt free to fly now. She yearned for stars she had never touched, sensing for the first time in her life what awaited beyond the threshold. Even as she reached out blindly, giving herself completely, she knew she didn't fear the unfamiliar experience that awaited. Croft was with her. Together they grabbed for the shimmering conclusion to the ever-tightening spiral of sensation.

"Yes, damn it, *yes,*" Croft's guttural command came as Mercy cried out her overwhelming need for release. "Take it, sweetheart. It's all yours."

She shuddered in his arms, sought for and found the unknown, hitherto undiscovered climax, and then reeled as it was thrust upon her.

"Croft, oh Croft, please, I can't stand it." She clutched at him, burying her face against his flesh. She could taste his perspiration on her tongue as she gripped him in an agony of satisfaction.

"Sweet Mercy, neither can I." He sounded awed with his own passion.

And then there was no more room for coherent words or demands. The storm of their desire broke, leaving them drenched and shuddering in throbbing release.

It was a long time before Mercy opened her eyes. Croft was still sprawled on top of her, his weight crushing her into the carpet. She smiled to herself, tracing small circles on his shoulders with the tips of her fingers. He had his head turned away from her, facing the mirrored wall as he rested on her breast.

Mercy was unaware that he was watching her in the mirror until she happened to glance in that direction and realized his eyes were wide open and very intent.

She grinned impudently at him. "What do you think you're staring at, Mr. Martial Arts Expert?"

"You."

"I don't recall giving you permission." She teased him with her eyes and a tilted mouth.

"I didn't ask." He lifted his head, slowly peeling himself away from her perspiration slick body. "Wouldn't be much point. You'd probably have said no. Just to be difficult." He brushed his mouth lightly over hers. "Christ. I had no idea just how difficult you were going to be when I saw that ad for *Valley* in the bookseller's catalog."

There was no good-natured amusement in his words, Mercy realized. He was having trouble adjusting to something and it showed. "Would it have mattered?"

He shook his head in a solid negative. "No. It wouldn't have mattered. What time do we leave in the morning?"

Mercy froze for a few seconds. Croft said nothing. He stayed where he was, crushing her into the carpet and waited. Just waited.

"Did you seduce me tonight in order to persuade me into taking you to Colorado?"

"No. I would have seduced you tonight regardless of whether or not you were leaving for Colorado in the morning. I wanted you very badly. I can't remember when I've wanted anything as badly as I wanted you tonight."

She looked up into his unyielding face and believed him. "I'm glad," she said gently. "Because I've never known anything like what happened tonight."

"Oh, Mercy. I know that. You're so damn transparent. Just like a watercolor." He smiled faintly and kissed the tip of her nose. "I saw the shock in your eyes when I first made you look into the mirror and watch us, and I felt the shock in you when you went wild in my arms a few minutes ago."

She flushed. "Proud of yourself, are you?"

His teeth flashed in one of his rare, predatory grins. "It's your own fault for giving me so much delightfully positive feedback."

"I'm not sure I like you being able to read me so well."

"You'll get used to it." He rolled lightly to his feet and reached down to pull her up beside him.

"Will I?" Mercy eyed him assessingly.

"Mmm." He touched the corner of her mouth with a gentle finger. "I'm looking forward to spending a few days with you in Colorado."

"You mean you're looking forward to trying to talk Gladstone out of his purchase."

Croft shook his head. "No. I have no interest in trying to talk Gladstone out of *Valley.*"

"Do you really mean that? Word of honor?"

"Word of honor. I swear I won't try to negotiate with Gladstone."

She ached to believe him, and when she searched his intent gaze she was finally convinced she could. "All right," Mercy said, coming to a decision.

Croft smiled again and reached down to scoop up their clothing. "I know it's all right," he said as he led her toward the bedroom.

Later, Croft lay quietly beside a sleeping Mercy and tried to analyze the shadows in the room. He wasn't having much success. He had already been over the same questions several times in his own mind and the answers eluded him. He was feeling restless again and it bothered him.

It was like looking at a watercolor. On the surface everything was crystal clear. He had achieved what he'd set out to do. Mercy had yielded to him physically, emotionally and intellectually. He would be going with her to meet the mysterious collector who had grabbed *Valley* as soon as it hit the catalogs.

But Croft wasn't satisfied and he knew why. It had to do with the way she had provoked him into losing his self-control earlier. Until that moment everything had been going just the way he wanted it to go. Mercy had been melting in his arms, surrendering with a sweet, enticing sensuality that Croft had enjoyed. Hell, he'd more than enjoyed it. He'd gloried in it, reveled in it.

He had been thoroughly aroused, obsessed with the idea of a gentle conquest that would tie her to him with what he hoped would be strong emotional bonds.

He hadn't been taking advantage of her, Croft had told himself earlier that day when he had planned the seduction. It was all for her own good. Lying now in her bed he had the grace to wince at the thought of how Mercy would greet such a rationalization for the volatile lovemaking that had taken place on her living room floor. But it was the truth. He was doing all of it to protect her.

But he admitted to himself that he needed her tied to him. He had deliberately set out to do exactly that. He wanted the emotional bonds in place just in case things got rough in Colorado. They could be crucially important. They might even save her life.

Croft knew he couldn't talk Mercy out of the trip or the book. That had left him no choice but to accompany her to meet Gladstone. She needed someone to look after her just in case Gladstone turned out to be a man who should have died three years earlier. And Croft knew he needed the entré into Gladstone's home if he was to discover the truth.

Everything was intertwined. There was no way yet to separate out parts of the whole without ruining the delicate pattern that was being woven. Repairing a broken Circle took care and patience and precision.

He was doing what had to be done, Croft assured himself. The seduction tonight had been necessary, as necessary as any of his other plans. He accepted that even though he had his doubts that Mercy would be able to accept it if she knew all he did about the situation. He had done what had to be done.

No, it wasn't self-chastisement that was keeping him awake.

What kept him from sleep was the knowledge that in the final analysis, he hadn't been completely in control of himself or the lovemaking. Instead he had been caught up by the overwhelming lure of Mercy's response to him. It had sucked him in, surrounded him, captivated him even as he told himself he was possessing her.

In the end he had not been the careful, deliberate seducer, able to guide every step of the action from start to finish.

He had been seduced himself.

Chapter
FIVE

Erasmus Gladstone lounged in the elegant white leather chair and gazed at the spectacular mountain scenery outside the sitting room window. He sipped at the glass of fine port Isobel had just poured and told himself for the thousandth time that this mountain retreat was exactly what he wanted. Beautiful. Isolated. Protected.

It was also equipped with several different escape routes. He had learned his lesson three years before when his escape had depended on a single, fragile old tunnel that could have collapsed on him at any moment. He hadn't paid much attention to having the tunnel properly prepared because he hadn't expected to have to use it. Here the tunnel had been prepared first, even before the vault was added to the house.

The workman who had helped him dig and reinforce the underground corridor had suffered an unfortunate accident on the mountain roads shortly after the escape route was finished. Gladstone felt safe now. No one else knew about the tunnel. Dallas and Lance and Isobel had not arrived until after it had been completed.

On the island he had thought himself safe. Geography had kept him safe from the laws of the United States and the small island governments that were scattered about the Caribbean. Business acumen had kept him safe from his competitors. The mindless fanaticism of his followers had kept him safe from betrayal, or so he had thought. Arming the more violent and fanatical among the faithful had kept him safe from the possibility of attack by a small mercenary army.

But he had not been safe from a single ghost who had appeared in the night.

This second time around Gladstone had decided he would not make the mistake of surrounding himself with an army of blithering idiots. He would not rely on fanaticism and dope to ensure loyalty. Such a method carried far too many risks—as he had learned to his cost three years earlier.

This time he had opted for simplicity. The isolated location in the mountains, the escape routes, the electronic security mechanisms, the dogs, the three handpicked bodyguards whose loyalty was ensured by blackmail, money and charm, these were the guarantors of his new life. It made for a smaller, more select crowd, Gladstone thought in amusement. A manageable group. Any stranger or ghost who appeared among them would be instantly recognizable.

Erasmus leaned his silvered head back against the chair, closed his vivid blue eyes and remembered the screams and the raging fire and the choking smoke. The scene was indelibly imprinted on his memory because he had almost died that night; almost died at the hands of a man he had never seen; a ghost, his followers had screamed in despair.

He knew the single warrior had been a man, not a ghost, in spite of the hysterical claims of the panicked members of the Society who had stupidly turned to their leader for salvation during those last frantic moments. He had had no time to worry about anyone except himself. But whoever had destroyed the island stronghold of the Society of the Graced might just as well have been a dark specter from hell as far as Gladstone was concerned. The results had been a disaster from which Gladstone knew he was only now recovering.

It had been a long struggle. Gladstone found himself thinking about the destruction of the island fortress every day of his life. He had operated with such power down in the Caribbean. It would be a long time before he could reestablish that degree of wealth and power again.

Unless he got hold of the book.

Valley of Secret Jewels held a priceless shortcut to what Erasmus Gladstone wanted.

"More port?"

He opened his eyes and saw Isobel bending down to refill his glass. Her breasts were round and full above the low neckline of her silk dress. He allowed himself the pleasure of just looking at her for a moment. Beautiful women were plentiful for a man of wealth, but few of them came equipped with Isobel Ascanius' particular talents.

"Thank you, my dear. You'll join me?"

"Of course." She smiled at him over the rim of her glass, responding as always to the sound of his voice.

Gladstone had learned early in life that his voice was a most useful tool. People invariably responded to that voice. It caressed the ear, charmed and beguiled the senses. Gladstone made good use of his secret weapon. "You've arranged to have the map ready for our Miss Pennington?"

"She'll receive it when she rents her car in Denver," Isobel assured him.

"And the motel?"

"I told her it was the only suitable one en route. She'll stay there. Why should she question our recommendation?"

"Why should she, indeed," Gladstone murmured thoughtfully.

"You're certain you want her to spend the night there before she comes here to us?" Isobel asked. "It seems a waste of time."

"It will give us a chance to make certain she's alone and is not being followed. If we have any doubts about her at that point we can take the book from her then. She will think she has merely been the victim of a motel robbery. No one will be able to prove anything else. Having her stay the first night at the motel is simply an extra precaution. The book is dangerous, my dear. Extremely valuable and extremely dangerous."

Isobel wandered over to the window, watching the light fade from the glistening mountain peaks. "I still think we're taking too much of a risk merely to obtain this book."

"You will understand how important the book is when I have it back."

"But you won't tell me its significance now, will you?" Isobel asked with a sad smile. "You still don't trust me completely."

"I trust no one completely, my dear. But rest assured that you are in my confidence to a greater extent than anyone has ever been." Gladstone took another sip of his port. "Everything is in order at the colony?"

"Of course. The members are all looking forward to the party."

Gladstone's fine mouth twisted wryly. "Yes, I imagine they are."

"You're certain you want to have the party while Miss Pennington is here?"

"Absolutely certain. It will provide excellent cover in case we decide it's necessary to do anything permanent about sweet Miss Pennington. Just another precaution, my dear.

You should be accustomed to my little eccentricities by now."

"I find your eccentricities quite charming, Erasmus." Isobel smiled at him. "I'm learning much from you."

"No doubt you are." Gladstone smiled back at her. Isobel was a beautiful woman, but she had known that since she was a young girl. She accepted comments on her beauty with the air of one who took them for granted. They bored her. The real key to charming her was to pay tribute to her intelligence and her various skills. She thrived on such admiration. The key to using her efficiently was to recognize and grant what she really craved: a genuine measure of power. She needed to feel she was finally on the fast track. She needed to know that one day she might have what Gladstone had. Isobel was an ambitious woman.

Gladstone had another innate talent aside from his compelling voice. He had the ability to find the right key to handle nearly anyone. Gladstone never let any of his talents go to waste.

Mercy awoke the next morning with the distinct impression that her whole life had undergone a significant change overnight. But the sense of impending fate that seemed to fill her senses was pushed aside almost immediately by a variety of surprising aches and twinges on the insides of her upper thighs.

Cautiously she flexed her legs under the covers. None of the aches and twinges could be called painful, she decided objectively. More like gentle reminders of the claim Croft Falconer had made on her. There was no real discomfort, but there was a deep awareness in her of what it had felt like to lie in his arms.

Mercy wondered if Croft knew the full effect he had had on her the night before. She was afraid he did. The man was far too perceptive. He seemed able to read her as easily as he would read a book.

But she had learned some things about him, too. Falconer was, for the most part, supremely in control of himself and the world around him, yet he had his limits and he could be pushed beyond them. He could be provoked into letting go of the internal reins he held. Last night Mercy knew she had succeeded in doing exactly that.

In the clear light of day she was amazed by her own daring. More than amazed. She was staggered by it.

Mercy opened her eyes and found the room filled with predawn light. A glance at the clock beside the bed told her it was five-thirty. A glance at the bed beside her told her that Croft was gone.

She frowned and sat up. Belatedly she remembered she had never gotten around to putting on a nightgown. As she climbed out of bed and reached for a robe, Mercy listened for the sound of the shower or the clatter of the coffeepot in the kitchen. The apartment was utterly silent, but she sensed it wasn't empty.

Tying the yellow sash of the scarlet robe around her narrow waist, Mercy padded to the bedroom door and paused again to listen. There was still no sound, but now she was certain Croft hadn't left. Silently she walked down the short hall to the living room.

He was sitting crosslegged on the floor in front of the window. He was nude and his hands rested easily on his bent knees. His whole attention seemed focused on a point on the horizon at the very limits of her tiny scrap of view. Mercy realized Croft was meditating.

Respectfully she withdrew and went back down the hall toward the bathroom. This discovery, she decided as she stepped into the shower a few minutes later, was fascinating. But then, everything about this man seemed to interest her.

The incident was illuminating in several respects, she

thought as she stood under the hot spray, but above all it illustrated just how little she still knew about him.

Common sense dictated that she slow down the affair that had sprung up like wildfire on a hot summer day. She had no doubt that Croft knew what he wanted and what he was doing. Unfortunately, she wasn't as in touch with her own wants and needs.

Perhaps she was the one who needed a period of meditation to try to get her thoughts in order.

Wrapped in a towel, Mercy emerged from the bathroom fifteen minutes later to find Croft in the bedroom, examining the copy of *Valley of Secret Jewels* that had been lying on the nightstand. He had put on a pair of jeans but that was all. The contoured muscles of his shoulders and back were well defined in the morning light. He glanced up, taking in the sight of her wet hair swept back in a neat, clinging wave, her freshly scrubbed face and the waterdrops that still glistened on her bare shoulders. The faint smile that lit his eyes could only be described as satisfied and possessive. He took a step toward her but halted immediately when Mercy went still. He held up the book.

"Don't forget to pack this."

"Don't worry," she retorted, "I wasn't planning on leaving it behind."

"Been using it for some late night reading, I see."

"Purely professional interest," she informed him loftily and turned away to search about in a drawer for her underwear. She knew she was turning pink.

"Professional interest. Is that what you call it?"

She heard the teasing quality in his voice and was torn between the pleasure of hearing his silent laughter and the annoyance of having him discover the book in such an incriminating location. "Yes, it was professional interest. I even formed a professional opinion about the author."

"Rivington Burleigh?" Croft walked up behind her and

put his hands on her bare shoulders. He dropped a feather light kiss on her wet hair. "What conclusion did you come to about him?"

"That he's a her."

"What?"

She could tell she had surprised him. Mercy smiled smugly. "That's right. A her. I think Rivington Burleigh was a woman."

"Eighteenth century porn written by a woman? Not likely."

"Why not? There were other women writers in the eighteenth century. Lots of them. And it wasn't uncommon for them to write under a man's name."

"But this kind of thing?"

"Are you one of those men who think women aren't interested in erotica?" She moved away from his hands, heading for the closet to find her jeans. "If so, I've got news for you. Our tastes in it might be different than men's tastes, but that doesn't mean we don't appreciate it on occasion."

"Oh, I believe you, Mercy," he drawled, his eyes gleaming. "I saw your face when you looked in the mirror last night, remember?"

She glared at him over her shoulder. "A gentleman would not remind me."

"A gentleman probably wouldn't have made you look in the mirror in the first place."

"That's an interesting point."

"Tell me what makes you think Burleigh might have been a woman."

Mercy held her jeans in one hand, thinking seriously. "Something about the sensitivity of the writing, I suppose. There's as much description of the main character's internal feelings during the sex scenes as there is of the actual physical activity. Male writers tend to concentrate on the mechanics of the action rather than the emotional responses."

"You're an expert on male-oriented porn? I had no idea your professional interests were so wide-spread."

"Well?" she challenged. "Isn't it true? Aren't men more into the physical side of things while women tend to concentrate on the emotional reactions involved? That's why an affair that's being manipulated by the man takes off with a running start for the bedroom. But I think one managed by a woman would be begun more slowly, with lots of time allowed for getting to know one another."

"Do I sense a turn in the conversation? Are we suddenly getting personal instead of professional?" Croft didn't move, but there was a new level of intensity in the room.

Mercy kept her chin firmly elevated although her fingers were clutched very tightly around the jeans she was holding. She met his gaze with a direct, level look. "Yes," she said, "I think we are."

"Say it straight out, Mercy. I don't want to have to pick my way through the jumble of your mysterious thought processes."

"All right, I will." She took a breath. "I think we rushed things last night. It was too soon. We need more time to get to know each other, Croft. If you're serious about . . . about this relationship of ours, then you'll have to agree with me that we should cool the physical side of things for a while."

"Well, hell."

Mercy was startled by his short, picturesque exclamation of disgust. She was also offended. "If all you care about is sex than you can damn well look somewhere else for it."

"You didn't have any objections to sex last night."

She didn't like the forbidding expression on his face. "In the heat of the moment that sort of thing can happen. It's very easy, very common for a person to get swept up by a strong, temporary physical sensation that—"

"Not you."

She narrowed her eyes. "What's that supposed to mean?"

"It's not easy and not common for you to get swept up by a strong, temporary physical sensation. You were swimming way out of your depth last night and I was the one you hung onto to keep yourself from drowning."

"That's a very colorful image, but it doesn't change anything!"

He took two long strides toward her, driving her back against the wall before she could think to dodge. His eyes were gleaming with a rare emotion that might have been anger or outrage or both. When she was backed against the wall he caged her there with a hand planted on either side of her.

"Do you really think that all I'm interested in is sex?" Croft asked far too softly.

Mercy made a grab for her composure. "Well, there's the book, of course. There's no denying you're also interested in it."

"Don't you dare mention *Valley*. Not right now. We are not discussing that damn book. We are discussing us. You and me. And I want to know if you really think my only interest in you is your performance in bed."

She flinched at that because she was very much afraid her performance in bed as well as on the carpet had been rather amateurish. Her experience was limited, and she knew it probably showed. "I'm sure this is a very common problem in relationships," Mercy said desperately.

"You're an expert on that subject, too?"

"Croft, stop it. You're deliberately trying to intimidate me. I have a valid concern and you owe me the courtesy of treating it with respect and consideration."

"Where is it written I have to treat your idiotic concerns with respect and consideration?"

"My concerns are not idiotic. Croft, we hardly know each other. You just appeared in my shop on Friday, for pete's sake. By Sunday you had me in bed. That's moving too fast by anyone's standards. By my standards, that's moving at the speed of light. I want to slow down, and if you're serious about coming with me to Colorado, then you'll have to agree to slow down."

"That's your final word on the subject?"

"Yes," she said fiercely, "it is."

He stared at her for an endless minute. The shadows in his eyes shifted rapidly, as if he were running through a variety of responses in his own mind. Abruptly he dropped his hands from the wall, shaking his head with grim disgust.

"How the hell do you do this to me?" he asked in a low voice as he turned away and stalked over to the window.

The question was so soft Mercy wasn't certain it was meant for her to hear. He was asking himself and it was obvious he didn't have an answer.

"Croft . . ."

He ignored her, running a hand through his dark hair as he stared out the window. "I've just spent a tough thirty minutes trying to clear my head for the day, and in less than five minutes you've managed to ruin everything I accomplished."

"Uh, Croft . . ."

He swung around, his gaze accusing. "Damn it, I *never* lose my temper."

"You mustn't get upset with yourself just because you're feeling a little impatient with me. You have a perfect right to be somewhat," she groped for the word, "*surprised* about the fact that I've decided to take charge of this relationship. You've got a dominant sort of personality, and for the past couple of days you have been more or less dominating this situation. Naturally, it comes as a shock to hear me say I want to put a hold on the physical side of things, but—"

He cut her off with a sharp movement of his hand. "Not another word, Mercy. I'm warning you. Unless you want to receive a few surprises and shocks yourself, you will close your mouth and keep it closed until I've had my tea and my breakfast."

Mercy, who had her mouth half open for another reassuring comment on the subject of expecting too much of one's self-control, closed it at once. Without a word she watched him stalk into the bathroom.

They said the way to a man's heart was through his stomach. She would whip up something extra special for breakfast, she decided. And she would keep quiet while she did it. Croft was obviously going through a period of adjustment and needed the time to think.

That decision couldn't stop the silent, laughing grin that suddenly curved her mouth.

Several hours later Mercy sat in the passenger seat of a rented Toyota and struggled with the large, folded map of Colorado she had picked up from the car rental agency. They had left the Denver airport, following Interstate 25 south according to the directions that had been neatly typed on a piece of paper and left waiting at the rental agency.

Once away from the big city haze around Denver, a perfect blue Colorado sky had beckoned. The late afternoon sunshine seemed stronger, more intense than it had back in Washington. On the right the massive barrier of the Rocky Mountains paralleled the interstate, challenging more adventurous drivers to leave the freeway and try their luck in a far more primitive environment. Most of the traffic ignored the challenge.

Croft was driving, his movements relaxed and economical, his full attention on the traffic around him. He had made the decisions at the rental agency, selecting a Toyota Celica for the mountain roads. Mercy watched him surreptitiously, aware of his quiet, focused concentration. He did everything that way, she realized. He had a way of aiming himself and channeling his energy on whatever task came to hand.

He was not the kind of man to get distracted from whatever he had originally set out to do.

That last thought had been bothering her off and on since that morning. It should have occurred to her earlier, Mercy chided herself. But the night before she knew she had wanted to believe that she had succeeded in distracting Croft on some important level. The bright light of day and several hours of contemplation had reminded her that wasn't really very likely. It would take a great deal to genuinely distract Croft Falconer, a lot more than the not-very-sophisticated responses of a woman who had practically tripped over her own feet falling into his arms.

"What's the matter?" Croft gave her a quick, questioning frown. "Did you make a mistake in the directions?"

Mercy wrinkled her nose. "No, I did not make a mistake in the directions. We're almost at the turnoff into the mountains. Just another couple of miles."

A reasonably normal level of peace had been restored between Croft and Mercy immediately following the homemade pancakes and pure maple syrup she had served for breakfast. That, however, did not mean they weren't still occasionally rather sharp with each other. For example, Croft had nearly gotten a cup of tea dumped on his head when he had made the mistake of complaining about having to make do with a tea bag. He had attempted to give his hostess precise instructions on the proper preparation of tea and had found himself looking up at a full mug being held threateningly over his head. He'd had the sense to cease and desist.

At first she had believed Croft's continued, periodic brusqueness was a hangover from his earlier flash of male temperament. But now she was coming to the conclusion that it was caused by something else. She had the strange feeling his mind was on a different matter, something more important to him than a recalcitrant woman. The realization made Mercy uneasy.

"Mr. Gladstone's note suggests we stay at a particular motel near the ski resort area this evening. It's one of the few that will be open at this time of year. Tomorrow morning we'll drive on to his home." Mercy leaned forward, reading the signs that were flashing by overhead. "This is the exit. Turn off here and head toward the mountains."

Croft obediently swung the car off the interstate and picked up the narrow two lane road that led into the steep terrain beyond. The mountains soon rose around them, hemming in the tiny swath of roadway. The sparse vegetation quickly thickened, turning into a forest of dark green that cut off the view of the distant peaks.

"I've never been very fond of mountains," Mercy remarked conversationally. "Everything always seems so oppressive in them. It always looks as though it's dusk or twilight during the daytime and at night it's downright dark. Too dark. And the trees make weird sounds."

"That's amusing, considering the fact that you live in the Pacific Northwest." Croft was concentrating on the increasingly torturous road. "Washington is famous for its mountains."

"I don't mind looking at them," she explained patiently. "But you may have noticed I don't actually live in them. I live near the sea."

"So do I."

Mercy nodded complacently. "I'm not surprised."

A smile edged the hard line of his mouth. "What makes you say that?"

"Maybe it's your interest in watercolors. They always seem more appropriate to seaside painting. Or maybe it's just that you're the kind of man who would appreciate the natural drama of living near the ocean. I'm not sure, I'm just not surprised to hear you have a home by the water."

"When we're through dealing with Gladstone I'll take you to Oregon."

She smiled. "It's a deal." It gave her a lift to hear him talk about the future. Then she thought about the odd phrasing of the sentence. He hadn't talked about delivering the book to Gladstone, he'd said when they were through dealing with Gladstone. Mercy's smile became a frown. She glared at the winding road ahead. "Hadn't you better slow down a bit? This road isn't an interstate."

"Don't worry, Mercy. Everything's under control."

She leaned back in the seat and sighed because he was right. The man drove with the precision and expertise of a professional race car driver. Each curve was met and conquered with perfect timing. The Toyota was responding to a master's touch.

"You've got awfully good reflexes, don't you, Croft?" It was almost an accusation.

"Yes," he said without any trace of pride. It was simply a fact as far as he was concerned.

Shortly before seven that evening Croft parked the rented Toyota in the lot of a somewhat shabby but clean looking motel. The structure was on the fringes of what was undoubtedly a lively ski resort during the winter. The two-story motel was probably much more cheerful and welcoming when it was surrounded by crisp white snow and flocks of eager skiers. Now, at the end of a drowsy summer day with long shadows already cutting off the waning sun, the place looked dreary to Mercy's critical eye.

Croft glanced at her expression as he started to take the luggage out of the car. "We could try to find another place farther down the line."

Mercy eyed the handful of cars in the parking lot. "We might as well stay here. It's getting late and there's no guarantee any other place would be open. At least they've got a coffee shop. I'm starving."

Croft hesitated, then shrugged and started toward the tiny lobby.

Mercy suddenly remembered something. She trotted to catch up with him. "Two rooms, Croft."

He said nothing, didn't bother to look at her. He just kept striding toward the entrance.

"And I like to be on the second level," Mercy added forcefully.

"Any other requests?"

She didn't care for the cold tone of his voice. "Yes. See if they have a safe. I think I'd like to put *Valley* into it for the night."

He stopped abruptly and stared down at her. "Why in hell do you want to do that? You haven't worried about keeping it in your apartment for the past few weeks. Why start fretting about it now?"

"I don't know," she said honestly. "Maybe it's because this place is so rundown looking. It doesn't exactly inspire confidence in the staff, does it? No telling who's working here. I'll bet the locks on the doors are the kind you can open with a credit card. Women traveling alone learn to take precautions, Croft. If some joker decided to prowl my room looking for cash while I was asleep he might accidentally find *Valley* and take it on a whim."

"You wouldn't have to worry about that if you were sleeping with me."

His logic was unassailable, so she decided to twist it. "No," she agreed tartly, "I wouldn't. You're not the type to prowl motel rooms going through ladies' purses, are you?"

"Not on my good days."

The clerk behind the desk proved helpful and courteous, to Mercy's surprise. After he had assigned them their rooms, he accepted the paper wrapped copy of *Valley* and put it in the motel safe. The safe was an ancient thing, but it looked solid enough, Mercy thought. She felt better knowing the nucleus of her business future was safely stowed for the night.

Over an uninteresting, distinctly greasy meal of hamburgers and fries in the empty coffee shop, Mercy attempted to keep up a cheerful conversation with Croft. But he hadn't been overly talkative all day and didn't appear inclined to change the situation now. Once again Mercy had the impression his mind was on other things. It was frustrating. It was also depressing.

So much for using this little jaunt to Colorado to get to know each other, she decided gloomily.

By the time Mercy crawled into the lumpy bed and turned out the light that had illuminated the plain, cheaply furnished room, she was seriously wondering whether anyone ever got to know Croft Falconer very well. She doubted it.

She lay in silence for a few minutes listening for sounds from the room next to hers. Croft had gotten the room next door. The walls were thin but other than plumbing sounds she couldn't hear any sign of him.

That was hardly surprising, she told herself. The man moved like a ghost. Mercy fluffed her pillow, turned on her side and closed her eyes.

Croft stood in darkness watching the shadows outside the motel room window. He had opened the window earlier in an effort to get some fresh air into the musty, damp smelling room. The pine and fir outside sighed in anguish. Mercy was right, he thought in fleeting amusement. The trees did make weird sounds. They also cut off most of the starlight that tried to filter through them. The darkness on the forest floor was very thick.

But unlike Mercy he didn't find the heavy darkness oppressive. He could understand her instinctive reaction. She was a creature of the light. Glowing, transparent, vibrant with color. He, on the other hand, was a creature of the night. He comprehended darkness, knew it on an intimate level, used it, acknowledged it, accepted it.

Half an hour before Mercy had finally settled down to sleep. He had listened to her rustle around the room, cataloging each sound and noting it as a part of her bedtime ritual. He had paid particular attention when he'd heard her open the suitcase. He could just imagine her taking out a prim, full-length nightgown.

Then he had listened with a sense of pleasant anticipation as she opened a closet door. She would be taking off the bright papaya colored shirt she had worn, unbuttoning it quickly and revealing the sweet curve of her breasts. The chill in the room probably caused her responsive nipples to tighten.

Next had come the jeans. He had heard her step out of them and had drawn a mental image of her nicely rounded rear clad only in filmy panties. In a moment the panties had followed the jeans. He had heard the slight, unbalanced movement she'd made when she had caught hold of the closet door to steady herself while she pulled them off. Then she was naked. He had imagined the way the light brown triangle of curls at the apex of her legs would have gleamed in the dull light from the overhead fixture.

The pleasant anticipation had given way to frustration as Croft had listened to Mercy climb into bed. His barely contained desire had made him restless.

Now, as he stood near the window, he contemplated letting himself into Mercy's room and joining her in bed. She would be drowsy and soft with sleep, not really in any condition to lecture him on the proper course of their relationship.

Relationship.

It occurred to him he didn't like the word. Probably because he didn't completely understand it. It was too vague, too imprecise, and it covered too much territory. It was a word he couldn't fully comprehend or understand, a woman's word. A female could use it and pin any meaning she wanted on it, leaving a man to flounder in search of a definition. Besides, it didn't begin to describe the bond that existed between himself and Mercy now that they had become lovers.

He remembered how she had surrendered completely in his arms and told himself that if he pushed just a little, she would do so again tonight. He liked that, liked knowing he could overcome her normal wariness.

Croft brushed aside the memories of how he had lost his own sense of control. It was easier not to think about that aspect of the lovemaking.

The tension in his body made him aware of the torture he was inflicting on himself. Deliberately Croft turned his mind to other matters. He was supposed to be working, he reminded himself grimly. The woman had a way of distracting him that was disconcerting and potentially dangerous.

Valley of Secret Jewels was the important thing at the moment. Croft frowned, thinking about Mercy's insistence on leaving it in the motel safe. He would have offered to keep it for her, but he had had a hunch she would have refused. She didn't like the notion that he was interested in *Valley*. It made her distrust him a little. He, in turn, hadn't liked the idea of her distrusting him, so he hadn't even brought up the possibility of giving him the book for safekeeping. It was all very convoluted when he thought about it.

Croft hadn't realized before just how complicated a "relationship" could get.

But one thing was clear: the more he thought about it, the more he disliked knowing *Valley* was sitting downstairs in that poor excuse for a safe. And his reasons for disliking the idea had nothing to do with his relationship with Mercy. Instead, they were simple and logical.

If Gladstone was a legitimate collector, there was no problem. But if he was the man who had once called himself Egan Graves, then by now he would know that Mercy was not traveling alone. Gladstone the honest book collector would probably not mind that his dealer had brought along a male companion. Graves, however, would be alarmed.

If he were alarmed, or even merely curious, *Valley* might be in jeopardy downstairs in that safe. The book would be more secure if Croft removed it from its present location and brought it back upstairs for the remainder of the night.

Croft made up his mind and turned away from the window. He would explain to Mercy in the morning that he had retrieved the book because he hadn't trusted the night clerk. Any clerk serving time in an out-of-the-way motel such as this one would naturally be curious about anything a traveler chose to put into the safe. Perhaps too curious.

Croft opened the door of his room without making a sound and silently moved down the hall toward the stairs.

Outside in the chilled darkness he discovered the motel's vacancy sign had been switched off for the night. The lights were also off in the motel lobby. Croft went up to the door and leaned on the bell. There was no echo from within and he assumed the clerk had probably disconnected it along with the flashing vacancy sign. Croft wondered if the motel's absentee landlord was aware of the minimal level of service available.

Then again, perhaps the landlord didn't mind. After all, there wasn't likely to be much traffic through this section of the mountains late at night in the summer.

Croft stepped back from the door, eyed the hinges critically and decided Mercy was right. This was the kind of place where the locks could be neutralized with a credit card.

A minute later he was inside the threadbare lobby, letting the door swing softly shut behind him. The odor of cheap wine assailed his nostrils immediately and Croft suddenly knew what the night clerk did for entertainment in the evenings. A faint snoring from a cot in the corner confirmed his conclusion.

The night clerk was out like a light. An empty bottle of cheap wine lay on the floor beside the cot. Croft made one attempt to shake the clerk awake and gave up in disgust. The guy had obviously found a surefire cure for insomnia. He wouldn't wake for hours.

Croft crossed the room and stepped behind the counter. The ancient safe stood on the floor of the small office, a hulking shadow in the darkness.

Croft opened only three desk drawers before he found the combination taped to the inside of one. Clearly security was not a major problem in this neck of the Colorado woods.

Chapter
SIX

Mercy awoke with a racing pulse and a chilled feeling that seemed to be centered in the pit of her stomach.

For a moment she struggled to orient herself. Her mind refused to identify the strange surroundings and the uncomfortable bed for several vital seconds. Two facts were stark in her mind: this wasn't her apartment and something was very wrong.

Mercy lay still under the covers as the shadows of the motel bedroom gradually took shape. Slowly she regained control over her quickened breathing. This was ridiculous, she thought. She had lived alone much too long to wake up tense and afraid of the dark. Nothing was wrong. She was simply in a strange room. All she had to do was calm down and get her bearings. There was nothing to worry about. Croft was right next door, after all. One small scream would easily penetrate the thin walls.

Sitting up slowly, she clutched the sheet to her throat and wished that Croft were closer. She wouldn't have minded if he were right there in the room with her. There was something very comforting about the thought.

Her pulse had slowed but still hadn't returned to normal. What on earth was the matter with her? she wondered. This wasn't like her.

The faint scratching sound outside her window instantly set her blood pounding again. The cold feeling washed over her. Now, at least, she knew what had awakened her.

It must be a tree branch brushing against the side of the building, she told herself. With a great effort of will, Mercy forced herself to climb out of bed. Damned if she would let herself be terrorized by a tree branch. A single woman living alone couldn't afford to have anxiety attacks in the middle of the night because of a tree branch.

Mercy marched determinedly toward the window. This sort of thing had to be faced squarely. A woman alone got used to getting up in the middle of the night to investigate odd noises. It was the only way to insure peace of mind. She would lean out the window, locate the troublesome branch and impress her overly active brain with the stupidity of its manufactured fears.

She was less than three feet from the window when the dark, distinctly human shadow glided into view on the other side of the glass.

There was a time for investigating strange noises and a time for being brave. There was also a time to call for help.

Mercy screamed blue murder.

The intruder outside froze as if he had encountered an electrified fence. But he came back to life before the echoes of Mercy's shriek had faded. The shadowed figure slid rapidly away along the window ledge and disappeared.

The pounding on Mercy's door sounded seconds later.

"Mercy! Open the door or I'll break it down."

Mercy leaped for the door. Croft didn't make threats, he

made statements of fact and she didn't feel like compensating the motel owners for a broken door.

She flung open the thin door and almost got trampled underfoot as Croft surged into the room. He not only moved very quietly, Mercy thought, he also moved very fast.

"What's going on?" He scanned the room as Mercy flipped the light switch.

"There was someone outside the window. A man's shadow. When I yelled, he disappeared."

Croft was already at the window, shoving it open and leaning out to examine the ground below. "He's gone. Headed for the trees, no doubt. If he knows what he's doing he can lose himself in that forest in six seconds flat. Probably has a car waiting near the highway."

"But what was he doing outside my window? Damn it, he's getting away. We've got to do something, Croft."

"What would you suggest? That I run after him barefoot while he escapes in a car?" He slammed the window shut with a controlled energy that spoke volumes about the level of his physical tension.

For the first time Mercy realized he was wearing only a pair of snug-fitting briefs. As he walked back across the room she saw the fluid slide of muscle under his sleek skin. Hazel eyes gleamed a dangerous gold. Croft was a frustrated predator who had just missed sinking his teeth into his prey.

"Actually," Mercy said cautiously, "I was thinking of something less ambitious. We ought to call the manager's office immediately." She reached for the phone.

"It's going to take more than a phone call to wake him," Croft muttered under his breath. "Hang on a minute while I pull on a pair of jeans."

"What do you mean, it's going to take more than a phone call? Croft? Come back here. What's going on?" Mercy slammed down the receiver and hurried after him as he strode out of her room.

"Never mind, I'll explain later," he told her through the open door of his own room. "Better put some clothes on if you're going to come downstairs with me."

Belatedly Mercy remembered that all she had on was her cotton nightgown. It was prim enough with its high neck and long sleeves, but she felt quite naked standing there in the hall. Glancing around quickly she scurried back to her room. None of the other doors were being flung open by alarmed guests. Her frightened scream would have awakened anyone else who happened to be sleeping on this floor. It appeared she and Croft were the only guests with rooms upstairs.

She was hastily sliding into her loafers when Croft appeared in the hall outside her room. He had thrown on a shirt and was still fastening his jeans as he spoke.

"Ready?"

She nodded quickly. "I'm ready."

They hurried down the stairs and outside into the chilly night.

"What do you think that man outside my window was doing, Croft?"

"I don't know, but it looks like you were right to be wary of motel prowlers."

Mercy nodded. "Good thing I put *Valley* into the safe."

"By the way," Croft began as Mercy reached the screen door of the manager's office, "I meant to tell you in the morning that I—" He broke off abruptly as he realized the office door was wide open. "What the hell?"

Mercy felt a new frisson of fear trickle along her nerve endings. "He must have broken in here first," she whispered, halting on the threshold. "Maybe he robbed the night clerk and then came looking for whatever he could find in the guest rooms."

Croft was already pushing past her into the small lobby. He reached out for a light switch just as Mercy followed him over the threshold.

"Damn."

Mercy peered around Croft's shoulder, trying to see what he was looking at. "Oh, my God." The night clerk lay in an awkward sprawl on the floor, blood trickling from a head wound. "The poor man." Mercy eased herself around Croft and hurried toward the stricken clerk. She was almost bowled over by the alcohol fumes that permeated the room.

"There was no need to bash the poor guy. He was already out for the count." Croft went down on one knee beside Mercy as she felt for a pulse.

"What do you mean he was already out? Croft, what's going on here?" Mercy didn't wait for an answer. "We've got to call whatever passes for the local emergency medic service around here. He's alive, but he's obviously badly hurt." Her hand came away from the clerk's head, her fingers sticky with blood. She wiped them absently on her jeans as she stared in concern at the man.

Croft watched the small action with a curious expression. "I take it you don't get sick at the sight of blood?"

"Self-employed entrepreneurs can't afford to have queasy stomachs. Between the IRS and the banks, life is too precarious. Are you going to call the emergency number or shall I?"

"Not much choice. We'll have to call someone in authority, I guess." He spoke reluctantly as he went to the phone. "There's a number for the local sheriff's office here in the front of the book. Better not move the clerk."

"I won't."

The phone was answered on the other end and Croft gave the necessary information in flat, economical sentences. "Yes, we'll wait."

He wasn't watching Mercy as he spoke in an impatient tone. His attention was on the scene inside the small, inner office behind the desk. It was a scene shielded from Mercy's eyes because of the open door. After a moment's further conversation Croft hung up the phone and glanced at Mercy. "They won't be long. They're just a couple miles away near the ski resort."

Mercy nodded as she continued to kneel beside the victim. "Who would do such a thing? This place is obviously run on a shoestring during the summer months. There couldn't have been much money on hand. There are only a few guests and I'll bet most of them paid for their lodging with a credit card, not cash. I wonder if whoever it was hit the coffee shop, too?"

"And then decided to make a clean sweep by checking the guest rooms to see if there were any stray wallets lying around? It's possible."

"You don't sound convinced."

"All the other guests are booked into ground floor rooms. You and I were the only ones on the second floor. Why would the guy risk going up the outside of the building when it would have been much easier and more lucrative to hit the rooms down below?"

"Who knows? Maybe he couldn't figure out which rooms were occupied and which weren't. At this time of night everyone's lights would probably have been turned off. It would be difficult—" Mercy was interrupted by a siren in the distance. "Good. The authorities are almost here."

"For all the good it'll do," Croft muttered.

"What's the matter with you? We had to call someone. What have you got against the local authorities?"

"Nothing. I just don't happen to have a lot of faith in the official enforcers of law and order."

"Honestly, Croft, sometimes you're very cynical." She got slowly to her feet and turned toward him. "It's too bad I didn't get a good look at the guy. All I saw was the outline of a man against the window. It was so dark outside and I—"

She broke off as for the first time she caught sight of what lay behind the open door of the inner office. *"Croft!"*

He followed her stricken gaze. "Take it easy, Mercy. *Valley* is safe."

"I didn't realize whoever it was had gotten into the safe!" She leaped toward the doorway, staring in horror at the open safe. One quick glance confirmed that there was nothing left inside. "It's gone. Croft, he took *Valley*. My whole future in the book business. He just walked off with it. Probably doesn't even know what he's got. Just assumed it was valuable because it was in a safe. Damn it to hell, if I ever get my hands on whoever did this I'll strangle him."

"Mercy, calm down." The sirens were louder now and the first of the emergency vehicles was pulling into the motel parking lot. Croft moved from the desk and gripped Mercy's shoulders from behind. "Listen to me, *Valley* is safe. I have it upstairs in my room." His tone was low and forceful.

She whirled around to face him. "You can't have it upstairs. I put it in the safe and someone's taken it."

"I took it out earlier this evening."

Confusion washed through her. "Why would you do that? When did you do it? And how would you get it out? I'm the one who had to sign for it. Croft, this is insane. I demand to know what's going on."

"I'll tell you later."

"You'll tell me now!"

He shook his head once. "No, not now. Now we have to talk to the sheriff and I want you to follow my lead."

"What are you going to do? Lie to him?" She was furious.

"I'm going to tell him the truth. It's always easier as long as you don't get carried away with all the little nuances and ramifications. We'll keep it simple."

"I don't understand, Croft." She was more than furious. She was totally mystified. None of this was making any sense, and the most worrisome part was that Croft seemed coolly in control.

"You don't have to understand it all right now. Just let me

do the talking. You can tell him about seeing the figure at the window, but let it go at that. I'll handle everything else."

Mercy wanted to tell him he was crazy, that she was not about to lie to the authorities. She wanted to inform him in no uncertain terms that she would not allow herself to be dictated to in such a manner. She wanted to scream at him that she was not stupid enough to let a man she had known only three days tell her what to do in such a serious situation.

But his hazel eyes were calm and reassuring as he tried to impress his quiet commands on her. His strong hands clamped around her shoulders seemed to be draining her will to resist.

"Mercy, you know you can trust me."

"No, I don't know that." But the protest was weak and she knew it. Outside in the parking lot a siren was choked off as the sheriff's vehicle came to a halt. A car door opened and someone got out. The uniformed figure started toward the office door.

Without any warning Croft's eyes went from calm and reassuring to terrifyingly ruthless. The hands on her shoulders tightened only slightly, but Mercy felt as if she were suddenly trapped in steel claws. Croft's will inundated her, a huge, silent wave of male power that could not be denied. She shivered as she looked up at him.

"Damn it, Croft, you have no right to intimidate me like this," Mercy hissed.

"I don't have any option. You'll do as I say. Follow my lead. We'll sort it all out later." He released her as the sheriff's boot sounded on the step outside. "Get hold of yourself and stop looking as though you've just seen a ghost."

Mercy could have cheerfully used the nearest lamp on his arrogant head, but it was too late to attempt anything so satisfying. The sheriff was walking through the office door and Croft was turning to face him.

Mercy watched Croft move toward the other man and decided resentfully that she had every right to look as though she'd just seen a ghost. The fathomless cold that lay beneath the surface of Croft's eyes surely had its origin in some spectral dimension.

Mercy sat stiffly on the edge of her motel room bed and watched Croft as he came through the door with the wrapped volume of *Valley of Secret Jewels*. The sheriff had departed a few minutes earlier and the still unconscious clerk had been taken off in an ambulance.

"All right," Mercy began aggressively as Croft shut her door, "so you do have *Valley* safe and sound. That only opens up more questions than it answers." She reached imperiously for the book.

He handed the package to her, raising his eyebrows in a faintly quizzical rebuke as she snatched it from him and tore open the tape on one end to check the contents. "Thank you for letting me handle the sheriff."

"Ha. Don't thank me. You terrorized me into cooperating with you." She slid *Valley* far enough out of its wrapper to be certain it was the right book and then began to carefully reseal the package. "You should be ashamed of yourself. You have no right to traumatize innocent people that way."

"I didn't terrorize you."

"Yes, you did. And I won't stand for it again, is that perfectly clear, Croft?" She gave him a vengeful look from between narrowed eyes.

For the first time that evening a slight smile touched his mouth. "If you'd been totally traumatized an hour and a half ago you wouldn't be sitting there ranting and raving at me now."

"I am not ranting and raving."

"You're not exactly cringing."

"Of course I'm not cringing. I'm furious."

"Then whatever terrorizing effect I had on you must have been short-lived."

"I have decided," Mercy told him with fine hauteur, "to give you a chance to explain yourself in private."

"Thank you."

"Don't try to sound humble. It doesn't work. Now tell me the exact truth. I don't want the Mickey Mouse version you gave the sheriff."

Croft glowered at her. "What I told the sheriff was the truth. I went down to the motel office a few hours ago and got *Valley* out of the safe. I didn't trust the desk clerk not to get bored enough or curious enough not to try to see what was inside the package."

"Tell me honestly, Croft, is the desk clerk going to remember any of this?"

"No. He'd been through a whole bottle by the time I knocked on the door. He won't remember a thing. If the amount of booze he'd consumed hadn't wiped out his memory, the concussion he got later would have done the trick. Just as I told the sheriff."

"Apparently he was functioning well enough to give you the combination to the safe and let you open it yourself," Mercy pointed out. "At least, that's what you implied to the sheriff."

"It's close enough to the truth." Croft shrugged.

Mercy's eyes widened. "The clerk didn't give you the combination?"

"Let's just say he conveniently left it lying around."

"Damn it, Croft, I want the whole truth."

"All right. The man was already passed out on the cot by the time I got there. Dead to the world. I tried to shake him awake and couldn't. I found the combination in a desk drawer in the office. You'd be amazed how many people keep computer access codes, safe combinations and important phone numbers taped conveniently at hand. I opened the safe myself and removed *Valley*. I took it back to my room and went to bed. End of tale."

"Why do I always find myself believing you even when you tell me the most incredible stories?"

Croft lowered himself into the single chair in the room. "Beats me. Must be my natural charm."

"I can think of another name for it," she murmured, remembering the frightening willpower that had poured out of him when he had been attempting to force her cooperation. "Why were you so intent on convincing the sheriff that the thief wasn't after *Valley?*"

"I didn't have to work very hard at that. The sheriff came to that conclusion on his own. After all, whoever opened the safe a second time also broke into the coffee shop, lifted a stereo from one of the cars in the parking lot and got three wallets from first floor guest rooms before he made his assault on our floor. It was obvious the intruder was just checking all possibilities."

"It looks that way, doesn't it?" Mercy frowned down at the package in her hand. It was true that the thief had covered a lot of territory. Surely anyone who had been after *Valley* wouldn't have bothered with a car stereo and a few wallets. "Who could have known about *Valley* in the first place? Unless the clerk told someone he'd put something valuable in the safe this evening. It doesn't make any sense."

"You're sure you didn't see anything of that man's face when he went past your window?" Croft asked quietly as he studied her bent head.

"No. It was just a figure in black sliding past my window. He halted for a second when I screamed and then he was gone." Mercy's head came up abruptly as she remembered exactly which direction the man had vanished. "He was headed toward your window."

Croft said nothing, watching her intent face as she worked through the possibilities.

"In fact," Mercy whispered slowly, "he could have gone onto your ledge, slipped into your room and—"

"Stripped off his clothes and appeared at your door a few seconds later in response to your scream?" Croft finished for her, not sounding particularly alarmed at the obvious conclusion. "Forget it. It wasn't me you heard going past your window tonight, Mercy."

His cool denial irked her. "You expect me to take everything you say at face value. How do I know it wasn't you running along my window ledge two hours ago?"

His eyes met hers. "Because if it had been me out there you wouldn't have heard a thing." There was no trace of boastfulness in the words, it was just a statement of fact.

A ghost. You didn't hear a ghost when it moved. He was right.

Mercy sighed and set *Valley* beside her on the rumpled bed. "Well, I guess that's it, then. Just a casual bit of roadside violence. The desk clerk will survive and the intruder gets away with a car stereo and three wallets."

"Mercy."

"Yes, Croft?"

"There is another possibility." He spoke far too gently as he leaned back in his chair, rested his elbows on the edge and laced his strong hands under his chin. His hazel eyes were brooding and thoughtful.

"Somehow," Mercy responded wearily, "I was afraid you were going to say that. I'm not sure I want to hear this, Croft."

"I think it's time you did. There are a few things you should know about me and *Valley of Secret Jewels*."

Mercy touched the paper wrapping around the book, aware of a deep sadness welling up inside her. Angrily she fought it down. She had sensed from the beginning that

Croft's presence in her life wasn't going to be simple and straightforward. Still, a part of her wanted to resist hearing the full truth. She was certain that everything would change once she did. "If there are things I should know, why didn't you tell me before this?"

"Look at me, Mercy."

She gave him one quick, resentful glance and then went back to staring at the package beside her. "Just say what you have to say and get it over with, Croft. But this time around why don't you save us both a lot of time and effort? Tell me the truth."

"I've never lied to you."

"Have you told me all the truth?" she countered tightly.

"No."

"Why not?"

"Because until now there's been no need for you to know. All I had was a handful of questions I wanted answered. No facts, no real leads, no hard information, except for that copy of *Valley.*"

Mercy yanked her fingers away from the package and sat waiting. "What about this copy of *Valley?*"

"It shouldn't exist. It should have been destroyed in a fire three years ago, along with a man named Egan Graves and everything in his collection."

"Why are you so concerned about its reappearance?"

"If *Valley* escaped the fire, there's the possibility Graves did, too."

"How do you happen to know all this?" Her voice was a thin reed of sound.

"I was there the night of the fire."

Mercy drew in her breath, afraid to move. "Where?"

"At Graves' estate down in the Caribbean."

"Did you set the fire?"

Croft shook his head. "No. It's not my way. I hadn't planned to use fire. There was a fight near the estate's electrical room. A guard threw a small grenade and something exploded. The fire just blew up and consumed everything. Or nearly everything. Afterward I thought it was all over. There was no evidence that Graves had survived. I didn't see how he or anything else could have made it through the fire. It was an inferno."

Mercy was dazed. "Croft, what were you doing there? What was it all about?"

"Egan Graves ran a dirty little operation down on a Caribbean island where the U.S. authorities couldn't touch him. It was supposed to be a religious commune, a place of enlightenment. Graves called it the Society of the Graced. It was a cover for a sex and drug ring that sucked in naive young people, both male and female, and turned them into virtual slaves. They were controlled with a combination of drug addiction and a bizarre brand of hypnotic hype. The Society used its victims as prostitutes, actors in the ugliest kind of porn films, drug dealers, thieves, and whatever else seemed useful to build up Graves' empire. And it was all done under the guise of religious enlightenment."

Mercy stared at him. "How do you know about all this?"

"I was asked to go down to the island and bring out one of the victims. The daughter of a friend of mine. He also wanted Graves. He wanted him very, very badly. I understood."

"My God. What happened, Croft?"

"I got the girl out, along with several others. But not all, Mercy. I didn't get all of them. Some were so far gone that when the fire broke out they raced into the flames searching for their guru instead of running to safety." Croft's eyes were shadowed pools. "And I didn't get Graves. He vanished in the fire. Or so I believed."

Mercy looked at him, her mind conjuring up the scene readily. *Too readily*. It was as if she were getting the images directly from his memories rather than her imagination.

There was a shattering sense of emotion overlaying the unwanted pictures. "There would have been screams," she whispered. "Terrible screams."

He looked at her oddly. "You know. How do you know?"

She shook her head, trying to clear her mind of the images that had flooded it. Impulsively Mercy lifted a hand as if to touch Croft. But she was too far away and she let her hand drop back into her lap. "You couldn't have saved all of them, Croft, especially not the really crazed ones. It must have been total chaos that night. Flames, people running around screaming, guards shooting. I can just imagine it. What a ghastly scene."

"Yes," he said softly. "It was." His eyes never left her face.

For a long moment they simply stared at each other. Mercy tried to work through what she had just been told, but it was difficult. She was torn between sympathy and fury. The combination of two such powerful emotions surging through her was disorienting. Carefully she tried to pick through the facts.

"You said your friend asked you to go down to this island?"

Croft nodded.

"He had some reason for thinking you could get his daughter out of there?"

"He had a reason, yes."

Mercy swallowed. "You'd done that sort of thing before?"

"Yes."

"Croft, what are you, for God's sake? Some kind of mercenary? Do you lease out your body and your skills to whoever pays your price?"

His expression hardened but he didn't move. "I worked for whoever needed me, *really* needed me, not just for whoever had the cash."

"I'm not sure I see the difference."

"I only took the jobs I wanted. I was sort of a private investigator, I suppose. My fees were high. I could afford to pick and choose my clients."

"Most private investigators do insurance claims and child custody work," she shot back.

He nodded in acknowledgement. "I didn't do that sort of work."

"I'll just bet you didn't." Mercy jumped to her feet and paced across the room to the window. She rested her forehead on the cool glass and closed her eyes. "Your talents lie in other directions, don't they? You said your field of interest was the philosophy of violence."

"I haven't done any investigative work for three years. I opened the schools when I got back from the Caribbean. It was time to stop doing the kind of work I had been doing."

"What are you trying to say, Croft? That you're no longer a violent man?"

"I am no longer a man who makes his living with violence," he said carefully. "Except indirectly by teaching self-defense."

She spun around. "You can say that? After going through all this trouble to accompany me to Gladstone's home? No more of your half-truths, Croft. I want it all."

He got slowly to his feet to face her. "I've told you the truth. The existence of *Valley* has raised some questions that must be answered. It's not a new job, it's old business. It must be settled."

She watched him intently, aware of the unyielding will in the man. "And you're the type who always takes care of old business, right?"

"The Circle must be closed."

"I don't want to hear any of your macho philosophy! Just give me facts. I can deal with facts. On the other hand, maybe I've already got more than I want. You're not interested in *Valley* because you want the book for your own collection but because it represents a link to something you thought had been settled three years ago."

"Yes."

"You're afraid you might not have finished the job you set out to do."

"Yes."

"And you're not interested in me because you find me fascinating and irresistible but because I'm another piece of the puzzle you're trying to solve. You're using me to follow the trail of the book."

Croft's brows came together in a hawklike frown. "That's enough, Mercy. Your logic is getting damned shaky. You and the book are two different issues."

"The hell they are. I can be just as logical as you, Croft Falconer. You're using me, and if you expect me to tolerate it you're out of your mind."

Croft sighed with genuine regret. "I'm sorry, Mercy. But you haven't got any choice in the matter. Things have gone too far."

She wanted to scream in frustration. Instead she fought for control. "Correction. I can stop them right here and now."

"You'd better take your shower and pack. It's almost dawn and I doubt if either of us is going to get any more sleep tonight." Croft turned and walked out of the room, closing the door softly behind him.

Mercy watched in helpless dismay. All thoughts of screaming in fury or retaliating with physical violence disintegrated.

What she really longed to do was cry. She felt trapped between Croft's rigid code of ethics and her own anger at being used.

Chapter
SEVEN

Croft kept his eyes on the winding mountain road as he drove into the dawn, but his mind was on the woman seated beside him. She was too quiet, he thought. He didn't like it. This much silence from Mercy meant trouble. It meant she was floundering inside her own head, looking for ways to put up barriers and erect defenses.

It wasn't good strategy to give an opponent too much time to think, especially not a woman like Mercy. She had already come to some dangerous conclusions. It was time to take a firm hand.

"Mercy, if you're finished sulking, we can talk about what we're going to do when we reach Gladstone's."

"I am not sulking. I'm thinking."

"I don't want to argue the point. But I do want to talk to you."

"If you want to talk to me, tell me why I'm sitting in this car with you when I should have dumped you off at the motel and driven on to Gladstone's alone."

"You're here with me because deep down you trust me and you know it." He felt a pleasant rush of satisfaction at the thought. It was the truth, and he'd known it for certain half an hour before when she had silently gotten into the car beside him and slammed her door.

"All right, I'll concede I believe your wild story. I think you are concerned about the fact that *Valley* has surfaced after three years. I think you're wrong to suspect a link between what happened three years ago and my client, however."

He shrugged negligently. "It's very possible I am. I hope to hell I'm wrong. I was certain that Graves died in that fire. But then, I was certain his book collection had also gone up in flames. None of the other books from that collection have shown up in any of the dealers' catalogs."

"You've kept track?"

Croft nodded shortly. "When I first set out to find Graves I spent a lot of time studying what little was known about the man. His passion for book collecting was the one thing he couldn't keep completely camouflaged—not if he wanted to add to his collection. He was very careful in his dealings with booksellers. Always used an intermediary and kept his own identity secret. But rumors have a way of leaking out and I was watching for them. I used Graves' book collecting mania as a way to trace him to the island. Believe me, I learned a lot about his areas of interest. He was very selective and specific. Most of the volumes were one of a kind. Some of them dated back to the sixteenth century. Most of them were extremely valuable simply because they were totally unique. *Valley of Secret Jewels* wasn't an important acquisition because it's not one of a kind. That's one of the reasons I remembered it when I saw your ad. There are a few other copies in existence. It's only worth a couple of thousand dollars. If someone had wanted to grab a really valuable book the night of the fire, he would have chosen something else to rescue besides *Valley.*"

"But you said most of those other copies were in the hands of European collectors. That doesn't mean this book hasn't made its way here from Europe."

"It's Graves' copy, Mercy. I'm sure of it. There's too much evidence, including an inscription on the flyleaf from the first owner to his mistress."

"All right," she allowed, "so it somehow survived the fire. That doesn't mean Graves did. It doesn't mean Graves is Gladstone or that he has come back from the, you should pardon the expression, grave to claim his copy of *Valley.*"

"I know, Mercy," he said gently.

"But you want to be certain," she retorted waspishly.

"I have to be certain."

"Let's get to the important stuff," she continued after a moment. "Are you telling me all this now because of that intruder last night?"

"I think it was too much of a coincidence that that particular motel was ransacked last night."

"Why would someone who was after *Valley* bother with a car stereo and a few wallets?"

"Camouflage."

"You've got a complicated mind," Mercy said wearily.

That annoyed him. "Just the opposite. I devote a lot of time and energy to keeping my thinking simple."

"Well, take my word for it, it only works when it comes to dealing with women. In that area, I'll agree you're very simpleminded. Outside of that you're devious and complicated and dangerous." She paused for a second. "And I'm probably even more simpleminded for agreeing to let you come with me to Gladstone's just so you can satisfy your curiosity."

"Mercy—"

"I suppose I can write off our relationship easily enough.

After all, I'm an adult and I've had to bite the bullet before. Heck, I once had to write off an entire engagement. Compared to that, a one-night stand should be chicken manure. But, I'm warning you, Croft, this book is another matter entirely. My whole business future is about to take off and if you wreck it by scaring away my first good client, I'll never forgive you."

"It was not a one-night stand and you know it. And you're not going to write it off that easily." Croft took a firm grip on his temper. She was deliberately goading him. That knowledge didn't bother him nearly as much as the fact that she was succeeding in making him struggle to contain his rising temper. He had never met anyone else on the face of the earth who could push him so easily to the edge of his self-control. "Damn it, Mercy, how do you manage to do this to me?" Even as he said the words he remembered it wasn't the first time he had voiced the complaint.

She gave him a fulminating glance. "I don't know what you're talking about."

"Sure you do, but I suppose you feel you're justified. Is this your idea of revenge whenever you don't like the way things are going between us? Do you get some satisfaction out of pushing me and seeing if you can get away with it?" He realized he was genuinely interested in her response. There were times when he was sure he comprehended the pattern of thoughts and emotions that formed the basis for Mercy Pennington's actions. He felt he understood how her mind worked and knew he understood the important things about her excitingly responsive body. But occasionally Croft acknowledged that there were some areas of Mercy's mind that remained an absolute mystery.

"If you don't like the way I push you around," she said far too sweetly, "you can always get out and walk back to Denver. As far as I'm concerned we never have to see one another again."

Croft was startled. He took his eyes off the road long enough to stare at her for an instant. "That's impossible now."

"I'll admit it would be a long walk."

"I'm not talking about the walk to Denver. Lady, if you think you can get rid of me that easily, you really are simpleminded. You can't ditch me until I've discovered what it is about you that makes it so easy for you to push me to the edge of my self-control."

"Is there a danger of pushing you too far, Croft?" Her eyes were wide with brilliant, mocking interest. Mercy turned slightly to regard him more intently. She tucked one foot under her thigh and rested her left arm along the back of the seat. "I'm astonished. You seem to have been totally in control of me and the situation right from the beginning. I was just a puppet on your string, wasn't I?"

"Some puppet," he muttered. "You're already whipping out a pair of scissors trying to cut your strings. But it won't work, Mercy. You can't break the bonds between us that easily."

"We'll see," she shot back. "Tell me something. Did you ever think of playing fair with me right from the start? You could have walked into my shop on Friday and told me exactly what was going on and why you were interested in *Valley*."

He shook his head once. "No. I considered that approach and discarded it."

"Gee, thanks for the vote of confidence. Mind telling me why?"

He almost winced at the scathing tone of her voice. Then he tried to give her a complete answer. "First of all I had to be sure you weren't involved as anything more than an innocent bystander."

"Good grief! You actually thought that I might be connected with Graves?"

"There was always the possibility that you were using the ad in the bookseller's catalog to contact him. As soon as I met you, I rejected that idea."

"I suppose I didn't strike you as smart enough to be involved. I don't have the cunning mind of the true criminal, is that it? Or was it something about my beautiful eyes that convinced you I was innocent?"

"It probably was your eyes," he said reflectively and had the satisfaction of seeing her struggle to decide if he was joking or not.

"Uh huh. And after you came to the conclusion that I was just a dumb bystander, how did you justify misleading me?"

"I decided there was no need to alarm you unnecessarily. I wanted to check out my speculations before I got you involved any deeper than you already were. I didn't want you worrying if there was no need."

"In other words, you did it for my own good?" Her tone was oddly neutral.

Relief spread through Croft. *She understood.* "That's right." He took a deep breath and began to relax. "For your own good. If everything had been on the level with this deal with Gladstone, I wouldn't ever have had to say anything. We could have had a pleasant trip to Colorado and used the time to get to know each other better, just as you wanted to do. If something did go wrong, I would be there to handle it."

"Croft, has anyone ever explained to you that the worst excuse in the world for screwing a woman is to tell her it's for her own good?"

Mercy's hand on the back of the seat was clenched into a tight little fist. Croft saw it out of the corner of his eye and decided he had been wrong. It was much too soon for him to relax. "This conversation is getting us nowhere. Let's talk about how we're going to handle Gladstone."

"Yes," Mercy said rashly, "let's talk about that. It just so happens I have a few ideas on the subject. But let's find a place to stop for breakfast first. It's been a busy night. I'm hungry."

Twenty minutes later Mercy sat across the table from Croft in a small cafe they had found in a tiny mountain community on the edge of another ski area. She waited patiently while Croft ordered his morning tea with as much care and as many precise directions as possible. The middle-aged waitress, wearing scuffed sneakers and a stained uniform and still half asleep, listened to the instructions with weary patience. Mercy, who had listened to the same relentless list of directions the morning before, empathized with the poor woman.

"I assume you haven't any loose tea," Croft said grimly. "And if you did, it would probably be lousy. That means a tea bag. Please put it in the pot first and pour boiling water over it. I would prefer that you heated fresh water and make sure it actually boils. It has to boil in order to extract the full flavor from the tea, do you understand? Please don't use the warm water you keep in that pot on the coffee machine. Boiling water, please. It would be a great help if you rinsed the teapot out first with hot water before adding the tea bag and the boiling water."

When the tea arrived a few minutes later, the water in the cup lukewarm, a tea bag slung negligently onto the saucer, he accepted it with stoic resignation.

Mercy felt her first humorous lift in hours. She sipped her weak coffee and grinned at Croft over the rim of the cup. "Sometimes you have to be adaptable."

He didn't look up as he dunked the tea bag in the lukewarm water and tried to coax some color and flavor out of it. "You mean sometimes one has to compromise. But there are some things that are ruined with compromise. A cup of tea is one of them."

"Is that another aspect of your philosophy?"

"I guess you could say that."

He didn't seem to want to discuss the matter. Mercy therefore was perversely interested. "What are some of the other things that are ruined with compromise?"

"Honor, vengeance and love."

Mercy's eyes widened. "I can see you've given the subject some thought."

"Yes."

"Have you ever compromised on any of those things?"

He looked up from the pale tea. "I'm not totally inflexible. This isn't the first time I've had to compromise on tea. Does that answer your question?"

But she would bet he had never compromised on honor or vengeance, Mercy filled in silently. She should let this drop right now, she told herself, but she couldn't. Not quite. "What about love? Haven't you ever had to compromise in that department?"

"No."

"Have you ever been in love, Croft? Somehow I can't see you overwhelmed by such an emotion."

"You're right. I've never been in love. I can't see myself overwhelmed by it, either."

"Ah ha. Then you can't say whether you'd be willing to compromise in that area or not."

"Don't look so triumphant. I find it unpleasant at this hour of the morning to watch you glowing with triumph. Having to drink this lousy tea is bad enough."

She ignored the warning. "I'll accept that your philosophical standards are probably set in granite when it comes to tea, honor and vengeance, but it's obvious you can't speak from experience on the subject of love. You shouldn't make rash statements, Croft."

He raised his eyebrows. "It's possible to have an understanding of the nature of something such as love without having actually experienced it. The obligations, risks and rewards are all quite comprehensible intellectually. And you, lady, are the last person who should be handing out lectures on the danger of making rash statements. You have a reckless streak in you that leaves me breathless. Are you going to eat the rest of that toast?"

She eyed the two slices of toast that remained on her plate. "No, I don't think so. Help yourself."

"Thanks." He reached across the table and scooped up the two slices. "Let's talk about a more critical subject."

"The visit to Gladstone?" She would rather have argued about love, Mercy realized. She was certain Croft needed some straightening out on the subject. But it was obvious he wasn't in the mood for an extended discussion on anything that esoteric. Not at the moment, at any rate. "I don't see any problem. We behave in a perfectly normal, reasonable, honest manner. We're not going there to do undercover spy work. At least I'm not. I'm simply there to sell the man a valuable book and get a start in the antiquarian book business."

"You don't believe my theory?"

"That Gladstone might be a reincarnation of Graves? I think it's highly unlikely. Would you recognize Graves if you saw him?"

"The only pictures I ever had of him were long range photographs. I saw him from a distance the night of the fire. He was running through the flames. It wasn't the best view, believe me. But I would recognize him if he hasn't changed a great deal. Unfortunately, in three years a man can do a lot to himself."

"Like what?"

"Gain or lose twenty pounds, grow a beard, undergo plastic surgery. A lot."

"I see." Mercy considered that, her imagination taking off on a new tangent. "Would he recognize you?"

"No. He's never seen me."

"What about the night of the fire?"

"If he saw anything at all that night, which I doubt, it was only a shadow," Croft said unconcernedly.

"The shadow of a ghost," Mercy said to herself. "Croft, if by some fluke Gladstone really is Graves, what are you going to do?"

"Nothing while you're nearby," he said promptly. "The last thing I want to do is have you involved in that old mess."

"You'll give me your word that you'll behave yourself while I'm conducting my business with him? You won't attack the man at the breakfast table or anything?"

"I'll try to restrain myself," he said dryly.

"Croft, I'm not joking. I want to know what you intend doing while we're at the Gladstone place."

"All I'm going to do is take a quiet look around and try to figure out if there's any connection between Graves and Gladstone. I just want to answer a few questions."

"But what will it take to answer your questions?"

"One thing I'll look at is Gladstone's book collection. Even if he wanted them he couldn't have many of the same books as Graves had because so much of the first collection was unique. It's gone forever. But I'll be able to tell if Gladstone's area of interest and expertise parallels Graves'. That will be a very strong clue."

"And if a good look at Gladstone's collection doesn't answer your questions?"

"I'll try to get a look at his private papers. Do some research. Get a feel for the way he's making his money these days, that kind of thing," Croft said casually.

"Oh, my God. Is that all?"

"That's all. We'll leave on schedule. If I've confirmed any of my suspicions, I'll return later, on my own, to pursue them. Relax, Mercy. I won't carve him up at the dining room table with a dull bread knife."

Mercy went pale and choked on her last sip of coffee. She seized the water glass, her eyes tearing. Croft was startled. He got up and moved around the table to whack her lightly between the shoulder blades.

"Are you okay?"

She nodded furiously, still unable to speak. Slowly her throat relaxed. She tried another sip of water.

"That was a joke, Mercy." Croft sat down again, his eyes concerned. "I would never expose you to violence."

"You have a weird sense of humor, Croft," she gasped. "Kindly remember it's my future you're talking about when you make such horrible jokes."

"Your future," he said thoughtfully. "That's an interesting subject."

"I agree. I think about it a lot. But at the moment I have no intention of discussing it with you. Now, about this Gladstone visit. There is just one other point I'd like to settle." She leaned forward to pin him with narrowed eyes. "We have to decide on the nature of our relationship."

"I really don't like that word. I've given it a lot of thought and I've decided it's a useless word."

"Relationship? I find it very useful."

"Only because you don't have any problem with a certain amount of vagueness in your life."

"I keep telling you, Croft, it's important to be flexible. I think we're getting off the main subject here. About our relationship—"

"What about it?"

"I've been thinking. We can present ourselves to Gladstone as professional acquaintances who also happen to be friends. We'll let him think you're also a book dealer and that you accompanied me on this trip purely out of professional curiosity and because you hoped to interest him in buying through you as well as me."

"It won't work."

Mercy was offended. "Why not?"

"First, because business people do not pay calls on their clients accompanied by competitors. Also, if he's the suspicious type, all he has to do is pick up the phone and find out whether I've actually got a bookshop. Once he discovers I don't, he'll be very curious."

"He'd only go through all that trouble if he's really Graves or connected to Graves in some fashion." Mercy chewed on her lower lip, thinking quickly.

"Not necessarily," Croft surprised her by saying. "He's obviously something of an eccentric and he has a valuable collection. He could be perfectly innocent and still be well within his rights checking up on an uninvited guest. I'd do the same thing in his place. No, Mercy, I'm afraid we're going to have to pose as lovers. You'll be the rare book expert. I'll just be along for the ride. I decided to accompany you on this little jaunt because it meant we'd have a vacation together. The Gladstone visit is just a short detour in the midst of a passionate romp in the Colorado mountains."

Mercy glared at him. "I don't like it."

"You're stuck with it unless you can come up with something better and convince me it will work."

"How can I convince you of any idea I dream up? You're bound to be prejudiced against it right from the start."

He shook his head firmly. "I'm always willing to be reasonable and logical about strategy. I'm always reasonable and logical about everything."

Mercy stabbed a finger at him. "You're the most unreasonable, illogical man I've ever met."

"One of these days, Mercy, I'll have to give you a few lessons in logic and philosophy. You've spent too many years operating on instinct and emotion."

"If I operated only on instinct and emotion, I wouldn't have survived running my own business for the past two years," she tossed back triumphantly. "Are you ready to go? According to the map we should be at Gladstone's place in another hour or so."

His hand shot across the table in the blink of an eye, capturing her wrist and stilling her just as she was about to rise. Croft's eyes were suddenly very intent. The command in them was almost as powerful as it had been during the night when he had ordered her to let him handle the authorities. Mercy didn't move.

"It's understood that we will pose as lovers while we're at Gladstone's? I don't want any surprises from you, Mercy. Not while we're there. It would be too risky."

"You said that if I came up with a better idea you'd be open to it," she replied, feeling very uneasy.

"You won't come up with a better idea. I've already thought the problem through. A better idea doesn't exist. I want to be certain that you're going to act the part of my woman for the next couple of days."

"And if I don't agree?"

"Then we'll cancel the whole trip right now."

She was shocked. "You can't do that! This is my future we're talking about here. Don't you dare threaten me, Croft."

"I've told you more than once, I don't make threats."

The situation was infuriating but Mercy felt trapped. That morning she had tried to cut the emotional strings that seemed to bind her to this man's will, tried to tell herself he was using her and that she owed him nothing. But she knew now as she faced him across the table in the dingy little cafe that nothing about this situation was going to be simple or straightforward.

And there were, heaven help her, some undeniable facts to take into consideration, not the least of which was that

Croft had managed to instill unpleasant worries in her mind about the true identity of her valuable client. That alone was probably reason enough to take a companion with her to the Gladstone home.

But she couldn't ignore the fact that Croft had misled her, or rather allowed her to come to some false conclusions. She didn't doubt for a moment that he had behaved within the framework of his own eccentric, strict, but honorable personal code. As far as he was concerned he had unfinished business to handle. He was determined to protect her even as he used her to follow the trail of *Valley of Secret Jewels*. In his own way he was doing his best to meet the obligations of honor and vengeance he felt he had to fulfill. She was forced to respect that even as it made her seethe.

Set against the need to make certain the creator of the Society of the Graced was truly dead, Mercy supposed her desire to gain a toehold in the world of antiquarian books was rather unimportant to Croft. The best she could hope for was that Gladstone was the innocent, reclusive eccentric he appeared to be.

"All right," she finally said, knowing there was no other choice. "We'll pose as lovers."

The blazing forcefulness went out of his eyes in a single blink. When his lashes lifted again, Croft's hazel gaze was warm as his mouth tilted. "It shouldn't be too hard. That's exactly what we are. Lovers."

Abruptly incensed Mercy yanked her hand from under his as he relaxed his grip. "Whatever else we are, we're not lovers. This trip is turning out to be nothing more than what it was originally planned to be: A business vacation, pure and simple." She shot to her feet, reaching down to collect her shoulder bag.

"Mercy, don't try to deny our, uh, *relationship*. I won't let you pretend it doesn't exist." Croft was on his feet, picking up the grease stained check that had been dropped on their table earlier. He hurried after Mercy who was already several steps ahead.

She swung around and noticed the bare table behind him. "Aren't you going to leave a tip?" she snapped, keeping her voice low so the waitress wouldn't overhear.

Croft's eyes narrowed. "Why should I? She didn't bother to make the tea the way I asked. A tip is supposed to be given for good service. It doesn't make sense to reward lousy service. It only encourages more of the same."

"Spare me your philosophy on the nature of punishment and reward. That woman is working minimum wage at most. I wouldn't be surprised if she's divorced and raising a couple of kids on whatever she earns here. From the looks of things she'll probably be stuck in this berg for the rest of her life. That's punishment enough for a bad cup of tea. Leave her a tip, Croft."

He surrendered without a word and reached for his wallet. Mercy nodded once in satisfaction. Every time she was about to give up on him, she saw a small ray of hope. Croft could be managed. He could be pushed. He could be made to alter his ways. But a woman would have her hands full in the process.

Following Gladstone's directions, Croft turned off the narrow mountain highway fifteen miles past the small cafe where they had stopped for breakfast. The new road was even narrower than the one they had left. It was obvious that keeping it in good repair was not a high priority for the State. Croft slowed the car to thirty miles an hour as the Toyota began to protest the scarred, uneven road surface. The towering trees seemed to press in on the thin road as if trying to push it off the mountain altogether.

"I get the feeling this isn't the route to any of the major ski resorts," Mercy remarked.

"You were right when you said you thought Gladstone

liked his privacy. This road is definitely one way to keep visitors at bay."

They rounded a hairpin turn and without any warning found themselves confronting a desolate assortment of grayed and weatherbeaten shacks that occupied a small clearing.

"A ghost town," Mercy exclaimed in delight. "A real, live ghost town."

"I think that may be a contradiction in terms." Croft slowed the car even more as he drove through the crumbling remains of what had probably once been a thriving mining town.

Mercy avidly examined the ruined buildings, sagging doors, and empty windows. The remains of a planked, wooden sidewalk that had once connected a row of shops stretched along one side of the road. A partially decayed wooden wagon was overturned beside a building that still bore the faded legend Drifter's Creek General Store.

Some of Mercy's initial delight began to fade as she examined the scene. The tumbledown buildings didn't look quite real. There was an overall pall of eerie isolation to the place, as if it existed in another time or another dimension. Mercy had the feeling that if she actually got out of the car and tried to touch one of the crumbling boards on a nearby structure it would vanish beneath her hand. The soft sighing of the pines had an unnatural whine to it. It was nearly midday, but Mercy felt chilled. She rolled up her window.

"I think I see why they call them ghost towns, Croft."

"Yes." He said nothing more.

"But it's fascinating, isn't it? When we leave Gladstone's place, let's stop here and spend some time looking around. I've never had an opportunity to explore a ghost town."

"It's a deal."

He sounded unexpectedly pleased. Belatedly Mercy realized he probably saw the suggestion as an excuse to pursue the personal side of this trip. She wasn't quite sure how to take that. Croft guided the car around another sharp bend and Drifter's Creek disappeared behind them. Mercy felt warmer almost at once. She rolled the window back down.

A couple of miles beyond what was left of Drifter's Creek the roadway disintegrated further.

"I have a hunch the car rental agency would take a dim view of this," Mercy said.

"I think you're right." Croft slowed to a halt and switched off the engine. He folded his arms on the wheel and leaned forward to study the terrain in front of him.

"What's wrong? Why are we stopping?"

"Take a look. There's a fence up ahead."

Mercy peered toward the trees. Loosely connected logs emerged from the forest on either side of the road and met in the middle of the path. "Doesn't look like much of a fence. Just a wooden gate. There's something in the instructions Gladstone gave us about calling the house for access when we reach the wooden barrier. This must be it. See a call box?"

"Over there in the trees." Croft was already opening the car door. His expression was becoming remote, his hazel eyes alert and unreadable.

"What's wrong?" Mercy demanded, climbing hastily out of the car.

"I just want to see how rickety that fence really is." He strode toward the barrier and then, not touching it, turned to follow its path a short distance into the woods.

Mercy watched in curiosity. When he returned a few minutes later he looked satisfied.

"There are alarms every ten feet along the fence. It may look rustic and picturesque, but, believe me, you couldn't drive through that gate without someone knowing you were here. Better make the call to the house."

Mercy nodded and went to the call box that was half hidden by a sweep of fir. The moment she lifted the receiver it was answered at the other end.

"Yes, Miss Pennington. We've been expecting you. Stay right where you are. Someone will be down in a few minutes to guide you to the main house."

Mercy glanced at Croft. "I've brought a friend with me. I hope that's all right? I don't like to impose, but—"

"Just a minute, Miss Pennington."

There was silence on the line and then the voice returned. "Mr. Gladstone is quite happy to entertain your friend as well as yourself, Miss Pennington."

Mercy hung up the phone. "No one seems to mind that you're with me," she said slowly. "I didn't even detect much surprise. Whoever it was sounded very friendly and accommodating."

"Maybe I was expected," Croft murmured.

"Did anyone ever tell you that you occasionally exhibit an unpleasant tendency toward melodrama?"

Chapter
EIGHT

A short time later Mercy got her first look at Erasmus Gladstone's Colorado mountain estate and decided Croft wasn't the only one with a touch of melodrama in his soul. Erasmus Gladstone appeared to have a few leanings in that direction, too.

Gladstone's large, two-story home was a dramatically modern design of sheer, sweeping white walls and smoked glass windows set inside a walled compound. At first glance it reminded Mercy rather uncomfortably of a futuristic mountain fortress. The compound walls were a couple of feet taller than an average man and made of stone. A wide, steel barred gate set into the walls appeared to be the only point of access.

The gate stood open in what Mercy supposed was meant to be a welcoming fashion and a muscular, handsome young man dressed casually in slacks and a short-sleeved cotton pullover stood waiting to greet Gladstone's guests.

Mercy wondered where Gladstone hired his help. The

man at the gate wasn't the first attractive male she had met so far. The young man who had met her and Croft in a four-wheel drive vehicle was equally eye-catching. Both of the men struck her as the type one expected to find flogging their portfolios to acting and modeling agencies. Except for the bulging muscles. Mercy wasn't so sure that much musculature would have been easy to clothe in designer garb, although it probably would have looked good on screen.

The bulging contours of shoulder, chest, arm and thigh that marked Gladstone's hired help made Mercy realize the lithe, sleek form Croft's strength took. The power in his body had a far more subtle, restrained and graceful emphasis. Gladstone's men would have looked good lifting weights at a body-building beach in California. Put Croft on that same beach and he would have looked like a jungle cat taking a stroll among the muscle freaks.

The handsome driver of the four-wheel drive vehicle halted inside the compound, got out and motioned Croft to park the Toyota to one side.

"Mr. Gladstone said you were to go straight on into the house. Dallas will show you the way. I'll bring in your luggage and put it in your room."

"Thank you, Lance," Mercy said politely as she alighted from the front seat of the Toyota. She felt obliged to add an especially bright smile of gratitude when it became obvious Croft was going to ignore Lance altogether.

Croft saw the smile and shot Mercy a dour glance as he swung himself easily out of the Toyota. "No need to tip him," he muttered over the roof of the car. "I don't think he's working for minimum wage." He took Mercy's arm in a firm grasp and led her toward the house.

"Honestly, Croft, for a man who believes in doing things the proper way, you can be downright rude on occasion."

That observation seemed to cheer him. "I do my best."

A sharp, questioning bark sounded from the rear of the

compound. Mercy automatically glanced in that direction. There was a long, fenced dog run there and two sleek Doberman pinschers paced alertly back and forth behind the wire mesh, their attention on the newcomers.

"They don't look like pets, do they?" Mercy said under her breath.

"No," Croft agreed, watching the dogs thoughtfully, "they don't."

"No need to be afraid of the dogs. We only let them out at night to keep an eye on things," the man called Dallas said as he approached. He smiled, a wonderfully boyish grin that displayed perfect white teeth. "We're a little isolated up here. The dogs are just a precaution. Right this way Miss Pennington. Mr. Gladstone is waiting for you. And your friend, too, of course." Dallas nodded politely at Croft, who didn't seem to notice.

Mercy rushed to fill the small social gap. "What a lovely place Mr. Gladstone has. Fantastic view. The air is so clear here in the mountains. The peaks and valley seem so close when you look out over a range."

"Distances are deceptive up here. The altitude and the lack of city haze are the primary reasons," Dallas informed her. "A lot of hikers and climbers set out for what appears to be a reasonably close goal and find themselves walking for hours and days longer than they'd planned."

"It certainly is a unique location. I imagine you're cut off almost entirely during the winter. How do you manage?"

Dallas pointed toward the other side of the compound and Mercy saw a small helicopter sitting on a concrete pad.

"The chopper is one form of transportation. We also have snow mobiles as well as the four-wheel drives. We're never completely trapped up here in the mountains."

"A helicopter!" Mercy was astonished. "I don't think I've ever actually known someone who had his own private helicopter."

Dallas gave her his riveting smile. "Believe me, it beats driving back down that road, especially during winter. Mr. Gladstone usually makes sure all his guests get a ride while they're here. Great view of the mountains from the chopper."

Mercy shuddered. "No thanks. I don't care for small planes and I'm sure I'd be just as nervous in a helicopter. You'd never get me up in that machine in a million years."

That got Croft's attention. He frowned at her. "You're afraid of flying in small aircraft?"

"My parents were killed in the plane my father owned. They went into a mountain during a storm, I was told."

"So that's where you picked up the phobia? From hearing about the way your parents died?"

"Probably. I've never stopped to analyze my dislike of small planes. I just know I don't like them. Or helicopters. They always seem so frail and vulnerable." Mercy firmly changed the subject. "Look, that must be our host."

They were at the entrance of the expansive house. Wide aquamarine doors were thrown open to reveal a hall tiled in light Italian marble. A tall, elegantly attractive man in his late forties stood in the doorway. There was a vaguely European air about him, a certain indefinable style and sense of wealth that made one think of expensive Swiss ski resorts, Paris, Saint-Tropez and the Côte d'Azur. Mercy had never been to any of those places, but she had a vivid imagination. This, she knew, must be Erasmus Gladstone.

His hair had once been blond but was rapidly turning a brilliant shade of silver-gray. The combination of silver and gold was stunning. It highlighted the bluest eyes Mercy had ever seen. She couldn't put a name to the exact shade of blue, but it reminded her of something, perhaps a color she had created with her watercolors at some point.

Gladstone's nose and mouth were finely drawn and showed no sign of losing their elegance as the man went through middle age. He was dressed in a casually expensive style, a silk sport shirt, dark trousers and Italian leather shoes.

Whatever else he was, Mercy decided, Gladstone didn't look like the guru type. He looked even less like the type to involve himself in anything as dirty as sex, slavery and drug running. This man had class. When he smiled at her he also revealed an astonishing amount of masculine charm. Then he spoke and she realized his voice was even better in person than it was on the phone. A wonderful voice for reading poetry or reciting heroic ballads.

A voice that might, just possibly, be very useful for enthralling an audience of willing believers. Mercy deliberately pushed that thought aside. She would not let Croft's melodramatic conclusions influence her.

"Miss Pennington, I'm very happy to meet you. I'm Erasmus Gladstone. Please call me Erasmus." He turned his patrician head toward Croft and extended his slender, long-fingered hand. A small, discreet signet ring gleamed on one finger. "You must be the companion I was told about. What was the name again?"

"Falconer." Croft took the extended hand but kept the handshake brief and businesslike. "Croft Falconer. When I heard Mercy was going to be spending a few days in the Rockies as the guest of a man I didn't know, I decided to invite myself along. I'm sure you understand. I realize business is business, but . . ." He let the sentence trail off with a meaningful emphasis. A man to man communication.

Gladstone smiled. "Perfectly, Croft. A man must look after his possessions. There is always someone lurking about waiting to steal valuables. And I must admit Miss Pennington appears to be extremely valuable."

"Miss Pennington," Mercy interrupted with a scathing glance at Croft, "would just as soon not be referred to as a commodity."

Croft merely shrugged but Gladstone chuckled richly and glanced back over his shoulder. "I assure you, I understand Croft's feelings entirely. If my Isobel were to receive an invitation from an unknown male a couple of thousand miles distant I would react with a similar degree of concern. Come here and meet our guests, my dear. You're always complaining that we don't entertain frequently enough. You should enjoy the next few days. Mercy, Croft, allow me to introduce my companion, Isobel Ascanius. I would be very lonely here in the mountains without her."

Mercy saw a movement in the hall behind Gladstone and a moment later a stunningly beautiful woman appeared. She was almost as tall as Gladstone, which gave her several inches on Mercy. As she approached, Mercy realized the woman named Isobel was only a couple of inches shorter than Croft.

Isobel Ascanius appeared to be somewhere in her early thirties, but with her bone structure, Mercy decided, the woman would always look far younger than her real age, even when she hit her eighties. Her hair was as black and lustrous as obsidian and she wore it twisted into an elegant chignon that emphasized her high cheekbones and beautiful dark eyes. Her mouth looked like something out of a lipstick ad, glistening with just the right touch of coral. The coral color was repeated on her long, carefully shaped nails.

Mercy didn't doubt for a moment that Isobel and Gladstone were lovers. Gladstone's female companion was dressed as elegantly as her mate. Her white silk safari shirt and matching trousers glided over a strong, distinctly healthy looking body. She was a lushly built woman with full breasts, but there was nothing soft about her. Isobel's waist was model slim and was wrapped in a soft, black leather belt.

Mercy glanced involuntarily down at herself and wished

she had put on something—anything—besides jeans that morning.

When Isobel came forward into the sunlight to extend a graceful hand toward Croft, Mercy was uncomfortably aware of what a striking pair the two made. The other woman's height, dark hair and eyes were a beautiful, feminine version of Croft's height and coloring. The sleek, bright white outfit Isobel wore only seemed to emphasize the darkness of Croft's chinos and loose-fitting cotton shirt. When Isobel put her hand in his, Mercy thought her nails looked like delicate red daggers against Croft's bronzed skin.

Mercy swallowed and faced the fact that she was experiencing a fierce shaft of what could only be called jealous possessiveness. There in the crystal clear light of the mountains she looked at Croft and understood what was happening to her.

She was falling in love with the man.

Just as Croft released Isobel's hand, he turned his head and glanced at Mercy. She knew in that moment that he had undoubtedly seen what must be showing in her eyes. She was so transparent, he claimed, at least to him. He could see through her as though she were a watercolor painting. Mercy swiftly turned away, not wanting to deal with the speculation she saw in his eyes.

"Won't you come inside?" Isobel asked politely, leading the way into the marble tiled hall.

There was a wide staircase on one side of the hall with flights that led to a downstairs level as well as the upstairs. For the first time Mercy realized the house had what appeared to be a full-sized basement.

"I've had your rooms prepared on the second floor," Isobel was saying. "There's an excellent view to the southwest from there. When you've had a chance to refresh yourselves you must come downstairs for a guided tour. Erasmus is very proud of his home. And naturally, you'll be interested in the library."

Mercy suddenly remembered the real reason for her visit. "I have the copy of *Valley* in my luggage. I'm sure you're anxious to see it, Mr. Gladstone."

"Erasmus, please."

She smiled. "Erasmus. I'll unpack the book and bring it downstairs in a few minutes."

"No hurry." He smiled. "I've been waiting for it for quite a while. Now that I know it's within reach, I can wait a while longer. Still, I am anxious to view it and I expect you're equally interested in settling the final negotiations."

"Your bid on the book was very generous," Mercy said.

"I meant what I said about offering you one or two interesting items from my collection as part of the price."

Mercy grinned widely. "I can't wait to see them. I'm going to use them as the basis for my new career in the rare book business."

"I'm looking forward to discussing our mutual passion," Erasmus Gladstone said smoothly. "Do you share our interests, Croft?"

"I prefer my books straight off the bestseller lists." Croft reached for Mercy's wrist. "You can talk about books later, Mercy. Let's go upstairs." He pulled her up the wide staircase toward Isobel, who was already on the landing. When he had his captive half way up the steps, out of immediate earshot of both Isobel and Gladstone, he added in a low growl, "You're here to talk about books, not 'mutual passion.' Keep that in mind."

"Keep what in mind? The mutual passion?"

His fingers tightened warningly on her wrist, but there was no chance for Croft to respond verbally. Isobel was beckoning her guests down a high-ceilinged corridor. The walls inside the house were as bright as the outside of the structure, their unrelenting whiteness punctuated here and there by works of art. Mercy was no expert, but one of the paintings reminded her of Picasso and another, one with the bold bars of color, made her think of Mondrian.

She leaned toward Croft to whisper in his ear. "Do you think they're originals?"

"Yes," Croft said readily, not bothering to lower his voice. "I think they're originals."

Mercy blushed a fiery red as Isobel turned to smile in amusement. "You're quite right, Croft. The paintings are originals. Everything in the house is of the finest quality, including the artwork. Erasmus likes to surround himself with beautiful things."

"And people," Mercy added without thinking.

"Yes," Isobel nodded. "Erasmus prefers to have attractive people around him, just as he prefers beauty in his physical surroundings."

Mercy held up a hand in a gesture of mock pleading. "Please don't say anything more on the subject, Isobel, I'm traumatized enough as it is about dressing for dinner. I think I may have left the emerald necklace at home with my Saint Laurent gown and wouldn't you know it, the airline lost my little Ungaro number."

"You mustn't concern yourself with such things," Isobel said. "I would be happy to loan you something to wear."

Good grief, Mercy thought. Had the woman taken her seriously? "Um, I was just joking, Isobel."

Isobel nodded serenely. "Still, it's no problem. I will be pleased to open my wardrobe to you."

It was Croft who put an end to the discussion by saying bluntly, "Forget it. None of your clothes would fit Mercy. Is this our room?"

Mercy seethed in silence while Isobel stood back to wave them into a suite done in a light, graceful interpretation of Art Deco. Every item in the sunlit room was in proper geo-metrical proportion to the others. There was a sense of

1930's ornamentalism in the small sculptured nude that stood by the wide bed, but the overall design was clean and somehow very modern. Outside the window a sparkling backdrop of snowcapped mountains and endless green valleys stretched toward infinity.

"When you mentioned to Dallas that you were being accompanied by a male companion, Mercy, we assumed he was a *close* friend. I hope we assumed correctly?"

"You assumed correctly," Croft said flatly before Mercy could think of a more delicate response. She glared at him as Isobel smiled directly at Croft.

"Then I hope this suite will do. There is a connecting door between this room and the next which should provide the two of you with whatever degree of privacy you wish. Lance has been instructed to put your luggage in the other room, Croft. Feel free to make whatever adjustments you please. Erasmus and I wish only that our guests be comfortable. Now, if you will excuse me, I will go downstairs to make certain everything is prepared for the evening. Join us when you're ready. We will be having cocktails in an hour."

Mercy breathed a sigh of relief when the door closed behind Isobel. "Better check your wrists to make sure she didn't help herself to a little blood when she shook hands with you. I wonder how she got such perfect nails? The nearest manicurist must be a hundred and fifty miles from here."

"Something tells me Isobel doesn't do much housework," Croft said absently as he began stalking slowly around the room.

"That's an understatement." Mercy frowned. "I wonder who does do it. The housework, I mean."

"Dallas and Lance probably."

"Obviously very versatile young men."

"Obviously." Croft went down on one knee to study the power receptacle in the wall.

Mercy scowled, knowing what he was doing because he had explained it all to her while they waited for the arrival of their escort. He was checking for eavesdropping devices. He had told her he might not be able to locate them if they were planted by a very sophisticated professional and that she was to watch her conversation carefully unless they were outdoors. Mercy had agreed to the terse instructions primarily because she was learning that there was no point arguing with Croft when he was in certain moods.

"Well?" She silently mouthed an inquiry at him as he finished his check of the room.

"I think I'm going to take a shower." Croft calmly began unbuttoning his shirt. He nodded toward the bathroom that separated the two sleeping suites.

"Okay." Mercy casually walked toward the window to examine the spectacular view. "This scenery is absolutely incredible, isn't it?"

Without any warning he was directly behind her, his hand clamping around the nape of her neck. Mercy jumped in surprise. "Honestly, Croft. Must you always sneak up on me like that?"

"I said I'm going to take a shower." The words were low, spoken directly into her ear. "I meant for you to join me."

"Now, see here, Croft," Mercy began heatedly, intending to give him a stern lecture on the subject of the exact status of their relationship. But she never got to finish the tirade. Croft clamped a large palm gently across her mouth and dragged her toward the bathroom. She felt like a kitten being transported by the scruff of its neck.

"Hush, love," he murmured as he pulled her over the threshold of the spacious bathroom. "Sometimes you talk too much." He used one booted foot to shut the door behind them and then made his way to the huge tiled shower. He released his hold on Mercy and turned on the water. "There. Now you can talk all you want."

The roar of the shower made it hard to hear his low voice. Mercy glared at him and started to back away. "What?"

"I said," he reached out and caught her arm again, halting her retreat, "that now you can talk all you want. The shower should drown out whatever we say."

A lightbulb went on inside her head. "Oh." A curious disappointment coursed through her. Croft was clearly all business at the moment. He hadn't intended to hijack her into the shower for a sexy romp after all. A realistic appraisal of the man indicated he probably didn't go in much for sexy shower romps. Croft was more the midnight passion type. She lifted her chin. "Well, as it happens, I don't have anything to say to you. I've got a much bigger problem on my hands at the moment than whispering secrets in the bathroom."

"What problem?"

"I've got to find something I can wear downstairs to dinner." Mercy turned and marched out of the steaming bath. But at the doorway she halted, frowning. "Does he . . . does he look like him, Croft?"

Croft knew what she meant. "No."

Mercy smiled in relief and went to see if her luggage had been brought up to the room. The first hurdle was over. Erasmus Gladstone didn't bear any resemblance to the man called Egan Graves. Everything was going to be all right, Mercy told herself cheerfully.

Croft followed Mercy down the staircase and into a room that received virtually all of its color from the view that poured in through the windows. The low, clean-lined furnishings were in the palest shades of peach and sea green and ivory. Normally he liked quiet, understated colors, but somehow when he walked into this room it made him wish he was standing amidst the bright, ecclectic color scheme of Mercy's apartment.

Dallas was mixing drinks at a small bar in the corner. Isobel and Erasmus were seated near the window, talking quietly. They both turned with welcoming smiles as Croft and Mercy walked into the room.

As greetings were exchanged, Croft studied Mercy's dress with a critical eye and decided she needn't have worried about holding her own. She was wearing a narrow dress of some light, summery fabric splashed with yellow and white. It was a simple but sophisticated garment, especially paired with her upswept hair and high-heeled sandals. True, Isobel's ankle-length sweep of deep purple silk had undoubtedly cost a great deal more, but Croft had learned a long time ago not to judge the effect by the price tag.

"Ah, I see you have brought my prize, Mercy." Erasmus Gladstone reached out to take the unwrapped copy of *Valley of Secret Jewels* from his guest. "This represents the end of a long search. I almost didn't see your little ad in that catalog, you know. I've never had much luck with that particular publication and I'd almost decided to discontinue my subscription."

"The man who prints it was kind enough to accept my ad. I could hardly run off a whole catalog of my own." Mercy smiled as she handed over the book. *"Valley* was my first and only item that might have been of interest to a true collector."

Gladstone examined the book. Isobel watched him turn the pages, her gaze intent. When Gladstone finally closed the leather bound volume he looked very pleased. He cocked one imperious brow at Mercy. "There was no problem with the money that was wired into your account?"

"None at all," Mercy assured him.

"Excellent. Come with me and we will find a place in my library for *Valley.*"

Gladstone led the other three out into the hall and down the stairs to the lower level of the house. When he opened a glass door at the bottom of the stairs the scent of chlorinated water wafted through. The heavy odor of lush greenery accompanied it. The small party stepped out onto a small platform and found themselves in the midst of a tropical garden. The only thing marring the illusion was the odd hue of the lighting. It lacked the golden warmth of real sunlight. Croft watched Mercy's eyes widen in appreciation as she saw what was on the other side of the door.

"Good lord, an indoor pool and garden. It's magnificent! It looks like something out of a travel poster ad for Tahiti or Hawaii."

Gladstone smiled complacently and waved Mercy graciously toward the short flight of steps that led down from the platform.

The pool room was a giant, indoor tropical setting occupying most of the bottom floor of the large house. The place was filled with broad leaved plants and a variety of exotic ferns. The lighting was subdued and artfully camouflaged. If it weren't for the lack of a sky overhead, the whole setting might have passed for a small slice of tropical paradise, complete with a designer's idea of a waterfall at one end of the curving pool.

"One can't get all one's exercise skiing," Gladstone explained, descending the steps from the platform. "Isobel and I find the pool a pleasant alternative. In the middle of winter, a few hours in here does wonders to raise the spirits."

"I can imagine." Mercy started toward a path that wound its way through the heavy foliage to poolside. In a moment she disappeared from sight. Then her voice came clearly "Come here and look at this, Croft. It's incredible."

Croft went forward slowly, moving along a narrow stone path that was bordered by lush plants. The greenery in there was damn thick. A lot of it was higher than a man's head. From the platform near the entrance it was possible to catch glimpses of the meandering path, but once down on the floor, the viewer found himself in the middle of a small jungle. Croft looked around with interest, automatically noting the extent of the realism.

A man could hide in here. Or go hunting.

He rounded a bend in the path and saw Mercy standing at the edge of the pool, peering into the water. The pool was lit with underwater lights. Mercy was obviously enchanted. Her eyes were full of laughter and excitement.

"This is amazing. So real and so huge! Have you ever seen anything like it?"

"Yes, but the last place I saw that looked like this was loaded with insects and one or two snakes. This is a Hollywood version of the real thing."

"I'd rather enjoy this version than the one that has the snakes and insects. Darn it, I wish I'd brought my swimsuit."

Isobel moved out of the foliage behind them. "We keep suits on hand for our guests. You'll find one that will fit you in the cabanas near the sauna. Come. I'll show you where the changing rooms are. Please feel free to take a swim whenever you wish."

Croft trailed slowly after the two women, continuing his examination of the tropical swimming pool. The effectiveness of the illusion did not totally disguise the fact that they were in a huge basement. There were no windows. If the lights were turned off, this place would be a black cavern.

A few minutes later Isobel led the way out of the garden and indicated a large wooden sauna room and two cabanas.

"Check inside the cabana to the right for the women's suits. There are several pairs of trunks in the other one." Isobel smiled warmly at Croft.

Mercy made a pretense of ignoring the smile that was directed at Croft, but he saw the faint narrowing of her eyes as she turned away to open a cabana door. For the second time that day he wondered if she was jealous of Isobel Ascanius. It was an intriguing thought.

There was no time to pursue the idea, however. Isobel was already leading her guests out of the pool area and through another set of glass doors that opened into a very different room.

"Erasmus went ahead to open the library. He'll be getting anxious," Isobel explained with gentle amusement. "He is very eager to show off his collection to people who can appreciate it. We have so few guests."

The room on the other side of a second set of glass doors was furnished like an old-world private library. There were small reading lamps with green glass shades, overstuffed arm chairs and polished wooden tables. The only thing missing were the books. In the middle of one wall a large, walk-in vault had been built. The door was made of heavy steel and there was a sophisticated locking mechanism on it. Croft eyed the mechanism with interest.

Light and air-conditioned air spilled from the open door of the vault. Erasmus Gladstone was inside, waiting. When Croft and Mercy stepped over the high threshold they found themselves in a book-lined room. Ranks of leather bound volumes filled the floor-to-ceiling shelves. It didn't take an expert to realize at once that most, if not all, of the books were very old and extremely valuable. Mercy was immediately enthralled. Croft watched her move over to a row of books and read the titles and authors on the spines.

"Boethius, Chaucer, Marlowe." She breathed the great names reverently, her fingertips hovering just above the leather as if she didn't dare touch the books. "I've never seen anything like this outside of a museum, Erasmus."

He chuckled. "One must acquire a handful of items printed before 1500, of course, if one is to have a respectable library. I confess I'm still working on that portion of my collection."

"But to have so many fine examples," Mercy said with a slight shake of her head. "It's mind boggling."

"Money overcomes many obstacles in the auction rooms, my dear. Personally, I'm more pleased with my first edition of Darwin's *On the Origin of Species* than I am with my Chaucer. It was very difficult to find the Darwin, you know, even though it was printed in 1859 and is therefore relatively new." He crossed the room to another shelf. "Over here I have some rather interesting Henry Fielding, including an original 1749 set of the six volumes of *Tom Jones*. I was also lucky enough recently to pick up the first two volumes of Richardson's *Pamela*. They're dated 1741."

"I'd kill to get my hands on either the Fielding or the Richardson."

Gladstone smiled approvingly. "I like a bookseller with enthusiasm. We will come down here again before you leave and discuss which of the books you would like to take back with you as part of the price of *Valley*."

"You're much too generous." Mercy was obviously shocked. "I couldn't possibly take any of these. Not in addition to what you've already paid me."

"In the world of book collecting everything is relative. *Valley* was almost unobtainable and I wanted it very badly. I have been chasing it for some time. I'm feeling generous because you have given me something I might not otherwise have been able to locate."

Mercy's smile was a little shaky. "I'm overwhelmed."

"Let's put *Valley* in its proper place. I keep my collection of erotica over here." Gladstone went to the far end of the room where a small row of volumes was set apart from the rest. They appeared to be in more tattered shape than their more respectable comrades. "I thank you, Mercy Pennington, for enabling me to add Burleigh's fascinating work to my library. This is a very satisfying moment for me." He eased the book carefully onto the shelf. He stood looking at it for a long moment. When he turned around, Gladstone was smiling broadly, his unusual blue eyes alive with pleasure. Something about him radiated that pleasure outward, involving others to join in his happiness.

The man definitely had a charismatic charm, Croft thought wryly. From all reports, so had Egan Graves.

"We should return to our drinks, Erasmus." Isobel spoke quietly from the doorway. "Lance has dinner scheduled for seven."

"By all means." Gladstone moved forward, graciously taking Mercy's arm. "Don't worry, my dear. You will have ample opportunity to spend time in my library while you're here. But now I believe Isobel is right. We had best go back upstairs. This is going to be a lively few days for us. Has Isobel mentioned the small party we're giving tomorrow night in honor of my success in finding *Valley?*"

Croft was thinking that he needed more time in the vault to study its contents. The quick scan he'd just gotten wasn't sufficient. He caught Gladstone's question just as he stepped through the vault door. "A party? Here?"

"We entertain very little. As you can imagine, it's rather complicated," Gladstone said genially as he escorted Mercy through the door and turned to seal the vault. "It requires much planning. But I'm afraid I have become something of a patron for a colony of rather talented young artists located about twenty miles from here. Once a year I have them in for an evening. I provide everything, including the transportation. Artists can be such interesting acquaintances as long as one doesn't have to deal with them on a day-to-day basis. Very temperamental people, I'm afraid. Perhaps it goes with the talent. This year you'll be here for the event. I hope you enjoy it."

Croft glanced at Mercy and saw the dazzled expression in her eyes. He felt a surge of anger which he quickly suppressed. It was obvious she had never met anyone like

Erasmus Gladstone and she was more than willing to be charmed.

Croft knew he was going to have to take steps to make certain Mercy didn't fall under Gladstone's spell.

Tonight, Croft decided, Mercy wasn't going to sleep alone. It was time to reinforce the bonds that had been established the night he had made her his.

Chapter
NINE

Mercy was aware of Croft's presence the moment he entered the bedroom that night. He made no sound, but some anticipatory instinct made her open her eyes and turn her head on the pillow. She saw him silhouetted in the open doorway between the two suites, a dark shadow among even darker shadows. She knew then that she had been waiting for him.

The door between the suites had been closed until Croft had silently opened it a few seconds before. She had closed it deliberately after preparing for bed. Croft had been in the bathroom at the time. When he had emerged a few minutes later he had made no immediate attempt to eradicate the poor barrier.

Mercy had lain awake for a long while expecting to have her privacy rudely invaded. She had seen the calculating expression in Croft's eyes during dinner. He had watched her laugh and talk with Gladstone, saying little himself, but making his masculine disapproval clear in subtle ways Mercy hadn't missed. Their hosts might not have noticed the dangerously remote quality of his gaze, but it had burned Mercy's nerve endings.

Croft was either a little jealous of Gladstone or very annoyed with Mercy for having found Gladstone unthreatening. Of the two she had enough common sense to guess the latter was the case. Somehow, she didn't see Croft giving into any emotion as primitive as jealousy. But whatever the reason, Mercy had expected to find herself on the defensive later.

But there had been no sizzling lectures in the bathroom with the shower running to cover Croft's words. And when she had calmly closed the door between the two rooms later, he hadn't kicked it open. Mercy had crawled into bed and waited, but eventually the sense of wary expectation gave way to drowsiness. She didn't know how long she had been asleep, but when she opened her eyes in darkness she knew she was no longer alone.

She watched him leave the doorway and glide soundlessly toward the bed. It wasn't fair that the man could move like a ghost. What he did to her nerves wasn't fair, either. She could feel heat in her veins and told herself she would not let him sweep her away as he had the other night.

Mercy didn't kid herself. She knew what was behind his presence in her room. He wasn't motivated by an uncontrollable desire, overriding passion or undying love. As far as Croft was concerned, he was on a job. He viewed Mercy's enjoyment of Erasmus Gladstone's company as a potential threat to the completion of his mission. He probably feared she was being charmed by Gladstone. Croft was going to reestablish the claim he thought he had on her. He wanted to be very certain she knew where her loyalties lay.

She could tell him he had nothing to worry about, Mercy thought as Croft came through the darkness toward her. She could try reassuring him that she was keeping an open mind about Gladstone. But that sort of conversation was difficult to have when she had to watch every word out of fear of a hidden microphone in the bed.

Croft stopped beside the bed and looked down at her. He was wearing only his briefs. It wasn't difficult to tell that he was already partially aroused. His hazel eyes were devoid of color in the shadows, but Mercy could see the catlike gleam in them.

"Croft," she managed throatily, aware of the tension that was filling the atmosphere around them. It was time to talk. She had better do it quickly. "The bathroom—"

"No." His voice was a whisper of rough velvet. He put one knee on the bed and reached out to stroke her shoulder. The bed gave beneath his weight. "There's no need to talk. Not now."

She read his intent and her tension flared into a strange anger. She rolled out from under his hand, rising to her knees on the far side of the bed. Her breath came quickly as she faced him.

"Come here, Mercy. You know you want me. I can make you want me."

"Who the hell do you think you are to walk into my bedroom like this and try to seduce me? I'm not a convenience for you, Croft." Her own voice was just as low as his, a soft hiss of feminine challenge. The battle was to be conducted in whispers, it seemed.

"You know you don't want to fight me, honey. You want to feel what you felt the other night in my arms. You want to give yourself to me."

"Is that right? What are you? The all-knowing, wise male who thinks he knows exactly what women really want? I've got a much harder question for you, Croft. What do *you* want?"

"That's not a tough question. I want to be inside you. I want to feel you wrapped around me, shivering with your pleasure. I want to know exactly how much you need me."

"I don't need you any more than you need me." She didn't know whether she had meant the words as a plea for reassurance or as a defiant challenge. They sounded like a challenge.

"Come close and we'll find out how much we want each other." There was soft satisfaction in his voice.

"I won't let you do it, you know. I refuse to go to bed with you while you're in this mood. You're nothing more than a cold-blooded male on the prowl tonight. You're only intent on proving to yourself and to me that you can control me in bed and I won't have it. You got away with the heavy-handed seduction routine that first night, Croft, but it won't happen again."

"Heavy-handed?"

"Well, you have to admit it was very deliberate. You seduced me as part of your—" She saw his eyes narrow. Belatedly she remembered the warning about watching her conversation in the bedroom. Mercy didn't believe for one minute that Gladstone was a crook or that there were secret microphones in the room, but she had given Croft her word that she would be careful. "It was a deliberate act of seduction. There was no love involved, was there?"

"I wanted you very badly the other night. I want you even more tonight. If that seems like deliberate, heavy-handed seduction to you, then I can't argue. When it comes to emotional interpretations, everything's relative, especially for a woman. But I think you're being unfair to me and yourself to label our lovemaking that way. There are a hundred different avenues for desire. Most of them don't have names."

"Don't bother using any of your fancy philosophical logic on me. Not on this particular subject. I don't think you're any kind of expert, and I won't let you trip me up with your crazy reasoning tonight. I have to draw the line somewhere. I won't let you manipulate me."

"Easy, Mercy. Just relax and come here to me."

She leaped off the bed, sensing a slight change in the way he was balancing himself. "Stay right where you are. Don't you dare use any of your . . . your tricks on me."

His eyes gleamed in the shadows. The starlight that poured through the window provided just enough illumination to define the unyielding set of his jaw and the sleek contours of his shoulders. He had no trouble following her movements. Just as Mercy had known from the first, Croft was very much at home in the darkness.

As she bounced to her feet, Croft slowly stood up on the other side. He started to circle the bed, coming toward her with smooth, pacing strides.

"You're the one using tricks tonight, sweetheart. What game are you playing with me? I think it was a mistake to let you sleep alone last night."

She backed away from him. "I chose to sleep alone last night and I choose to sleep alone tonight."

"In a few minutes you'll change your mind."

"You talk about me playing games, but you're the one who plays them. That's exactly what you're doing with our relationship. You're toying with it the way a cat toys with a mouse, using it for your own advantage."

He grinned briefly. "You're not much of a mouse, sweetheart."

"I'm not joking, Croft."

"Neither am I. So let's stop talking about our 'relationship' and start talking about us. You and me."

He was very close now. Mercy risked a quick glance over her shoulder and found she was less than two feet from the wall. There was no more room to run. She looked back at Croft, tried to gage the distance as best she could, then dove wildly past him.

"Damn it, Mercy!"

For the first time that evening Mercy heard some genuine emotion in his voice. Unfortunately, that emotion was chiefly frustration and annoyance. She couldn't even take minimal satisfaction from it because his arm was suddenly in the middle of her flight path, coiling around her and whirling her gently to an abrupt halt. Mercy came up against Croft's chest with a silent thud and found her face pressed into his bare shoulder. The warm, sexy scent of him assailed her nostrils.

"Let me go." The words were muffled against his skin.

"Not yet, sweetheart." He started to fold her closer. "Not for a long time."

Mercy felt his other arm around her, locking her to him. She reacted instinctively, driving her small fist into his ribs. It felt as though she had struck a solid wall, but she had the satisfaction of hearing Croft's sharp intake of breath. His grip loosened slightly and Mercy danced back out of reach. A new kind of excitement washed over her.

He wasn't invincible.

"So, you're not all that tough, after all, are you?" Her mood was shifting with a rapidity that left her feeling euphoric. A wave of adrenaline seemed to have unleased itself in her bloodstream. Mercy found herself enjoying a heady sensation of power. "I warned you not to use your clever little tricks on me. I took a class in self-defense once."

"Is that right?"

"Damn right." She edged a few more steps away from him. The class in self-defense had been a three-hour seminar conducted by a policewoman the library had hired to instruct female employees in certain emergency measures. It had been over two years since she had had the class and Mercy was realistic enough to assume she shouldn't push her luck too far.

"Are you sure you want to turn this into a battle, Mercy?"

"What I'm sure of is that I want you to go back to your room and leave me in peace."

"I can't do that."

"Try."

"And leave you here by yourself to think about what a charming, educated, cosmopolitan man Erasmus Gladstone is? Not a chance. I want you to think about me tonight, Mercy."

She felt her breath catch in her throat. "Are you jealous, by any chance?"

His eyes were fathomless. "Is that what you want? Is that why you were hanging on Gladstone's every word tonight? Did you want to see if you could whip up a little jealousy?"

"Not much chance of that, is there?" she shot back, goaded to a rashness she knew she would probably regret. "You've got too much cold blood in your veins."

Something flashed in his gaze, and in spite of the precarious position in which she found herself, Mercy felt a flicker of triumph. It was dangerous to prod Croft Falconer, but at times it seemed the only way to find out what lay beneath the cool, totally controlled surface of the man.

"Maybe what I need is some of your warmth to take the chill off, Mercy."

He flowed toward her without any warning, his hand snapping out to catch her by the nape of the neck even as she tried frantically to duck back out of the way.

"Damn it, Croft," she hissed, "I'm not going to make this easy for you." She brought her hands up quickly in an attempt to break his hold and shoved against the wall of his chest. When nothing happened, Mercy used both hands to try to dislodge the gentle grip on her nape.

He was drawing her inexorably toward the bed. She tried another rib punch, aware that she was severely hampered in the conflict because she didn't really want to hurt Croft. The knee-to-the-groin routine and the finger-in-the-eye bit were definitely off limits.

She wasn't fighting for her life or her honor. She was just trying to make one very thickheaded man aware of her on a vital level. She would force him to be just as emotionally involved with her as she was with him even if it meant a knock-down, drag-out battle royale.

Croft didn't seem to notice her side punch, but he must have felt her heel when she brought it down fiercely on his bare toes because he reacted immediately. He swore, something very short and very crude. Mercy had never heard him use the word before. He used his convenient grip on the nape of her neck to yank her off his foot and then he gave her a small shake.

"You little witch. I ought to turn you over my knee."

Mercy gave him a fierce, reckless smile that showed all her fine white teeth. "I think I read something about that technique in *Valley of Secret Jewels*. Does it work?"

"Use your heel on my toes again and we'll find out."

"Let go of me, Croft. I won't be dragged off to bed like this."

"It seems to be the only way to get you there."

She didn't use her heel this time, she used her whole foot. Mercy hooked it around his ankle and tugged violently. Croft didn't lose his balance, but he finally lost his temper.

"That does it," he said between clenched teeth. "If you want to do this the hard way, we'll do it the hard way." He swung her off her feet and into his arms, ignoring her wriggling, twisting efforts to free herself.

In two strides he reached the bed and tossed her lightly down across the rumpled sheets. Her bare legs dangled over the edge. Before Mercy could scramble out of the way, Croft stepped between her knees. He spread his own legs into a wide stance that had the instant effect of prying Mercy's thighs far apart. Her prim cotton nightgown was scrunched up around her buttocks, providing no modesty or protection at all. Mercy lay open and vulnerable, her hair tumbled around her shoulders, her eyes widening with the realization that she might have gone too far. Hands on hips, Croft stood looking down at her.

Mercy caught her breath at the implacable, deeply sensual expression that etched his mouth and filled the bottomless pools of his eyes. She could feel the new level of tension radiating from him. He was no longer the cool, calculating lover who had entered her bedroom intent upon a cold-blooded seduction. She had his full attention now, on every level. She tried to tell herself it was what she had wanted, but the assurance didn't do much to cut through the belated sense of wariness that was growing in the pit of her stomach.

When all was said and done, she knew very little about Croft Falconer. She was taking chances with a stranger that she hadn't ever taken before in her life with any man. She was trusting her instincts when she probably ought to be listening to reason.

"Anything else you learned in that self-defense class you'd like to try before we stop playing games?" Croft asked with silky menace.

Mercy levered herself up on her elbows, aware of the crisp hair of his legs against the inside of her wantonly spread thighs. She felt so very vulnerable. "If you think I'm going to give you any advance notice of the next move, you're indulging in wishful thinking. You'd better be very careful of what you decide to do next."

His eyes glittered as he shoved his briefs down off his hips and kicked them aside. "Don't worry, little witch, I'll be very, very careful." He reached out to touch her with one hand.

Mercy stared, mesmerized by the sight of his huge, pulsing shaft as it thrust toward her. Then she flinched and gulped for breath as his fingers combed boldly through the triangle of dark hair that guarded her warm secrets. She was aware of the shocking, sweet sensitivity of his touch in every fiber of her body. It freed a wild excitement in her and at the same time reassured her. No man who ever touched a woman in this exquisitely sensitive way would ever hurt her.

"Croft," she breathed, his name a whisper of longing in the darkness. Still braced on her elbows she trembled and knew he could feel the tremors in her legs as he stood between her thighs.

"Do you like playing such dangerous games, sweetheart?" His touch became more intimate.

He slid one finger across the small pleasure bud hidden in the soft hair and Mercy sucked in her breath. Part of her felt so excruciatingly vulnerable and sensitized that she didn't think she could bear the deliciously erotic caress. The other part of her wanted to arch her lower body closer to his hand in a silent plea for more. The conflicting sensations came together in a hot spiral of emotion. Not knowing which action she wanted to take, Mercy settled for the safer of the two. She used her elbows as a lever and tried to scramble backward on the bed.

Croft's other hand grasped her upper leg and held her in place. "You're not going anywhere, honey. Not until you've apologized for all the trouble you've put me through tonight."

"What about the trouble you've put me through?"

"Your problems have just begun," he informed her with deep satisfaction. He stroked his finger lower, finding his target easily.

"Oh! Croft, *please.*" Mercy gasped for breath and her nails dug into the rumpled sheets. Her eyes squeezed shut and her head tipped back as she felt his fingers tracing an intricate design around her heated flesh.

"Please what? Please touch you here?" He parted her with the tip of his finger and Mercy shivered. "Or here?" He edged his hand a little lower. "You're going to have to spell it out, sweet Mercy. You're going to have to tell me exactly what you want. And then I think I'll wait until you're begging me before I take you completely. I'm in a mood to let your punishment fit your crime tonight."

"Damn you!" But it was more of a plea than a curse.

"Try again. I want the sweet, hot words, Mercy. All of them." He edged her thighs another inch or two apart and his thumb moved over the small nubbin again. Another large finger was circling the opening of her body, coaxing forth a honeyed flood that dampened his hand. This time Mercy didn't try to pull away. This time there was no uncertainty or confusion in her reaction. She wanted more of him inside her. She lifted her hips against his hand.

"Say it, sweetheart. Tell me exactly what you want. Then we'll both be sure." Croft's words were even hotter than the flowing warmth between Mercy's legs.

"Touch me. Please, touch me, Croft. There. Yes, like that. Inside me. *Deeper*." The plea was squeezed out of her, infinitely hard for her to say aloud, but even harder, apparently, for him to resist.

Croft watched her face, drinking in the signs of her mounting passion as she quivered under his hand. Mercy knew he was watching her intently and it only seemed to add fuel to the fire within her. When he teased her with his finger, easing just barely inside her and then withdrawing, Mercy grew impatient.

"More," she begged.

"How much more?"

With a low moan of frustration, Mercy reached down to catch his wrist and force him to penetrate her more deeply with his finger. She shuddered as he willingly obliged.

"Ah," Croft said softly. "Is that what you want?"

"I may strangle you when this is over."

"Think of it as justice. Sweet justice." He introduced another finger into her and when she cried out with excitement he began slowly separating his fingers, stretching her gently.

He released his grip on her thigh and used his free hand to lightly graze the throbbing bud of her desire.

Mercy nearly came apart in his hands. She was wild for him now, arching upward, clutching at him in an effort to drag him down across her body.

"Now, Croft. Please, now, or I'll go crazy."

"We're going to find out what happens when you go crazy. I want to watch."

"I *will* strangle you. I swear it."

"But not just now, right?"

"Did anyone ever tell you that you can be a real bastard?"

"Yes. But somehow it sounds different coming from you."

"You're laughing at me!"

"No, I'm making love to you." He edged the two fingers deeper, widening the slick, hot channel. When she trembled violently, he sank down on his knees between her legs.

Slowly he withdrew his fingers. Mercy cried out in protest, but when she felt his hands on her inner thighs, she suddenly realized what was about to happen. Croft's warm breath fanned the damp, glistening curls at the juncture of her legs and Mercy's overwhelming excitement metamorphosed into overwhelming panic. She had never been kissed like this.

"Croft, don't. Stop it. Not like that. I don't want you to do that . . . I've never. . . ." She was flushing furiously, starting to struggle.

He paid no attention to her stammering pleas. His fingers clamped gently into the soft skin of her inner legs, holding her in position, and then his tongue was on her in the most intimate of all kisses.

Mercy gasped at the unfamiliar caress. She tried desperately to retreat from the silky touch of his tongue. And then her panic changed back into the most unnerving kind of desire. The wildness returned, claiming her completely. She shuddered again and again as Croft tasted the heart of her.

Then she lost control completely. The coiling tension inside her gave way with a convulsive snap that sent incredible pleasures lashing through her.

Croft released her and came down on top of her before the convulsions had dimmed. He drove himself into her, groaning thickly when her body tightened instantly around him and sucked him deeply inside. Mercy could feel him, hot and huge inside her, filling her to the limit, stretching her body and the bounds of sensation until another shivering release cascaded through her.

Croft tried to pull out a short distance but ended up surging back into her hot sheath, unable to resist the pull of Mercy's climax. It sparked his own, a bolt of lightning in a hot, dry forest. The wildfire consumed him.

Mercy clung to him as she felt him spill himself inside her. For a timeless instant she was bound to Croft and he was chained to her. She could feel the invisible forces linking them and hope washed through her even as the last of the sensual pleasure faded from her veins.

It may not have been the safest way to let Croft make love to her, but at least she knew for certain she was getting some genuine emotion from him. She didn't want to think about the emotion he was getting from her. She was certain there was far too much of it. It was dangerous to let him know she was this vulnerable to him, but there was no way to avoid it. All she could do was endeavor to take him with her whenever she lost control in his arms.

Croft opened his eyes slowly, still half intoxicated by the warm, spicy scent of Mercy's perspiration damp body. One of her legs was still curled around his. Her fingers were trailing across his shoulder and around the back of his neck as if she were conducting an idle survey of him.

He stretched slowly, flexing his back muscles as he carefully eased himself out of Mercy's clinging warmth. He looked down at her and saw her watching him through a veil of lashes. He realized he felt totally replete and completely drained. It was an effort just to move off of her and lay down beside her, but he managed it. A moment later his legs dangled over the edge alongside hers. He put a hand on her thigh, squeezing gently.

He felt good. Better than good. He felt magnificent. All-conquering, all-powerful and filled with a gracious, generous tenderness toward the vanquished.

The only problem was that once again he wasn't quite sure which of them was the vanquished. How did she do it to him? he wondered. How did she pull him so thoroughly into the sensual storm? He had intended to ride that thunder and control it, but it never seemed to work out that way. Instead she pushed him and goaded him and beat on him until he lost the self-control he had taken for granted for years. The next thing he knew he was sucked into the heart of the whirlwind, his emotions raging as wildly as Mercy's.

Croft grinned suddenly in the darkness. At least they went over the edge together. She was such a stubborn little thing, so bound and determined not to be the only victim of the seduction. Well, he could afford to overlook her initial stubbornness. She had learned her lesson and he had gotten more than he'd bargained for when he had decided that it was time to remind Mercy where her loyalties lay.

"You're a reckless woman, Mercy Pennington. One of these days you're going to get into real trouble."

"With whom?"

He laughed softly, hearing the teasing tartness in her whispering voice. "With me, of course. You think I'm going to let you mess around and get into trouble with anyone else? Try asking permission just once to go out and play with some other man and see what happens."

"If I have to ask permission to get into trouble with anyone else, I *am* in real trouble," she observed thoughtfully.

"Your logic is impeccable, sweetheart. You've got it in one." Croft decided not to dwell on the primitive, satisfying sense of possession in which he was wallowing. He knew enough to realize there were some reactions it was better not to question or analyze. It was like trusting instincts. Some things a person just accepted and accommodated.

He raised himself on one elbow and decided that it would be more comfortable for both of them if he adjusted his and Mercy's positions on the bed.

"Up you go," he murmured, sitting up beside her, changing position and tugging her back down onto the pillows. "That's better."

"Croft?"

He glanced at his watch, frowning at the time. "It's late, sweetheart. Better get some sleep." The household should be settled down by now, he decided. Unless Gladstone really did have a listening device planted in Mercy's room. The image of the elegant Gladstone, attired in a silk smoking jacket, hunched over the receiver as he got hard and frustrated listening to Mercy climax in Croft's arms was amusing. Croft decided not to mention it to Mercy, however. She probably wouldn't find it humorous at all.

"Croft, I think we should talk."

He leaned over and kissed her mouth, effectively closing it. "Not here. Not now. Go to sleep, honey."

"But, Croft—"

He put his mouth to her ear. "Bugs."

"Oh." Her eyes widened faintly. It was obvious she had temporarily forgotten the possibility of hidden microphones.

"Sleep." He made it an order and smiled to himself when she gave a resigned sigh and obediently closed her eyes.

There were advantages to letting Mercy think her every word might be monitored, although Croft was privately certain the room was clean. The lady was too unpredictable and much too rash. She needed to be lightly but firmly reined in, he told himself.

He was beginning to think he was just the man who could handle that challenging task.

Croft let another forty-five minutes go by before he reluctantly released Mercy's soft, curled body. Then he got out of bed without making any sudden distributions of weight that might awaken her. He made his way back to his own room on silent feet and pulled on a pair of jeans.

He let himself outside into the hall. He was already adjusted to the quiet shadows. All he had to do was make himself one of them. He wouldn't use the stairs. The possibility of a weight-sensing device under the carpet was too strong.

Croft took hold of the railing along the landing, tested it briefly with his hands, then vaulted lightly over the side. He dangled for a moment, his hands around the railing, and listened intently. When he heard nothing to alarm him he began making his way downstairs using the supporting posts of the banister for hand holds. A moment later he dropped soundlessly to the main level of the house.

One more level to go.

Chapter
TEN

Mercy discovered she was tired of waking up in the middle of the night with a sense of something being wrong. This sort of thing, repeated on a regular basis, could turn a woman into a devoted insomniac. At least this time she was able to figure out the problem as soon as she stretched and wriggled one foot under the quilt.

Croft was gone.

The bastard. Mercy sat bolt upright, fuming. Who the hell did he think he was to believe he could just walk into her bedroom any time he pleased, take a quick, flying leap into bed with her and then walk out again before dawn? The man was definitely a diamond in the rough in spite of his fancy meditation habits and his persnickety tastes in tea. If he was going to insist on hanging around her, she decided as she threw back the covers, he was going to get some polishing.

Shape up or ship out as her Uncle Sid always said.

She hurried across the room, grabbed her lightweight traveling robe and went briskly through the closed connecting door. Once on the other side she stopped, letting her eyes adjust to a different set of shadows. It didn't take her long to realize Croft wasn't in the room.

Feminine pique gave way to dread. Mercy reached out to steady herself with a hand against the door. She had almost forgotten that Croft still considered himself on a mission of sorts. She might have no real doubts about Gladstone's honesty and integrity, but Croft would not be so easily convinced. It was very likely he had gone in search of evidence.

Visions of humiliating discovery and embarrassed, awkward explanations flashed into her mind. She could just imagine what would happen if Dallas or Lance came across Croft going through desk drawers or fiddling with the lock on the library vault.

The vault.

It was the most obvious place. If Croft were out skulking around he would undoubtedly head straight for the vault. He had once claimed he had originally traced Egan Graves through his book collecting habits. He'd said he intended to start his current investigation by trying to get a better look at Gladstone's collection so that he could compare it with what he knew of Graves' book buying habits. But heaven help her and Croft both if he was discovered nosing through the vault. Mercy was positive no one was going to be very understanding.

Mercy didn't waste any more time getting agitated over the situation. She would find Croft and drag him back to his room before they both found themselves trying to explain to Gladstone that they weren't trying to rob him blind.

One way or another, it seemed Croft was determined to squelch her budding career in the rare book business. He would probably sacrifice anything to finish his stupid mission of vengeance.

The thing about Croft, Mercy decided as she let herself

out into the hall and tiptoed down the stairs, was that he was extraordinarily committed. Once he made up his mind about something he just wouldn't quit. Under certain circumstances that might be reassuring. If he learned to love her, for example, he would probably never stop.

He was behaving in an infuriating manner, but she couldn't doubt his basic integrity. He was sure he was doing the right thing, taking the steps required to close his Circle or Ring or whatever he called it. He was no Aaron Sanders out to steal from an unsuspecting, trusting victim. Croft was on a three-year-old mission of vengeance.

It would have been so much easier to deal with him if he were simply another Aaron Sanders, Mercy decided gloomily.

There was no sound from either the main level of the house or the upstairs. Mercy breathed a sigh of relief as she stood for a moment on the first step that led down to the tropical garden pool room. When she was convinced no one heard her moving down the hall, she padded down the flight of steps. Fortunately the Dobermans weren't house dogs. They would be outside doing sentry duty.

The glass doors to the darkened garden gave easily when she turned the handle. Mercy went through onto the little platform. The lights were still on in the pool, but the wealth of foliage was shrouded in complete darkness. There weren't even any windows to provide a modicum of starlight. There was only the eerie glow from the swimming pool. From her vantage point on the platform Mercy could see portions of the pool as it wound its way among the overhanging ferns and wide-leafed palms. The blue tinged light looked oddly unnatural.

The scent of the thick greenery was strong. It seemed to overpower even the trace of chlorine that hung in the air. It was like looking into a night darkened jungle, and for the first time Mercy wondered how easy it would be to find her way through it to the room that held the vault. That afternoon it had been simple enough because of the ample lighting overhead and planted among the foliage. Tonight it would be a different matter.

She didn't even know where the light switch was and wouldn't have dared use it even if she had been able to locate it.

There was no time to waste. She had to go on the assumption that Croft had already found his way into the vault room. She wondered how he expected to open the vault itself. Mercy gathered her courage and her sense of direction and went down the steps into the night shrouded garden.

She stumbled onto one of the delicate gravel paths more by luck than planning. Once on it she managed to follow it by feel. It wasn't all that difficult. When she accidentally tended to veer off she felt the gravel change to moist loam beneath her toes. A second or two later she stumbled into a palm frond or stumbled over a fern.

It was strange how disorienting it was trying to walk through the elaborate garden in the darkness. She tried to use the faint glow of the pool to navigate but it wasn't very easy. There were several points along the way when the pool light was completely hidden by the heavy growth between the path and the water's edge.

This was stupid, Mercy decided a few minutes after she had started. Progress was slow and somewhat painful. Gravel didn't provide the most comfortable path for bare feet. What if Croft hadn't gone into the vault room? she thought to ask herself with blunt disgust. This wretched jaunt could be a totally wasted trip. He might even now be merrily sifting through the contents of Gladstone's upstairs study.

Stupid, crazy, ridiculous and potentially humiliating. When she found Croft she was going to give him a piece of her mind.

She never even sensed the movement in the air behind her. When the large masculine hand slipped across her mouth and the arm went around her waist, Mercy didn't have so much as a split second's warning. One instant she was laboriously making her way through the overgrown garden; the next she was held prisoner against a man's body.

Mercy wanted to scream and couldn't breathe a word. She wanted to struggle and found herself immobilized. When she made a furious effort to employ some of the more brutal tricks she had learned in the three-hour self-defense class she realized in horrified shock that it was totally useless. She went limp. It was the only action left to her.

"You stupid little idiot. What the hell are you doing wandering around here in the middle of the night?" Croft's voice was a furious breath of sound against her ear. He seemed to realize she couldn't answer him as long as he had his palm flattened across her mouth. Slowly he withdrew it. "Keep your voice down."

Mercy gasped for air. "My God, you scared me to death. Don't you ever jump out at me from the bushes like that again. Do you hear me?"

"Damn it to hell. You're supposed to be upstairs asleep."

"I was asleep until I realized you had gone gallivanting off on your own. You have no business flitting around Gladstone's house in the middle of the night. You were heading for the vault, weren't you?"

"How long have you been out of the bedroom?"

She blinked, trying to see his face in the shadows. She could barely make out the vague outline of his shoulder. He was just an extension of the darkness around her. "I don't know. I wasn't looking at my watch. A few minutes, I guess. Why?"

"Just close your mouth and do as you're told. We probably don't have more than a few seconds. Come on." He manacled one of her wrists and led her straight into the heavy foliage that fringed the path.

"What are you doing? What's going on?" She stumbled against a palm and then found herself on another path. Croft was yanking her along it with no regard whatsoever for her bare feet. She wondered how he could see so well in the dark. It had to be the ghost in him, she decided resentfully.

"Take off that robe."

"Forget it. I'm not playing Jane to your Tarzan. Once was enough tonight."

"The Tarzan bit comes later. Right now we're going swimming."

He broke through the foliage that ringed the pool, pulling Mercy with him. She found herself on the tiled edge looking down into the glowing blue water. "No thanks," she muttered, realizing abruptly what he intended. "I don't feel like a swim tonight. I want you to come back upstairs to our suite before you get us both in trouble. Can you imagine how embarrassed I'm going to be if anyone discovers you were prowling around the vault in the middle of the night?"

"Your embarrassment would be the least of our problems." His hand was already on her robe, wrenching free the sash and pushing the garment off her shoulders. Underneath she was naked. The sight obviously did not inflame him to any great degree of lust. He seemed oblivious of her nudity. "In the pool," he ordered in a soft, dangerous voice. "Now."

Croft was already unzipping his jeans and shoving them down over his hips. Mercy didn't argue any more. There was no point. The man might be crazy, but he was serious. She knelt down at the edge of the pool and slipped cautiously over the side. Croft was right behind her.

"Ah," Mercy sighed, relaxing immediately as she slid into the water. "This is wonderful. What are we doing in here, Croft?"

"Guess."

She groaned. "I was afraid of that. This is camouflage, isn't it? In case someone heard us come down the stairs?"

"Not us. You. No one heard me come down the stairs."

"Why not? Did you levitate?"

"Keep your voice down."

"You sound irritated."

"Probably because that's the way I'm feeling."

Mercy nodded. "I'm learning to take what I can get in the way of honest emotion from you." She flipped a hand through the water, sending a small wave in his direction. It broke harmlessly against his broad chest. "I thought it might be a bit nippy in here, but this is like bath water. Perfect. Do you know something? I've never gone skinny-dipping in my life."

Croft glanced at her curiously as he began stroking leisurely toward the far end of the pool. "You've led a sheltered life, haven't you?"

"It was my aunt and uncle's fault. They were a little old-fashioned." She turned languidly in the water, enjoying the novelty of a late night swim in the nude.

"They raised you? This aunt and uncle?"

She was mildly surprised by his continuing interest in the subject, especially at the moment. Until now he hadn't shown much real curiosity about her past. "They got stuck with me when I was three after my parents were killed in the plane accident. Aunt Ruth and Uncle Sid already had two boys of their own who were starting into their teens when I arrived. Just when they'd begun looking forward to getting their own kids raised and out of the house they had to start all over again with me. I think they were a little stricter with me because they'd never raised a girl before. They gave up a lot to take on the job of rearing me."

"That explains it," Croft said quietly.

"Explains what?" They were both speaking in whispers, she realized, just as they had earlier in her bedroom. Maybe she was fated to conduct every meaningful conversation with this man in a barely audible tone.

"Your feelings of gratitude toward them. You think you owe them something, don't you? You feel indebted to them in a way a child doesn't normally feel toward a parent. And you're very conscious of your debt. I noticed your attitude the day you told me the story of your ex-fiance trying to use you to fleece your aunt and uncle. You weren't just hurt personally, even though it was your engagement that went down the tubes. In the final analysis you were more concerned about what had almost happened to your relatives. You took responsibility for it, didn't you? You felt that it was all your fault."

"Well, it was my fault. I'm the one who got hoodwinked by Aaron Sanders. I'm the one who introduced him to them. And I do owe my aunt and uncle a great deal. They didn't have to take me in, you know. They could have let the state put me into foster care. They had no obligation toward me."

"When Sanders tried to take them to the cleaners, you blamed yourself for having been stupid enough to believe he loved you."

"It was stupid of me to believe it." Mercy didn't like the way the conversation was going. On the one hand she welcomed more intimate, revealing, honest discussions with this strange man. But on the other hand, she didn't particularly want to be the one who made all the intimate, honest revelations.

"What I'm trying to point out, Mercy, is that you reacted as you did because you felt responsible, even though you were just another victim yourself. It was a matter of honor for you."

Mercy stopped swimming and began treading water. "Just what is the point of this conversation?"

Croft stopped swimming too and hovered in the water only a short distance away. He seemed to float without effort. There was no mad churning of his hands or scissoring of his legs to hold his position. He just *floated*. The uneven, unearthly blue light from beneath the rippling surface gave his hard-edged face a disturbing illumination. "I want you to understand that I did what I did tonight because of a similar sense of obligation."

Mercy raised her eyebrows. "Are you by any chance trying to justify yourself to me?"

He frowned. "I was just trying to explain."

"You've already explained," she said stiffly. "I know why you came down here tonight. I know you feel you have to do this, even though you could easily jeopardize my future in the rare book business and get us both arrested for sneakiness or something."

His frown turned to an arrogant scowl. "If I'm wrong I'll take full responsibility."

"Terrific. When future clients refuse to deal with me because my reputation as a reliable dealer is in shreds and I've got a prison record, I'll just casually mention that it's really all your fault and that you take full responsibility. I'm sure that will solve everything."

"Mercy, I—"

Whatever Croft was going to say next was cut off abruptly when the overhead lights and the camouflaged garden lamps came on with no warning. Mercy gave a small yelp of surprise and automatically whirled around in the water to stare toward the doorway. Unfortunately the foliage was too thick to see whoever stood on the platform from this angle.

"Is anybody down here?" The voice was Isobel's.

"Over here," Croft called back readily. "In the pool."

"For pete's sake, Croft," Mercy muttered. "I don't have any clothes on."

"I told you, this is camouflage," he whispered back.

"Being stark naked in the water with all these lights on is not my idea of being camouflaged." Mercy launched herself toward the side of the pool, intending to grab her robe. She could hear footsteps on the graveled path and knew Isobel was making her way through the greenery. With all the lights turned on it was an easy trip. She would appear in a matter of seconds.

As it happened she appeared just as Mercy had herself halfway out of the water. Isobel stepped out of the shrubbery at the side of the pool, her expression concerned. She was dressed in a flowing robe of silver satin, her long black hair loose and streaming around her shoulders. Mercy had time enough to notice that the exotic black mass fell all the way to the woman's waist before she realized Isobel was not alone. Lance was right behind her.

Mercy gave another muffled gasp and dropped back into the water. Lance looked at her immediately, his eyes going from her flushing face to the broken image of her nude body under the surface of the water.

Mercy opened her mouth again to demand some privacy, but before she could voice the words there was a flash of broad-backed, naked male in the water in front of her and an instant later Croft was surfacing to stand between Mercy and Lance's interested gaze.

"Sorry about this, Isobel," Croft said coolly. "We couldn't resist a midnight swim. You said something about feeling free to use the pool at any time and we took you at your word. Mind giving us a little privacy while Mercy and I put on some clothes?"

"Of course not. I'm the one who's sorry." She nodded at Lance. "As you can see, there's no problem. Thanks for alerting me. You may go back to bed."

Lance accepted his dismissal without a word and vanished back into the bushes.

Isobel smiled at Croft, who was still standing in front of Mercy. Her dark gaze slid over his nude frame with what Mercy could only describe as professional interest.

"Don't let me interrupt your swim," Isobel said. "You are quite welcome to finish it. Lance and Dallas have rooms at the back of the house on the floor above. Lance happened to be up getting himself a drink of water or something and thought he heard a noise. We have to take strange noises seriously up here in the mountains. We're so isolated and Erasmus has so many valuable things here in the house. But now that I know what the problem is, I won't disturb you further. Good night and enjoy your swim. I'll turn out the overhead lights on my way back up the stairs. Shall I leave on the path lamps? It's a little difficult to find your way down here when they're off."

"That would be great," Croft said. "Thanks. And sorry again about alarming everyone."

"No problem. See you at breakfast, unless you'd prefer to sleep in."

"We'll be at breakfast," Croft assured her.

Mercy exhaled in relief as Isobel disappeared down the garden path. "Good grief. How embarrassing."

"If you want to save yourself further embarrassment in the future, try not giving Lance an eyeful."

"Don't you dare blame me for this. Everything that's happened tonight is all your fault." Mercy scrambled out of the pool and grabbed her robe. "And I'm not the only who who got leered at tonight. I saw Isobel staring at you. That water doesn't conceal much, you know. It was obvious you didn't have on a swimsuit."

Croft planted both hands on the edge of the pool and hauled himself out in a single, smooth movement. Then he surprised Mercy with an unexpected grin. "You can stare all you want, honey. I won't mind."

"Thank you very much." Primly, she turned away and fastened the sash of her robe. "But I think I've seen all I want tonight."

Croft shrugged. He glanced regretfully toward the far end

of the room. "I haven't seen all I want, but I guess I've seen all I'm going to see tonight," he muttered quietly. "Now that the hired hands are awake and alert, I can't risk going back into the vault. Somebody might be paying attention this time. I'll have to try again later." He followed Mercy out of the garden room and back up the stairs.

When Mercy walked into her own room and closed the connecting door he didn't try to open it.

For a long while she sat on the edge of her bed staring out at the endless mountain sky. Tomorrow, she decided, she was going to have a serious talk with Croft. She would insist he take her for a hike to some place where she wouldn't have to keep her voice low and watch every word.

It occurred to Mercy that this business of having to worry about listening devices in the bedroom was very useful for Croft. It was an effective way to keep her from asking too many questions or making too many demands. The man definitely had a talent for getting his own way.

Croft wasn't thinking about his talent for getting his own way the next morning as he sat down to breakfast with Isobel, Gladstone and Mercy. He was giving grave consideration to the limitations on his time at Gladstone's mountain fortress. The party was scheduled for that night. The next day he and Mercy would be leaving. Last night had very nearly turned into a full-scale disaster; that left only tonight to try to accomplish something useful.

Breakfast was a delightful meal served in a glass walled room that had spectacular views on three sides. Dallas and Lance served the fresh fruit, heated silver racks of toast, Colombian coffee and goat cheese omelettes. Croft was served tea perfectly brewed in a pre-warmed ceramic pot. The tea was a very find blend of Ceylon and Indian leaves, full-bodied with an excellent color and aroma.

The room was filled with morning sunlight. It reflected

very nicely off the sterling and crystal. The peach colored nappery and a beautifully restrained arrangement of peach gladiolus provided just the right hint of color in the elegantly light room.

Croft knew that from a purely aesthetic point of view he should admire the flower arrangement. It was quite perfect, austere and subtle. Isobel was no doubt responsible for it. But the more he looked at it, the more he found himself wondering how Mercy would have handled the flowers. He suspected she would have chosen a more brilliant shade of flower to start. And then she would have given full scope to the flower's inherent lush qualities in her design. The final effect would have been a bright, brash, intriguing counterpoint in the elegant room. Croft knew he would have been charmed by the result even if he did feel compelled to criticize it.

Gladstone was in an engaging mood, talking animatedly with Mercy about books. There was no doubt but that the man was a devoted collector who knew his field. Mercy was once again hanging on his every word, participating eagerly in the discussion while Croft and Isobel listened politely.

"You must tell me how you came across *Valley*," Gladstone said as he helped himself to dry toast. "No offense, my dear, but I would have expected it to turn up in one of the East coast or English auction houses rather than a second-hand bookshop out in Washington. It is a rather valuable item."

"That's the great thing about the book business, isn't it?" Mercy smiled happily. "You never know when you're going to unearth buried treasure. I got *Valley* in a trunkful of books I picked up at a flea market. I had no idea it was inside. I thought the whole trunk was full of used paperbacks and some assorted junk."

"You must have been very excited when you realized what you had."

Mercy nodded. "I wasn't sure at first, but I spent a few years as a librarian and I had enough training to know *Valley* might be valuable. I also had enough training to go about finding out if the book was really worth anything. As soon as I'd verified that it was an original and not just a clever reproduction, I put the ad in that catalog you happened to see."

"Did anyone else call about the ad?" Gladstone asked casually.

Croft saw Mercy blink, but she never missed a beat as she replied immediately. "No. No one else telephoned. I was delighted when I got your offer, believe me."

"You must have wondered about my, er, interests when you got my call. Did you think I was the prurient sort?"

"Of course not," Mercy said instantly. "It's obvious *Valley* is hardly an example of run-of-the-mill pornography. The copper plate illustrations are beautifully done and the writing is very literate. The original owner must have spent a fortune to have it bound in that beautifully tooled Moroccan leather. Many collectors who have a general collection would want such a fine example of, uh, curiosa on their shelves. That sort of thing is so rare."

"It is, indeed. I didn't take the time to show you the other night, but I have some even more valuable examples of what might be termed curiosa down in the vault. There are one or two particularly fine seventeenth century Japanese painted scrolls. Not true books, perhaps, but I was unable to resist them when they came on the market. The Japanese have done some exquisite erotic art, as have the Indians and the Chinese. That section of my collection is not my chief area of interest, but I want it be as excellent as possible. I believe in acquiring only the best."

Croft saw Mercy's gaze go briefly to Isobel, who didn't appear to notice. "You are fortunate to be able to indulge your interests. Not all of us can afford to do so."

Gladstone chuckled. "Inheriting money from several generations of shrewd ancestors is extremely helpful." Without any warning he turned to Croft. "Tell me, Croft, do you share any of Mercy's interest in the rare and the valuable?"

Croft looked at Mercy. "Occasionally I'm fascinated by rare and valuable things." Perhaps that explained his growing fascination with Mercy Pennington, Croft thought. She was so rare and so very valuable and she had absolutely no idea of her own uniqueness. She bloomed for him like one of the beautiful flowers in the mountain meadows, unselfconsciously delightful.

"I have always sought to surround myself with the beautiful and the rare and the valuable," Gladstone went on conversationally. "Some people say we are what we eat, but I believe we are just as influenced by our environment. Do you agree?"

Croft was watching Mercy eat a strawberry. She was thoroughly enjoying the fruit and it showed. He realized it gave him great pleasure to see her pleasured. Reluctantly he took his gaze from the sight of the plump red strawberry disappearing between her lips and looked at Gladstone.

"The ability to appreciate the rare or the exotic or the beautiful is largely a matter of education and the development of a certain kind of sensitivity. It has nothing to do with whether the viewer has any of the equivalent human virtues. Surrounding an evil man with works of fine art and great beauty would not alter his basic nature."

"In other words," Mercy said as she reached for another strawberry, "you can't make a silk purse from a sow's ear."

"Exactly," Croft murmured. But one might be able to disguise the ear for a long time so that few would recognize it for what it was, he added silently.

Mercy pursed her lips. "Speaking of valuable things, aren't you worried about having a house full of people tonight? What about security? Won't it worry you to have so many people in the house at the same time?"

"Dallas and Lance handle that end of things for us," Isobel explained. "But there is really very little need to concern ourselves with the possibility of theft. The artists in the colony are all quite grateful to Erasmus for his patronage. It's unlikely any of them would abuse his generosity."

"I see." Mercy started in on her goat cheese omelette.

"What would you two like to do today?" Gladstone asked genially. "We want you to enjoy yourselves."

"I'd like to take a walk this morning," Mercy said, glancing determinedly at Croft. "I haven't really had a chance to enjoy the scenery firsthand."

"An excellent idea," Gladstone approved. "We have several examples of Alpine meadows within walking distance and the views are superb. I would suggest you take a topographical map and a compass, however, or else stay within sight of the house. It's far too easy to get lost out there. One must never forget this is true wilderness, some of the last left in the States."

"We'll leave right after breakfast," Mercy said enthusiastically. Then she smiled benignly at Croft. "I'll bet Croft knows how to follow a topographical map and read a compass, don't you, Croft?"

He saw the mischief in her wide-eyed, innocent green gaze and realized just how much he was learning to enjoy that element in her nature. She didn't fool him for a minute, though. The sweet, sexy little witch was determined to get him out of the house where she could lecture him to her heart's content. Croft surrendered to the inevitable. It occurred to him that he usually did around Mercy.

"We won't get lost," he said equably and went back to his omelette.

An hour later they walked away from the house, following Dallas' directions toward a meadow that he assured them was in full bloom. Mercy was wearing her jeans and a pair of white Nikes along with a flower patterned camp shirt. She had her hair in a short ponytail and Croft thought she looked very fresh and enticing. It was a fine morning to be setting out on a hike with this woman.

"Of course we're not going to get lost," Mercy murmured provokingly as she strode along beside him. "I knew right away you'd be an expert at hiking in the wilderness, just like you are at everything else."

"I'm not an expert at everything and we're not going very far." He didn't like the taunting note in her voice. She was looking for a way to bait him again. He just knew it. "Don't," he advised.

"Don't what?"

"Don't spend the whole morning trying to provoke me. I know you think it's your only form of retaliation at the moment, but I'm not in the mood for it."

"Retaliation?" She looked more innocent than ever. "Why would I want to retaliate against you? Just because my whole future is hanging in the balance and I'm scared to death you're going to do something that will cut the thread that's holding it, why should I feel like retaliating?"

"Don't exaggerate. Your whole future is not hanging in the balance."

"Oh yes it is. You'd better exercise a great deal of caution while you're investigating Gladstone, or I'm the one who will pay the price. I don't want any more embarrassing scenes like last night."

"It wouldn't have even occurred if you'd stayed upstairs where you belong." He slanted her a quelling glance but she didn't seem to not.ce.

"I won't take the blame for what happened. It was all your

fault. I suppose you're going to make another foray tonight while the party's going on?"

He cocked an eyebrow, mildly surprised by her shrewd guess. "I don't have much choice. We leave tomorrow. If I'm ever going to get the proof I need, it will have to be tonight."

"I take it you never got inside the vault last night?"

"I didn't have a chance. I heard you clumping through the garden just as I was starting to crack the lock."

"You're a cat burglar, too? You pick locks? My, what a talented man."

He decided to ignore the sarcasm. "I am not a cat burglar, but I've had to learn a few things about locks in the past."

"Ah, yes. Your past," Mercy said with grim determination. "That's something I've been wanting to discuss with you. I think now is the time to do it."

He felt suddenly uneasy. "Forget it, Mercy. My past isn't something I spend much time discussing with anyone."

"You'll discuss it with me. Now."

"Is that right? Why should I?"

"Because," she announced with gleeful satisfaction, "I'm going to blackmail you into it."

Croft halted on the rocky trail. "You want to run that by me again?"

"You heard me. I'm going to blackmail you for some answers to my questions. Either you talk or I'll blow the lid off your investigation. Gladstone will kick you out of the house so fast you'll never know what hit you."

He stared at her. He could pick her up in one hand and dangle her over the edge of a ravine until she screamed in panic and she wouldn't be able to do a thing about it. She was as delicate as a flower, but she seemed to have absolutely no fear of him. Mercy didn't seem to realize the extent of her own vulnerability.

Then Croft smiled faintly. She probably didn't realize the extent of her own integrity, either. She wouldn't betray him because deep down she was incapable of betrayal. Besides, she trusted him.

"You're bluffing," Croft said finally. And with that he started down the narrow path toward the meadow.

Chapter
ELEVEN

Mercy was infuriated. So much for clever tactics.

"How do you know I'm bluffing?" she demanded as she dashed down the small incline behind him.

He looked back at her over his shoulder. "Watch your step The flowers in these meadows are very delicate and they've got a very short growing season. Summer doesn't last long around here."

"I know all about the fragility of mountain flora and fauna," she informed him stiffly. "I am not a complete idiot."

He smiled and sat down on a nearby boulder, one of many that had been carelessly tumbled into a small heap at that end of the meadow. "I know you're not an idiot, Mercy, but sometimes you are a little rash or naive. Come over here and sit down and enjoy the flowers. This is something you don't see very often, a high mountain meadow in full bloom."

"Have I told you that I really don't like it when you turn

patronizing and start playing the intellectually superior male?"

"You've probably mentioned it, but not within the last five minutes."

Mercy eyed him warily as she walked over and sat down on a sun-warmed rock. Croft's dark hair was lightly ruffled by a breeze. He was wearing his black chinos and, as usual, a dark shirt. He had one knee drawn up and was resting his arm on it as he gazed out over the bright wonderland spread before them. His darkness was a vibrant counterpoint to the sunlight and color surrounding them.

Something stirred in Mercy's mind, a sudden image of Croft gliding between two dimensions, his own and the one she inhabited. Like the ghost town they had passed on the way to Gladstone's estate, Croft didn't always seem completely in touch with this world. It was as if he was in it, but not always a part of it.

He needed an anchor, Mercy thought with sudden insight, something to tie him firmly to the here and now. He could too easily detach himself and retreat into his own world, a world where everything could be comprehended in terms of complete and incomplete Circles. He had difficulty accepting the eccentricities, irrationalities and unpredictableness of those who inhabited the real world. But with a flash of insight Mercy suspected he had even more trouble accepting the possible existence of some of those qualities within himself.

Mercy tore her gaze away from Croft and made herself study the landscape. She had to admit it was magnificent. Clumps of fragile wildflowers bloomed in bewildering profusion, giving their all in the short span of time allotted them. The grassy carpet in which they grew was a verdant green. Beyond the meadow snow glittered on distant peaks. The sun was warm on her shoulders.

"Falconer priorities," Mercy said on a sigh.

"What's that supposed to mean?"

She shrugged. "Only that it's typical of you to be more concerned about the possibility that I might smash a wild-flower than about the possibility I might blackmail you."

"Mercy, we both know you're not capable of blackmailing me. Don't make threats you can't carry through."

"You won't tell me about your past?"

"Not now. Maybe not ever. Believe me, honey, you don't really want to hear about it."

She wondered about that. "Maybe you're right. Okay, I accept your right to remain silent about that side of things. But I want some questions answered about this Gladstone business. It concerns me and I want to know your plans."

"I've told you my plans. I want to find something, any-thing, that might tie Gladstone to Egan Graves."

"You think you'll find evidence in the vault?"

Croft nodded. "It's the most likely spot. If not there, then maybe in his office. I should be able to check both places tonight during the party. Isobel says there should be almost fifty guests."

"That many more chances you'll be discovered."

He shook his head. "That much easier to disappear."

Mercy shuddered. "I wish you'd let it go, Croft."

"I can't."

She heard the simple truth in his words and sighed. "No, you can't just let it go, can you? You're Croft Falconer and that means you have to close all the doors, seal all the gaps, stop all the leaks. Nothing must be left to chance. No ques-tions can remain unanswered."

"A closed Circle."

"What was she like, Croft? The young woman you went down to the Caribbean to rescue?"

He hesitated and then, to Mercy's astonishment, he an-swered her question.

"Eighteen years old. Pretty. Blonde. Athletic. Full of life. When I pulled her off that island she was no longer eighteen, pretty, blonde, athletic or full of life. She was strung out on drugs, believed Egan Graves was the local representative of heavenly salvation and thought she was doing her duty to the church when she slept with Egan's business acquaintances."

"Grim."

"Yes."

Mercy chewed on her lower lip for a while. "How is she now?"

"Her father said it took a year to get her off the drugs and convince her Graves was nothing more than a pimp and a dealer. But two years ago she started college and she's still there."

Mercy breathed an unconscious sigh of relief. "So she's going to be all right."

"Looks like it."

"You saved her," Mercy said quietly. "She would probably be dead by now if you hadn't rescued her. Does she ever talk to you? Do you see her sometimes?"

"No. She doesn't remember me. She was hysterical that night. So were the others I managed to keep from throwing themselves into the flames. I turned them all over to Ray before dawn that morning. He was waiting in a boat a couple of miles offshore. I never saw any of the kids again and they never really got a good look at me. I told Ray that Graves was dead."

"Ray?"

"Ray Chandler. It was his daughter I was supposed to pull off the island. He was the one who desperately wanted to get his hands on Egan Graves."

"He's the one who asked you to go?"

"Yes."

"You didn't take a fee for your services?"

Croft gave her a strange glance. "Not from Ray Chandler," he said quietly. "I owed him."

"Why?"

"Ray works for the government. He did me a favor once. Looked the other way when I needed some answers from a top secret file."

"So when Ray came to you for help, you returned the favor?"

"Some people call it maintaining good karma. Others call it keeping your honor clean. I call it keeping the Circle closed. I told you, I owed him."

She looked at him. "That's how you live your life, isn't it? You keep this . . . this Circle closed around you. Everything must be kept under control. Including me."

"I don't think you know just how much of a wild card you are in all this, Mercy. Just when I think I've got you pinned down, you do something that scares the hell out of me. Like following me downstairs last night. Don't ever do that again."

A wild card? Mercy experienced a rush of recklessness. "You know what I think, Croft? I think you need to be shaken up from time to time. You're too rigid, too set in your ways. You get upset if you miss your morning meditation or if a waitress brings you tepid tea water. You think your way of doing things is the only way to do them and you turn tyrannical when someone tries to argue. This business of keeping the Circle closed sounds like a very limiting kind of philosophy. It makes you inflexible. Maybe it keeps you from being able to fall in love." Mercy shook her head wisely. "Doesn't sound like a healthy lifestyle to me."

"You think yours is any better? You're naive and reckless and unpredictable. You deliberately try to goad me into losing my temper or my self-control. Yes, you do," he said forcefully when she opened her mouth to deny the accusation. "Last night was a classic example. I didn't come into your bedroom intending to play bondage games."

"No, you thought you'd just sashay in and give me a little thrill with a quick, off-the-cuff example of your seduction skills. In the process you'd make sure you still had me under control. I know how you try to use sex against me. I'm not *that* naive. You think that if you've got me tied to you with sexual bonds I won't question your orders or demands. You don't like me thinking for myself, do you? It worries you that I might be viewing this Gladstone situation with an open mind. That's dangerous for you because it means I might decide the man is totally innocent. Which, for your information, I have just about decided, in spite of your bedroom karate."

His mouth tilted in a wry grimace. "So much for my skills at sexual bondage."

"I thought you'd better know it's not working."

"I appreciate the warning."

"Anytime." She realized she was the one feeling goaded and provoked now.

There was a long silence and then Croft spoke quietly. "About last night."

"If you're going to apologize, make it good. I'm not in the mood for any halfhearted attempts at rationalization."

"You want me down on my knees?"

"Sounds perfect."

"I seem to recall being on my knees in front of you last night at one point," he began thoughtfully. "Doesn't that count?"

"Why you son of a—Last night I told you I would strangle you. Today I will." Mercy flew off the rock with the speed of an exploding grenade. She launched herself at Croft, heedless of the danger.

He caught her easily, cushioning her against his solid frame so that she didn't injure herself on the rocks. Croft absorbed the momentum of her flying charge and then, holding Mercy tightly, he rolled gently off the boulder and onto the grass. He used one arm to manage the small impact for both himself and his wriggling burden.

Mercy felt the rock-hard security of Croft's grasp, closed her eyes as the sky spun overhead, and then found herself flat on the ground. Croft was sprawled on top of her. When she lifted her lashes she found herself looking up into laughing hazel eyes.

It was the golden laughter that defused her short-lived flash of anger. It captivated her and charmed her as nothing else could have done. Mercy realized she loved to see Croft laugh.

"You think you're the slickest thing I've come across since sliced bread, don't you?" she asked, unable to resist running her fingers through his hair.

He grinned. "If we had world enough and time I'd make love to you out here in the sunshine. You look good on a carpet of flowers."

"Aren't you afraid I might have squashed one or two?"

"It's worth it to see your hair spread out on the grass."

"I take it we don't have world enough and time?"

"Disappointed?"

"Even if I were I'd never admit it," she said. "You're already far too sure of yourself. Besides, I know why you want to head back to the house as soon as possible. You're on a mission and nothing must get in the way. First things first, business before pleasure, keep the Circle closed, etcetera, etcetera."

He brushed his mouth across hers. "Why do you have to fight me every inch of the way, honey? Why can't you just accept the way I am and the way things are between us?"

"Mostly because I haven't been able to figure out how things actually are between us." Mercy pushed against his shoulders and Croft sat up slowly. She glanced back to see how many dainty daisies or delicate blue columbine she might have crushed. But Croft, with typical proficiency, had made certain she missed the flowers.

"I've told you from the beginning you're safe with me," Croft said. He reached out toward the petals of a starry little columbine growing between some rocks. His touch was so delicate the purplish-blue petal barely quivered. "And I think you've trusted me from the beginning. So why do you keep arguing with me and provoking me?"

"It isn't a question of trust. Well, maybe it is in a way. It irks me to admit it, but I do trust you, Croft. I trust you to be true to yourself and your own brand of philosophy. But I'm not sure where that's going to leave me. I can't avoid the feeling of being used. The last time a man used me, it was easy to hate him, easy to be thoroughly repulsed by him and everything he had done. Easy to walk away from him. But I seem to be trapped with you."

"And you don't hate me."

Mercy heaved a forlorn sigh, thinking of the previous night. "I guess that's only too obvious, isn't it?"

His gaze turned remote and austere. "I'm aware that when this is all over, regardless of how it turns out, I'm going to owe you. I always pay my debts, Mercy, and I'll pay this one. I swear it."

"That's just ducky." She sprang to her feet, dusting off the seat of her jeans. "I'll have to think long and hard about exactly what to ask of you in the way of repayment, won't I? I'll want to be sure I get my money's worth."

She started through the meadow, aware that Croft was following with his usual silent tread. The sun was still warm and the flowers just as gemlike, but some of the brightness had gone out of the day. Mercy understood now that as far as Croft was concerned, he was going to come out of this tied to her with the bond of indebtedness.

He would owe her.

Mercy didn't see how a debt of honor, especially one based on Croft's rigid personal code, was going to translate very easily into a bond of love.

"Mercy, wait."

Croft reached out to catch her hand and drew her to a halt. She looked up at him. "What is it, Croft?"

"I was wrong," he said a little thickly as he framed her face with his strong hands. "We do have world enough. Hell, we've got this whole mountain meadow. It's a world unto itself."

"And the time?" she whispered.

"We'll make the time."

The brightness came back into the day as Croft lowered Mercy down onto the grass. She put her arms around his neck and thought about how badly he must want her if he was willing to change his mind about making love to her. She smiled.

Croft saw the smile and groaned as he stretched out beside her. "You really must be a witch." He trapped her legs beneath his thigh and his fingers went to the buttons of her camp shirt. "Just feel what you do to me." He took her palm and put it on the burgeoning hardness that was already pushing against the fabric of his pants. "I don't seem to have any control around you."

Mercy threaded her fingers through the thickness of his hair, her eyes misty with a loving invitation. "It works both ways, you know. Look what you do to me."

"I'd rather feel what I do to you. You always feel so good when I touch you." He pushed the shirt off her shoulders and started on her jeans. He worked quickly, his impatience evident in the swift, sure movements he used to undress her. A few minutes later Mercy was lying naked in a field of wildflowers, her skin warmed by the sun and the touch of the man who held her as if she were a part of him.

"Your clothes," she murmured in husky protest as he

didn't bother to undress himself. Her trembling fingers went to the buttons of his shirt.

"Forget my clothes," he muttered. "I'll take care of them." He unzipped his pants, sat up in a cross-legged position and caught hold of her hand again. "Now you can help me." He guided her fingers back to the opening in his pants.

"Croft?"

His expression was a little wicked and altogether sexy. His eyes gleamed. "How long are you going to keep me waiting?"

Goaded, she slipped her hand inside the open zipper, found the pocket of his briefs and then her fingers closed around his hard shaft. Warm, masculine flesh pulsed eagerly against her palm. Gently Mercy freed Croft's eager member from its confinement. She touched him delicately, wonderingly and Croft groaned. A drop of moisture formed at the blunt tip of his shaft, dampening Mercy's fingertip.

"Come here, honey. I can't wait any longer." He reached for her, pulling her down onto his lap in a sitting position.

Mercy gasped, filled with a sudden, wild abandon when Croft positioned her so that she was astride him. She clutched at his shoulders as she sat facing him, her thighs spread wide, the secret place between her legs fully exposed. Croft's unyielding manhood pressed against her inner leg, heavy and waiting.

"Croft, I'm not sure this is. . . ." She couldn't think of a logical protest. She could not think at all. Mercy just knew she felt outrageously wanton as she sat there straddling Croft's lap.

"Relax," he whispered. "Just remember that you're always safe with me." Then he touched her, exploring her with a deliberate possessiveness that made Mercy tremble. She cried out softly and closed her eyes. He moistened his finger in the dampness he elicited between her thighs and then coaxed her small bud of desire into a tingling fullness.

When he was satisfied with her reaction, he drew his finger lower. He used her womanly lubrication to ease his path. Mercy shuddered as he slipped his questing finger inside her and then went lower still to find the sensitive flesh just below her soft, wet channel. There he drew an exquisite little pattern that nearly drove Mercy over the edge.

"Croft!" She wriggled on his lap, trying to get more of the delicious sensation. "Oh, God, *Croft*."

"I know," he muttered, his voice dark and husky with passion. "I know what you want. I'm going to give it to you. Now." He stopped his sensual exploration and cupped her buttocks in both hands. With infinite, excruciating slowness, he guided her down onto his upthrust manhood.

Mercy was fiercely aware of every throbbing centimeter of him as he entered her. Her whole body tightened in anticipation as Croft filled her completely. She wanted to hurry now. The excitement was already starting to ripple through her and she could not control it. It gripped her, claimed her and thrilled her. And the dark glitter in Croft's eyes told her he was with her every step of the way.

When he had buried himself in her softness, Croft began to guide the primitive rhythm. He used his hold on her thighs to establish the movements of the sensual dance.

It was an act of urgency and claiming and Mercy was as aroused by it as she was when he teased and tormented her with his caresses.

There was a different type of excitement in this sudden fierce need. It proved just as compelling as the other kind.

The onrushing climax that shook them both seemed as natural and magnificent as the vista of mountains and meadows that surrounded them.

Croft's shout of exultant satisfaction echoed across the meadow.

When it was over they collapsed in each other's arms until the brisk air and dazzling sunlight restored their energy.

* * *

Isobel Ascanius stood at the window and watched Croft and Mercy walk back into the compound. She saw Falconer halt for a moment and pause to brush some bits of grass and dried leaves from Mercy's hair. It didn't take much imagination to know that at some point during the morning walk Mercy had found herself lying on her back in a mountain meadow. Isobel found herself feeling strangely envious.

She couldn't remember the last time a man had made love to her in the grass under a sunny sky. Isobel maintained a carefully groomed appearance of exoticism. Hers was a beautiful, cool, sensually challenging facade that never failed to attract and compel. She required her lovers to be skillful and sophisticated. Her image was clearly not that of a woman who would tolerate a simple tumble in the grass. Few men would dare to suggest it. She couldn't even begin to imagine Erasmus Gladstone suggesting such a thing, for example. Gladstone was an accomplished lover, but sometimes he repelled her. His passion was cold and mechanical, satisfying but never fulfilling.

Isobel told herself that Gladstone's emotionless lovemaking was sufficient. Sex was a low priority on her personal list of needs and desires. She took her real pleasure in knowing that Gladstone respected her skills as a professional security consultant and bodyguard and she planned to impress him with her abilities as a strategist. She would find ways to convince him he needed her.

She had started working for Gladstone because she sensed that he would one day be powerful enough to promote her into the level of power she craved. Someday she, too, would be the head of a lucrative network based on providing the titillating, illegal products demanded by a spoiled, ego-centric, shortsighted clientele. She would be rich beyond her wildest dreams, a woman with the power of life and death over others. Her goals were clear and shining; and she would not abandon them.

But as she watched Mercy returning to the house, Isobel found herself wondering what it had been like out there in the meadow with Croft Falconer.

"Everything is under control for tonight?" Erasmus asked from behind her.

"Of course. You're certain it's necessary to get rid of Falconer?"

"Better to be safe than sorry," Gladstone murmured. "On the surface he is nothing more than a very ordinary, very uninteresting man. The perfect lover for our dull little Miss Pennington, I imagine. But something about him bothers me. He moves very well, have you noticed?"

Isobel glanced out the window again. "I've noticed."

"I don't like the fact that things went wrong that first night at the motel. Somehow Falconer got the book out of the safe before Dallas could get it. And I don't like the fact that you discovered Falconer and Mercy in the garden last night. Too close to the vault. But most of all, I don't like the fact that you haven't been able to trace Falconer."

"I know," Isobel agreed quietly. "I should have been able to find out more about him by now."

"Precisely. Given the facts and the suspicious lack of information, I think it's better to get rid of the man."

"And Miss Pennington?"

Gladstone made a dismissing gesture with his hand. "I insisted she make the trip here with the book so that I would have an opportunity to evaluate her and decide just how much she knows. There was always the possibility that she had learned of the real value of *Valley* and was setting a trap or planning to work a blackmail scheme. If such were the case I knew it would be far easier to get rid of her here than in her own territory. But it's clear she's nothing more than what she appears to be. A naive little twit. Still, if Falconer is more than he appears, it would probably be best if Miss Pennington eventually suffered a fatal accident, too. I want nothing and no one around who can follow the trail of *Valley* back to me."

Isobel inhaled deeply, wondering again what it was going to be like to kill for Gladstone. She told herself she was committed now. With cool logic she had made up her mind to pursue this path and she would not quit. All her training had been focused on making her into the perfect female mercenary, the perfect security consultant for a wealthy, powerful man. She would not balk at the first kill. This was the route to the power she wanted. Someday, if her plans were fulfilled, she would be the one hiring people to do her dirty work.

But the peculiar dread she was feeling alarmed her. There was no doubt that it would be easier on her if she could avoid the necessity of having to get rid of Falconer and the woman. Logically it would be safer, too. Deaths always brought questions, and questions always left one vulnerable.

"If Miss Pennington is that silly and naive, then you might be able to get her to tell you something about Falconer. We might be able to verify just how dangerous he is before we act. I've seen your skill with hypnosis."

Gladstone smiled. "That's a thought. It would be interesting to know more about him, even though we're going to get rid of him soon. Knowledge is always useful. It would be interesting to know, for example, if he was in the employ of someone else or working for himself." He paused, thinking it over. "You're right, my dear. I'd better have a little chat with Miss Pennington and I'd better do it this afternoon. You'll have to provide a distraction for Falconer."

"I don't think that will be a problem," Isobel said smoothly. "Lance mentioned that Miss Pennington has a horror of small aircraft. Falconer, on the other hand, seems like the kind of man who would find a helicopter flight around the vicinity interesting."

Gladstone's blue eyes were unreadable. "I shall rely on you, my dear, to set up an entertaining afternoon for both of us."

Isobel glanced out the window again. Perhaps if Gladstone satisfied himself that Falconer was harmless he could be talked out of arranging the "accidents" he had planned for Croft and Mercy.

But regardless of the outcome of Gladstone's chat with Mercy, Isobel told herself, she would do what she had to in order to insure her own future.

There was a first time for everything, including killing.

Shortly after lunch Mercy stood at the huge plate glass window in the living room and watched Isobel Ascanius lift the small helicopter off its pad and point it toward the south. Croft was sitting beside Isobel in the passenger seat. He didn't bother to look back and wave at Mercy.

Somehow it didn't come as any great surprise to discover that Isobel was Gladstone's pilot. The woman looked like she could handle anything.

Mercy still wasn't quite certain how she and Croft had gotten separated, but she suspected it was all Isobel's idea. As the other woman had climbed into the cockpit she had looked quite competent and dashing in her multi-pocketed khaki flight togs, leather boots and mirrored sunglasses.

The invitation to take an aerial tour of the region had been issued over a lunch of cold poached salmon and chilled asparagus with hollandaise. Croft had accepted with enthusiasm. Mercy had winced at the thought of skimming the peaks in a sardine can sized helicopter and had regretfully declined. So now she stood all alone with no one but herself to blame.

"There you are, my dear." Erasmus Gladstone's voice

came from the doorway behind Mercy. "Don't worry about having to miss out on the sightseeing. We all have our little phobias. Isobel is an excellent pilot, but to tell you the truth I'm not all that keen on flying, myself. I use the copter only when necessary. Sometimes in the dead of winter it's the only practical transportation."

Mercy turned away from the window, summoning up a polite smile for her host. "I'm sure the scenery would be magnificent from the air, but, as you say, we all have our little phobias."

Gladstone smiled with great charm. His unusual blue eyes seemed to be alight with the force of that charm. "As it happens, I was going to suggest we do some sightseeing of our own. The kind of touring that only people in our field of interest can truly appreciate. How would you like to go down to the vault, Mercy, and spend the afternoon wallowing amid my treasures? I must admit, there's nothing I like more than showing them off to someone who can appreciate them."

Mercy's mood lifted at once. "I'd love it."

"Good." Gladstone glanced at his watch. "We should have a couple of hours to ourselves. Dallas and Lance seem to have everything in order for this evening's affair and the guests aren't due to start arriving until after four o'clock. Let's escape to our own version of paradise on earth, Mercy."

It was a pity, Mercy decided resentfully, that Croft hadn't trusted her with a detailed account of the kind of information he sought in the vault. Not that she had encouraged him to do so, Mercy admitted to herself. She had resisted his notions of Gladstone as a crook right from the start. Still, this would be the perfect opportunity to do some investigative work for him. But Croft had not told her what to look for. He'd only said he wanted to see if the contents of Gladstone's collection fit with what he knew of Egan Graves' tastes in rare books. It was typical of Croft to want to limit her involvement as much as possible. He was so damned aloof and independent.

Nevertheless, Mercy decided to make a mental note of as many titles as possible. Perhaps she could provide Croft with a shortcut in his detective work.

Forty minutes later Mercy was carefully turning the pages of a fine copy of Fuller's *The Worthies of England*, printed in 1662, when she began to notice the growing warmth inside the vault. It had seemed almost chilly when she and Gladstone had entered earlier. Perhaps having the door open had upset the interior air conditioning system.

She frowned down at the title page of Fuller's laboriously compiled national biography, studying the roman numeral date and the accompanying illustration of the author. Thomas Fuller, DD, appeared to have been a robust, serious man. He stared out of his portrait with a gaze that told the reader he expected proper attention to be paid to the biographies he had written.

"Now over here, if I can just find it," Gladstone was saying half to himself, "I have a first rate copy of White's *Natural History of Selborne*. Beautiful binding. Where did I . . . Oh, yes, here it is." He pulled the volume down from the shelf and started to hand it to Mercy. He frowned in concern. "Anything wrong, my dear?"

"No, not at all. I was just thinking it was turning a little warm in here."

"I'm afraid that happens when the door stands open for a while. Throws off the air conditioning a bit. It all returns to the proper temperature when we close the door. Allow me."

Before Mercy could protest, Erasmus reached out and swung the heavy vault door shut. Instantly the small room seemed even smaller, more the size of a large coffin. Mercy noticed the locking mechanism on the inside of the door for the first time and wondered why anyone would have a lock on the inside of the vault as well as on the outside.

"Uh, maybe it would be better to leave the door open," Mercy said weakly.

"Nonsense. We'll get the temperature back to normal in here and you'll be more comfortable." Gladstone moved back to the shelves. "I want you to take a look at this. A particularly fine collection of some of William Morris' private press books. I'm especially proud of his Chaucer. Exquisite, isn't it? When you've finished examining it, I really must show you my prizes in the field of medicine."

His words were almost melodic, Mercy thought bemusedly. Gladstone had a wonderful speaking voice. In the confines of the vault it seemed to be even more beautifully modulated. It promised wisdom and understanding and sensitivity. She listened to him as he continued to discuss his collection, beginning to find more pleasure in the actual sound of his voice than she did in the content. She became less aware of the confining feeling of the closed vault.

"I'm afraid my passion for books almost consumes me at times. Isobel occasionally complains during the long winter months that I spend more time in my library than I do with her." Gladstone reached for another volume. "But I expect you understand how it is, don't you, Mercy?"

"Well, I certainly spend a great deal of time in my bookshop," she agreed, not certain she would ever develop Gladstone's level of enthusiasm for collecting old books. She found the prospect of dealing in them fascinating, but she didn't think she was likely to become quite this impassioned about it. After all, there were other things in life. "Will your vault be open tonight for your guests?"

Gladstone shook his head firmly. "No, I'm afraid I draw the line at putting my books on display. Dallas and Lance can keep an eye on the paintings and sculpture, but books

tend to be too small and too easily removed. There will be
nearly fifty people in the house tonight and I wouldn't want
to put too much temptation in anyone's path. Some of these
artists are living on a shoestring," Gladstone added with a
knowing chuckle. "And while they may be grateful to me for
past favors, it might occur to one of them that selling just
one of these books would keep them in paint and assorted
recreational drugs for a couple of years."

He continued talking about his hobby and Mercy tried to
absorb the wealth of information that was flowing her way,
but for some reason it was becoming harder and harder to
concentrate. Every time Gladstone looked at her she was
very aware of his eyes. She was beginning to realize they
reminded her of another blue she had seen recently, an odd,
glowing blue that she couldn't quite place.

". . . I was overjoyed when this fine example of some of
Rudolph Ackermann's aquatint work turned up at an English
auction house two years ago." Gladstone breathed the words
the way a lover would say that he had had the finest climax
of his life. "So many great English artists did their appren-
ticeship as aquatint artists for Ackermann's books."

The word aquatint jarred her, distracting Mercy slightly
from the compelling sound of Gladstone's voice. The word
made her think of water. Of blue swimming pools, to be
exact. She gazed down at the pictures in the book Gladstone
had just handed her. "They're beautiful."

"Very. Are you sure you're not too warm, Mercy? We
could leave the vault and have some iced tea if you like."

"Oh, no, I don't want to miss a minute." She smiled
faintly. "This must be a pleasant, cozy place to spend a cold
winter's evening. Do you worry about losing power during
the winter? I noticed you don't have any fireplaces."

"None at all." For the first time Gladstone's voice lost a
measure of its melodic luster. "I noted earlier that we all

have our little phobias. I don't like fireplaces or, indeed, any source of naked flames."

"I can imagine it would be a risk to your collections," Mercy said quickly, realizing she'd definitely struck a sore point.

"Yes. A grave risk. A man in my position must take many precautions. No, I am very careful with fire, Mercy. I respect it. It's very clean, very certain, very sure."

Mercy glanced toward the solid door and wished it were open. The room didn't seem to be getting any cooler. "Do you ever worry about getting trapped in here?"

Gladstone chuckled, his voice shifting back into the charming, beautifully modulated, hypnotic tones. "Believe me, you are in no danger. This vault would be a trap for others, but not for me. There are many kinds of escape, Mercy, intellectual, emotional and physical. This vault contains all three for me. Now, let me show you a few of my other beauties. Why don't you sit down on that little stool over there? Some of these books are quite heavy. I'll just set them in your lap."

Mercy sat down obediently and struggled to listen to every word. She might never get another chance like this. She made a valiant effort to take in everything Gladstone was saying, but she simply couldn't concentrate.

The sound of Gladstone's voice and the drowsy warmth seemed to envelope her. She found herself seeking eye-to-eye contact, drawn by the vivid blueness of his gaze. She was certain she had never seen anyone else with eyes quite that color. Perhaps he wore contacts.

Still, that particular blue shade was so familiar.

She closed her eyes, trying to remember where she had seen that shade. Dimly she heard Gladstone's voice. He was murmuring on and on. She thought he asked her a question but she couldn't find the energy to open her eyes and answer it.

Very rude. Incredible that she could even think of dozing off while in the midst of this splendid collection. Whatever would her host think of her?

Blue eyes. Such strange blue eyes. Somewhere she had seen that shade, though. It was a glow, an eerie color, not a normal sky blue.

He was asking her something. She couldn't quite understand the question.

". . . Falconer, my dear?"

Croft's name jolted her. "I beg your pardon?" Mercy whispered. *Falconer*. Gladstone was asking her something about Croft. That didn't make sense. He should ask Croft if he wanted to know anything about him. Lots of luck, she thought. Gladstone wouldn't get any answers from Croft unless Croft wanted to provide them. And it was equally useless for Gladstone to be asking her about Croft. It would be a kind of betrayal to talk about the man she loved to Gladstone. Never in a million years could she betray Croft.

". . . so curious about him, Mercy. Have you known him long?"

Mercy frowned, bewildered. No, she hadn't known him long, although she wouldn't admit it aloud. She ignored the question and thought about Croft, focusing on him as if his name were a meditation mantra. She wasn't sure why it was suddenly so important to concentrate on her lover, but she obeyed the instinct without question.

An image of Falconer filled her mind, blocking out all of Gladstone's questions and neutralizing the compelling quality of her host's perfect voice. Right now Croft was flying through the blue skies of Colorado with Isobel Ascanius, Mercy remembered. At this very moment Isobel was probably making plans to initiate him into the legendary mile-high club. Disgusting. Impossible, too. They were already well over a mile high before they even got off the ground. No need to make love in a helicopter to join the stupid club. Maybe there was a two-mile high club. . . .

". . . seems like an interesting man. . . ."

"I. . . ." What color were Gladstone's eyes, anyway? Mercy kept her mind primarily focused on Croft, but a part of her attention took up the question of eye color and mulled it over.

An eerie blue light.

Water that glowed from the lights beneath the surface.

The swimming pool in the tropical garden.

Mercy's eyes snapped open. The room still seemed too warm, but she was no longer feeling drowsy. In fact, she was feeling quite amused to discover she had found the answer to her question about eye color. Erasmus Gladstone's eyes were the same color as the swimming pool in the next room. She would have to tell Croft.

Mercy smiled. Croft's image was still planted firmly in her head, but she no longer needed it for some reason. It had been a shield and a defense for a while, although she could not say exactly what she had been shielding and defending herself from. But now she was safe again.

"Good grief, I had no idea I was getting so sleepy. Please forgive me, Erasmus. This is terribly embarrassing. I think I need some fresh air and that glass of iced tea, after all."

"By all means," Gladstone said. There was a peculiar note of regret or perhaps irritation in his voice. "I'll have Dallas fix us both a glass. I could use some myself. We can spend more time in the vault tomorrow before you and Croft leave. We have yet to decide which of these books you will be taking in partial payment for *Valley*."

"That would be wonderful." Mercy hurried out of the vault, almost overcome by a sense of relief. She felt as if she were escaping from a steel trap into which she had accidentally wandered.

No, not accidentally, she reminded herself with a feeling

of deep unease. She had been drawn there by Erasmus Gladstone, held there by a closed door and the hypnotic sound of Gladstone's voice. If she had not been able to focus somehow on an image of Croft and her own inner knowledge that she must not under any circumstances betray him, she wasn't sure what she might have said or what might have happened.

As it was, she had been so busy trying to keep her senses tuned into reality that she hadn't made much of a mental list of the contents of the vault. So much for impressing Croft with her investigative skills. Quickly she ran through the few titles she could recall.

Then Mercy shook off the unpleasant sensation that still hovered around her consciousness. It was amazing how one's imagination could run wild under certain conditions.

But it was even more amazing how one could become mesmerized by strange blue eyes and a charismatic voice.

She hoped Isobel wouldn't keep Croft up in the air for much longer. Mercy decided that if she was going to let herself be mesmerized, she would rather become the willing quarry of Croft's dark sensuality than the unwary victim of a room that was too warm, eyes the wrong shade of blue, and a voice that was too compelling.

Croft thought he had handled Isobel's pass rather well. Mercy would have been proud of him. Maybe. Actually, it was a little tough to decide just how Mercy would feel about the situation.

Of course, the process of dealing with Isobel's sensual invitation had been made easier by the fact that the woman hadn't exactly thrown herself at him. Nothing embarrassingly obvious or awkward from Isobel Ascanius. Nothing overly forthright and honest. There was no sign of genuine emotional need. That would have been far too unsophisticated.

In short, it was nothing like the kind of pass Mercy might have delivered in similar circumstances, assuming Mercy could have worked up the nerve for such a blatant sexual assault in the first place.

Croft smiled to himself at the thought of Mercy trying to actively seduce a man. She would be very genuine and quite passionate about it, probably even reckless. The man in question would find himself in no doubt about the nature of the invitation.

He would also know that before Mercy could bring herself to do such a thing she would have to be totally and irrevocably in love. That would make the business of accepting her invitation all the sweeter, Croft thought. Such a pass from Mercy would probably be impossible to refuse. The lure of her complete surrender would be far too tempting.

But the kind of invitation Isobel had issued was another matter. Very polished, very sophisticated, very smooth. And very easy to ignore without embarrassing either party. On an intellectual level Croft had to admire it. She was one hell of a pilot and it took considerable skill to fly these mountains and try to seduce a man at the same time. On an emotional level he felt nothing. If it had been Mercy sitting next to him right now he would be rock hard already.

"Erasmus is a fascinating man, very wealthy, very brilliant. But I'm afraid he views me as just another item in his collection." Isobel pitched her voice over the roar of the rotor blades.

She was giving him one more chance, Croft decided, just in case the first pass had been too subtle. "I gather his main interest is his art and his books."

Isobel's glance was unreadable because of her mirrored glasses. "I admire him tremendously. But he has certain physical problems. Most unfortunate."

"Physical problems?"

"Certain male problems. I'm sure you understand," Isobel

said smoothly. "He has suffered such problems for some time. There was an accident, you see. He never quite recovered. It makes life difficult at times for me."

"I think I get the picture." Croft leaned forward to study the terrain below the copter. He wondered if Gladstone really was impotent as Isobel was implying and whether the "accident" which had caused the problem was related to a fire. "This country is absolutely amazing, isn't it?"

"Fantastic," Isobel murmured. "The beauty of this machine is that I can set it down almost anywhere. There is a perfect meadow over there." She glanced at him inquiringly, silently asking if he would like her to set down the copter.

"If we had time, I'd take Mercy there," Croft said, as if he hadn't understood exactly what she was offering. "But it looks like we won't be able to make the trip. We'll be leaving tomorrow."

"I understand," Isobel said, her voice smoothly masking her twinge of regret.

Croft rather thought she did. It was always nice to talk to someone who appreciated subtlety. "You're an excellent pilot, Isobel."

"Thank you."

"Does Gladstone also fly?"

"He had me give him some basic lessons a few months ago, but he's not an expert yet. He just wanted to know enough to take the controls in an emergency. It was a wise idea."

As Isobel turned the little helicopter back toward Gladstone's estate, Croft began worrying about Mercy's ability to interpret certain forms of subtlety. He hadn't liked the idea of leaving her behind, but he had wanted the aerial view Isobel was offering. It paid to know the terrain. Croft had also wanted a chance to discover more about Isobel Ascanius' interesting assortment of talents.

He was satisfied with the first goal. He now had a good internal picture of the landscape surrounding Gladstone's mountain fortress.

As for the second goal, Croft wasn't so certain. But there was no doubt that Isobel was a very formidable female.

Chapter
TWELVE

Mercy didn't bother to offer a protest early that evening when Croft suggested they go upstairs to dress for the lavish buffet dinner. Most of the guests had arrived in a bus that had been chartered for the occasion. They were an exotic throng that appeared to favor avant garde clothing, jagged hairstyles and vivid makeup.

Several people had descended immediately to the pool area and the tropical garden was swarming with semi-naked and a few fully nude Adams and Eves. The laughter from the pool could be heard throughout the house.

Dallas and Lance had taken turns ferrying the new arrivals from the first gate where the huge bus had been forced to halt. Now both of Gladstone's good looking house boys were busy mixing drinks and putting the finishing touches on the buffet.

"I can't get over how useful Dallas and Lance are around the place," Mercy observed as Croft tugged her into their suite. "Good help is so hard to find. I must ask Erasmus where he picked up those two. I'm not sure Isobel is so useful, but then nobody's perfect. Where are we going?"

"To take a shower."

"Work up a sweat during your aerial tour?" Mercy asked far too sweetly.

"Do I detect a slight waspish note?" He pulled her into the bathroom, shut the door and turned on the shower.

"Don't blame me, I've had a hard afternoon," Mercy said.

He leaned against the sink counter and folded his arms. "Tell me about your afternoon."

"Well, it probably wasn't as exciting as yours, but it had its moments. I almost went to sleep in the vault."

"Gladstone gave you another tour?"

"Uh huh. And in the process I picked up the following information which is probably totally irrelevant and utterly useless. Gladstone doesn't have any fireplaces in this house because he's afraid of open flames. He's also rather curious about you."

Croft's gaze sharpened. "About me?"

"I don't think you should read too much into this, Croft, but there was a time there in the vault when I felt so sleepy I almost dozed off. But Erasmus just kept talking. He has a very unusual voice, have you noticed? And I kept listening. I could hear him asking me questions about you. It was a weird feeling. Made me wonder what it would be like to be hypnotized."

Croft was quietly alert. "What did you tell him?"

"Nothing. I knew you'd throttle me if I told him a single thing about you. That alone was enough to make me careful."

Croft smiled with cool satisfaction. "I doubt if you could betray me if you tried."

"I don't know about that, but I found myself concentrating on his eyes, instead. I've decided they're the same color as the swimming pool when the lights are on under the water. Then I told him I wanted a glass of iced tea and he. being the gracious host he is, got it for me right quick. End of story. Frankly, I don't think it means much, but I knew you'd find all sorts of ominous clues in it. You have such a wonderfully melodramatic bent to your character. I was going to impress you by making a complete mental list of the most important titles in his collection, but that sleepy feeling got in my way. I can, however, give you some idea of at least part of his book collecting tastes." She quickly ran through the titles and authors she had had a chance to study.

"Interesting," Croft commented when she had finished. "Definitely a different emphasis, although the materials are just as rare. Sounds like a much more generalized collection than Graves'."

"You still think Gladstone is Graves, don't you?"

"My gut feeling is that they're one and the same. It all comes back to *Valley*, though. I want another look in that vault tonight."

"Why?" Mercy demanded.

"It intrigues me. It's the most secured place in this house. Far more secure than it needs to be. The Picasso and the Mondrian aren't given any special protection and they're individually every bit as valuable as the books. But even a relatively unimportant book like *Valley* goes in the vault."

"I think you're putting too much emphasis on the importance of that vault," Mercy said uneasily.

"I'm only putting a lot of emphasis on it because it's obvious Gladstone does. That business of being able to lock it from the inside interests me. It makes the vault a fortress within a fortress. A final retreat."

"Or a prison." Mercy shivered, remembering her feelings of claustrophobia.

"Yes," Croft agreed thoughtfully. "A fortress or a prison. But if Gladstone is really Graves, he will have made certain that he always has a way out. This time around he will be more cautious than ever."

"Assuming this is Graves' second time around. Now tell me every single detail about your helicopter jaunt. Did Isobel make a pass?"

Croft tilted his head to one side. "How did you know?"

"Instinct. Thank goodness we're leaving tomorrow. The next thing you know, she'd be wanting to take you on a wildflower crushing expedition. What did she tell you?"

"About what?"

"About Gladstone. Come on, Croft, I know you didn't waste that whole trip playing slap and tickle with Isobel. Learn anything interesting?"

"Not unless you consider the fact that Gladstone's apparently been impotent for the past three years interesting."

"Not particularly. Did you believe her?"

Croft shrugged. "Why not?"

"Why not? I'll tell you why not. You may take my word for it. Isobel Ascanius is not the kind of woman who would stick devotedly by a man she no longer found useful in bed." Mercy tapped one nail on the marble counter top and frowned at her image in the mirror. "She's a smart woman and she's a beautiful woman. She could find another sugar daddy if she wasn't getting what she wanted from Gladstone."

"Maybe she is getting what she wants from Gladstone. And maybe what she wants isn't sex," Croft suggested softly.

"What more could she want besides sex and money?"

"You really don't like the woman, do you?"

"Nope."

Croft smiled faintly. "I'll tell you what else she might be getting from Gladstone. Respect and power."

That brought Mercy's head up sharply. "Respect for what?"

"For such things as her skills as a pilot. I told her she was a good pilot this afternoon and you'd have thought I'd told her she was the most beautiful woman in the world."

"And power? What kind of power?"

"I'm not sure yet, but I'll tell you one thing. She's impor-tant around here, Mercy. She's not just a decorator item Don't forget she was the one who found us that night in the pool. It wasn't Gladstone who responded to the alarm you tripped. It was Isobel."

"And Dallas."

"True, but I think we can assume Dallas and Lance are at the bottom of the hierarchy around here."

Mercy considered that. "Okay, but I don't see where that takes us. So what if Isobel is something more than Glad-stone's mistress? What's that prove?"

"Nothing. It's just an interesting piece of the pattern." Croft moved away from the edge of the counter, rubbing his jaw. "I guess I'd better shave, huh?"

Mercy couldn't resist. "Did Isobel complain about a five o'clock shadow?"

"No." Croft began unbuttoning his shirt.

"Croft, tell me what happened after Isobel made her pass."

"Nothing." He removed his shirt and reached for his shaving kit on the counter.

"Absolutely nothing?"

"Absolutely nothing."

"Good," said Mercy, satisfied.

He caught her eyes in the mirror and arched his brows "You believe me?"

"Sure. In some ways, Croft, you're completely trust-worthy."

"But in other ways?"

"In other ways you're as hard to pin down as a ghost. In

fact, there are times when you bear a distinct resemblance to one."

"A ghost?"

"Yup. The only thing that makes me think you're not is that there are parts of you that are amazingly hard and substantial." Deliberately she let her eyes skim the territory beneath his belt buckle. Mercy tried to keep the assessing look cool, arrogant and casual, but she could feel the heat rising in her cheeks even as she made a point of heading for the door. She really wasn't very good at this sort of sexual provocation. It was the thought of Isobel making a pass at Croft that had driven her to such boldness. She was already regretting whatever imp had gotten hold of her tongue.

Croft's hand snaked out, closing around the nape of Mercy's neck without any warning. He pulled her back against him and kissed her with deep thoroughness. His tongue slid between her teeth and his fingers moved enticingly under her hair. Mercy heard her own soft moan and knew that Croft had heard it also. When he released her she was breathless. His eyes were brilliant as he looked down at her.

"I'm not a ghost, Mercy. When this is all over I'll take great pleasure in letting you prove to yourself just how solid and substantial I can get."

Mercy fled from the bathroom. She ought to ask Isobel for pointers, she decided.

By ten o'clock that evening Gladstone's party was in full swing. Mercy was torn between fascination and a distinctly uneasy sensation. She had never seen anything quite like this crowd, even though she had been raised in California. As Croft had once observed, she had apparently led a sheltered life.

For some odd reason the noise level bothered her most. A sophisticated music system was piping progressive jazz and rock to all three levels of the house, but that wasn't the main problem as far as Mercy was concerned. The increasingly high pitch of the laughter and the rising decibel level of the conversations were what was really beginning to bother her. She didn't see how anyone was managing to communicate at all in the living room or anywhere else on the first floor.

She did overhear several shouted arguments about the merits of some of the artwork that filled the house, but Mercy decided that they couldn't really be classified as conversations. Everybody involved appeared to be interested only in what he or she personally had to say. Other people's input was obviously a distraction and an annoyance.

It was a strange self-centered group of people, not quite real in their wild, arresting clothing and their obviously intense need to focus interest on themselves.

The wine and liquor were flowing freely, but Mercy suspected that wasn't all that was contributing to the general gaiety. Here and there she caught whiffs of the acrid scent of marijuana along with some less identifiable aromas. She had seen more than one person exit the room discreetly and return a few minutes later looking unnaturally euphoric.

Croft might think her naive, Mercy decided, but she wasn't stupid. And she *had* been raised on the West Coast.

"Why are you standing in a corner looking so serious? This is supposed to be a party. Act happy, Mercy."

Croft's voice came from her left, sounding strangely cheerful. Too cheerful, considering the situation.

"There you are." She realized she was feeling both relief and acute anxiety. "I was wondering where you'd gone. I couldn't see you in the crowd and I was afraid—" She broke off uneasily, glancing around. But no one seemed to be paying any attention, and any listening devices that might be planted in the living room would already be awash with static. She glared at Croft. "Why are you smiling like that? You almost never smile. Are you all right?"

"You know, you're kind of cute when you snap at me." He took another sip of the drink in his hand. "I am fine. Peachy keen, in fact. Rarely have I felt better."

"I'm glad to hear it because you're looking a little frayed around the edges."

"Camouflage," he said in a conspiratorial whisper. "Got to appear to be part of the crowd."

"Right. Well, you're doing a good job of it."

"You're not. You're standing around looking morbid. What are you drinking?" He peered at the glass in her hand.

"Water."

"Ah ha. That explains it."

"Explains what?"

His brows came together and he gave his head a small shake, as if to clear it. His eyes darkened briefly. "Never mind." He glanced around at the loud, colorful throng. "Time for all good ghosts to be about their business, hmm? Time to practice disappearing and materializing and assorted skills."

Mercy leaned toward him. She was intensely worried now, not just nervous but downright scared. "Croft, are you sure you want to do this? Isn't there some other way of answering your questions about Gladstone? If you get caught—"

"I won't get caught."

"That's very reassuring," she snapped, annoyed with his blithe lack of concern. It struck her as both unnatural and un-Croftlike. "But what happens if you do?"

"You pretend to be as shocked as everyone else."

"What are you talking about?"

He patted her head as if she were an eager puppy and said with exaggerated patience, "If I get caught you just pretend to know nothing about what I was doing in the vault. You tell everyone you're shocked and stunned. Appalled, even. I must have been using you to get access to Gladstone's valuable collection. You're an innocent dupe."

"I've already played that role once too often around you. Croft, listen to me, I think you should reconsider your plan tonight. There are bound to be a bunch of people downstairs in the gardens and the pool. Any one of them might notice you sneaking into the vault room."

"Nope." He smiled genially at a striking young thing who was wearing hair dyed to match her green, skintight dress. The woman smiled back and floated on past as she inhaled deeply on a long cigarette.

"What do you mean, nope?" Mercy wanted to slap him in order to get his full attention. There was a distracted quality about him that was alarming.

"No one downstairs in the pool room now. I just went down and checked. Place is empty."

"I didn't see you leave."

He winked wickedly. "Trust me. It's empty." He took another sip of the red wine he was holding. "Did you try the salmon canapes? They're great. I've had several."

Mercy shook her head. She hadn't been able to eat a thing or drink anything besides water since the perilous evening had started. There was something not quite right about Croft's mood. She had never seen him like this. Why was he chatting about salmon canapes at a time like this?

If she hadn't known him better she would have sworn he had had too much to drink. But that was impossible. Croft never drank to excess. He was as restrained about his drinking as he was about everything else. Something else must be going on. . . .

"Dallas and Lance probably cleaned out the pool room during the last hour," Mercy noted thoughtfully. "Gladstone's insurance might not have covered twenty or thirty artists getting drunk and falling face down in the swimming pool. On second thought, I don't see a man as wealthy as

Gladstone being overly concerned about his insurance policies. Where is Gladstone, anyway?"

"Over there by the window, talking to that guy with the beard."

Mercy glanced across the room and saw Gladstone involved in what appeared to be a serious conversation with an intense young man. Isobel stood politely beside the two men, listening with an expression of what Mercy assumed was artistic interest.

"That's Micah Morgan. I met him earlier," Mercy told Croft. "Gladstone says he's going to be the hottest thing on the art market in three or four years. Needless to say, Gladstone is collecting him now. Those pictures in the sitting room are Morgan's."

"Why don't you join them?"

Mercy stirred the ice in her glass. "More camouflage? You want me to distract Gladstone and Isobel while you go downstairs and play cat burglar?"

Croft beamed at her. "Will you do that for me, sweet Mercy? Dallas and Lance are so busy up here running the bar and the buffet that I don't think they're likely to wander downstairs unexpectedly."

"I don't think you need my help in this project," she retorted. "You seem to be able to appear and disappear without any assistance from me."

"It never hurts to have a little extra insurance."

"Oh, all right." Resentfully Mercy started to move toward the window where Gladstone and Isobel stood. But something made her turn back once more to confront Croft. "Are you sure you're up to this tonight? How much of that wine have you had?"

"Half a glass. Just enough to look sociable." He smiled again. "Stop worrying, honey. I'm in complete control."

"I wonder why that doesn't reassure me." Without waiting

for a response, she plunged into the crowd, heading toward Gladstone and Isobel.

Croft thought about the expression in Mercy's eyes as he made his way through the jungle of plants in the pool room. She didn't approve of what he was doing but she was going to help him. She was committed to him, he decided. That pleased him enormously. He liked having her feel committed. When this was all over, he intended to have a long talk with her about her sense of commitment. She was the kind of woman who would stick with a man through thick and thin. For richer, for poorer, in sickness and in health. . . .

Damn it to hell, he knew for certain now he wasn't feeling normal. Marriage rarely—if ever—crossed his mind.

Another wave of queasiness jarred him and he yanked his thoughts back from Mercy to his stomach. This was the third time during the past half hour that he had been aware of a wave of nausea. Nothing bad yet, but potentially dangerous. Nausea could stop a man as effectively as a fist in the face.

Croft couldn't remember the last time he was sick to his stomach. What the hell was wrong with him? Maybe it was something he had eaten from the buffet table. But all he had had was a couple of slices of the smoked salmon and some crackers. There was the half glass of wine, but that was hardly enough to have this kind of effect. Besides, it had been an excellent Bordeaux, not some rotgut vinegar.

Rotgut vinegar. That was a joke. As if Gladstone would serve anything but the best wine. Croft realized he was grinning. It was damned amusing when he thought about it. Gladstone serving cheap wine. What a scandal. Croft almost laughed aloud.

A small sense of shock went through him. The last thing he wanted to do right now was laugh out loud. The whole idea was to make absolutely no noise at all. He was good at that kind of thing. He could tiptoe through a swamp full of alligators and never wake one of the beasts.

What was it Mercy called him? A ghost. That was it. He'd go in like a ghost. Get in, get a close look at the inside of the vault and get out. If he didn't find anything he would slip upstairs to the study. Somewhere there had to be something in the house that would give him the answers to his questions. His gut instincts told him that Gladstone was Egan Graves. There were too many similarities in style. This business about being the chief patron for an isolated artist colony, for example. Too much like running a cult. And that voice. Ray Chandler had once told Croft that his daughter still talked about the compelling quality of her ex-guru's voice. Then there was Gladstone's obvious preoccupation with security. The Rocky Mountain estate reminded Croft in some ways of Graves' Caribbean setting. Except for the dogs. They were a new addition.

There were a myriad other small hints and clues. Croft was sure Gladstone was a reincarnation of Egan Graves. All he had to do was prove it. As soon as he had, he would get Mercy away before doing anything more. Above all he had to take care of Mercy.

The nausea faded again, leaving behind a strangely pleasant sensation. Croft tried to analyze the feeling. This light-headedness wasn't quite normal. True, it had been three years since the last time he had had to play ghost, but he would never forget the feeling of all his senses working together in a faultless rhythm. He knew what the adrenaline rush felt like, remembered the exquisite, almost painful tension, recalled the exhilarating feeling of walking along the sharp edge of an abyss.

He remembered all those feelings very well, just as he remembered his own deep fascination with them.

But he was only getting bits and pieces of those sensations tonight. Everything seemed to be overlaid by this strange sense of easygoing, light-headed cheerfulness. And the cheerfulness was only occasionally interrupted by the sick feeling in the pit of his stomach.

Croft drew in a deep breath, trying to suppress the abnormal giddiness. He should be feeling a lot of things, but not giddiness. Something was wrong. Under ideal circumstances he would have called off tonight's mission and postponed it until he had his body more completely under control.

It was dangerous being out of control, he reminded himself wisely. He never allowed himself to lose that fundamental sensation of being completely in command of himself. Never.

Except when he made love to Mercy.

Every time he took her in his arms he was sure he would be able to handle himself and her. But it always ended in a storm of wild, uninhibited abandonment. He wished he understood what happened when he was around Mercy. It worried him that he couldn't explain his passions or his sense of protectiveness or the strange bond that seemed to link him to her.

Well, she wasn't with him now. He had no excuse for feeling unsteady and unnaturally cheerful. Something was wrong, but it was too late to turn back. He had to get the answers that night. There wasn't going to be another opportunity. Even if he could have persuaded Mercy to stay another day or two he wouldn't have risked it. She was safe enough for the moment, but if Gladstone and Isobel were starting to ask questions, it was time to get Mercy out of these mountains.

The last thing he wanted to do was put Mercy in real jeopardy. Finishing what happened three years before was important, but not more important than protecting Mercy. Mercy could get into trouble so easily.

Croft smiled fondly as he thought about her penchant for

recklessness. She definitely needed him to keep an eye on her.

That thought led immediately into another. A mental picture of Mercy lying nude on a field of wildflowers formed in his mind. She was so damn sexy, so warm and soft and inviting and she didn't even realize it.

Croft shook his head again, trying to force the stray, disrupting images from his head. What the hell was the matter with him? He was getting hard, for crying out loud. This was all wrong. Normally he never had any trouble clearing his mind for this kind of work. He had to be able to focus everything on the task at hand. It was the only way to assure the degree of mind-body coordination needed. He couldn't afford to distract himself with images of making love to Mercy.

Christ. He was going to screw this up if he didn't get hold of his erratic thoughts. With a sudden grimness Croft tried to concentrate on regaining his customary physical, emotional and mental control. He had spent years training himself to be in control regardless of what was happening around or inside him.

Another wave of nausea interrupted the process. It only lasted for a few seconds this time, however. At least he seemed to be getting some form of control over his stomach. Must have been the salmon. Hell of a time to get food poisoning.

Funny, he understood why his stomach might be feeling queasy if he had gotten some bad fish, but he had never heard of a food poisoning victim enjoying this pleasant euphoria. This was almost like being drunk.

But he never got drunk. *Never.* He had never allowed himself to become what his father had become, not even for a few hours. He didn't dare. He knew his limits and respected them strictly. And it had only been half a glass of wine from a bottle Dallas had used to pour drinks for several other guests.

Croft glanced around, vaguely aware that the overhead lights had been turned off before he had entered the garden room. The swimming pool still glowed faintly. He caught glimpses of it as he moved along the path toward the vault room. The garden itself had a weird green shadowy ambience because of the lamps that had been left on under the leaves. All in all, a nicely exotic effect. Should appeal to the artsy crowd upstairs. Too bad there was no one there besides himself to enjoy it.

It might be fun to make love to Mercy in the middle of a tropical forest.

Croft came through the far side of the garden and leaned heavily against the glass doors that opened onto the vault room. He could see the heavy metal door sealed shut in the wall. When he pushed against the glass doors he was amazed by how heavy they seemed. He hadn't noticed their weight the night before.

Once inside the room, he made straight for the sealed vault. He had to stop and think about the technique he had used the previous night to unlock it. He knew on some level of awareness that he shouldn't have had to pause while he tried to recollect the method. He had memorized it, after all. He had wanted nothing to slow him down now. Slowly he pulled the delicate little tools out of the seam of his shirt.

For an instant he stood, swaying slightly and staring down at the small lock picking implements. He was an old hand with these. The knowledge it took to use them was imbedded in his fingers after years of practice. So he shouldn't be standing here trying to recall exactly how to use them.

Impatiently he turned toward the vault door. There wasn't much time.

It took a few embarrassingly awkward attempts, but the sophisticated lock finally surrendered, just as it had the night before. Every lock was vulnerable in some way. A moment later, Croft started to ease the heavy door open.

He didn't just want another look inside the vault, he remembered vaguely. He also wanted one more look at *Valley*. That damn book was still the key. He had studied it a number of times but he knew he must be missing something. The door handle moved in his hand.

It was then that he knew there was someone else nearby.

There was nothing tangible on which to base the sudden knowledge but Croft didn't require hard evidence. He had stopped relying solely on his five senses years before. Surviving in his unique line of work had often meant listening to a sixth sense.

Another wave of nausea hit him at that moment. Christ. Just what he needed.

He staggered slightly as the sick feeling threatened to overwhelm him. It took a fierce act of will to fight down the queasy sensation. He had to control it.

The nausea faded. Croft took advantage of the returning euphoria to make his way to the door. He left the vault unlocked but closed behind him. He stepped out into the shadows of the garden, remembering his first thought when he had seen the pool room.

A good place to hunt or hide.

Gravel crunched under his booted foot. A false sense of well-being must be making him careless. Or had the crunching sound come from someone else? He ought to be able to tell the difference, damn it.

A heavy palm frond blocked his path. Croft put out a hand and shoved it aside with a sense of impatience. There was someone else in the garden, he was sure of it. Not a guest. A guest wouldn't have cared how much noise he or she made. Whoever it was was trying to hide.

Time to play hunter, Croft told himself, feeling suddenly

invincible. Mercy was always saying he reminded her of a ghost. Well, now was the time to play ghost.

Another crunch of leather on gravel. His own footstep or someone else's? Croft wiped the back of his hand across his forehead and discovered he was sweating.

Couldn't be nerves. He knew what fear tasted like and he wasn't tasting it tonight. Not yet at any rate.

Instinctively he headed toward the pool. There was more light in that direction. He would force the other hunter to reveal himself against the blue glow of the underwater lighting. He chose another path and started toward the center of the garden.

What a truly brilliant idea, he thought. Make the other guy reveal himself. Too bad Mercy wasn't here to appreciate his brilliance. Croft got the feeling that on occasion she didn't think too highly of his strategic planning capabilities. Little did she know. He was good at this kind of thing.

Damn good.

But not good enough that night.

Croft sensed the movement behind him but his body didn't react the way it had been trained to do. Everything went wrong.

He tried to turn and stumbled, slightly off balance. The movement hardly qualified as a stunning example of training and coordination, but it probably saved his life. The blow that had been meant to land on the back of his head caught him mostly on the shoulder.

Croft had a distant impression of someone hovering in the bushes, watching him. But he couldn't concentrate on his unseen opponent. Searing pain shot through his arm and up his neck. It was followed by a sense of rage that would have been earth shaking if he had been in any condition to give voice to it.

The only thing he could do was go with the flow. He let

the force of the blow send him over the edge of the pool and into the water.

Blind, dumb instinct kept him from moving so much as a muscle as he hit the surface. He floated face down in the water and concentrated on holding his breath. After all those years of breathing exercises, he ought to at least be able to hold his breath for a while. Croft knew his survival probably depended on his assailant assuming that he would quickly drown.

It was a logical assumption under the circumstances. Drunks who got struck on the head and wound up facedown in a swimming pool usually did drown.

Croft opened his eyes and stared down through the depths of the glowing water. Mercy was right. The color of the pool water bore an uncanny resemblance to Gladstone's eyes.

Mercy. Sweet Mercy, I need you.

Chapter
THIRTEEN

Much to Mercy's surprise, she found herself interested in the conversation with Micah Morgan, Gladstone and Isobel. Micah's enthusiasm was contagious, and if Gladstone's comments weren't always amazingly insightful or brilliant, one could always take pleasure in just listening to his marvelous speaking voice.

"The important thing about working in Santa Fe," Micah was explaining very seriously, "is the fact that there would still be a couple thousand miles between me and New York. You wouldn't have to worry about me being influenced by the East Coast art establishment. You were absolutely right two years ago when you told me I needed to get out of New York. But I'm changing again. I really think it's time I left the colony. I'm beginning to feel stifled there."

"Moving to Santa Fe isn't the answer for you, Micah. Too much West Coast influence there now," Gladstone told him soothingly. "The hard edges would bleed through into your work. You need time to solidify your unique style before you try to take it to either L.A., New York or Santa Fe. Trust me. You need the control and isolation of the colony for a while longer. It's done wonders for you."

Micah's head bobbed up and down like a yoyo on a string. "I know, Erasmus. It has done a great deal for me. I'll admit you're usually right, but—"

Isobel smiled benignly. "Erasmus is always right. You must trust him when it comes to this kind of thing."

Micah sighed. "Don't worry, I do. So do most of the people in this room." He smiled at Mercy. "All of us here tonight have reason to be grateful to Erasmus. Without his help and financial encouragement, most of us would be trying to make a living doing advertising layouts or department store windows. Are you going to be joining the colony?"

Mercy smiled self-deprecatingly. "I'm afraid I'm a business person, not an artist. But I've seen your work in the sitting room across the hall. It's wonderful. I love your nice, clean colors and shapes."

"Micah has an extraordinarily fine sense of color and shape," Erasmus interjected.

Micah looked thrilled. "Can I get you another drink?" he asked Mercy.

She looked down at her empty glass and decided not to mention that she had been drinking water. She started to respond as she handed her glass to Micah, but nearly tripped over the polite words as an image of water flickered through her mind.

Blue, glowing water. Water the color of Erasmus Gladstone's eyes. Unable to help herself, Mercy glanced quickly at Gladstone. He was saying something to Isobel that was making the other woman smile politely. Then they both turned away to talk to a woman dressed in a glittering, iridescent leotard.

"Mercy?" Micah Morgan cocked a quizzical brow.

"A glass of . . . water sounds good."

"Just water? Nothing in it?"

"If you don't mind."

"Sure," Micah said amiably. "Be right back."

Mercy watched him disappear into the crowd. Then she glanced again at Gladstone and Isobel, who appeared to be deeply involved in their new conversation.

Glowing blue water rippled through her mind again. She wondered uneasily how Croft was doing down in the vault. Automatically, as she had every few minutes, she checked to see that Dallas and Lance were still in the room. Dallas was tending the bar and Lance was just coming in from the kitchen with another loaded tray of canapes. She had seen him go into the kitchen a few minutes earlier.

Damn it, this was ridiculous. There was nothing to worry about. She couldn't really bring herself to believe Erasmus Gladstone was the evil Egan Graves in disguise, and even if she did believe it, there was no denying Croft was more than capable of taking care of himself. He always seemed to know what he was doing.

The water image faded from her mind, but the sense of uneasiness did not. Mercy began wondering how long it took to thoroughly explore the interior of a man's private library vault. How long before someone noticed Croft had disappeared?

One thing about this crowd, it did provide good cover. There were a number of men dressed in black or other dark colors scattered around the room. Croft's absence wasn't immediately noticeable.

Nothing should be wrong, but something was.

After having awakened more than once now with this strange, uneasy feeling in the middle of the night, Mercy was not inclined to ignore it when it struck, even if it did so in the middle of a party. Being around Croft seemed to have caused her to develop a sixth sense of awareness.

She remembered his unusual cheeriness earlier. For the

first time she wondered if Croft really had had too much to drink before he undertook his trip downstairs. He had claimed he hadn't, but he'd had half a glass of wine in his hand and there was no telling how much he had had before she saw him last.

The idea of Croft drunk was ludicrous. But if she hadn't known him better, she would have sworn he had been dangerously close to overindulging just before he left for the basement.

Mercy waited no longer. A glance across the room showed that Micah had gotten sidetracked by a blonde in a pair of red long johns and three-inch high heels. Gladstone and Isobel were still occupied with their leotarded friend. Mercy slipped through the crowd toward the door. No one paid her any attention.

Outside in the hall she heard a few voices whispering and laughing from the elegant sitting room. Someone had turned off the lights and it was obvious the couples who had retreated to that room had not gone there to enjoy the starlit view of the Rockies.

Mercy waited a minute to make certain no one noticed her and then she headed for the staircase. The sounds of laughter and the smell of marijuana and tobacco faded rapidly as she descended into the lower level of the big house.

An eerie silence and the familiar combination of chlorine and growing plants hit her as she pushed open the glass doors and stepped out onto the platform. The glowing blue of the swimming pool drew her eye. The room was dark because the overhead lights were off, but not as shadowed as last night when all the lights except those in the pool had been dimmed. Tonight the green glow from the undergrowth lit the paths that led toward the water.

She was never really certain what made her start toward the pool. Theoretically, she told herself, she ought to check the vault room first. But the aura of the glowing blue water drew her. Lately she seemed to be haunted by that shade of blue. Mercy found herself moving quickly along the white gravel path.

She saw the dark shape floating in the pool within seconds after leaving the platform. Shock went through her. She got only a glimpse through the palm fronds and ferns of what looked like a black pant leg billowing languidly in the water, but it was enough. Someone was in the pool and whoever it was, he wasn't moving.

It was the color of the pant leg material that added the extra dimension of horror to the scene. Mercy broke into a run. It was true a few other men had worn dark clothes to the party, but she was willing to bet those guests were all still upstairs. The man in the pool was Croft.

He couldn't be dead. Not like this. Croft Falconer wasn't the kind of man who would end his life by getting ignominiously drunk and falling into a pool.

"Croft! Oh, my God, Croft, don't you dare drown like this. *Don't you dare.*" Mercy reached the edge of the pool, stumbled slightly as she kicked off her high-heeled sandals and then she dove into the water. Croft was floating as if he were unconscious or dead.

The skirt of her dress became a heavy, soggy weight almost instantly. But she was only a couple of feet away from Croft. Mercy stroked fiercely and caught hold of his arm.

Croft moved at her touch, rolling over in the water like a seal and smiling complacently.

"I knew you'd get here sooner or later," he said. "Never had to depend on anyone else before. Dangerous. But I knew I could depend on you. Strange, huh?"

Mercy released him as though she had been burned. "What is this?" she demanded through set teeth. "Some kind of game? Croft, you had me scared to death."

"Not you," he informed her as if he had given the matter some thought. "You're not the kind who gets scared to death. You might be terrified, but you'd keep moving, keep fighting back. It's your nature, you know. By the way, I can see your nipples through that wet material you're wearing. Very sexy."

"You idiotic bastard," she breathed, staring at his abnormally pleasant expression. "You *are* drunk."

"I never get drunk," Croft said and smiled wickedly. "But it might be interesting to see you when you're tipsy. Would you lose all your inhibitions and crawl all over me?"

"There's no point trying to talk to you now. You're too far gone." Mercy began tugging him toward the edge of the pool. He drifted happily along in the direction she was aiming him, neither helping nor hindering her efforts. "We've got to get out of here. For pete's sake, Croft, it's a miracle you didn't drown yourself."

"I can hold my breath a long time," he confided proudly.

"Is that so?" She got him to the steps and struggled to get him balanced on his feet in the water. "How long can you hold it?"

"A while."

"Oh, that's just terrific. How long have you been floating here in the pool practicing your breath holding skills?"

He swayed upright in the water, blinking water out of his eyes. "A while," he said again. "A long while." Then he leaned forward as if imparting a confidence. "I was just about to cheat and take a breath when you showed up."

"How very intelligent of you." She held her dripping skirts with one hand and yanked on his arm with the other. "Come on, Croft. Move, damn it."

"Don't swear at me. No need to swear. Unbecoming in a lady." His words were only slightly slurred as he staggered up the steps and reached out to steady himself on the rail. "Good thing I didn't have to take a breath. Would have tipped 'em off. They were watching, you know. Wanted to make sure. But now you're here they'll have to pretend everything's hunky dory."

"Croft, I haven't the faintest idea what you're talking about, and if you don't want me to swear at you, try behaving yourself."

"I am behaving. Perfect gentleman. If I weren't behaving, know what I'd be doing now?"

"I don't think I want to hear this," she muttered as she pulled and prodded him to the top step. Out of the water Croft was a lot harder to maneuver.

He was leering cheerfully at her. "If I weren't such a perfect gentleman I'd drag you off into the middle of this phony tropical garden, take off your clothes and make love to you until you couldn't scold me or swear at me or yell at me. By the time I was finished with you you wouldn't even be able to glare at me the way you're doing now. You'd just lie there under me, clinging to me, pleading with me, whispering my name until you went up in flames. I'm getting hot just thinking about it."

It was his eyes that seemed to be turning into flames. Mercy felt herself growing warm beneath the hungry, anticipatory expression in Croft's hazel eyes. She wasn't sure if her uncomfortable flush was a reaction to the softly voiced sexual threat or if it was merely the result of sheer outrage. "I can't believe you allowed yourself to get into this condition," she muttered, releasing him to look for her shoes. "I just can't believe it. It's disgusting."

He reached out to touch her breast, which was clearly outlined by the wet dress. "I didn't do it on purpose, you know."

She brushed his hand away. "That's not exactly reassuring."

He glanced around, apparently looking for something. "Where is it?"

"Where's what? A towel? Taking a swim was an impromptu decision on your part. You didn't bring a towel with you. Next time plan ahead." Water was dripping off her in long rivulets. "Wait a second. There's one on that lounger over there. One of the guests must have left it behind this afternoon." She picked it up and thrust it at him.

Croft's brows came together in a heavy line as he stared at the towel in his hand. He shook his head impatiently. "Not a towel. The book."

Mercy went still, her fingers pausing over the second shoe. She looked up at him. "Croft," she said as gently and clearly as possible, "did you get into the vault?"

He blinked owlishly down at her. "Sure. It's what I came down here to do, remember? I always finish what I start."

Mercy rose slowly to her feet, automatically wringing water out of her skirt. The water had been warm and the garden room was even warmer but she was suddenly experiencing a genuine chill. "Did you bring a book out of the vault?"

"Meant to." He frowned again. "Wanted to take another look at it."

"Was it *Valley*, Croft?" Mercy grasped his damp sleeve, trying to get him to focus his attention on her. "Did you take *Valley* out of the vault? Damn it, why am I trying to carry on a coherent conversation with you while you're in this condition?"

His mood shifted again. The frown disappeared and the cheerful, blatantly sexual invitation was back in his eyes. "You want to look at the pictures with me, Mercy? We could look at *Valley* together and see if you get hot."

"Women," she informed him sharply, "do not respond to visual sexual stimuli nearly as much as men do."

"Is that right?" He appeared fascinated. "You'd rather have the real thing, huh? That's okay by me."

"Croft, stop it. You've got to get hold of yourself."

"No need to do it that way. Very lonely that way. Now

I've got you to hold. Much better." He draped a heavy, wet arm around her shoulder. Some of his cheeriness faded again as he stumbled against her. It was obvious that the unfamiliar lack of coordination was puzzling to him, even in his present condition. "What's the matter with me?"

"You're drunk. Come on, O Great Ninja Master, time for you to go to bed."

He shook his head but didn't pull away when she wrapped an arm around his waist and started to guide him down the path. "Not ninja. That ninja stuff is for television."

"Yeah, well, that's about your speed tonight. If you get real lucky, you might be able to kick in a picture tube."

"The book," he said abruptly.

"The book is safe." She sensed the lightning shift of his mood. It was disturbing having him switch from a state of silly, stupid inebriation to one of clear concern about *Valley*.

"Safe? You got it?"

His head came around quickly and for just a few seconds Mercy thought she saw the spark of normal reasoning in his eyes. Then she decided it was more likely a trick of the poor light.

"I don't have the book. It's in the vault," she reminded him patiently.

"Get it."

"What?" Mercy came to a halt on the path. "Are you crazy? How can I get into the vault?"

Croft wiped water off his forehead with the towel. "I left it open."

"The vault?"

"Must have left it open. I was in there when I realized someone had followed me. Closed the door but didn't lock it when I went to see who was in the garden." He stopped and grimaced. "Shit. I think I'm going to throw up after all. Thought the sick feeling was gone."

"Your stomach is upset? Croft, pay attention to me."

He took a deep breath. "There. It's gone. Damned nausea."

Mercy was getting frustrated and scared. She caught hold of the lapels of Croft's wet shirt and tried to shake him. He blinked and looked down at her.

"Did you find someone out here in the garden?" she demanded softly.

"Didn't have to," Croft explained. "He found me. It was a man. Must have been Dallas or Lance. Embarrassing. He shouldn't have been able to get that close without me knowing it. Something's wrong with me, Mercy."

Mercy was suddenly the one feeling nauseous. "Did he throw you in the pool?"

Croft considered that. "I think he tried to knock me out and throw me in the pool. But I tricked him." He grinned in memory of his own brilliance. "I went into the pool all by myself."

"Oh, Lord." Mercy yanked on his arm, hurrying along the path once more. "We've got to get out of here."

Croft abruptly stopped cooperating. He didn't actively fight her grip, he simply came to a halt in the middle of the path. Mercy couldn't budge him.

"Not without the book," he said. "Got to get the book."

Mercy was feeling frantic. "If I get the damned book, will you come with me?"

He nodded happily. His sexy grin returned. "Sure. Always happy to come with you, Mercy. I like to come with you and in you. I like to make you come, too. I like to watch your face when it's about to happen. I like to feel you get all hot and tight and wet around my—"

"*Shut up.* We are in serious trouble here. If you don't stop talking about sex, I'm going to throw you back in that pool, do you hear me, Croft Falconer?"

"Geesh, what a grouch. Lucky for you I'm so good-natured, huh?"

She decided the only thing she could do was ignore most of what he was saying. The book seemed to be the one thing he was really concerned about. If she got it, he might be more amenable to following her orders.

Mercy came to a decision. It looked as if she was going to have to give a few orders to Croft tonight. He had finally succeeded in convincing her that something was very wrong at the Gladstone estate. The only sane thing to do was leave. It was very obvious he was incapable of organizing the retreat. That left her to manage things.

"Croft, listen to me. I'm going to get that copy of *Valley* for you if I can get into the vault. Then we're going upstairs. If anyone sees us, we will pretend you're so drunk you have to go to bed. Once upstairs we will pack our things and go down the back way to where the car is parked. Got that?"

He smiled and nodded his head in pleasant agreement. "Anything you say, sweet Mercy. I am yours to command."

"Remember that." She guided him off the path and into the depths of the garden. She drew him to a halt under a huge palm. "All right, Croft. Here's the first command. Sit here and don't move until I get back with the book. If anyone comes out on the platform, he won't be able to see you. Just sit perfectly still and don't move. Pretend you're meditating. Think you can do that?"

"No sweat." He sank down immediately into a neat, cross-legged position and looked up at her for approval. "Slick, huh?"

"Amazing," she muttered.

"I don't suppose you want to try making love in this position again?" he asked hopefully. "You know, the way we did in that meadow? You could sort of sit on my lap and wrap your legs around my waist. Then I could—"

Mercy began to feel desperate. "Hush! I'm going after that book now. Remember, don't move until I get back."

A flicker of more sober intelligence briefly appeared again in his eyes. "You're going to get the book?"

"Yes."

"Good. Hurry."

"Believe me," she said as she turned and started through the garden, "I will."

Maybe Croft was wrong. Maybe he hadn't left the vault unlocked. If she couldn't get inside to retrieve *Valley*, she would simply lie to him and tell him she had it hidden in the folds of her skirt. In the shadows of the garden he might not be able to tell, and in his present mood he might not be inclined to demand proof.

The room in which the vault was housed was dark. Mercy thought about turning on a light and decided that would be the height of stupidity. Summoning up a mental image of the approximate location of the heavy steel door, she made her way carefully across the room and groped along the wall.

Her memory turned out to be reasonably accurate. Her nails skidded across metal a few seconds later. She found the handle and didn't know whether to pray it would turn or hope it wouldn't give an inch.

It turned easily. Croft had, indeed, unlocked the door earlier and left it unlocked. An amazing accomplishment considering his obvious condition. Mercy took a deep breath and stepped inside the cool, metal room.

Now she had to have light. There was no way she could find the copy of *Valley* by memory or touch. But she couldn't risk having a sliver of light leak out into the main room. She would have to close the vault door behind her while she switched on the interior light and searched for the book. The thought of letting the massive door swing shut behind her was almost enough to make her forget the entire project.

Mercy remembered questioning Gladstone about being trapped in the vault. But he had assured her the vault was no trap for him. Just the opposite. Mercy set her back teeth and let the door swing silently shut. Then she reached out and turned on the light.

The sudden brilliance made her blink rapidly while her eyes adjusted. Then she went quickly to the section of the room where Gladstone shelved his small collection of curiosa. Burleigh's *Valley of Secret Jewels* was sitting right where it had been left. Mercy snatched it down off the shelf.

"You've caused me nothing but trouble, Rivington Burleigh. I wonder if you know that. This is what comes of writing erotica, I suppose. Why couldn't you have been a metaphysical poet or something?"

She held her breath again when she switched off the light and reached for the door. For a terrible instant the heavy door didn't budge when she pushed against it. She was terrified she had accidently tripped the interior locking mechanism. Mercy was nearly swamped with visions of being locked in the vault. She had never thought of herself as being claustrophobic, but in that moment when the vault door didn't seem to be moving, she knew she had a very strong fear of being trapped in a small, confining space.

Then her weight overcame the normal inertia of the solid door and it swung silently outward. Mercy hastened over the raised metal threshold and closed the door behind her. She hesitated and then decided to reset the lock. With any luck at all Gladstone might not guess that anyone had been inside. She reached out and pushed the small button on the door.

There was a nearly inaudible click as the lock took hold.

Mercy realized she was starting to shiver in her wet dress. Clutching *Valley,* she picked up her limp skirt once more and slipped out of the room and back into the garden. It would be a grim joke if Croft had decided to play games by hiding from her now.

But he was right where she had left him, sitting quietly in

his meditation pose. His head turned as she came toward him through the shadows.

"Hello, sweetheart," he said, his voice thick and dark as molasses.

"I've got *Valley.* Let's go." She reached down to catch hold of his wrist and draw him to his feet. She felt another abrupt shift in his mood. "Are you okay?"

"Feel sick again," he mumbled.

"Oh, Croft, not here or now. Wait until we get upstairs."

"You're damn bossy at times, you know that?"

"I'm not nearly as bossy as you are. Give me that towel."

"Why?"

"So I can drape it over *Valley,* you idiot. I don't want someone to see us going up the stairs carrying this stupid book. How would we ever explain taking it out of the vault?"

"Good point," Croft said with an air of grave admiration.

"Come on, let's hurry."

They made it to the first level of the house before encountering anyone. Mercy was guiding Croft past the darkened entrance of the sitting room when an amorous and quite inebriated couple lurched through the doorway and nearly collided with Croft.

"Better watch out," Croft advised politely. "I might throw up on your shoes."

The woman, dressed primarily in glittering eyeshadow, gazed up at him with a shocked expression. Her companion yanked his foot out of Croft's path.

"You sick?" the woman inquired sympathetically.

"Yeah," Croft admitted cheerfully.

"You're wet," the man observed.

"Went swimming."

Mercy tugged on Croft's wrist. She kept the towel-wrapped *Valley* as discreetly out of the way as she could. Holding the book, the towel and her wet skirts in a tangled

mass helped minimize the odd shape under the large, thick
terrycloth. "Let's keep moving, honey. We don't want you
disgracing yourself in the middle of the party."

Croft gave his new acquaintances a knowing grin. "She's
trying to get me upstairs so I can seduce her."

"Croft!"

"Okay, okay, honey. I'm on my way. Don't want to keep
you waiting."

He had one wet boot on the first step that led up to the
second level of the house when Isobel Ascanius appeared in
the hall. She stared at the couple on the stairs, her eyes sharp
and questioning.

"Mercy? What's wrong? You're both soaking wet. Are
you all right?"

"Hi, Izzy," Croft said good-naturedly, his words sounding
slightly more slurred. "Is that a new pilot suit? Looks great.
Oughta set a whole new trend."

"Ignore him," Mercy said with a sigh. "He's bombed out
of his skull. Decided to take a midnight swim and nearly
drowned in the process. I'm going to take him upstairs and
put him to bed."

Isobel looked at Mercy. "Do you need any help with
him?"

"No," said Croft before Mercy could decline. "She
doesn't need any help with me. Just a little practice, is all.
I'm gonna see she gets plenty of practice." He leaned forward confidentially and nearly fell over. "Mercy's a little
shy, you know. Kind of inhibited 'bout some things, if you
know what I mean. But she's learning."

Mercy clamped a hand over his mouth. "That's enough
out of you," she hissed. "You're embarrassing me." He
gazed at her over the edge of her palm, a ludicrously hurt
expression in his eyes as Mercy turned to Isobel.

"Please excuse us, Isobel. This is so humiliating. I'm

going to take him straight upstairs to bed and let him sleep it off."

"I didn't realize he had had that much to drink."

"He doesn't hold his liquor well."

There was a "humph" of protest from behind Mercy's hand. She felt Croft's tongue on her palm and hastily removed her fingers. He smiled in triumph, satisfied with the small victory.

"Behave yourself," Mercy snapped. She turned back to Isobel, still clutching the hidden book against her wet skirt. She tried to stand at an angle, using Croft's body to shield the woman's gaze from the towel. "If you'll make our apologies to Erasmus?"

"Of course. You're sure you don't need any help?"

"No, thanks. I can manage." She started up the stairs and Croft followed obediently, his body still hiding most of her slender frame. He waved at Isobel until she was out of sight.

"Hell of a pilot," he said as Mercy pushed him down the hall and into the suite.

"If you're so enthralled with her, why did you get drunk at her party and make a fool of yourself?" Mercy began unbuttoning his shirt.

"I'm not enthralled. Just making an observation. She's a good pilot. I think I'm enthralled with you, though." He looked down at Mercy as she shoved the wet shirt off his shoulders and went to work on the buckle of his belt. "It works better if you take the boots off first."

"Why didn't I think of that?" Thoroughly irritated, but even more thoroughly scared, Mercy shoved him down to a sitting position on the bed and knelt in front of him. She set *Valley* down beside him.

Croft ignored the book. "You gonna undress me and throw yourself on my body?"

"No, I'm going to throw you in the shower."

"I'm already wet."

"We're both cold. We need a quick, hot shower and fresh clothes. And we need to hurry." She finally got his boots off and hastily rose. "Take off your pants and get into the shower."

He frowned and fumbled with his zipper. "Need help."

"Oh, Lord, I can't believe this." Her own fingers were trembling, partly with cold, partly with her frantic concern as she unzipped his trousers and helped him step out of them. It was not an easy task. Croft kept having trouble with his balance. For some reason that genuinely alarmed him.

"I'm not drunk," he muttered as he lurched, naked, through the bathroom doorway. "Can't be drunk. Never get drunk. *Never*. Can't risk it. Might turn out like my dad. Might hurt someone I don't want to hurt. *I never drink too much.*"

Mercy stared at him, listening to his mumbled protest. It occurred to her again that he was probably right. He couldn't be drunk. Croft had had a mission tonight. The last thing he would have done was have too much to drink before tackling the vault.

She caught his arm just as he was about to step into the shower. "Croft, if you haven't had too much to drink, *what's wrong with you?*"

"Goddamn it, don't know." He put a hand to his head. "Feel dizzy."

Mercy waited no longer. She reached for one of the paper cups that was housed in a dispenser beside the sink, filled it with water and handed it to him. "Here, start drinking."

"Not thirsty." But he took the cup and drank.

When he was finished, she filled it again and made him consume the liquid. He started to protest when she refilled it a third time.

"No more," he muttered. "Feel sick."

"Good, that's exactly how I want you to feel. But first I want to dilute whatever was used to poison you. Then you can be sick to your heart's content. We'll try to get out whatever's left in your stomach. Drink the water, Croft."

He stared at her over the rim of the cup. "Poison?"

"If you really aren't drunk, then you must have been poisoned or drugged. *Hurry.*"

He finished the third glass of water and made a face. "Now what?"

"Now I get to stick my finger down your throat and make you gag."

Croft swung suddenly toward the porcelain bowl. "I don't think you're gonna have to use your finger," he said.

Mercy steadied him while he was thoroughly and violently ill.

Isobel went in search of Gladstone. When she found him she drew him off to one side. She knew he wasn't going to be pleased.

"She got him out of the pool before he drowned, but he's pretty far gone," Isobel said quickly. "She thinks he's drunk and she's taking him upstairs to put him to bed."

Gladstone's eyes burned for a moment. "He should be dead by now. It was supposed to look like a simple drowning accident. A drunk guest slips and falls into the pool. Nothing to worry about at an autopsy."

"I know. Something went wrong."

"I do not like incompetence."

"Dallas or Lance failed. Whichever one of them slipped away for a moment to knock Falconer unconscious and toss him into the pool bungled the job."

"He should have made certain Falconer was dead!"

"He couldn't hang around the pool for more than a minute or two," Isobel reminded him. "That was the plan, remember? If the authorities were to ask embarrassing questions somebody here at the party might have noticed that one of the hired hands was missing for a critical few minutes. It had to happen very quickly. Besides, Falconer should have been unconscious when he went into the pool. He should have drowned without any further assistance!"

"I do not tolerate failure."

"This failure can be remedied," Isobel assured him.

"It had better be remedied. I do not like the way things are going. Falconer should not have escaped the trap. The drug should have given him all the symptoms of drunkenness."

"It did. He seems very obviously inebriated. The problem was that Pennington pulled him out of the pool before he drowned."

"Keep an eye on Falconer and Pennington."

Isobel nodded. "Of course, but it's doubtful they're going anywhere. Falconer can barely stand. Soon he won't be able to do even that. In any event they can't get away without us knowing it. If they try, they will only make things easier for us. A drunk, a car and a mountain road. All the ingredients needed for an unfortunate accident. It might, in the end, be the simplest way. It will take care of both of them at once."

Gladstone nodded thoughtfully. "Yes. It might indeed be the simplest way. Did Falconer get into the vault?"

"No. It's still locked. Dallas just checked."

Gladstone nodded again. "Excellent."

Chapter
FOURTEEN

Croft was shaking by the time Mercy got him into the shower. Beneath the natural bronze of his skin he was pale. His eyes were stark in his harsh face and it was obvious that the sheer force of his will was the only thing keeping him on his feet.

But he seemed to be thinking more clearly. At least that was what Mercy told herself as she stripped off her own wet clothes and got into the shower beside him. The hot water felt good. She realized just how chilled she had gotten.

Croft watched enigmatically as she stepped into the shower. "I get the feeling you're not here to join me in some fun and games." He stood braced against the tiled wall with one hand, letting the water pour down on his head.

"You're right. I'm in here to keep you from falling flat on your face."

"Why stop me now? I've been doing a damn good job of it since this whole thing started. Christ, I can't believe I screwed up this bad. This job is coming apart the way my last one did three years ago." He closed his eyes and put out his other hand to help hold himself in an upright position. "What a mess."

"You don't normally screw things up, huh?" Mercy knew he was in no condition to continue the ribald teasing he had been indulging in earlier, but she still felt awkward sharing the shower with him. This was a purely therapeutic effort, she reminded herself as she carefully kept her back to him. As soon as they were both warm, she had to get them out of the house.

"Three years ago I did a fairly good job of screwing up," Croft said thoughtfully, as if caught up in a sudden need for a dose of self-chastisement. "But other than that and this bit tonight, no, I don't usually screw things up."

"Well, aren't you Mr. Wonder Man."

He opened one eye. "You're mad."

"I'm scared." She reached out and turned off the shower. "Come on, Croft. We've got to get out of here. I'll pack for you while you're getting dressed."

"I don't think I'm in any condition to drive out of these mountains tonight," Croft said quietly, watching her as she tossed him a towel.

"You won't be driving. I will."

"Are you a good driver?"

"Under the circumstances, I'm the best available."

His mouth crooked slightly. "A valid point."

Mercy wasn't sure if his faint smile was caused by the remnants of whatever drug had been used on him or if he found the situation genuinely humorous.

She quickly finished drying herself, wrapped the towel around her body and then reached out to snatch his towel out of his hands. "That's enough, you'll do. Now let's get you into some dry clothes. The party is still going strong. By now most of the guests are stoned out of their minds on something. I figure we can get downstairs and out to the car without anyone noticing we're even gone."

"I doubt it." Croft allowed himself to be led out into the bedroom. He was totally unself-conscious of his nudity. He seemed more concerned with the faint trembling in his hands. The weakness obviously alarmed him.

Mercy shot him a quick, worried glance as she shoved a clean shirt at him. "What do you mean, you doubt it?"

"Sounds too simple."

"But with all these people here, no one would dare try to stop us, even if someone did see us leave. There would be fifty witnesses."

"Maybe. Maybe not." He started buttoning the shirt, giving the task close attention.

Mercy was exasperated. "Have you got any better ideas?"

"No."

"That's just great. Well, until you come up with a spiffier plan, why don't you quit taking potshots at mine?"

"It's a deal. No more potshots at your plan until I can think of a better one. Where are my pants?"

"Here." She tossed him a pair of jeans with one hand as she dragged his small overnight bag out of the closet. Quickly she raced through the room, gathering up the few items he had left out of the bag.

"My boots are wet. I'll go barefoot." Croft glanced around the room, frowning intently.

"All right. I'll get my things. Stay right here and don't move, understand?"

His gaze snapped back to her anxious face. "You can stop treating me as if I were a drunken husband who's just embarrassed you at a party. My head is clearing."

"Don't worry, I'm not in any danger of mistaking you for my husband, drunk or otherwise. Now hold onto this." She shoved the bag into his hand. "I'll be right back."

She was ready within minutes, her things pushed carelessly into her small suitcase along with the copy of *Valley*. When she returned to the other room Croft was standing where she had left him. He smiled brightly.

"I didn't move."

"Do you think you can now?" she asked with concern. He might not be shaking as badly as he had been earlier, but he still looked as though the only thing keeping him on his feet was his willpower and her nagging.

"Lead the way, boss lady. I still haven't come up with a better plan."

She held out a hand. "Got the car keys?"

He thought a moment. "In here." He patted the bag he was holding. He unzipped a pocket and handed the keys to her.

Mercy grabbed them, aware that her fingers were also trembling. Too bad, she chastised herself. She was going to have to drive, anyway. Maybe tomorrow she could find time to have a nervous breakdown, she told herself consolingly. But for the moment it looked as if she was in charge whether she wanted to be or not. Fortunately, Croft was being cooperative. "All right, let's get this show on the road."

The hall outside their suite was still empty when they emerged from the room. The laughter, music and conversation were as loud as ever, floating up through the house. Mercy led Croft down the carpeted hall toward the back stairs.

They encountered no one en route, but when they slipped out into the cold night air two sleek, dark shapes materialized in front of them.

"The dogs," Mercy whispered, halting immediately. "I thought they'd be in their pens."

The Dobermans made no sound, but their small, pointed ears were held stiffly alert. They moved closer. Mercy shrank back.

Croft didn't move. Instead he extended a hand to the closest Doberman. "Easy boy," he said softly. "We just came out for a little fresh air." He kept talking quietly to the animals in a voice that was so soft Mercy could barely hear the words.

The dogs cocked their heads to one side, listening attentively. Whatever questions they might have had in their canine brains seemed laid to rest by Croft's quiet words.

"It's okay," Croft finally said to Mercy. "They won't bother us."

"Are you sure?"

"I'm sure."

"I never did like Dobermans," Mercy whispered as she eased past the watching animals. "They always look like they're ready to attack."

"That's because they are always ready to attack."

"That explains it. How did you get to be such good friends with these two?"

"Dogs and I get along well. We . . . understand each other."

"Maybe you're in the wrong business. Maybe you should be raising dogs."

Mercy and Croft threw their bags into the back seat of the Toyota. Mercy slide into the driver's seat. She turned the key in the ignition as Croft got in beside her and closed the door. As she started backing out of the drive, Croft leaned over to peer at the gas gage.

"Well, we got lucky in two respects."

"How's that?" Mercy's attention was on her driving as she started toward the compound gate.

"No one emptied the gas tank and I know how to open the gate."

Mercy's fingers tightened on the wheel. "You think maybe that's a combination of too much luck?"

He leaned his head back against the seat. "It's a possibility."

"Croft."

"Don't get cold feet. This was your brilliant plan, remember?"

She brightened. "Maybe it's working because it was a spur-of-the-moment thing. After all, no one expected us to sneak off tonight."

"That's true. They expected me to end up face down in a pool. As for you. . . ."

"Yes, what about me?"

"I don't know, Mercy." Croft spoke wearily. A deep tiredness seemed to be replacing the alternating episodes of drunken euphoria and sickness. "I can't think straight yet. Let's just get out of here."

"How do you feel, Croft?"

"Exhausted." He held his hands up in front of him, examining them in the glow of the dashboard. "But I think I can still handle the gate."

A few minutes later he proved himself right. The lights of the big house faded as Mercy eased the Toyota through the compound gates and started to descend the steep road. They reached the outer gate a few minutes later without incident.

"You could probably have driven through this one if you'd had to." Croft observed matter-of-factly when he climbed back into the car after unlocking the gate. "But it looks like our luck knows no bounds tonight. We must live right."

The huge bus that had brought the crowd of guests stood in the starlight looking for all the world like a slumbering dinosaur. Mercy edged the Toyota around it and started into the first of the endless curves that shaped the mountain road for miles. Tires squealed as she came out of the first curve.

"I take it you haven't had a lot of experience driving mountain roads?" Croft noted after a few minutes.

"Don't worry. I'm a fast learner."

"Good." He closed his eyes again.

The isolation as well as the sharp, never ending switchback curves were enough to give anyone an anxiety attack, Mercy told herself as she concentrated on her driving. She had only gone a couple of slow, torturous miles when she noticed the brief flash of headlights in the rearview mirror. They disappeared almost immediately, cut off by a bend in the road behind her, but she was sure she had seen them. She shoved her foot down on the gas.

"Croft!"

His eyes snapped open, focusing instantly on the hairpin turn she was approaching at high speed. "Uh, Mercy, you want to slow down a bit? Even my Porsche can't take turns like this at this speed."

"Someone's following us."

"Well, whoever it is won't have to worry about finding us if you go off the edge here, will he? We'll make a nice, big hole in the guard rail."

"Maybe that's what he wants. Maybe he wants us to go over the edge." Nevertheless, Mercy reluctantly slowed the Toyota to a more reasonable speed. She whipped it around another curve. Tires squealed in protest as they clung game-ly to the road surface. Croft winced.

"You know, you're developing a streak of melodrama as wide as mine." Croft turned in the seat and glanced back through the rear window. "It's got to be Dallas or Lance—or both. I don't think you're going to be able to outrun them."

"Thanks for the vote of confidence." Mercy's foot eased back down on the gas pedal. The next curve came up much too fast in her headlights.

"Forget the Grand Prix act. I said you aren't going to be able to outrun them. Whoever's driving knows this road a hell of a lot better than you do. That gives him a distinct advantage."

"Look, if you can't offer any really helpful suggestions, maybe you'd better just keep quiet and let me drive." Mercy's mouth was dry.

"You're getting tense," he observed.

"What a brilliant observation. We're a real pair, aren't we? You're falling asleep as the bad guys close in, I'm totally traumatized, and we're both shaking like Aspen leaves in the wind."

"Drifter's Creek," Croft said succinctly.

"What?"

"Just get us to that little ghost town we came through on the way up here. Drifter's Creek."

"What are we going to do there? Panic?"

"Only if all else fails. Just get us there, honey. I think we've got a little time. Whoever's coming after us doesn't seem to be in a hurry yet. Probably just wants to keep us in sight until we're closer to the main road."

"Why?"

"The accident will look more accidental if it happens on the main road."

"*Accident?* Oh, God, Croft, do you really think—"

"They wanted an accidental drowning, at least in my case. But barring that, this plan probably struck them as equally useful. And it would definitely be better if it happened on the main road. That way there won't be anything to connect us with Gladstone. If it happens on this road, someone might wonder how we happened to be on it at this hour of the night. Not that the inquiry would go much farther than that. If worse came to worse, Gladstone would probably just tell the truth. We were a couple of houseguests who had a few drinks, left the party early and went over the edge of a convenient cliff."

"I wish you'd stop using the past tense." Mercy came around a bend and found herself on a short, straight stretch of road. She increased her speed as much as she dared. The Toyota seemed to be hitting every pothole and rut in sight.

"The trick to this kind of driving," Croft said patiently, "is to brake going into the curve and accelerate coming out of it."

"Croft, this is not a good time to give me lessons in anything, especially driving." She rounded another bend and saw the first tumbledown buildings of Drifter's Creek looming up in the glow of the car's headlights.

"Kill the lights," Croft said quietly.

"Are you kidding?" She was startled. "I won't be able to see a thing."

"Then stop the car and let me take it from here."

"But Croft, you're in no condition to drive, you said so yourself. If you think I'm going to let you drive us out of these mountains without the lights you must have taken one too many karate chops on the head."

He didn't respond, but his bare foot was suddenly on her side of the car. He used it to yank her foot off the gas pedal as he reached over and flicked off the lights. The next instant he was slamming on the brakes. "Get out. Now." He was already crowding her out of the car as he moved over into her seat.

"Damn it, Croft." But she stopped arguing. Shoving open the car door, Mercy scrambled out into the chilled night air and dashed around to the passenger side. Croft had the car in motion before she had even closed the door. "What are you going to do?"

"Hide the car over there in the trees."

Mercy glanced in the indicated direction. All she could see was a mass of dark limbs and branches. "There's no room for the car in among those trees."

"There's room." He steered the car carefully off the road. The wheels dipped into a ditch and then the Toyota pulled itself up on the far side.

"I assume you have better than average night vision?" Mercy didn't bother to hide the sarcasm.

"Better than average," he agreed.

She glanced at him quickly but could barely make out his profile. He was concentrating on his driving, easing the vehicle over the rough terrain.

The trees loomed closer, a dense, solid looking cluster of shadows. Then the car was nosing its way into the thick darkness. There was a swishing sound as a limb grazed the windshield. Mercy stared straight ahead. She could see a little, but not nearly enough to drive into this maze. Croft was driving very slowly, but he seemed very sure of what he was doing. She remembered her earliest impression of him: A creature at home in the darkness.

Croft brought the car to a halt and switched off the engine. "That's as good as it's going to get. Can you open the door on that side?"

Mercy unlatched the door and opened it carefully. "Yes. Just barely. Boy, is the rental agency going to have a fit."

"Why? I haven't scratched the paint." He was climbing out of the car as he spoke, closing the door behind him.

"You must have scratched the paint. You just drove through all those trees. You can't have avoided scratching the paint." She didn't know why she was pursuing such a stupid, meaningless accusation. It had to be a reaction to stress.

"We'll worry about it later," he said placatingly.

Mercy knew by the tone of his voice that he was humoring her. He was very sure he hadn't scratched the car. She peered through the shadows at where he stood near a tree. He stood very still, listening, apparently. It was hard to see him. If she hadn't known he was there she probably wouldn't have seen him at all. The realization gave her a new case of shivers. Then she remembered Croft's uncertain condition.

"How do you feel?"

"Like hell."

Not reassuring. Mercy fought a sudden urge to scream or cry. "Are we going to hide here in the trees with the car?"

"No. The car's too big. I've done the best I can to conceal it, but there's a good chance whoever's following us will find it. Come on."

"Where are we going?" Mercy eased her way around the Toyota until she was standing near him. When she looked up into his face all she could see was the colorless gleam of his eyes. The eyes of a ghost.

He took her arm and started leading her through the grove of trees. "Into town."

Mercy started to ask for more details, but the questions went out of her head when she caught a brief flash of light in the darkness. "Whoever it is, he's almost here." She couldn't tell if Croft was still trembling because her own nerves were performing a high wire act.

Croft glanced back along the road that wound down the mountains from Gladstone's estate. Headlights appeared for a second and then disappeared. Mercy was right. They didn't have much time. He felt her shivering under his hand and wondered critically which of them was in worse shape. He moved out into the open, yanking Mercy along with him as he started toward the nearest of the old shacks.

This was all his fault, he told himself fiercely as he loped toward the leaning building. Mercy was in danger because of his stupidity. He felt her stumble over a pine cone she hadn't seen lying in her path and quickly jerked her back to her feet. He had to remember she couldn't see as well in the dark as he did. Few people could.

His night vision was just one of the odd assortment of physical talents with which he had been born and had spent years honing. Useless talents, for the most part. All they were good for was getting him into situations where he was likely to get himself or someone else killed. If he had been born nearsighted, with a tendency toward a beer belly and a dislike of too much internal speculation and analysis, he would have had a completely different life. He might have found happiness working on an assembly line or in an accounting office. He was good with details.

But, no, he hadn't been that lucky. He had found himself endowed with a keen sense of mind-body coordination and a connoisseur's appreciation of violence. Most unfortunate of all, he had been cursed with enough intelligence to understand just how dangerous that made him, both to himself and others.

"You want us to hide in one of these old shacks?"

Mercy was panting, not so much from the exertion of the short dash across the open field, but from her own adrenaline. Croft had seen the syndrome before. It took training and willpower to conserve the wild rush of energy adrenaline caused. Mercy was holding up amazingly well. He was aware of a new level of respect for this woman.

"I'm going to put you in that one over there by the creek. It's set back behind the others. Not likely to be one that will be searched right away."

"Searched! You expect whoever's in that Jeep to look for us here?"

"If they spot the car in the trees they'll start looking for us. There's a good chance they won't spot the Toyota, though. They'll just keep driving, thinking we're still ahead of them on the road."

"You don't sound too sure of that possibility."

He smiled ruefully, in spite of himself. "Sometimes you're too perceptive for your own good, Mercy."

"I've had the feeling lately that hanging around you is the cause of the problem." She came to an abrupt halt as he stopped to push open the door of the old cabin. There was a squeaking sound as the rusty hinges groaned under the unfamiliar exertion. "I'm not going inside, Croft."

He heard the deep conviction in her voice and felt the

resistance in her body as he tried to draw her over the threshold. "You'll be safer in here than you will be out in the open, especially if they've got guns."

Mercy was staring into the black shadows inside the cabin. "I'll take my chances out in the open with you."

"No you won't. I have to be free to move. I can't look after you and handle whoever's in the Jeep at the same time." He would try sweet reason first, Croft decided. She was a smart woman. She was just a little nervous at the moment. He tried to make his voice sound reassuring, but the knowledge that time was running out made it difficult to be patient.

"I'll feel trapped in there, Croft." She swung around, her eyes wide and pleading in the starlight. "I won't be able to stand it. I'd rather be hiding in the trees. I want to be able to run."

He heard the fear in her words and wanted to gather her close to tell her she didn't have to be afraid, that everything was going to be all right. But there wasn't time to treat her terror with sensitivity. His hands closed roughly around her shoulders and he gave her a small shake.

"Listen to me, Mercy. I'm having a hard enough time holding myself together. I can't spare even a few minutes to explain why it's better for you to be hiding in here rather than out in the open. Just take my word for it that you can't outrun a bullet. Now, I don't want to hear another word from you. That Jeep will be here in a matter of seconds. Get inside, get down on the floor and stay there until I come back for you."

"But what are you going to do?"

"What I'm good at doing. Playing ghost. Get inside."

She shook her head. "I don't want to go in there, Croft."

There was no point arguing further. Croft opened the door further with his bare foot and hauled Mercy over the threshold. She started to struggle and then went limp in his hold.

He knew she had decided not to fight him. He pulled her close for an instant, pressing her face into his shirt.

"You'll be okay here, Mercy. Just stay down and don't make a sound, understand?"

She nodded against his chest and said nothing. When he released her and moved to the door she still said nothing. He doubted if she could see anything more than the bare outline of his body in the darkness of the old shack, but her head turned to follow his soundless movement. He was slipping outside into the cold night when her voice came softly.

"Croft?"

"What is it, Mercy?" He could hear the Jeep's engine clearly now. His attention was focusing on it, not Mercy's small, tense voice.

"Be careful."

"I'll be careful. You be quiet. Very, very quiet." He let the old door swing shut.

The Jeep roared around the last bend and raced into sight on the road that curved through what was left of Drifter's Creek. The headlights cut a bright swath through the darkness, momentarily throwing a handful of the empty, weathered shacks into stark relief.

A couple of minutes later the Jeep was through the town and charging into the next series of curves that led down to the main road. Croft stood in the shadows of the general store and watched the vehicle disappear. He wasn't going to count any chickens before they hatched. Sooner or later whoever was driving would realize the road ahead was empty. The next realization would be that the only place a car could turn off the road was Drifter's Creek.

The Jeep would be back soon.

Another wave of debilitating shivers went through Croft. He wrapped his hands around his upper arms and forced his mind to steady itself. At least he seemed to be over the bouts of nausea, thanks to Mercy's first aid treatment. The aching tiredness was getting worse, though, and he was still getting brief flashes of dizziness. He had to stimulate his internal resources. He needed a good dose of adrenaline to keep him moving.

Croft leaned back against the wood boards of the old store and closed his eyes while he concentrated on focusing what remained of his energy and willpower. He had to stay on his feet and in command of the situation. Mercy's life depended on how well he could pull himself together. She had saved his life earlier this evening. The least he could do was repay the debt.

Mercy, sweet Mercy. He had to do this for her.

Slowly he turned his attention inward, finding the quiet place in his mind where strength and energy swirled together in a calm pool. Another bout of shivers went through his nerves, distracting him for a few seconds, but Croft fought his way through them.

The night air was fresh and invigorating. It stirred ancient hunting instincts and revived old senses that most of the modern world had long since forgotten. Croft inhaled deeply.

He soon found himself on the familiar mental path, following the serene spiral of energy to its focal point. This was where he went when he meditated. This was the place he had found when he had finally acknowledged the potential for violence that lay in his own mind. He had known then that unless he found a counterpoint to that lethal element in his nature he would be destroyed by the raw, destructive energy it produced.

Long ago Croft had come to the conclusion that in some ways he was a throwback to a more primitive era. Violence came all too easily to him. It seemed to be built into his genes. His reflexes and instincts would have made him a good survivor, a valued member of society perhaps if he had been born in a different time and place. A part of him had always understood the primitive ways of survival.

But he hadn't been born in the past. He had been dropped into a more civilized society where violence was only an occasional event, not a way of life. The closest most Americans in the latter quarter of the twentieth century ever got to real violence was reading the headlines in the morning paper. True, most people feared violent crime, but the reality was that few would ever be a victim of it. Few civilized people needed the primitive survival instincts their ancestors had once depended on for hunting and defense. Whatever was left of those instincts lay dormant within the average individual.

Unfortunately for Croft, in him those instincts had never been dormant. Always he had been aware of them, simmering just below the surface. They had always been fierce, strong, and very much alive. They would have taken him over years ago if he hadn't found the other side of his nature, the part that could be civilized, analytical, rationally serene. This part of him could control the other side of his being.

Paradoxically it could also be used in some strange way as a source of energy, a means of stimulating the more aggressive elements within himself. Croft had a theory about how that actually worked. It involved the realization that civilized behavior actually required more willpower and emotional strength than did aggression and violence. The force needed to ensure civilization was every bit as strong as the fiercer elements within man. It had to be in order to have allowed civilization to triumph at all. But this force was less understood and less controllable.

From the moment he had discovered it, Croft had thrived on the challenge of controlling that inner source of power. It was his salvation. It kept him from becoming a beast at the mercy of his own, more aggressive and violent instincts.

Tonight he needed it in a way he had never needed it before. The other side of him was exhausted, its resources devastated by the effects of poison or drugs. And tonight he needed that side of himself.

It must have been in the goddamned fish. He would never eat smoked salmon again. But no. The poison or drug had probably been in the wine.

Drunk. The poison or drug had made him feel and act drunk. Was that how it had been for his father?

He pushed the stray thoughts aside. They were a weakening influence on him and he could not afford any more weakness.

He needed strength. He found the source of it within himself, sensing that he would be draining all his reserves when he tapped into what remained of his energy.

In the distance he heard the muted roar of the Jeep's engine. Whoever had followed them from the Gladstone estate had finally realized the quarry had taken a detour at Drifter's Creek.

Croft moved farther into the shadows, his mind steadying on the focal point of calm strength that was his only hope now. He realized he had temporarily stopped shaking.

It was cold in the starlit shadows, but there was a sense of rightness as well. The darkness offered concealment while allowing his primitive senses full rein. Mercy would probably say this was his kind of place, Croft thought grimly, a ghost town.

The Jeep roared back into town and halted abruptly at the end of the street. Two male figures leaped from the front seat. Croft saw the odd shapes jutting from their hands and knew that Dallas and Lance were both carrying guns.

Chapter
FIFTEEN

Mercy huddled in the shadows of the ruined structure and listened to the sound of the returning Jeep. Croft was right, as usual.

Mercy wished disappearing was a viable option. Under the circumstances it looked like the best way out of an untenable situation. She inched carefully toward the wall, wary of unseen objects lurking the shadows waiting to trip her. There was one window in the old shack, but it had been boarded up long ago, her questing fingers discovered. Fortunately there were plenty of cracks and knotholes in the wooden walls. When she pressed her face close to the boards she could see a couple of other disintegrating buildings looming in the shadows outside. Their outlines seemed a little clearer now than they had earlier. Maybe her eyes were getting more accustomed to the darkness.

She hugged herself against the chill. It wasn't just cold in Drifter's Creek. There was something more. She remembered the vague uneasiness she had experienced when she and Croft had first driven through the ghost town. Croft hadn't seemed aware of anything out of the ordinary, she recalled.

Possibly because the strangeness she had felt hadn't seemed particularly out of the ordinary to him, Mercy thought wryly. The man was an enigma. It was awkward being in love with an enigma.

Mercy caught the flash of the Jeep lights between a staggered row of buildings as the vehicle stopped right in the middle of the road. Whoever was driving probably wasn't unduly worried about blocking oncoming traffic. There wasn't much likelihood of any traffic on this road, especially at this hour of the night.

The lights of the Jeep were left on to illuminate the road between the dry, rotting hulks of buildings. The vehicle itself was in deep shadow, but Mercy thought she saw a shape jump out of the front seat and move forward to crouch beside the fender. Perhaps there were two shapes. She couldn't be sure. It seemed very probable that Dallas and Lance traveled as a pair. Snakes were said to do exactly that.

She knew she couldn't be seen, but Mercy drew back instinctively, wondering where Croft was. She glanced around blindly, desperately trying to quiet the panic that threatened to inundate her. She hated being cooped up like this. She felt like a trapped animal waiting for the arrival of the hunters.

She had to get out.

Under normal circumstances it was possible Croft could handle the situation outside. There was a terrifying kind of strength in him that had its roots in the emotional as well as physical side of his being, and he freely admitted that violence held some sort of fascination for him. Mercy forced herself to acknowledge that he was one of the hunters of the world, a predator who was at home in the darkness.

But tonight Croft was weakened by whatever had been

used to poison or drug him. The thought of him trying to take on Gladstone's two musclemen was appalling.

Croft could get himself killed out there in the shadows and she wouldn't even know it until Dallas and Lance finally tracked her down in her poor hiding place.

Mercy shuddered. She hated this dark, cold room. She wondered what it had been when Drifter's Creek was a flourishing mining community. It wouldn't surprise her to find out this particular building had once served as the town's morgue.

The thought made her almost sick to her stomach. She tried telling herself that towns the size of Drifter's Creek wouldn't have had morgues, but somehow the image of a dead body sprawled on a table nearby wouldn't vanish.

She could see the body very clearly in her mind's eye. The dead man was dressed in miner's clothing, his dirty shirt stained reddish brown from the bullet wound in his chest. The town doctor was leaning over him, shaking his head. It was too late. Just another victim of a claim feud.

The miner's small store of personal belongings were stacked on another table. A gun in its holster, an iron shovel with a wooden handle, a battered hat.

He had never had a chance to draw the gun.

Mercy gasped and came back to her senses with a start. She was going to drive herself crazy. Even if Croft did survive to fetch her he would find a crazy woman waiting for him. It was no good. She had to get out.

Mercy bolted for the door and nearly went sprawling as she stumbled over an object in the darkness. Her scrambling hands encountered a long wooden object and instinctively closed around it. It was a length of wood that was surprisingly round in shape.

Rising to her feet, Mercy headed once more for the door. She clung to the wooden stick as she let herself outside into the shadows. It wasn't much, but the stick gave her a feeling of being armed, albeit poorly.

She felt a little better outside in the open. Lately she seemed to be developing a sizable case of claustrophobia. First it was the fear of being locked in Gladstone's vault, and then those nightmare images of a dead man inside the old cabin a few minutes before. Hanging around Croft was proving uncomfortably stimulating to her imagination. His streak of melodrama was definitely starting to rub off on her.

Mercy made her way cautiously along the wall of the gutted structure in which she had been hiding, keeping the building between herself and the view of the road. A faint gurgling sound warned her of the small creek a few seconds before she would have stumbled into it. Glancing down she could see the dark swath of water. It would have been bitterly cold. That made her think about Croft running around in the chilled night without his boots.

Overhead the wind sighed in the treetops, an eerie, desolate sound. She hated that whispering cry, Mercy thought. It was the epitome of loneliness and isolation. Just like Croft. He was out there somewhere, the burden of protecting her and himself resting squarely on his shoulders. She knew instinctively that he was accustomed to facing this kind of thing alone. He probably wouldn't appreciate help from an amateur.

But he was in a seriously weakened condition. He needed her help. She had as big a stake in the outcome of this night's work as he did. Mercy was convinced now that both she and Croft were fighting for their lives.

The shot, when it came a moment later, crackled through the night, startling Mercy into realizing just how serious matters had become. She froze, waiting in an agony of suspense for a shout or cry from one of the three men who were hunting each other through the ruins.

"Over there, damn it. I saw him." The voice belonged to Lance.

Mercy closed her eyes and silently told Croft that he couldn't be dead. She wouldn't allow it. Then, clutching the stick, she moved away from the shelter of the cabin and edged toward the shadow of the next ruin. More voices drifted toward her. She caught bits and pieces of conversation from Lance and Dallas. The clear night air carried sound very well.

"What about the woman?"

"No problem. We'll find her later. Falconer is the one we have to worry about. Are you sure you saw him?" Dallas sounded angry and impatient. He also sounded a little worried. Perhaps this business of hunting ghosts at night wasn't his cup of tea.

"Something moved."

"It could have been anything," Dallas muttered.

"He's not armed. We know that. And he's fighting that stuff I put in the wine. You saw the condition he was in when the woman pulled him out of the pool. He can't last much longer. That stuff should have made him pass out by now." Dallas sounded as if he were trying to convince himself.

"Don't bet on it. He should have keeled over in the garden and he didn't. I don't know how he stayed on his feet. I was lucky to get him into the pool. He almost got me, instead. I'm telling you, Dallas, the guy's fast and strong."

"You should have made sure of that scene in the pool. If you had, we wouldn't be here now. Gladstone's not happy. Stop worrying about how fast the bastard is. With that stuff still in his system Falconer can't be anything but dead slow by now." Lance sounded satisfied with that deduction.

"I like the sound of that. Dead slow. Yeah, that's what he's gonna be all right. You want to split up or handle this together?"

"Let's split up. We can cover more ground that way. But pay attention if you use the gun. It's dark and we don't want any mistakes. Make certain you're aiming at Falconer or the woman and not me."

"Gladstone wants this to look like an accident, remember? We're supposed to dump them both over the edge of a cliff, not put a bullet in them."

"You think the local cops are going to be looking for bullet holes if they find two charred bodies in the wreckage of a burned out car?" Lance scoffed. "Once they find the fake alcohol in Falconer's system they won't ask any more questions."

"Yeah, but Gladstone—"

"Stop worrying about Gladstone. We'll handle this our own way."

A cold breeze was stirring the branches overhead. The increased moaning of the tree limbs covered whatever response Dallas made to Lance's comment. Mercy retreated behind another shack and crouched low, trying to listen for footsteps. It would be awkward if she blithely rounded the corner of one of these old buildings and ran straight into Dallas or Lance. Or Croft, for that matter, she added silently. In his present state he could easily mistake her for the enemy before he realized who she was.

For the first time she realized that was a very real danger. Perhaps she should have stayed in that horrible place Croft had left her.

The unfortunate second thoughts were shattered by a man's shout and the rapid firing of two more shots.

"I got him. Over here, Dallas. I got the bastard."

Mercy cringed as heavy, running footsteps came straight down the narrow alley between buildings where she was hiding and passed by. Her first reaction was complete denial. Lance couldn't have shot Croft. It wasn't possible. But earlier that evening she would have sworn it was impossible for

Croft Falconer to get drunk and wind up face down in a pool. The man might be part ghost, but he wasn't completely inhuman.

Mercy's second reaction was to follow Lance. If Croft was wounded, she was his only hope. Grabbing her rounded stick, she got shakily to her feet, listening for Dallas, who was calling for his buddy.

"Lance? Where are you? Are you sure you got him? What about the woman?"

But there was no answer from Lance. Warily Mercy stepped out into the narrow strip of uneven ground that separated the two rows of shacks.

There was no exclamation of triumph or anger. No call for help. Nothing. Not a sound except the moaning of the wind. It appeared that Lance had simply run down the aisle between the row of wooden hulks and vanished into the darkness at the far end.

The looming structures on either side of Mercy seemed abruptly less substantial than they had a few minutes before, once again taking on that aspect that made them seem half in and half out of the real world. Rocky Mountain starlight played unpleasant tricks on the eyes.

"Lance! Where the hell are you, man?"

Dallas' voice sounded from behind Mercy. Automatically she stepped out of the dim starlight back into the dense shadows between two buildings. There was still no response to Dallas' call.

"Goddamn it, Lance, what the hell's going on?"

There was real fear in the man's voice now. Mercy recognized it and thought it strange. Dallas was the one with the gun. Interesting that he should be starting to panic. Ghost hunting in Drifter's Creek was not turning out to be the sporting game he had originally thought it would be, apparently.

There was a hesitant footstep nearby and then the crashing

sound of a sagging door being thrown open. Dallas was on the broken porch of the building to Mercy's right. The flashlight he held cut a jerky path through the darkness. Mercy flinched as he fired into the black shadows of the interior. It occurred to her that Croft was right. She had led a very sheltered life. She had never, for example, heard a gun fired at such close range. It made her ears ring.

"Shit. Where the hell are you, you bastard?" Dallas spoke in a confused, angry whisper. *"Where are you?"* It wasn't clear if he was speaking to his silent partner or talking about Croft.

Mercy heard his footsteps on the porch and then a thud as rotting wood gave way beneath Dallas' foot. He swore violently, yanked his foot free from the splintered trap and leaped off the porch.

His lurching jump took him directly into the narrow path between the shacks where Mercy was hiding. His flashlight picked her out immediately.

For a split second Dallas simply stared at her. "Goddamn bitch." And the hand holding the gun came up in a swift, smooth arc.

But Mercy was already moving, closing her eyes against the blinding glare of the light and running straight at him. She held the stick in both hands as if it were a sword aimed at his chest.

There was a muffled thud and a furious gasp as Mercy found her target. Dallas flailed awkwardly, staggering backward as he lost his balance under the impact. The gun in his hand went off and Mercy thought that this time she would lose her hearing, the sound was so close and so loud.

Without any warning Croft was there, materializing in the alley behind Dallas as the other man floundered in an effort to keep his balance. Dallas seemed to sense that he suddenly had another enemy in the small space besides Mercy. He swung around awkwardly, trying to bring the nose of the gun up to aim at Croft, but it was too late. Croft was already reaching out for him.

Mercy was watching the whole thing, but later she couldn't describe what happened. One instant the man in front of her was trying to aim a gun at Croft, the next Dallas was lying in an unconscious sprawl on the cold ground.

Croft stood quietly, his bare feet slightly spread in a balanced stance, his hands at his side. He glanced down at the man on the ground and then looked at Mercy.

"Are you all right?" Croft asked, his words unnaturally even.

Mercy gasped for breath and nodded, staring at him. "What about you?"

"It's cold out here."

He appeared vaguely surprised, as if he were noticing the mountain chill for the first time. Mercy glanced down at his bare feet.

"Yes," she said. "It's cold." But the shiver that went through her had nothing to do with the mountain air.

"You should have stayed in that shack where I left you." There was no masculine outrage or chiding complaint in the words; no male fury over disobeyed orders. There was no emotion whatsoever. There was only perfect calm.

Mercy wasn't sure how to respond. She wasn't being chastised, so there was no reason to launch into a passionate self-defense, although that was her first instinct. She wanted to scream at Croft in an effort to break through the unnatural serenity that gripped him. She wanted to throw herself into his arms and be soothed and comforted while she offered soothing comfort in return. She wanted to hear him chew her out for having disobeyed his orders so she could have the release of yelling back at him.

The potent cocktail created in her bloodstream by the aftermath of violence was causing her to tremble with reaction. She wanted to seize Croft and shake him while she pointed out that although this might be a normal occurrence for him, it certainly was not for her. She craved some sort of emotional explosion, needed it to use up the nervous energy flooding her system.

But one look at Croft's remote, too-serene expression was enough to keep Mercy still. Somehow it seemed futile to use emotion of any kind as a weapon against such an impregnable fortress of self-contained isolation. She hardly knew this man.

Croft went down on one knee beside the unconscious Dallas. He started going through his victim's pockets. The process was a curiously detached one, methodical and totally without emotion.

"I think we'd better get out of here," Mercy offered tentatively. She found herself groping helplessly for words as she tried to communicate with the stranger in front of her.

"Yes," he agreed, pulling Dallas' wallet out of a back pocket. He flipped it open.

"What are you looking for?" Mercy whispered.

Croft didn't bother to respond. He was slipping a credit card out of its plastic envelope. He picked up the flashlight and used it to glance at the name on the card.

"Well, I'm glad to know you have some normal human limitations," Mercy heard herself mutter before she stopped to think. "I was beginning to think you might even be able to read in the dark."

Croft glanced up. "This credit card doesn't belong to Dallas."

She frowned. "Whose is it?"

"My guess is that it came from the wallet of one of the guests in that motel we stayed in on the way to Gladstone's."

Mercy's eyes widened. She crouched down to look at the card. The name etched in plastic was Michael J. Farrington. "You don't think Farrington is just Dallas' real name?"

Croft pulled out another card. "This one's in the name of

one Andrew G. Barnes. I'll bet Gladstone would be furious if he knew his hired muscle had stashed a little on the side for himself after that robbery. Dallas and Lance were probably supposed to get rid of all the evidence, but they were too greedy to dump the credit cards."

Mercy nodded. "As long as they keep purchases under a certain minimum, they can use the cards a long time without anyone checking for authorization. You've made your point, Croft," Mercy said ruefully as she got to her feet. "It's probably safe to say these cards don't belong to Dallas. Lance probably has a few stray souvenirs in his wallet, too." She bit her lip. "Where is Lance?"

Croft rose smoothly beside her. He nodded in the direction Lance had run while firing his gun. "At the other end of that row of buildings."

"Unconscious or . . ." Mercy glanced uneasily down the narrow path. She realized she was afraid to complete the question.

"Unconscious," Croft said.

"Thank heavens." Mercy wasn't aware she had spoken aloud until Croft responded, his voice still devoid of inflection.

"Did you think I'd killed him?"

Mercy hugged herself. "I didn't know what to think. He just went racing up this little alley and disappeared. You've mentioned your interest in the philosophy of violence and I—"

"I'm interested in violence. Not death."

"Is there a difference?" she snapped, goaded.

He looked at her. "They're frequently linked, but yes, there is a difference. All the difference in the world."

She knew he could see her expression much more clearly than she could see his. Mercy turned away, lifting her hands to clasp herself against the chill. She realized she was still holding the stick she had used to defend herself.

"Where did you find that?" Croft asked, taking the stick from her and examining it briefly.

"I found it in that horrible cabin where you left me. I couldn't stay in that place, Croft. It was awful. I couldn't stand it another moment."

He wasn't paying any attention. "It looks like a shovel handle."

Mercy stared at the piece of wood as Croft tossed it aside. Images of a dead miner flowed back into her mind. The miner's personal possessions were stacked on a table. Camping gear. A battered hat. A shovel.

"Let's get out of here, Croft."

"As soon as we tie these two up and leave them in one of the buildings. The general store would be a good place, I think."

"What are you planning to do about them? We ought to call the sheriff's office."

"We will. An anonymous tip. We'll tell the authorities that if they're interested in solving the motel robbery, they might check the general store in Drifter's Creek. We'll let the sheriff take it from there."

"As good citizens, we ought to go straight to the authorities. We shouldn't turn in an anonymous tip over the phone."

"Good citizenship is not high on my list of priorities at the moment." Croft stepped out into the corridor between buildings. "I have other things to do."

"Croft, you can't handle this sort of thing on your own. You're supposed to call the cops when you get into a situation like this." Mercy hurried after him as he made his way down the alley. "We've got proof that Dallas and Lance were probably involved in that motel robbery and some indication that Erasmus Gladstone might be Egan Graves or at least connected to him. We should turn everything we've got over to the sheriff and let him take it from there."

"Take it where? He might be able to build a case against Dallas and Lance, but they're unimportant. Gladstone is the one who matters, and Gladstone is too well protected to be hurt by Dallas and Lance. He would never let himself be vulnerable in that way. If the sheriff questions him, he'll simply say he's shocked to learn he'd hired two thieves to work for him. No one will believe that Gladstone sent his hired help to steal a couple of wallets and open the empty safe of a rundown motel. It's obvious he doesn't need the few dollars and the stolen credit cards."

"I guess you've got a point," Mercy said uncomfortably. "And Gladstone's already paid for the book, so who would think he'd want to steal it. It will be obvious to everyone that Dallas and Lance were probably operating on their own. No one would think Erasmus Gladstone was a common thief. But what about what happened to you tonight?"

"I got drunk and fell in the pool."

"You were poisoned or drugged."

"There are forty or fifty artists at Gladstone's estate who will say I was drunk when they last saw me."

Mercy chewed on her lower lip. "Maybe blood tests would turn up some evidence of poison or drugs."

"I doubt it. Whatever Gladstone used will probably look like alcohol in my blood, if there's even enough left of the stuff to detect in a test. These new designer drugs are getting more sophisticated every day. Just like Gladstone to be at the forefront of the technology."

"You're looking for excuses. You don't want to go to the authorities," Mercy accused.

"You're right. I don't deal well with authority. I prefer to operate on my own."

"Well, you're not on your own," she said through gritted teeth. "I'm here, remember?"

He stopped and turned around so quickly she almost ran into him. "Believe me, I'm well aware of your presence."

Mercy opened her mouth and then closed it abruptly. Croft had told her he never made threats, so what she saw in his eyes had to be a statement of fact. He did not want to hear any more arguments on the subject of good citizenship. Mercy decided to shut up.

Croft studied her face, nodded once in satisfaction and then continued down the alley.

There was no point arguing with a ghost, Mercy told herself.

She maintained her silence while Croft collected the unconscious bodies of Dallas and Lance, tied them hand and foot with a cord he found in the Jeep and left them in what had once been the Drifter's Creek general store.

Mercy kept quiet while Croft did a quick survey of the contents of the Jeep, turned off the lights and then drove the vehicle to the side of the road and hid it among the trees. He wiped off the steering wheel and door handles when he got out.

She didn't say a word as the Toyota was carefully extracted from its hiding place among the trees. It was Croft who finally broke the silence.

"You'll have to drive. I've used up everything I've got. I need rest. Get as far as you can before dawn and then find a motel." He didn't wait for her response. He handed her the keys and went around to the passenger side of the car.

He fastened his seatbelt, leaned his head back against the head rest and closed his eyes.

Mercy could have sworn Croft was asleep before she drove the car through Drifter's Creek.

I've used up everything I've got.

His words floated through Mercy's head frequently as she made the long drive through the mountains that night. The man beside her in the car wasn't just napping or dozing. He was sunk deep in a heavy sleep that bordered on unconsciousness. She wondered once or twice if she should try to find a doctor, but something told her Croft wouldn't appreciate the act.

She realized she was experiencing a strange combination of exhaustion and tension that would have made it impossible for her to sleep. She probably shouldn't be driving, either, Mercy told herself. But Croft had said to get as far as she could before dawn.

So she drove on into the night, her eyes never leaving the excruciatingly twisted pavement that flowed endlessly into the path of the headlights. Her hands were frozen on the wheel. Her nerves continued to dance with the remnants of adrenaline. She was aware of the exhaustion waiting to ensnare her, but her mind and body were too keyed up to give into it.

She couldn't have surrendered to sleep, anyway. Croft had said she had to drive. He would never have ordered her to do it if it hadn't been necessary. Someone had to get them out of the mountains and he couldn't do it.

I've used up everything I've got.

Croft was not really a ghost, Mercy thought. He was just a man. Any resemblance between Falconer and a supernatural specter was purely coincidental.

She wondered if Dallas and Lance would have believed her.

The first pale shift in sky color appeared as the mountain road widened and began branching off in different directions. She picked one of the side roads at random and wound up in a small town a few miles from the interstate.

There were two motels. Mercy picked the larger one which seemed to be favored by truckers. There were three big rigs in the lot. She parked the Toyota near one of them.

Croft spoke without opening his eyes. "Use a fake name, fake license and pay cash."

"How can I fake the license? They can check it."

"They won't."

He was right, Mercy reflected. Motel desk clerks rarely doublechecked the license plates of the cars in their parking lots.

A few early risers were already stirring, checking out at the front desk and carrying their bags to their cars. The desk clerk didn't seem to think it strange that Mercy was checking in so early in the morning. He was probably accustomed to truckers' driving hours.

Mercy collected the key and went back to the car, wondering how she was going to get Croft upstairs. If she couldn't wake him long enough to get him out of the car, she would have to leave him where he was. She certainly couldn't carry him.

He didn't move as she approached the passenger side of the car, but his eyes suddenly opened.

"We're checked in," Mercy said gently as she unlatched the door. "Can you make it upstairs?"

He glanced at the two-story building ahead of him. "Yes." He got out of the car and followed her silently up to the room. It was the heaviness of his tread as he wearily climbed the steps that told Mercy just how exhausted he still was. Normally he moved soundlessly. When she unlocked the door he stepped inside.

"I'll get the luggage," Mercy said.

When she got back to the room she found him sprawled on the bed, sound asleep.

She needed sleep, too. Mercy set down the luggage, aware of the weariness in her body. She went into the bathroom and stared at her drawn face in the mirror. The sight was not inspiring.

A few minutes later she curled up beside Croft and closed her eyes, wishing for the same deep slumber he had found so easily.

Twenty minutes later she was still awake. She began to wonder if she would ever be able to sleep again.

Chapter
SIXTEEN

Croft awoke with something less than his usual instant awareness, but he knew he had slept off most of the effects of the poison or drug as well as the additional adrenaline he had forced into his system to deal with Dallas and Lance.

The additional dose of adrenaline had probably helped eat up what had remained of the poison or drug after Mercy's first aid. But the combination of the two had left him totally drained. He had never been so exhausted in his life.

He had a vague memory of following Mercy up to the motel room sometime around dawn. The bright mid-morning sunlight was visible between the curtains now. Croft stretched, testing his muscles and strength. Then he turned his head on the pillow and looked for Mercy. She should have been sound asleep beside him but she wasn't even on the bed.

He shouldn't have made her drive out of the mountains the previous night, Croft thought, but there had been no other option. He had wanted to put distance between them and Gladstone and knew he wasn't capable of driving.

As usual, he thought with an inner wince, he hadn't given Mercy much choice. He never seemed to give her much choice.

Mercy hadn't complained or argued, though. She had simply gotten in the car and driven out of the mountains, even though she must have been tense and tired herself. And even though she had witnessed more violence within a span of a few hours than most people saw in a lifetime.

A good woman and a good friend. The kind he could depend on in a crunch. She had proven that more than once last night. He still remembered what it felt like to be staring down into eight feet of glowing blue water.

Croft levered himself up on one elbow and looked for Mercy. He wondered why she wasn't sleeping beside him on the bed. Maybe she was in the bathroom. Or perhaps she had awakened and gone out for breakfast.

But she wasn't in the bathroom and she wasn't at breakfast. She was sitting cross-legged on the worn carpet, still wearing her jeans and the pullover she had tossed on before leaving Gladstone's estate. Her eyes were closed and her hands were resting palms up on her knees.

She was meditating, Croft realized. He was so surprised he spoke without thinking.

"Mercy? Are you all right?"

Her eyes snapped open and her head turned quickly. He saw the unnatural brightness in her gaze and realized tension was still consuming her.

"No," she said starkly, "I am not all right. I can't sleep, I can't think, I can't settle down. My insides feel as if they're racing along at a hundred miles an hour."

"It's the stress," Croft said quietly, understanding what was happening to her. "Sometimes it hits you like that afterward."

"After what, Croft? After finding you nearly drowned in a swimming pool? After being hunted through a ghost town by a couple of jokers with guns? After driving out of the mountains in the middle of the night when any sane person would have waited until daylight? After deciding not to report attempted murder to the authorities? Don't be ridiculous. Why should a few little incidents like that bother me? They sure don't seem to bother you. You've been sleeping like a log."

She was wound up tighter than a bed spring, Croft realized. He sat up slowly, pitching his voice to a low, soothing level. "It's okay, Mercy. Calm down. Everything's going to be all right. You just need some rest. You're a little highstrung at the moment, but after you've had some sleep you'll be fine."

"The hell I will. And I'd appreciate it if you wouldn't speak to me as if I were one of those Dobermans. I've been sitting here for an hour trying to use meditation to calm myself down, but it doesn't seem to work for me."

"It takes practice. Years of it."

"Well, I haven't got years. I need something *now*." She sprang to her feet, her eyes glittering. "This is all your fault."

"I know."

"Don't you dare sit there and assume full responsibility for everything."

He blinked. "Mercy, you just said it was all my fault and I agree."

She threw up her hands in outrage. "Don't try to humor me. I am not a child. It's true you used me to get to Gladstone, but there's no point apologizing. We both know you'd do it again given the same set of circumstances. It's your nature to do what you feel you have to do. You don't let anything get in your way, especially not a woman who. . . ."

"A woman who what, Mercy?" he asked curiously.

"A woman who loves you, damn it!"

Croft went very still, absorbing her words. He had never seen Mercy like this. She was flushed with a heat that, under other conditions, he would have assumed was a sign of sexual arousal. Her eyes were glittering, green pools of fierce, feminine energy. She was riding a wave of residual tension that burned like fire in her, feeding on her nerves.

She didn't know what she was saying.

"Mercy, be still," he said firmly. "Sit quietly. I'll help you meditate. I'll help you get into the calm part of yourself. Just listen to me. I'll give you the words—"

Without any warning except an enraged yelp, Mercy exploded across the room. She launched herself across the bed, sprawling on top of Croft before he fully realized what was happening. The force of her impact pushed him back against the pillow. Her legs tangled with his and her nails dug into his shoulders as her eyes burned into his.

"Listen to me and listen good, you arrogant bastard. You've used me and manipulated me right from the start. You've even had the nerve to admit what you were doing while you did it. You've given all the orders and made all the decisions. You've had the unmitigated gall to make love to me because you thought you could control me more effectively if you turned me into some sort of sexual slave."

"A sexual slave? I think that's overstating the situation a little, Mercy."

Her nails tightened on his shoulders. He was going to have marks on his skin, Croft thought.

"Shut up. I am not interested in your fine points of logic or philosophy. I'm doing the talking and I'm not finished with you yet. I've never met anyone as arrogant as you, Croft Falconer, but things are going to change. Until now everything has gone your way, but this morning I'm going to have things my way."

"Mercy, honey, you're upset. You need to clear your mind. You need to calm down."

"The only reason I'm in this condition is because of you. So you're going to do something about it."

"I will," he promised. "I'll help you."

"Damn right, you're going to help me," she muttered as she yanked at the buttons of his shirt. "But I'm not in the mood for any more meditation. And I don't want to listen to any more of your noble talk about assuming responsibility for this mess we're in. We already know it's all your fault. I need more than words. I need something to help me get to sleep. I am, as they say in California, stressed to the max. I need to work off all this nervous tension. That means I need a physical release. You know what? I'm going to use you to get it. It's about time I got to use you for something."

"Mercy, honey, calm down," he urged softly, realizing at last what was happening. She didn't know what she was doing. He tried to clasp her wrists but she ignored him, yanked her hands free and went back to unbuttoning his shirt.

"I'm not going to calm down, so you might as well save your breath. I figure I can either use you for a punching bag or a stud. Take your pick, but you'd better choose fast."

"If you won't calm down, then slow down," he ordered gently. "Mercy, I need a shower." She was squirming on him as she worked her way down his chest. She got the shirt unbuttoned and began plucking furiously at his belt buckle. He could feel her heat as she slid down over his lower body.

"I don't want to slow down and you can take your shower later. For once we're going to do something my way."

She unzipped his jeans so quickly Croft sucked in his breath. "Mercy, be careful."

"Why should I start being careful now? I haven't been careful since I met you." She wriggled further down his legs, tugging furiously at the jeans. She got them past his hips and then lifted her head, her eyes challenging him.

"Well? Do you want me to use you for a punching bag or a stud?"

"For crying out loud, Mercy, this is ridiculous." He didn't know whether to laugh or shake her until she gained a semblance of normal behavior.

"Forget I gave you a choice. I've decided I'll get more use out of you as a stud than a punching bag. Sex is what I want, not a gym workout." She grabbed the waistband of his briefs and stripped them down to where his jeans were caught just above his knees.

He felt his stiffening manhood fall into her waiting hands.

"Hang on a second, honey. If you want me to make love to you, just give me a minute and I'll do it right."

"You don't have to worry about doing it right. We're not doing this your way. We're doing it the way I want it done. You don't have to say or do anything except perform on command. Close your mouth and concentrate on being useful. You might try meditation. Here, I'll give you something a little different in the way of mantras."

Croft didn't realize what she intended until he felt her hair flowing around his thighs. Then her soft mouth found him in an overwhelmingly intimate caress. A shudder went through him.

"Oh, Christ."

Mercy didn't respond. She was too busy exploring him with her tongue.

Croft realized she had never done anything like this before in her life, but that didn't seem to be slowing her down.

She was cautious at first, tentative, but eager, and what she lacked in skill she was more than compensating for with sheer determination. She didn't seem at all interested in advice or suggestions from her victim. Her fingers cradled the heavy globes at the base of his throbbing shaft while she learned the taste of him.

Croft felt the edge of her teeth skim lightly over the most

vulnerable place on his body and he nearly exploded in her mouth.

He had told her once that there was a fine line between pleasure and pain. Mercy had found it.

She had claimed she was doing this for her own pleasure. It was her own release she sought; a way to relieve the nervous tension and anxiety that was driving her. But Croft found himself enthralled by the sensual assault. He had never experienced anything like it in his life.

He had spent years learning to master himself. Self-mastery made it easy to master others. He was always the one in control, even in the rare moments of sexual climax.

Except when he was with Mercy.

She had already demonstrated that she could provoke him into sharing a wild, shimmering release with her. Now she was teaching him that she had the power to overwhelm him completely. She had the power to force his surrender. No woman had ever treated him like this.

No woman had ever wanted him this much.

Croft groaned as the tip of Mercy's tongue circled him. He was torn between grabbing her and pinning her beneath him and a surprisingly strong impulse to simply lie back and enjoy the unfamiliar excitement of surrender. It was his nature to dominate, yet with Mercy he was learning that there were other ways to find pleasure.

Mercy had said she was going to use him to achieve her own gratification, but surely no woman could make such intoxicating love to a man unless she felt something more than lust.

Croft closed his eyes, twining his fingers into Mercy's tousled hair. Driven by the spiraling desire that was rapidly threatening to overtake his senses, he lifted his hips, wanting more of her sweet, hot kisses. Mercy answered the silent plea for more with a final butterfly caress, and then she was pulling away from him.

"No," Croft muttered, opening his eyes to discover her kneeling between his spread legs. "Don't stop. Not now." His momentary fascination with finding himself a victim of Mercy's assertiveness faded quickly. She had aroused him too fully. He couldn't let her quit now. Croft started to reach for her.

"Don't you dare move," Mercy ordered. "I've got you exactly as I want you. Stay put." She grabbed the hem of her pullover and yanked it over her head, heedlessly tossing it aside.

Croft breathed deeply when he realized she was wearing nothing underneath. The taut peaks of her high breasts were dark against her pale skin. He ached to take a gemlike nipple into his mouth. He lifted a hand, letting his fingers brush lightly across the tip of one soft white breast.

But Mercy ignored him. She was too busy shimmying out of her jeans. When she shoved the denim down over her hips, she removed her panties at the same time. The tawny triangle of hair glistened in the morning sun.

Croft caught his breath, his whole body tight and heavy with his need. All his instincts urged him to pull her down beneath him so he could drive himself into her. He had had enough of this passive surrender bit. It was an interesting novelty, but now impatience was consuming him. His hand closed around Mercy's thigh, his fingers sinking into her resilient, warm flesh.

"Take your hand off me," she hissed as she finished kicking off the denims.

"Mercy, what's the matter with you? You want me. You've said it yourself."

"I've had it with you taking control. I'm in charge here. Lie down and shut up."

She moved on top of him and Croft allowed himself to be pushed back into the pillows once more. She was all over him with a vengeance. Her fingers pushed through the hair on his chest, her lips were buried against his throat, her soft inner thighs clasped him tightly.

He stirred and groaned thickly when she lowered herself over his rigid shaft. He felt the heat of her femininity seconds before he felt the dampness. Croft thought he would go out of his mind.

She levered herself up, her small hands planted solidly on his chest as if to pin him down while she took him. Then she slowly began to ease him into her velvety sheath. Croft heard her draw a deep, impatient breath at her body's initial resistance.

"Damn it," she muttered, wriggling in an effort to accommodate his size.

She was small and sensitive and delicate. Didn't she realize she couldn't rush this part of things? Croft wanted to laugh, but the sexy wriggling as she forced herself down onto his shaft was nearly his undoing. The amusement he had felt briefly because of her impatience faded beneath the much stronger desire to grab her hips and pull her down until he was completely inside her. He clamped his hands on her thighs, unable to resist the need to take charge of the lovemaking. He was wild for her now.

She pushed his hands away at once. Croft swore softly, but he found himself letting her get away with the action. She didn't seem to realize just how vulnerable she was, he thought, his mind clouded with a savage desire. He could pick her up with one hand, toss her down on the bed beneath him and cover her body with his own. He could put an end to this act of feminine aggression in two seconds flat. She must know that if he chose to take control she couldn't possibly stop him.

But she seemed to have no fear of him, Croft realized dazedly, no sense of being the smaller and more helpless one in this assault; no fear that he would override her commands and become the aggressor.

In some perverse manner, it was a measure of her trust in him.

Then his frustration and exultant anticipation reached new heights as, with a small cry, Mercy took him inside her.

"Sweet Mercy." It was an exclamation of wonder, an impatient curse against the gentle, feminine domination and a muffled shout of pleasure. *"Mercy."*

Her nails were digging into his shoulders as she established a slow, surging rhythm that left her and Croft both shuddering. Croft opened his mouth when she leaned over him and sought his lips with her own. Her tongue slipped inside in an aggressive penetration that was an exciting reversal of the penetration lower down.

Croft tightened his arms around her, glorying in the soft, hot feel of her. He sensed she was losing her own self-control now, becoming swamped by the sizzling sensations she had sought to command. He knew how it felt. On the occasions when he had made love to her, it had always ended like that for him. In the final analysis there was no winner or loser, only a passionate bonding and shimmering climax that had to be shared together.

Mercy cried out and her teeth sank into his earlobe when the coiled spring inside her finally released. The small convulsions squeezed him demandingly and Croft dimly heard his own muffled, exultant shout. His body surged deeply into hers one last time and then he was erupting inside her.

Mercy clung to him as tightly as he clung to her and together they rode out the fabulous storm that tore through their bodies.

Together they slowly returned to the here and now.

Together they sank back into the rumpled sheets, their legs entwined, their perspiration slick bodies gliding against each other.

Together.

Croft lay still for a long time, enjoying the feel of Mercy

in his arms. It was a while before she stirred, slithered off and curled up beside him. He turned his head to look at her and found her watching him through heavy-lidded eyes. She blinked sleepily and yawned like a cat.

"It's okay, honey," he said gently. "I know you didn't mean it."

"Mean what?" Her eyes were closing as she nestled her head more comfortably into the pillow.

"What you said earlier about being in love with me. It was the tension and your nerves talking. And you have a tendency to say rash things before you've thought them through."

"I really wish you'd stop putting your foot in your mouth, Croft." She turned over on her side, presenting her back to him. "It's going to be hard enough as it is to respect you in the morning."

She was asleep before he could even begin to formulate a response to that one. Croft gazed at the curve of her bare shoulder for a long while before he finally got up, pulled on his jeans and sought solace in his meditation.

Mercy awoke to find herself alone in the motel room. Judging from the position of the sun, she guessed it was early afternoon. She probably hadn't had more than four hours of sleep, but it seemed to be sufficient. She felt rested and the frazzled feeling was definitely gone.

She stretched luxuriously, letting her mind drift back. The events in Drifter's Creek seemed very distant in the light of day. Ghosts always faded in the sun.

Except for Croft. He seemed as real and substantial as ever, even in full daylight.

Mercy tossed the covers aside and padded into the bathroom for a shower. While she stood under the driving water she wondered if Croft had done his civic duty and telephoned the authorities.

I don't deal well with authorities. Mercy recalled his words and wondered what they meant.

Mercy finished her shower and put on her jeans and a fresh shirt. She was busy securing her hair into a no-nonsense twist that would keep the tawny mass out of her eyes when Croft materialized in the doorway.

As usual there had been no sound of the door opening, no footsteps to warn her, no knock. The door was simply closed one instant and the next he was in the room with her. Croft was obviously back to normal. He was carrying a paper sack that had come from a restaurant.

Mercy met his eyes in the dressing table mirror and her hands stilled on top of her head. As memories of her early morning aggression returned she determinedly fought down the blush that threatened to turn her face a vivid pink.

"Is that coffee? Good. I could use a cup. Did you call the sheriff about Dallas and Lance?" She kept her voice bright and chatty and hurried to finish pinning her hair in place.

"Coffee for you, tea for me. Yes, I called the sheriff. About two hours ago. Anonymously from a pay phone." He walked over to stand behind her, his eyes never leaving hers in the mirror.

It was Mercy who looked away first, pretending to be searching for a hairpin. "So they'll pick up Dallas and Lance."

"If Gladstone hasn't found them first."

"Do you think he'll have gone looking for them?" Mercy demanded.

Croft set the cup of coffee down on the table, leaned over and dropped a lingering kiss on the exposed nape of her neck. Mercy shivered and her eyes flew back to meet his in the mirror.

"No." Croft straightened, apparently satisfied with the

telltale shiver he had induced in her. "I don't think Gladstone will have found them. I doubt he even looked for them. When Lance and Dallas failed to return last night, he probably assumed they were dead."

"Dead!"

"It's how he would have left them if he'd been in my place." Croft shrugged. "By now he'll have something more important on his mind."

Mercy chewed her lower lip. "Escaping?"

Croft shook his head. "I don't think he'll run very far. Not yet. There are too many loose ends. But that helicopter makes him too damn mobile. With any luck he'll decide he's safe enough where he is for the time being. Even if Dallas and Lance turn up in the hands of the sheriff, Gladstone isn't in danger of anything more than having to answer a few polite questions."

"Won't he be afraid we'll lodge a complaint against him?"

"I don't think so," Croft said. "He'll probably assume we're operating on our own. That's what I want him to think. That means we aren't likely to complain to the cops. Even if we did, all Gladstone has to do is deny any knowledge of Dallas and Lance's activities."

"You really do believe he's Egan Graves, don't you, Croft?"

"I'm almost sure of it now. But I can't move until I know where he's going to go to ground. As soon as I find out . . ." Croft let the sentence trail off as he paced to the window and stood looking out. He sipped his tea. "That book is still the key to this mess." He looked at Mercy over his shoulder. "And we've got it because you had the guts to go back into the vault and get it last night. Thanks, Mercy."

"Don't thank me," she told him waspishly. "I didn't have any choice. You refused to leave the pool room without it, remember?"

His smile was rueful. "Vaguely."

Mercy's brows came together. "How are you feeling? Any sign of a hangover?"

"No. Whatever it was seems to be gone from my system."

"It's amazing you could function at all last night, let alone handle Dallas and Lance. You were on the point of collapse."

"You were the one who got me out of the pool and got us out of the house."

Mercy set her back teeth. "So you owe me, right?"

He nodded seriously. "Right."

"Oh, goody. I can't wait to collect."

He surprised her with a fleeting expression of mischief. "I thought you already did. Bright and early this morning."

Mercy lost control over the blush that had been threatening her since he had walked into the room. She tried to brazen her way through the embarrassing little scene with a deliberately lofty smile. "I'll admit you make a very interesting sex slave."

"Thank you. My only goal is to please. Tell me the truth. Do you still respect me?"

She wasn't sure what to make of his provoking banter, but her pride wouldn't let her back down. She felt obliged to hold her own. "There are certain aspects of you that definitely command respect." She let her eyes drop to a point below his waist.

"So help me, Mercy, one of these days—"

She didn't see him move, but suddenly he was across the room. His hands closed around her shoulders and he hauled her lightly to her feet. When she jerked her startled gaze up to meet his she found herself staring into hazel depths filled with a combination of laughter and exasperation.

There was no sign of the too-familiar remoteness in Croft's eyes, no evidence of detachment. Mercy was entranced.

"About this little matter of respect," Croft began warningly.

Mercy smiled, her eyes brilliant. "I want to assure you, Croft, that you have my sincerest respect."

The laughter faded from his gaze to be replaced by an unreadable expression. The look he gave her wasn't remote or distant this time, just enigmatic. He leaned down to kiss her slowly and possessively.

"I guess that's a start," he said.

"Croft?"

He released her and went back to the window. "We have to talk, Mercy."

"I know."

He threw her a narrow glance. "About Gladstone. Or Graves, or whoever he is."

She sighed. "I know. What happens now?"

"You're going to phone your bookshop and alert the woman who's covering for you that someone will be trying to reach you through that number. She's to take the caller's number and then give it to you when you check in with her. Keep it casual. No need to alarm her. But make sure she knows she's not to give the number here to the person who calls her looking for you."

"What are you talking about? Who's going to call Dorrie looking for me?"

"Gladstone will call her," Croft said with absolute certainty. "It's the only contact point he has."

"But why would he try to reach me?"

"Us," Croft corrected absently. "He'll be trying to reach us and he'll figure we're waiting to hear from him."

"But why, damn it?"

"Because he wants the book back, of course. By now he'll have realized it's gone again. He went through too much, risked too much, took too many chances to get that copy of Burleigh's *Valley*. He'll want it back."

"He's a collector. Collectors will do a lot to get an item for their collection."

"Not Gladstone. He wouldn't risk exposing his new identity. None of the other books in that vault are duplicates of the ones he collected when he was known as Egan Graves. He's not trying to rebuild his old collection. In fact, judging from what you saw in the vault, he's deliberately avoided picking up the kind of books he wanted when he was Graves. He's smart enough to know he shouldn't do anything that might make someone suspect his old identity. Trying to duplicate his old collection of rare books would be too big a risk. If someone were watching and waiting for him to reappear—"

"Okay, I get the point. He's not trying to duplicate his old collection, but he went through a lot of trouble to get *Valley*."

"*Valley*'s an expensive book, but it's not exactly priceless. It's valuable but not a true treasure—not to a man like Gladstone. It's not special enough to go into his collection."

"Yet he tried to kill us because of it?"

Croft nodded. "That book is the key. He's going to keep trying to get it back."

"I wonder why?"

"I wish I knew." Croft ran a hand through his hair. "I looked through it again this morning while you were sleeping. I didn't see any signs of altered pages, but that doesn't mean there's not a code of some kind imbedded in the text."

"A code!" Mercy was struck by the possibility.

"Don't look so thrilled. I'm grasping at straws, believe me. I'm just trying to come up with a reason why Gladstone wants that book so badly." He came away from the window again, finishing his tea. "Let's go get something to eat. You can call your shop and alert Dorrie that someone might be trying to reach you. But whatever you do, don't tell Dorrie where you are, understand? She might accidentally mention our location to Gladstone and that could be awkward."

"When you're not indulging your streak of melodrama, you have a nasty way with the classic understatement. Tell me something. What will Gladstone hope to accomplish by contacting us about the book?"

"By now he'll be fairly certain we're not representing the forces of law and order. That means we're just small-time opportunists who've stumbled into the biggest deal of our lives and are trying to take advantage of it. He'll probably assume we're holding *Valley* for ransom now that we know how important it is to him. I imagine he'll offer us a real deal."

Mercy eyed him warily. "But we're going to refuse it, right?"

"No," said Croft. "We're going to accept. On our own terms."

Chapter
SEVENTEEN

"I don't like it, Croft. I don't like it one damn bit." Mercy paced up and down in front of him, her brows drawn into a straight line. This was not the first time she had made her impassioned plea for common sense. She had been arguing with Croft off and on all afternoon. It was nearly time for dinner and she still hadn't made any headway. He was stubbornly determined to handle the Gladstone situation on his own.

"You don't have to like it, Mercy. I'm the one who will handle things from here on in." He was reclining on the bed, his back propped against a stack of pillows, his arms folded behind his head.

There was the same note of abiding patience in his voice as they went through the argument for the umpteenth time as there had been when they went through it the first time. Mercy was convinced that his endless patience was beginning to bug her as much as his endless stubbornness. "This is stupid. This is crazy. We should be running to the cops."

"No."

"What have you got against the cops? We pay taxes so they can handle this kind of thing."

"They can't handle Gladstone. They couldn't touch him when he was Egan Graves and they can't touch him now. He's too well protected. Too careful. It's obvious he's involved in something as dirty as his guru scam down in the Caribbean, but it's going to take some doing to prove it."

"But he has acted illegally. He sent Dallas and Lance to run us off the road," Mercy pointed out.

"Prove it. Dallas and Lance were a couple of hired, two-bit hoods who snuck around during their leisure time and robbed motel guests. The cops will be lucky to make that much stick. There's no chance of making attempted murder stick."

Mercy swung around and confronted him with her hands on her hips. "Do you have this lack of trust in all authority or is it just the law you don't trust?"

"I told you, I don't—"

"Deal well with authority figures. I know. You want to know why?" She pointed a finger at him.

He smiled at her, his eyes strangely curious. "Why?"

"Because you are one, yourself. People who tend to dominate don't take to *being* dominated. Somewhere along the line you never learned to relax occasionally and let someone else take charge."

"That's an interesting theory. Were you giving me a lesson in how to let someone else take charge this morning when you assaulted me on this bed?"

"Forget this morning. I'm not finished with my observations on your behavioral eccentricities. There's more," Mercy said threateningly.

"Yes?"

"Yes," she muttered, resuming her pacing. "It isn't just that you're a dominant personality, it's that you're so isolated, so self-controlled. You operate in your own universe —which just happens to collide once in a while with the real world. Occasionally, probably only when absolutely necessary, you try to cross over into this world, the one where people like me live."

He gave her an odd look. "Is that why you call me a ghost? Because you think I don't belong in your world?"

She sighed and flopped down on the foot of the bed. "Maybe. Except that you're not a ghost, Croft. You're as real and as human as anyone else. But you've found a separate place for yourself, haven't you? How did you manage that?"

To her utter shock, he answered her wistful question. "I had to find that place very early in my life."

Mercy looked at him, willing him to explain. "What happened, Croft?"

He shrugged. "Nothing that hasn't happened to a lot of other kids. But it changed things for me."

"What was it?"

He hesitated, clearly sorting through old memories and emotions. "My father drank. Heavily."

"Oh, Croft."

"I told you, it's not an uncommon problem. He tried, I think. He worked at whatever job he could get, factory work, day laborer, crop picker, you name it. He married my mother when she was eighteen and pregnant. But after a few years of living hand to mouth, my mother decided she couldn't take the life and left for the bright lights of Los Angeles. I was five or six. We never saw her again. I think that's when Dad started drinking. It got worse as I got older. He used to go on some real binges and when he was lost in the booze he was...violent. Dangerous. It was as if the liquor released all his inner rage. I finally got smart and learned to hide until it was all over. I think I hated him."

Mercy swallowed at the calm way Croft said that. "It must have been terrible."

"When he was sober it was okay. We could both tolerate each other. But when he was drinking, yeah, it was rough. I think he knew he was dangerous when he was drunk but he couldn't control himself. I think he was afraid that one day he'd really do some damage."

"To you?"

Croft nodded. "Either that or he realized that I was getting bigger and that one day I might stop disappearing when he started drinking. I might start fighting back. Whatever his reasoning, he began going into town on the weekends to do his boozing. I was glad to see him go. I had signed up for self-defense classes at the Y. I told myself at first I just wanted to be able to protect myself from my father when he was drunk. But I guess I became fascinated with the world of martial arts and the underlying philosophy of mind and body control. I found a refuge in my classes at the gym, a place where I could go and be strong."

"Another world."

"In a way. The instructor at the Y was good, but he had his limitations and he knew them. He told me I needed to travel, to find other teachers who could help me get the most out of myself. He gave me some names of men who might be persuaded to take me on as a pupil. I didn't have the money for that kind of travel and tuition. I felt trapped. Then I decided I couldn't hang around any longer. I would have left earlier but I had some crazy idea my father might die if I weren't there to look after him. But on the day I turned eighteen and packed my bags, he went into town and didn't come back."

"What happened?"

"He got himself killed in a stupid, meaningless back alley brawl. Somebody rolled him for the few bucks that were in his wallet and a bottle of cheap wine."

Mercy closed her eyes and a premonition of what was about to come took hold of her. "Did they ever find out who killed him?"

"The cops didn't spend a lot of time on the case." Croft's voice had shifted into that dangerously neutral tone. "My father was just another drunk who got himself killed in an alley. Happens all the time. The authorities have better things to do than try to solve that kind of crime."

Mercy realized dimly that she was digging her nails into her palms. "So you decided to go looking for the killer, didn't you?"

"No one else was going to do it. I thought I hated my father, but after he was killed I couldn't walk away from the fact that he was my father. He'd done his best by me."

"So you did your best by him. You decided to see that justice was done. You went looking for the killer?"

"I found him. It wasn't hard. I just went to the section of town where my father used to hang out and started asking questions. For some reason people talked to me."

"I'll just bet they did."

Croft shook his head. "It wasn't like that. I didn't have to beat the answers out of anyone. There were people on those streets who wanted someone to find the killer. My father wasn't his first victim. They were all potential victims and they knew it. They would have been frightened of cooperating with the cops, but they weren't afraid of a young kid who wanted to know what had happened to his old man. I got the help I needed. And I found the man who had stuck a knife in Dad."

"What happened to the killer?" Mercy wasn't sure she wanted to hear the answer.

Croft gave her a cool, level look. "I didn't kill him."

"Almost but not quite?"

"Not quite. I left him unconscious on the front steps of the police station. I also left enough incriminating evidence in his pockets to tie him to my father's murder and the murders of a couple of other transients."

"Where did you get the evidence?"

Croft shrugged. "He was still carrying around some of the things he'd taken off his victims' bodies. And he had the knife that had been used to kill my father. Not the brightest killer in the world. The cops were more than happy to have three murder cases cleared up without any real effort on their part. They didn't try to look a gift horse in the mouth. They even managed to get a confession out of the guy. Justice, after a fashion, got done."

Mercy didn't flinch from his direct gaze. "A closed Circle."

Croft's mouth twisted slightly. "Yes."

"What happened next, Croft?" Mercy kept her voice steady even though her stomach was tying itself into a knot.

"I learned something about myself during the process of tracking down the bastard who killed my father. Something that I might have been better off not knowing. It scared me."

"Let me guess," Mercy said softly. "I think you found out two things. The first was that you could do it. You actually found the killer and took your vengeance. You were able to do on your own what society couldn't do. The second thing you learned was that you found your new line of work . . . interesting? Is that the right word?"

His eyes never left her face. "Fascinating is the word. And I had an aptitude for it. After I found the man who murdered Dad, I knew that in a sense I had found myself. I had to know more. But there was still the money problem. So I joined the Army, and that's when I realized I really didn't deal well with authority, especially blind, bureaucratic, senseless authority that operates most of the time without reason or logic. But the military gave me training, the kind of training I hungered for."

"And after that?"

"My aptitude didn't go unnoticed," Croft said dryly. "I was invited to go to work for a special unit, but it wasn't long before I knew I wasn't going to make a very good team player. So I left when my hitch was up, took the money I had saved and went looking for some of the names on the list my old instructor had given me. I found a few. I traveled and studied and learned and everything I learned was dangerous in some way, either mentally or emotionally or physically. So I had to learn how to control the things I learned. And I didn't stop there. I put what I learned into practice. There was a market for my skills. An insatiable market."

Mercy smiled in spite of herself. "Don't waste your time trying to frighten me with veiled hints of how dangerous you are, Croft. It won't work. I know you too well."

"You aren't scared of me, are you?" he asked quietly. "Not on any level. I wonder why. You're such a soft, gentle little thing."

"Just because I'm smaller than you and maybe a bit softer in certain areas—although certainly not in the head—that doesn't make me a 'soft, gentle little thing.' I'm not afraid of you because even though you seem to be interested in violence and physically adept at it, you're not crazy. You're not out of control. You've come to terms with yourself and your nature. In some ways you're one of the most civilized men I've ever met. All of us have a streak of wildness in us. Few of us have had to learn to control it and integrate it into our day-to-day lives. But you have. Maybe that's the true definition of being a civilized human being."

Croft closed his eyes and leaned his head back against the wall behind the bed. "Don't romanticize what I am, Mercy."

"I'm not romanticizing you. I'm trying to understand you."

His lashes lifted, revealing a betraying hunger. "Why?"

"I've already given you the answer to that question. I love you."

He sat up in a smooth rush, his expression stark. "Mercy, you don't know what you're saying."

The phone rang shrilly. Mercy reached to answer it. "Of course I know what I'm saying. I'm not a complete idiot."

"Mercy."

She ignored him as she listened to the familiar voice on the other end of the line. "Hi, Dorrie, how's everything going? Any messages yet?"

"Just got one," Dorrie said easily. "Wait a second until I find my note. Here it is. A Mr. Glad called. Is that the person you were expecting to hear from?"

Mr. Glad. Mercy's gaze swung to collide with Croft's. It had to be Gladstone. At that point Mercy realized she hadn't really expected Gladstone to contact them. Obviously an example of wishful thinking. "That's him, Dorrie. What's the message?"

Croft was hovering over the phone as if he wanted to snatch the receiver out of her hand. He gave Mercy a pen and a pad of motel paper. "Get everything down."

Mercy nodded, listening intently.

"Just a short note," Dorrie said. "You're to call him at this number." She rattled it off. "Got it?"

"Got it. Thanks, Dorrie."

"Hey, what's going on? I thought this deal was all settled."

"So did I," Mercy said with a sigh.

"I guess this is what it's like in the big time world of rare book negotiation, huh? Offer and counteroffer and all kinds of maneuvering. It's exciting, isn't it?"

"Yes," Mercy said softly, "it's exciting." She hung up the phone and sat staring at Croft, the note pad clutched in her hand. "He wants us to call."

Croft snapped the note from her hand. "He's still at the estate."

"How can you tell?"

"I checked the number on the phones while we were there. This is it. It's unlisted, naturally, but even people who worry about their numbers getting out still make the mistake of putting them on the phones where any visitor can see them."

"Perhaps Gladstone wasn't all that concerned about his number getting into the wrong hands," Mercy said.

Croft nodded abruptly. "He's been fairly safe tucked away up there in the mountains with only a few handpicked people around him. Probably learned his lesson about the risks of trusting a multitude of not-necessarily devoted followers. I wonder what kind of games he's been playing with that artist colony he runs."

"You think it's a front for something illegal?"

"I think it's a front for something very profitable and very illegal and very rough. Gladstone is still Graves inside. He needs power and money. Lots of it. And he's learned how to get it. He's using those artists for something. The setup is too similar to what he had going down in the Caribbean. The money making end of things probably includes drugs this time around, too, just as it did last time. It's the field Gladstone knows best. At least we know for certain where he is now. And we've forced him to make the first move. That makes him a little more vulnerable." Croft studied the number in his hand. "So he wants us to call, does he?"

"Just like you said."

"Yes." Croft reached for the phone. "Let's not keep the man waiting."

Croft saw the expression on Mercy's tense face as he dialed the number on the note pad. She was scared. Not of him, but of what was going to happen next. She probably had a good hunch about the next logical step in this deadly game. He wished he could quiet her fears but that was impossible now. Things had gone too far to turn back. He hadn't been able to turn back since the day he had seen that ad for Burleigh's *Valley of Secret Jewels*. She seemed to realize that, but it wasn't going to make her any less fearful of the final outcome.

The phone rang once. It was answered by Isobel, her low, husky voice clear and controlled. "Hello."

She knew who was calling, Croft thought. "Let me speak to Gladstone." There was no sense revealing he knew that Gladstone was really Egan Graves. The goal now was to assure Gladstone that Croft was just an opportunistic hustler who had lucked into the biggest deal of his life.

"We've been expecting your call, Mr. Falconer. Just a moment."

So much for being on a seductive first name basis. Croft waited quietly until Gladstone's warm, charming voice came on the line.

"Ah, Mr. Falconer. Why do you wish to cause me all this trouble?"

"We aren't all born rich, Gladstone. Some of us have to take advantage of our opportunities as they arise. I assume you're interested in getting your book back?"

"You assume correctly. I'm a reasonable man. You have a certain figure in mind?"

"I have a large figure in mind."

"I was sure you had. That book is very important to me, Mr. Falconer, as you must have guessed by now. It has great sentimental value."

"That's the first time I've ever heard anyone call pornography sentimental, but to each his own, I guess."

"Just how large is the price tag you've placed on my book?"

"Fifty thousand."

There was a beat of silence from the other end of the line. "You're not bashful, are you, Mr. Falconer?"

"Mercy tells me there aren't many copies of this particular

volume around. I think you took advantage of her in the first set of negotiations."

"And she's empowered you to negotiate this time?" Gladstone asked.

Croft looked at Mercy. "Let's just say she's put everything in my hands."

"Isobel was correct. You and Miss Pennington are, indeed, besotted with each other. How strange. Well, in the meantime, you and I must deal. I can meet your figure, Mr. Falconer. In cash. How soon can you get here with the book?"

"You want me to come back to the estate?"

"Isobel can meet you anywhere you choose with the helicopter."

"No thanks. I prefer to get there under my own power. I'd just as soon not have to depend on Isobel to fly me back out of the mountains after you and I have made our deal. I'll be there at dawn."

There was another pause on Gladstone's end before he asked smoothly, "How far away are you?"

"Far enough."

"You can't get here any sooner?"

"I'm afraid not. It's going to be a long drive. Dawn is the earliest I can make it. Have Isobel take the money down to the first gate at sunrise. I'll meet her there."

"With the book, I presume?"

"All I want is the money, Gladstone. You're welcome to the book. It's not my kind of thing, anyway."

"No, I'm sure it isn't. You undoubtedly prefer a more modern style of such fare."

Croft noted a trace of condescending disgust lacing the man's voice. Gladstone was giving into his private sense of intellectual snobbery, he realized, though he also wondered how anyone could be snobbish about preferences of erotica.

"I don't want to see anyone except Isobel at that gate, Gladstone."

"There's no one left to meet you except Isobel or myself. Lance and Dallas are in the hands of the authorities, as I'm sure you're aware."

"And you're not going to go bail, right?"

"For a couple of thieves who had taken advantage of my generosity?" Gladstone sounded appalled at such an idea. "I wasn't aware they both had criminal records when I hired them. I was very shocked when the sheriff informed me."

"I can imagine. Everyone must be feeling sorry for you. So the cops aren't worried about any possible connection between them and you?"

"The authorities understand that I am merely an innocent, victimized employer. Apparently Dallas and Lance robbed a motel the other night. They gave the sheriff some nonsense about having been sent by me to do it, but the sheriff didn't buy that ridiculous tale for a minute. I'm afraid their past is against them."

"Somehow I'm not surprised."

"The story they gave the sheriff about how they came to be tied up in a ghost town, however, was far more interesting," Gladstone continued thoughtfully. "They claimed they were chasing a burglar down the mountain and that this man vanished in Drifter's Creek. When they stopped to search for him they found nothing but ghosts. They remember very little of the incident. I, of course, informed the sheriff that nothing was missing from my home and that I had to assume Lance and Dallas were involved in another private scheme. I did hint, however, that there might be a third man involved and that there might have been a falling out among thieves. That would explain how my two employees came to be found with such incriminating evidence in their possession."

"So the sheriff is now looking for a third thief?"

"Relax, Falconer, I don't think he's looking very hard. He

assumes the man will have left the area after having abandoned his buddies. The sheriff is pleased to think that trouble has moved out of his neighborhood."

"All neat and tidy."

"I like things neat and tidy, Mr. Falconer."

"So do I," Croft said. "Make sure Isobel is at that gate at dawn." He hung up the phone before Gladstone could respond.

Mercy sat on the bed, waiting for the details. Her hands were clasped tightly in her lap and her eyes were very large in her face. "Well?" she asked bluntly.

"It's all settled as far as Gladstone is concerned. He thinks I'm a petty thief who's willing to turn *Valley* over to him for fifty thousand."

"That's hardly a petty sum."

Croft shrugged. "I had to make the number big enough to convince him I meant business but not so huge that he might suspect I thought the book was really priceless to him. Fifty thousand doesn't sound like a vast sum of money to a man like Gladstone."

"Everything's relative," Mercy agreed with a sigh. "I could open a couple of bookstores with that kind of money."

"Everything is not relative. Some things are absolute."

"I know. Properly prepared tea, honor and vengeance."

"And love."

She ignored that, eyeing him intently. "So now what? I heard you say you're going to meet dizzy Izzy at dawn. It's not going to take you all night to drive back into those mountains. It's a four-hour drive at the most. Believe me, I timed every minute of it last night. If you left now, you could be there by eight o'clock this evening."

"I was planning on getting there around nine. I prefer to work in full dark."

Mercy took a deep breath. "You're not really planning to

meet Isobel in the morning, are you? You're going to try to get into the compound tonight."

"I want this finished by dawn," Croft said. He waited for her to absorb the implications.

"What about Isobel?"

"I don't care about Isobel. It's Gladstone I want."

"You're sure he's Graves?" Mercy pressed quietly.

"I'm sure. Even if he wasn't Graves I would still have to do something about him now."

"Because he sent Dallas and Lance to kill us?"

"Because he probably meant to kill you after I suffered my 'drowning accident' and because he definitely sent Dallas and Lance to kill you after we escaped from the party." Croft got to his feet. Perhaps she didn't understand that the moment Gladstone had ordered Dallas and Lance to get rid of Mercy, he had signed his own death warrant. Even if he hadn't been certain now that Gladstone was Graves, Croft would have had to act. He knew he was no longer going after Gladstone just because of the unfinished business of three years before. There was now a much more immediate, more pressing reason for getting Gladstone.

That reason was Mercy Pennington, who had twice claimed she loved Croft Falconer.

"Croft?" Mercy watched him anxiously.

"I've got an hour before I have to leave, Mercy. I want to meditate. I need to clear my mind."

"Yes, but what about me?"

"You'll be safe here. No one knows where you are."

She jumped up, anger replacing the anxiety in her face. "I'm not talking about my safety. I want to come with you."

That shocked him. "Absolutely not. You've been exposed to far too much danger already because of me. I'm not about to take you with me."

"But Croft, I've been in it this far. I don't want to let you go alone the rest of the way."

He realized she was serious and was amazed she would even consider going along. "Forget it, Mercy. This is what I do best. And I always operate alone."

"You might need help."

"No."

"Damn you, you're always so blasted sure of yourself. So self-contained. You think you can do everything alone, don't you? You don't need anyone—or at least you won't admit you need anyone. One of these days that's going to change, Croft."

It was already changing but he didn't know how to say it.

Later, Croft promised himself. Later he would tell her that she was realigning his whole world along a different axis, finding a connection between the dimension in which he existed and the one in which she lived. There wasn't time to tell her now, and besides, he couldn't fully explain it to himself yet.

"We'll talk when I return, Mercy."

"I want to come with you," she said once more.

He shook his head. "No." He knew from the helpless way she looked at him that she was accepting the inevitable.

"You're so stubborn. So arrogant," she whispered.

"This is the way it has to be, Mercy."

"Oh, shut up and go meditate. I'm going out to get another cup of coffee."

She whirled around and slammed out of the room before he could think of a response.

Croft stared after her for a long moment and then opened the window. He sank down onto the carpet and let the sunlight warm him. The distant sounds of traffic and occasional voices floated in through the open window, but Croft tuned them out. He could tune out almost anything when he was meditating.

But that afternoon he found it difficult to clear his mind of the memory of green eyes that reflected emotions as clearly as a watercolor reflected light. Wonderful, transparent eyes that a man could read like a book.

Mercy had said she loved him and he had looked into her eyes when she had said it. Croft had told himself that she had been under too much stress to know her own thoughts clearly, but he had lied to himself. He knew that as he sat quietly freeing his mind of all extraneous thoughts. Slowly he focused on the point of light within himself and his mind cleared.

He could no longer doubt Mercy. She knew what she was saying. He had seen the knowledge in her eyes.

She loved him.

Croft took that knowledge into himself, learning it completely, turning it over in his mind, examining it the way he would examine a flower or a sunset or the sea at dawn. He wanted to know what it meant to be loved by Mercy. He wanted to know it in every fiber of his being.

He let the knowledge that Mercy loved him flow through him until it filled him, satisfied him and gave him peace of mind.

It was a different kind of peace than the sort he achieved through meditation and the strengthening movements of his physical training, but it was related to that deep calm in some ways. It was more emotionally satisfying, more filling. In some sense it was a more complete kind of peace. It encompassed the other and surpassed it.

Croft realized that he had never known a complete love before in his life. Perhaps that was why he hadn't recognized it or had tried to deny it when he felt it growing between himself and Mercy. He had thought he understood love on an intellectual basis, thought he knew its demands and requirements, but he hadn't really comprehended its power.

But he accepted the truth now. He had no choice.

He was in love with Mercy. As much in love with her as she was with him. It was a combination of passion, friendship, respect, even the exciting, stimulating friction of disagreements and differing interpretations of important concepts.

A complete Circle.

Croft studied the new Circle as it came together in his mind, watched as it coalesced around the point of light that was his focus. It was perfect. Even the parts of it that couldn't be completely understood were part of that perfection. There was no such thing as total knowledge. Some mysteries always remained and he sensed that between a man and a woman those unknown regions were as important as the portions that could be comprehended. He accepted them; accepted the whole. Mercy belonged to him and he belonged to her.

Satisfied at last, Croft went on to another aspect of his meditation. It was time to summon the clearheaded logic and stamina he would need during the next few hours.

Time passed. But when Mercy cautiously opened the door of the room a half hour later, Croft was ready. He turned his head to see her standing hesitantly in the doorway, a white paper sack in her hand.

"I brought you something to eat. And a cup of tea. It's made with a tea bag but I made them boil the water first. Are you finished with your meditating?" She pulled two cups out of her sack and handed one to him while she uncapped the other for herself.

"I'm finished." He got to his feet, feeling serene and yet fully alert. All his senses were awake and aware but they were all under his control. It was the way he always felt before he explored the boundaries of violence and learned anew the thrill of existence.

It was the way he always felt when he made love to Mercy, except that there were times with her when she took him even farther. With her he could actually lose control and still know that he was safe.

Croft uncapped the cup of tea and took a sip. "I love you, Mercy," he said calmly.

Mercy nearly choked on her coffee. "What?" she sputtered, gasping for breath. Her eyes watered with the effort.

Croft slapped her lightly between her shoulders, ignoring her frantic question. "I have to go now. I'll eat the sandwich on the way. I'll be back around dawn tomorrow. Good-bye, Mercy."

He brushed her mouth lightly with his own and then he walked out the door without looking back.

Chapter
EIGHTEEN

He loved her.

As usual, Mercy was torn between wanting to shake Croft and a passionate longing to throw her arms around him. He had managed to frustrate both possibilities by walking out on her directly after making his grand announcement.

It was typical of Croft to do things this way, Mercy fumed as she stalked up and down the small motel room. No passionate proclamation of undying love over a candlelit dinner, no surprise engagement ring, no intense discussion of his emotions and feelings. Just a factual statement before he walked out the door to risk his neck.

It must have happened during his meditation session, Mercy decided.

He had clearly worked something out in that convoluted mind of his, meshed his growing attraction to Mercy into his private world view and completed one of his damn inner Circles. When everything was in place, understood and accepted in that labyrinth loosely termed a male brain, he had presented the finished product calmly, as if it were nothing more or less than a fact of life and the universe.

Then he had left without allowing Mercy any emotional farewells or prolonged pleas to be cautious. She was stuck there while the man she loved and who claimed to love her went off on his lone crusade for truth, justice and the Way of the Circle.

She must be crazy to be in love with him. She barely knew him.

Except that she *did* know him. That was the puzzling part. Somehow, in the few days they had been together, she had come to know him better than she had ever know anyone in her life. The paradox of the matter was that she really knew very few facts about him. The short, bleak history he had given her that afternoon in a rare moment of confidence was the only summary of the details of his life she had gotten, and that summary had made no difference one way or the other in her feelings for him. She would have loved him even if he had chosen never to confide the details of his life.

Her understanding and acceptance of him had happened on another level entirely, one that had little to do with facts or logic. From the first moment she had met him she had been aware of a new and different sense of awareness around him. It was as if he had the power to bring to life something within her that had slumbered, undetected, all these years, a sixth sense that did not have much to do with facts. That preternatural sense of awareness had its own means of bypassing facts and logic.

What good were facts and logic in a situation such as this, anyway? After all, Mercy reminded herself grimly, she had had plenty of facts about her ex-fiance. She had known everything about him from the schools he had attended to the stores in which he preferred to shop for his designer running shoes. She had discussed his career goals with him and his tennis scores. She knew his taste in films and his taste in cars. She had known everything important about Aaron Sanders except the most important thing of all: He couldn't be trusted with a woman's love or with her valuables.

Mercy was willing to stake her entire investment in Pennington's Second Chance on the bet that Aaron Sanders had never spent more than two seconds in his entire life contemplating his own sense of honor or integrity, let alone building a philosophical base on which to ground himself.

That wasn't entirely Aaron's fault, Mercy decided. A person couldn't spend much time contemplating something that didn't exist.

Restlessly she moved across the room and opened her suitcase to take out the copy of *Valley*. It was nerve wracking to know that Croft was going to risk his life because of the stupid book. He had almost gotten himself killed the previous night because of it. They had both nearly been killed.

What was it about the book that made it so important to Erasmus Gladstone?

Mercy took the volume over to the small table by the window and sat down to study it. She had read a great deal of the thing already, and although it certainly made interesting reading, she had a hunch it wasn't Gladstone's kind of erotica. She was convinced now that it wasn't written for men at all. There was too much romance in *Valley*, too much genuine passion, too much emotion to be a man's kind of erotica. It was more sensual than sexual. When all was said and done, Burleigh's *Valley of Secret Jewels* was a love story, not a mechanical treatise on exotic sex. And while it was valuable, it certainly wasn't rare enough or unusual enough to warrant such interest on Gladstone's part.

On the surface, *Valley* simply wasn't worth attempted murder.

The conclusion was obvious. There was something else about the book that made it valuable to Gladstone.

Mercy turned the book over in her hands, examining the

worn leather binding. If there was a secret code imbedded in the text, there was no point in her looking for it. She had trouble getting through the crossword puzzle in the daily paper.

But she did know a few things about old books.

Mercy turned the thick pages slowly, letting her mind toy with possibilities. The beautiful, high quality paper used in the eighteenth century still felt good to the touch and it was still in excellent condition. The scattered handwritten notes that appeared in some of the margins were clearly very old. The ink was faded and the handwriting itself was in a two-hundred-year-old style that was extremely difficult to read. Mercy didn't see any margin notes that looked recent. New margin notes would have lowered the value of the book, but notes that dated from the time the volume was published were another matter altogether. They added an element of interest as far as many collectors were concerned, especially if the notes had been made by an important historical figure.

Outside the motel room window the afternoon was fading rapidly. Mercy wondered where Croft was. He was undoubtedly making excellent time. Without her in the car he would probably be driving the mountain road at a much swifter pace than he had the first time. His excellent reflexes and eyesight would make it easy for him to take chances on the curves that would have sent chills down Mercy's spine. The only limitations would be those of the car itself. Croft would respect those mechanical limits, but he would probably push the Toyota to the edge of its abilities.

Mercy stared thoughtfully out the window for a while, worrying about Croft and resenting her own helplessness. Then she glanced down at *Valley* again. The long rays of afternoon light caught the binding in a particularly revealing way. It was possible to see every crack in the leather, every nuance of detail left by the binder's tools. Whoever had purchased *Valley* had gone to great expense to have the book bound by an expert.

Most books of *Valley*'s era were issued by the publisher in paper covered boards. The purchaser was the one who sent it out to a skilled craftsman to have it bound in leather. Collectors loved to find volumes from the period that were still in their original boards, but the next best find was a book that was in a binding contemporary with the time period in which it was published. *Valley* was such a book. Since it had been privately printed in an extremely limited quantity, it was possible the printer had seen to it that it was bound before it was sold.

Mercy fingered the spine of the book, examining it in the full glare of the afternoon light. It was slightly loose. Perhaps the book had been dropped at some point during its lively past. There was something slightly uneven about the inside edge of the spine, too, as if the leather had been torn or cut and then carefully repaired. The faint mark was a thin line that was only visible in strong light, but it was definitely there. That new extra sense of awareness she seemed to have developed lately told her the mark was not a simple scratch.

Mercy sat very still for a long time, weighing her options. She could assume her imagination was functioning on overtime and forget her wild fancies. Or she could pry apart the leather at the point where it appeared to have once been cut and risk lowering the value of the book by deliberately damaging the already worn binding.

She thought of Croft on his way to Gladstone's and she thought about how convinced he was that *Valley* was crucially important to his quarry. There was something about this book that made it worth a murder or two.

Mercy didn't hesitate any longer. She went to her suitcase and dug out her cosmetic bag. There wasn't much in it, just toothpaste, toothbrush, a comb and brush, a few assorted cosmetics that she usually forgot to use and a small mending kit. She removed the tiny scissors from the mending kit.

It took nerve to insert the point of the scissors into the almost invisible seam in the leather. The book she was assaulting was two hundred years old and worth a great deal of money. One didn't attack such a thing lightly—one did it with unsteady fingers and a lot of ambivalence. The line in the leather might not be a new seam. It might simply be an old mark or a binder's error.

It was a shock when the leather began to separate under the probing of the scissors to reveal that the repair in the leather had been done with glue and was a very modern addition to the old binding. Whoever had attempted to reattach the leather to the spine of the book had done a neat but far from inaccessible job.

Or just perhaps, Mercy thought, whoever had done this had intended to be able to undue his work at some point in the future.

It took long minutes of painstaking work, but eventually the seam separated completely and Mercy found herself looking into a narrow opening between the spine of the book and the binding. She put down the scissors and angled the spine to catch more afternoon light.

There was a piece of paper imprisoned inside the leather.

She had been nervous when she had first cut into the valuable book, but Mercy was trembling with excitement when she withdrew the slip of paper.

It was a very ordinary slip of paper, very modern. It was a piece of writing paper from a common tablet. It had been cut and folded to form a narrow envelope.

When Mercy turned the makeshift envelope upside down and shook it a strip of microfilm fell out onto the table. She sat staring at it for a long time. It didn't take much imagination to figure out that this was what made *Valley of Secret Jewels* so valuable to Erasmus Gladstone. Whatever was on this microfilm probably dated from the days when Gladstone had been known as Egan Graves. It was important enough to Gladstone that he had risked his new identity to reclaim the film.

The phone rang shrilly just as Mercy picked up the strip of film and held it to the light. She jumped a good two inches and promptly dropped the film back onto the table. She nearly tipped over her chair as she grabbed for the phone.

"Hello?"

"Mercy? It's Dorrie. Are you all right? You sound kind of strange."

"I'm all right." Mercy took a breath. This whole mess was getting frighteningly out of hand. Croft would be furious if she called the authorities, but there were times when even Croft had to have help. She suspected this was one of those times. It wouldn't hurt to talk to someone levelheaded like Dorrie. "Dorrie, I'm glad you called. I want to talk to you about something that's happened. I need some help."

"Okay, but first I've got a message for you," Dorrie said easily. "Mr. Glad called again."

Mercy's fingers clenched around the phone. "When?"

"Just a few minutes ago. That's why I'm calling you. He asked me to give you another message."

"Oh, hell."

"What?" Dorrie sounded concerned.

"Never mind. You'd better give me the message." This was going to be awful, Mercy was sure of it. Something was going terribly, terribly wrong. She could feel it in the pit of her stomach.

"Hang on a second while I get my notes. He was very particular that I get the message straight. How's the deal going with him, anyway? He sounds so nice on the phone. I never thought you'd have the nerve to haggle like this with your first big client."

"I've had a lot of inspiration lately. What's the message, Dorrie?"

"Calm down, I've got it right here. He says to tell you that there's been a slight change in plans. Mr. Falconer has arrived early and the two of them have agreed to terms. You're to call him at home as soon as possible."

Mercy went cold. The chills that crawled along her spine were reminiscent of the ones she had experienced the previous night in Drifter's Creek. She sat staring blindly out into the early evening sunlight. It would be dark in another couple of hours. "I'm to call him at home," she repeated.

"That's right. Do you need the number?"

"No," said Mercy. "I've got it. Thanks, Dorrie."

"Mercy, are you sure nothing's wrong?"

Everything was wrong. "I'm sure. Thanks again, Dorrie. I'll talk to you soon."

"I hope you get that deal settled quickly. At this rate you won't have any time for a vacation. Your whole trip will be spent on business."

"It's beginning to look that way. Good-bye, Dorrie."

"Take care and have a good time." Dorrie hung up with a cheery farewell.

Mercy put the receiver back in its cradle and sat staring at it as if it were a snake. Then she glanced at the strip of microfilm.

Mr. Falconer had arrived and he and Mr. Glad had agreed to terms.

It wasn't possible.

Unless one considered the helicopter.

It *was* possible, just barely, that somehow Gladstone and Isobel had intercepted Croft at some point on the road leading up to the estate. The small helicopter was no doubt highly maneuverable. A skilled pilot might be able to set it down on a straight stretch of mountain road.

Isobel was a skilled pilot. Croft had said so himself, and he didn't give praise lightly.

A surprise landing by the helicopter coupled with Gladstone and a gun could have ruined all Croft's carefully set plans. He might even now be a prisoner. Gladstone might be holding him hostage for the microfilm.

It all made a terrifying kind of sense.

There was no point putting off the inevitable. Mercy picked up the phone again and carefully dialed Gladstone's number. Isobel came on the line after the first ring. Her low, throaty voice held smooth satisfaction. It also held a certain degree of strain.

"Miss Pennington. We've been expecting your call."

"Let me speak to Gladstone."

"You will speak to me. I am authorized to deal with this on Erasmus' behalf. Now then, I assume you got our message from your friend, Dorrie?"

"I got it."

"Excellent. Then you know that Mr. Falconer is once again a guest of ours."

Mercy hunched over the phone. "Let me speak to him."

"I'm afraid that's not possible at the moment."

"I'm not doing anything until I speak to him."

"You have my word your lover is alive and well, if not particularly happy."

"Your word isn't worth much."

"I'm sorry you feel that way," Isobel said. "But my word is all you have right now."

"What exactly do you want from me?" Mercy asked cautiously, staring at the strip of film in front of her.

"We want you to join us, of course. Our house party came to a somewhat abrupt end and Erasmus is afraid that we might have made you and Mr. Falconer feel unwelcome. We'd like to make up for that."

"You want me to come back to the estate?"

"I assumed you'd want to under the circumstances. You and Mr. Falconer being so close and all."

They were threatening to kill Croft unless she came back. "It will take me several hours to get there."

"We wouldn't think of asking you to drive all that way," Isobel assured her. "I'll meet you en route. Give me a point where you can be within an hour. That will still give us an hour of daylight to get back here. Choose an isolated place and don't bring anyone along, is that clear? I won't land if I see that you're not alone or if I think you're being followed."

Isobel was going to meet her with the helicopter. Mercy cringed at the thought. Reluctantly she reached out to pull a map toward her. "There's a resort area a few miles from the motel Croft and I stayed in the first night."

"I know it. A little too busy. But there's a meadow five miles east of the motel. Be there within an hour."

"It will take me longer than that. Probably an hour and a half."

"Then you'd better get moving."

"Damn it, it's not that simple. I don't have a car." Mercy realized she was getting angry. It had the therapeutic effect of driving off some of the fear.

"Then you'll have to rent one. You'd better get going, hadn't you? When you reach the meadow park the car out of sight. There's a stand of fir behind a bend in the road. You should be able to conceal the car there."

"I suppose you want me to bring the book with me?" Mercy asked grimly.

There was a pause on the other end of the line. "Most definitely," Isobel finally said with a new note of urgency. "You are to bring us the book. That's the whole point of this little exercise, isn't it?" She hung up the phone in Mercy's ear.

Mercy frowned at the receiver. She could have sworn Isobel sounded almost surprised, as if she hadn't known Mercy had the book. But if Isobel and Gladstone had Croft, they would know by now that he hadn't taken the book with him.

A new horror washed over her as Mercy forced herself to consider the possibilities. If there had been a fight when Isobel and Gladstone had tried to intercept Croft, it was possible Croft had been hurt, or even, God help her, killed. Or they might have assumed he had hidden the book before he was taken prisoner.

In which case Isobel and Gladstone might not know what had happened to the book. That would account for Isobel's surprise at hearing Mercy offer to bring *Valley* with her.

Mercy reached out and picked up *Valley*. Experimentally she closed the book. In that position the fine crack inside the spine was sealed shut again and hidden from view. Isobel and Gladstone had no reason to believe that their secret had been discovered.

The microfilm was the only real bargaining chip in this dangerous game.

If Croft were alive—and for her own sanity Mercy had to believe he was—then all he would need would be an opportunity. It was up to Mercy to provide that opportunity. Once she turned the microfilm over to Gladstone she would have nothing left with which to negotiate.

Somehow she was certain Croft was still alive. She would know if he were dead. The new sense that seemed to have been awakened by his presence in her life would also be dead.

Her mind made up, Mercy set the book down on the table and picked up the film. She needed a hiding place for the dangerous strip of microfilm.

After a few minutes of thought during which she considered and discarded most of the obvious places in the small room, Mercy took a motel envelope out of the desk drawer and addressed it to herself in Ignatius Cove. If she didn't return to Ignatius Cove within a few days, Dorrie would check Mercy's mailbox and see the envelope. Eventually the envelope would be opened by someone, hopefully someone in authority who would know what to do about such a bizarre situation.

Following a few more minutes of consideration, Mercy wrote a carefully worded note listing everything she knew or suspected about Gladstone. If she were making a mistake by going into the lion's den, then this note and the film might conceivably still be used to expand the options for her survival as well as Croft's.

When she was finished, she took it down to the motel lobby, bought a stamp and dropped the envelope into a mailbox. One could only hope that the U.S. mail was still relatively sacrosanct. Then she inquired about renting a car.

After filling out the paperwork on the car, Mercy bought a small bottle of glue at an old-fashioned general store a few blocks from the motel. She spent several precious minutes regluing the tear in the leather spine of *Valley*. When she was done she looked at it critically and decided the quick fix would probably pass inspection as long as someone wasn't looking too thoroughly. The glue dried quickly.

A few minutes later she was on her way to meet Isobel Ascanius in an isolated mountain meadow.

It was unfortunate, Mercy thought, that she really disliked small aircraft. But she was learning that one terror could counter another. Her fears about what might be planned for Croft were more than enough to control her fears about flying in the helicopter.

Mercy heard the relentless chopping sound of the rotor blades within minutes after she parked her car amid the trees as Isobel had stipulated. She got out slowly and watched as Isobel set the helicopter down in the middle of the meadow with absolutely no regard for the wildflowers.

Croft would not have approved.

Clutching *Valley*, Mercy moved toward the idling helicopter. Isobel sat inside, signaling imperiously for Mercy to hurry. The cabin door on the passenger side was open. The blades created a wild, violent wash of air that caught at Mercy's hair as she ducked instinctively and climbed into the cockpit.

"You have the book?" Isobel said loudly, eyeing the packing in Mercy's arm.

Mercy nodded and reached for the seat belt. Her stomach twisted abruptly as Isobel lifted the helicopter back into the air. The meadow fell away beneath Mercy's feet and the peaks of the mountains stood out like teeth against the sunset. It would be so easy for those teeth to snag the small craft and drag it down from the sky.

The trick was to focus on something else, Mercy thought. She tried to remember what Croft had said about meditation. You had to clear your mind, concentrate on a centered, focused image. . . .

"Is Croft all right?" Mercy asked, wrenching her mind away from images of shattered aircraft.

"You will soon see for yourself." Isobel's classical profile was not marred in the least by her reflective sunglasses. They just served to give her an added touch of exotic mystery. Her hair was in a chignon and somehow the khaki jumpsuit she wore seemed to be the height of fashion.

"You'll never get away with this, you know," Mercy called above the noise of the rotor. "I know that probably sounds trite under the circumstances, but it's true."

"Get away with what? The book is ours. We are merely retrieving it."

"You tried to kill us!"

"Nonsense. You both got drunk and went for a joyride down the mountain at midnight. You're lucky you both survived."

"Tell me something, Isobel. Do you like doing this kind of thing for a living?"

"You tell me something, Miss Pennington. Have you ever been so dirt poor that you had to sell your body to a man for the night in order to have enough to eat?"

"No, and I don't believe you've ever been that poor either. There are always alternatives."

"You don't know what you're talking about. You're a sheltered, naive little creature. Well, I have been that poor and I am very determined never to be that poor again. I am determined that no man will ever use me again. I am the one who will use them. One of these days I will be controlling people like Erasmus Gladstone and his kind. I will do whatever I must to achieve my goals."

Mercy heard the conviction in her voice and decided there was nothing more to be said. She sat back in her seat and concentrated on keeping her stomach under control. In the end she had to close her eyes against the images of deep ravines and clawing peaks. Once more she sought for the calm circle of light within herself.

The trip wasn't quite as bad as she had anticipated, but the faint relief she felt on that score was wiped out by her fear of what awaited her at the other end of the trip.

When she opened her eyes twenty minutes later, Mercy saw that Isobel was making her descent into the compound of Gladstone's estate. The sun had set and the last of the twilight was rapidly turning into darkness.

"Inside," Isobel ordered as she shut down the helicopter. "Erasmus is waiting for you."

"Geez, if I'd known that I would have hurried." Mercy slowly unbuckled the belt. She half expected Isobel to snatch *Valley* from her grasp, but the other woman made no move to do so. Instead she walked beside Mercy toward the main entrance of the house. The dogs barked from inside their wire pen.

The door opened as the two women approached. Gladstone stood on the threshold, looking very much as he had the day he had welcomed Mercy and Croft to his luxurious mountain fortress. The difference this time was that he held a gun in his right hand.

"Come in, my dear, I am relieved to see you again. You have given us a great deal of trouble."

Mercy wrinkled her nose and glanced at Isobel, who was silently escorting her toward the door. "Do you really like taking orders from this bozo? You could do better than him, you know. I don't think Gladstone is the world's most reliable employer."

"If you are wise, you will watch your tongue," Isobel advised coolly. "You are nothing but a nuisance in this affair. Now that we have the book, there is not much reason to keep a nuisance around."

Mercy wondered when she should mention that the microfilm was no longer inside the spine of *Valley*. She decided to wait until she saw Croft. Perhaps he would have an idea of how best to play their last ace.

Gladstone saw the book in Mercy's grasp and nodded approvingly at Isobel. "I see you have made up for some of your recent incompetence, Isobel. We now have the book and soon we will have this entire affair under wraps. Here," he handed the gun to Isobel. "You can take care of this. You know how much I dislike weapons. They are your responsibility. Give me the book."

Isobel inclined her head in acknowledgement as she accepted the gun. She held the weapon with the ease of long familiarity as she motioned Mercy inside the house.

Mercy held her breath as she saw Erasmus give *Valley* a cursory glance. He didn't seem concerned with what he saw. Probably because he didn't think she had the brains to have uncovered his secret, Mercy decided grimly.

"You certainly are handy to have around the place, Isobel," Mercy remarked as she stepped into the marble hall.

Gladstone chuckled. "Most useful, except when she makes a mistake as she did last night. Isobel is my bodyguard and my personal servant, Mercy. My safety is her responsibility. She is also in charge of making sure I get what I want. She knows that if she fails in either capacity she will no longer be of any use to me. You made her quite nervous last night, my dear, when you managed to pull your lover out of the swimming pool."

Mercy stopped and turned to stare at Isobel. "What about Dallas and Lance? Just a couple of extra servants?"

"Dallas and Lance reported to me," Isobel answered. "I made certain when I hired them that they could do no lasting damage to Erasmus in the event they screwed up and got picked up by the police. Their records are against them, you see. And we knew things about them that were not on their prison records, things that would have sent them back to jail for life."

"So you kept them under control with blackmail?"

Gladstone smiled. "I also paid them very well. They were reasonably content, I think, until recently."

"You sent them to get *Valley* that night at the motel, didn't you?" Mercy asked.

"When we learned you had brought someone with you Isobel became worried," Gladstone explained genially. "Falconer's presence raised several disturbing questions. She decided to find out what she could about your little surprise by sending Dallas and Lance to the motel to have a look through his room. She also decided that we might as well pick up *Valley* in the process just to make certain some elaborate switch hadn't been executed. If matters were falling apart unexpectedly, we would at least have our hands on the book."

"But you didn't get hold of it."

"Unfortunately we were forced to go back to the original plan, which meant letting both of you into the estate," Gladstone said. "We felt the situation was controllable and we had to get the book. You didn't particularly concern us, of course. We were almost certain you were exactly what you appeared to be, an innocent little bookseller who had lucked into an important find and who wanted nothing more than to make a legitimate deal. We invited you to deliver *Valley* in person because we wanted to make absolutely certain you didn't know the true secrets of the book. We thought we could tell that by having you under our roof for a few days. Genuine naivete and stupidity are not hard to diagnose. But Mr. Falconer was something else. We could learn nothing about him in the short span of time we had available, and that struck us as dangerous."

Mercy swallowed. She must not let her imagination drive her crazy, she told herself. She must stay calm and controlled. "How did you know I'd put *Valley* in the motel safe that night?"

"The night clerk mentioned it when Dallas asked a few questions and offered him a small bribe. The clerk was also obliging enough to tell Dallas where the combination was kept. We chose that motel for you precisely because we knew the clerk had a drinking problem and would be manageable." Isobel regarded Mercy with a gimlet gaze. "Dallas and Lance were instructed to make the robbery look like the work of a thief who was interested in getting everything he could, so they hit a few of the guest rooms as well as the safe. Dallas decided to try your room when they found the safe empty. But you apparently woke up at an inopportune moment."

Gladstone smiled charmingly. "It's unfortunate for both you and Mr. Falconer that you awoke when you did that night. If Dallas and Lance had been successful in retrieving *Valley*, we might have canceled our invitation to you both and sent you away when you arrived at the first gate. As it is . . ." He let the sentence trail off into a small, regretful shrug.

Mercy stared at him. "I don't believe you. You would still have wondered who Croft was and why he was with me."

Isobel smiled. "She's not as stupid or as naive as she looks, Erasmus." She turned to Mercy. "You're quite right. Mr. Falconer was an unknown factor in the equation and we could not afford to ignore him. We would probably have had to arrange an accident for him sooner or later, just to be on the safe side. You might have been luckier."

"I doubt it," Mercy said dryly. Isobel merely smiled. "Are you going to take me to Croft?"

"He will soon be joining you."

Mercy allowed herself to be nudged toward the staircase that led down to the garden room. "Where is he?"

"With any luck we'll all soon find out," Gladstone told her as he followed the two women down the stairs.

Mercy halted at the glass doors, turning to pin Isobel with a savage glance. "He isn't here? You said you'd captured him!"

"We will capture him, Mercy, using you as bait."

Mercy felt ill. Croft was going to be furious. For some reason that was her chief concern at the moment. She pushed it aside and made one last effort. "Why do you need to draw him into a trap? You've got your precious book."

Gladstone nodded. "True, but I am a careful man, Mercy. I do not like to leave any loose ends. And I'm much afraid your Mr. Falconer constitutes a very dangerous loose end. Much more tidy to get rid of him before he can do any more damage."

Mercy was nearly blinded by her own fury. She had been so stupid. Now she had put Croft in danger as well as herself. She reached for the glass door and yanked it open, wanting Isobel to think she was going to make a dash for the cover of the gardens.

Isobel reacted instinctively, stepping toward Mercy in an attempt to grab her. But instead of dashing futilely out into the gardens, Mercy whirled around and startled Isobel by hurling herself toward the other woman.

"Damn you!" Isobel raised her gun hand in a desperate effort to ward off the whirlwind, but Mercy managed to collide with her and knock her to the ground.

There was a brief, savage scramble on the steps. Mercy concentrated her attention on getting hold of the gun. She tried everything she remembered from her short course in self-defense, but in the end it was all useless.

Erasmus Gladstone simply stepped forward and slammed the copy of *Valley* against the side of Mercy's head.

Mercy didn't sink into unconsciousness, but she saw stars for several seconds.

By the time she had recovered from the dazed sensation she was being pushed into Gladstone's rare book vault.

The heavy door closed immediately with a final sounding thud.

A terrible silence and an even more terrible darkness descended instantly.

Chapter
NINETEEN

Croft stood in the shelter of a stand of aspen and watched the helicopter set down inside the Gladstone compound. The last of the twilight was going quickly, but the lights installed around the high walls gave a clear view of what was happening. A bleak anger tightened his gut as he watched Mercy get slowly out of the craft and start toward the front door.

As soon as he had heard the ominous sound of the helicopter returning to the estate, Croft had been prepared for the fact that something had gone very wrong. Now he knew just how wrong. Mercy was Gladstone's prisoner.

From his vantage point on the hillside Croft watched as Gladstone appeared in the doorway. A moment later Isobel, Mercy and Gladstone disappeared inside the house.

"Shit." Croft stared at the empty compound.

It didn't take much of an exercise in logic to figure out that Gladstone planned to use Mercy as bait. Croft decided he could assume Mercy had been told that Croft, himself, was already a captive.

And she had come dashing recklessly to his side, even though it had meant flying in the small copter and facing Gladstone's gun. Croft shook his head, thinking about how much Mercy must love him. She would do just about anything for him, apparently.

Except obey orders. She really did have a thing about doing what he told her to do. When this was all over, he was going to make love to her until she was limp, and then he would read her the riot act on the subject of staying put when he told her to stay put.

Whereupon, Croft decided, she would probably tell him she was not a dog, that she didn't like someone else telling her what was good for her, and that anyone who had as much trouble dealing with authority as Croft did had no right to give her lectures on following orders.

When that argument was done, he would give up trying to reform her and just take her to bed again.

But first he had to get her out of Gladstone's compound and that wasn't going to be easy. Getting in was no problem. He had already figured out how he was going to do that. Getting at Gladstone might be more complicated, but Croft was confident he could handle it. Isobel was a factor, but she could be dealt with if she got in the way.

The problem, Croft realized, was to get Mercy out of there before he went back for Gladstone. Mercy was the number one priority. As long as she was in Gladstone's hands, Croft was also held in check. Apparently Gladstone had figured that out for himself.

Croft continued to stand silently in the trees for a while, thinking. He was distantly aware of the chill in the night air, of the breeze that was making the aspen leaves shiver and of the sounds of the night around him. He let himself meld with his environment, accepting it and being accepted by it. Then he started to think as Gladstone would think.

It was possible Mercy would be locked in an upstairs bedroom. It was also possible she was being held downstairs at gunpoint. But as things stood now, Gladstone and Isobel didn't quite know what to make of Croft. He was a mystery to them, an unknown factor. They wouldn't know when or where to expect him. As far as they knew he might be keeping to the original agreement, in which case they wouldn't see him until dawn.

But they would have to be prepared for the possibility that Croft might try something unexpected, in which case Gladstone and Isobel would want their hands free. They wouldn't want to have to worry about Mercy. She was merely a nuisance to them at this point. People like Gladstone and Isobel frequently made the mistake of not taking people like Mercy seriously. They didn't look beneath the surface. They would keep her alive until they had Croft, but they wouldn't want to be bothered with her until they had achieved their main goal. They would want her out of sight and out of the way.

The vault was the most secure room in the household, a natural and logical choice as a jail cell. It would be much more secure than an upstairs bedroom and much less taxing on the captors than holding a gun on Mercy for several hours. And instinct told Croft the vault was more than it appeared to be at first glance, just like Gladstone/Graves, himself.

Gladstone, Croft decided finally, would probably have stuffed Mercy into the vault and locked the door. Mercy wouldn't have a chance of figuring out how to open the trap from the inside.

Croft turned the logic over in his mind one more time and decided it was sound. The vault was the first place to go looking for his sweet, reckless Mercy. If she wasn't there he would go through the house until he found her.

He continued to stand among the aspens for a long while, letting dark settle in around him until it dominated everything. The lights blazing on the compound walls were the only bright spot in the enveloping shadows, and as far as Croft was concerned, their glow would prove to be only a futile attempt to hold back the night.

He could see twin spots of darkness moving about in the compound now. The Dobermans had been released. The dogs were the least of Croft's worries. He understood them and they responded accordingly.

The easiest way into the compound was over the wall at the back of the house. He would have to avoid the electronic security cameras, but that would be no problem. The discreet monitors were set up to see human beings, not ghosts, he told himself wryly.

The next step was to get to the helicopter and the one remaining vehicle that stood inside the walls. A few minutes with the machines was all he needed. After that he would enter the house.

He took a deep breath of the clear, cold air, letting the energy of it sift through his senses. The darkness was a friend and companion. He was a shadow among shadows. He followed paths that could not be seen by others; moved with a silence that could not be detected by others. All this was natural to him. He was a part of it.

The night was his.

Inside the vault Mercy fought a silent battle within her mind. She had thought at first she would be able to handle the confined sensation, especially after she managed to find the interior light switch. After the utter darkness, the illumination was a blessed relief.

But the relief was short-lived. As time passed it became increasingly difficult to block out the closed-in feeling. Mercy found herself prowling the small room the way a zoo animal paced in its cage. The restless movement only seemed to make things worse, yet she could not stay still.

She studied the locking mechanism for a while, but that was futile and she soon gave up on the project. Croft might have been able to deal with the complicated lock system from the inside, but Mercy was a bookseller, not a locksmith.

Gladstone had said this room was not a trap for him but that it would be for anyone else. Mercy shuddered.

When the brief shudder became a more long lasting shivering sensation, Mercy really began to worry about the state of her mind. It was cool in the vault but not cold. There was nothing wrong with the air, she told herself. Eventually she might need a bathroom, but she would deal with that problem when it cropped up. In the meantime, other than being confined she wasn't in any great discomfort.

The little lecture didn't help very much. Mercy kept prowling her cage and time passed. Isobel appeared once, unlocking the outer door and motioning Mercy silently into the downstairs bathroom. Mercy tried a few sarcastic remarks but her captor ignored them.

When they returned to the vault Isobel made Mercy stand to one side while Gladstone stepped inside the metal room and quickly removed a number of books from the shelves.

"I'll take only the most exquisite volumes," he told Isobel. "The rest can be replaced." He left the vault.

Mercy didn't like the sound of those cryptic words but she didn't say anything. There wasn't anything useful to be said as far as she could see.

When the door was sealed shut again Mercy's shivering began to occur more frequently and lasted for longer periods. As the time passed, the free-form anxiety that was preying on her mind grew to swamping proportions. The worst part of all this was not knowing where Croft was or what was happening to him. Hours passed. She dozed at one point but awoke with a start to find her anxiety worse than ever.

She would have given a great deal for even a small measure of Croft's bottomless well of detached calm.

Throwing herself down into a corner, Mercy hugged her knees and stared straight ahead of her at a shelf of valuable old books. As she had in the helicopter she tried to find an inner point of focus. She needed to get herself under control. Whatever was destined to happen, she would be able to handle it better if she could find some strength and serenity. She needed to find the kind of calm Croft could find when he meditated.

Surely it couldn't be that hard.

A few more minutes passed. Mercy was not aware of any great tranquilizing sense of serenity descending upon her, but her mind, for some reason known only to itself, began to play with stray thoughts.

Gladstone's words hounded her. The vault was a trap for others but not for him. What was it Croft had said? Something about Gladstone always leaving an escape route for himself.

The vault locked on the inside. The only logical reason for such a bizarre arrangement was that Gladstone had constructed it with the idea that someday he, himself, might be in there.

And if he had planned for the eventuality of having to lock himself in he would most certainly have provided a way out.

Mercy took a deep breath and got to her feet. With no idea at all of what she was searching for, she started systematically going through the books on the shelves. Carefully she pulled each one off and stacked it on the floor.

She decided to start with the section of shelves Gladstone had not had an opportunity to show her on her previous trip into the vault.

Once or twice the book lover within her paused in wonder. She studied the elegant Latin on one title page and decided she was looking at a work by Thomas Aquinas. Mercy was awed by the precious book in her hand until common sense reminded her the volume was not going to do her much good in her present situation.

It was when she bent down to carefully place the volume beside the others on the floor that she lost her balance slightly and had to reach out to steady herself. She grabbed the upright support on the section of shelving and was startled when it moved a fraction of an inch.

Mercy released it instantly and stepped back. Then, tentatively she tried to move the upright again. This time nothing happened.

Maybe she was starting to hallucinate.

Mercy was giving serious consideration to that possibility when the vault door opened without any warning. The next instant the lights inside the small room were doused with a flick of the switch. Mercy whirled around, biting back a scream, and found herself confronting a solitary dark shadow.

"Croft?"

"Hush," he said in the softest of whispers, "not a sound, Mercy."

She went toward him instantly, a vast relief welling up inside her. There were a thousand things she wanted to say, most of them variations on the theme of how glad she was to see him, but she obeyed his instructions and kept silent.

He took her hand and turned to lead her out of the vault room.

They got three paces before the lights went on all around them. Isobel stood in the doorway that opened onto the garden room, the gun in her hand pointed not at Croft, but at Mercy.

"Did you think I would depend only on the electronics?

Not a chance. Not when it comes to a man like you, Mr.
Falconer. I've been waiting for you. Don't move or I'll kill
your sweet Miss Pennington."

The warning came too late. Croft was already moving. It
happened so fast Mercy didn't have time to think. She found
herself spun around and shoved over the threshold into the
vault. Croft was throwing himself in behind her, yanking the
door closed behind him.

The heavy steel door clanged shut just as the sound of the
gun exploded in the outer room. Croft found the light switch
and bent quickly over the inside locking mechanism. "Isobel
is going to have to learn that if she wants to make a success
of herself in this line of work, she's going to have to shoot
first and brag later."

"What are you doing?" Mercy demanded.

"Locking us in and Isobel out." He pushed against a bar
and when it didn't give, he pushed a little harder. The metal
bolt moved ponderously into position.

"I hate to point this out, but we're trapped in here."
Mercy rubbed her shoulder. It was bruised from where she
had hit a bookshelf when Croft had tossed her back into the
vault. She decided this was not the time to complain about
that point. She had another, more serious complaint to
lodge. "Croft, you shouldn't have taken the risk of trying to
rescue me. Now we're both stuck inside this damn vault."

He turned around to face her, his gaze hooded and enigmatic. "Are you all right?"

She winced at the neutral tone of his voice. She hated it
when he talked in that remote, detached manner. "I'm okay.
I'm sorry, Croft."

"What happened?" No accusations, no anger, just curiosity, as if he were a stranger inquiring about how she came to
be there.

Croft was working, Mercy realized. When he was working that was the way he was. It was silly and dangerous to expect any sign of emotion from him at this stage of events.

"I got a message from Gladstone and Isobel through Dorrie," Mercy explained quickly. "The implication was that you'd been captured and were being held until I brought the book. Like an idiot, I took the threat at face value and came running."

"How did they know you still had the book?"

Mercy frowned. "I don't know. They hadn't got hold of you, so they couldn't possibly have known . . . I guess it was my fault. When they said they had you I just assumed they knew you hadn't brought the book. So I, uh, offered to trade it for you."

"They wanted to get you here so they could use you to get their hands on me."

"Yes. I figured that out on my own eventually."

"Then they planned to kill us both. Gladstone learned last time not to leave any loose ends."

"That's one of the things I admire about you, Croft. You don't mince words in the crunch."

"Not much point."

"I guess not." She watched him, wishing she could throw herself into his arms but sensing this wasn't the moment. "What now?"

"Now we wait. It will be easy enough for us to open the vault but we can't risk it until we know Isobel has gotten tired of sitting out front with her Smith & Wesson."

"Well, if we're just going to stand around and chat for a while, there's something I want to show you." Mercy put a hand on the shelf upright that had moved earlier. She told herself she would be just as cool and professional about this as he was. "I don't know if it's important, but it's a little unusual and if this doesn't work, I've got something else to tell you. Something about *Valley*. You'll never guess—"

"Mr. Falconer. You have accepted my hospitality for the

last time." Erasmus Gladstone's disembodied voice blared into the small room through a tiny speaker in the ceiling.

Mercy and Croft both looked up at the small grill. Mercy started to say something, but Croft silenced her by the simple expedient of putting his hand over her mouth. When her questioning eyes met his over the edge of his palm he silently shook his head. She nodded her understanding and he dropped his hand.

"I know you can hear me, Falconer. I also know you think you are at least temporarily safe from Isobel's gun. But there was never any intention of killing you with a bullet. Even our local sheriff might feel obliged to investigate thoroughly if you and Miss Pennington were found to have died from bullet wounds inside the vault. Fire is so much cleaner, don't you think? I've had some experience with fire."

Mercy's eyes widened as she stared at Croft. He glanced at her and then answered Gladstone.

"Apparently fire wasn't clean enough last time, Graves. I found you again, didn't I?"

"Ah. So you do indeed know who I am. I was afraid of that." There was a wealth of sad satisfaction in Gladstone's voice. "While I waited for you this evening I gave a great deal of thought to that unfortunate incident on the island. And I had come to the probable conclusion that you might have been involved in that episode. Was it you? If so, you destroyed several million dollars' worth of free enterprise three years ago. I still don't understand how you did it. My men reported no sign of an assault force, no evidence of high speed government chase boats, no helicopters or planes. It would have been impossible for any sizable group to have landed on my island and escape detection."

"It's dangerous to think in terms of impossibilities," Croft said toward the intercom. He motioned to Mercy and mouthed the words, a question about what she was going to show him.

"You're wrong, Falconer. I think in such terms all the time. I also think about possibilities. And I have analyzed what might have happened that night in the Caribbean. A large group could not have infiltrated my estate. Not without giving themselves away long before they got inside the walls. But it is just barely conceivable that one man might have gotten inside. You were that one man, weren't you?"

Mercy pointed to the shelf upright and soundlessly explained that it moved. She took hold of it and tried to demonstrate. The upright stayed rigidly in place.

"Falconer?" Gladstone's voice rang imperiously from the intercom grill. "You were the man who ruined everything for me three years ago, weren't you? I want to know for certain. I do not like loose ends."

"Neither do I." Croft ignored Gladstone's voice and concentrated on examining the shelving support. "Which way did it move?" he asked softly.

"Left. I stumbled and grabbed for it and it just sort of shifted a bit." Mercy leaned forward and tried to wriggle the metal upright. "Gladstone told me once that this vault would be a trap for others but not for him. And you said he'd always have an escape route. So I started looking for one. It wasn't like I had a whole lot else to do during the past few hours."

Croft nodded. "Logical. After the close call on the island, he'd want to make certain he had his new escape routes well planned. There's a reason he made it possible to lock this vault from the inside."

"Falconer! Answer me, damn you." Gladstone's voice rose a notch.

"He's getting upset," Croft remarked, not bothering to lower his voice this time.

"He obviously has severe emotional problems," Mercy said in a normal tone, sensing it would infuriate Gladstone to be discussed in clinical terms. "Maybe that's true of all really evil men. They're emotionally sick."

"No," Croft said with absolute certainty. "Gladstone knows what he's doing. He's made conscious choices all the way down the line. That's why he can't be forgiven or forgotten. He has to be destroyed."

Gladstone's voice roared through the grill. "You will both be dead soon, you know that, don't you? Locking yourselves in the vault won't do you any good."

Croft stroked the upright as if it were a long-stemmed chrysanthemum. His fingertips moved delicately over the surface from top to bottom, probing, prodding and pushing with light pressure. When he reached the bottom section something gave slightly. "I need a little time to figure this out," he muttered quietly. "We'll have to keep him talking."

Mercy nodded, reaching down to lift some of the valuable books off the shelf so Croft would have more room to work.

"You will answer me when I speak to you, Falconer," Gladstone thundered.

"What makes you think you'll get away free and clear this time?" Croft asked Gladstone carelessly.

"Last time the fire was an unexpected catastrophe," Gladstone said eagerly. "But I learned from it. I leaned how effective it was. Everyone thought I died in that fire, didn't they, Falconer? Even you. I almost did die. Anyone else in that situation would have. But I'm not anyone else. I always take the precaution of ensuring myself an escape route. In this case it was old and dangerous and nearly became a death trap for me. I had to go through a wall of flames to reach that island tunnel and when I got there it was already filling with smoke. But I survived and I learned from that, too. You can't begin to guess how much plastic surgery was required at a discreet private clinic in Switzerland before I could show my hands and face in public. But it was worth it, because when I did, no one recognized me. I realized then that there was nothing to stop me from starting over. There was, after all, a nice nest egg waiting for me in my Swiss bank account. I do not leave such things to chance."

"How many lives did you consign to oblivion to get that nest egg, Gladstone?" Croft changed his grip slightly on the metal upright and pushed more firmly against it.

"One must work with the material at hand," Gladstone responded. "The beauty of it is that there is always so much raw material available to a man who understands that most people in this world actually prefer to be told what to do. They want all the decisions made by someone else. They crave surrender and need an authority figure. So few people really like to think for themselves, Falconer, have you ever noticed?"

"I've noticed." The upright began to slide to one side.

"Offer such people a new religion, a cult, a sense of being special and apart and elevated from the normal run of humanity and they flock to you begging for direction."

Mercy watched Croft as she asked, "Was your private artist colony supposed to be the start of another source of slave labor for you, Gladstone? I've always thought artists were a fairly independent crowd. What made you think you could manipulate them?"

"You are very astute, Miss Pennington. More so than I would have assumed at this point. You're quite right. My artist colony was to be the start of a very useful power base. I made the mistake of having my followers too close to me last time. Ultimately that was a weakness. It enabled one lone man to invade my sanctuary. He was able to use the sheer numbers of people around me as camouflage. This time I deliberately ensured that my naive assistants, as I call them, were kept at a distance. They knew nothing of their real purpose. They had no idea of how useful they were to me. They assumed they were simply transporting their art supplies and luggage to various points around the country and the world. As for controlling them, well, artists may be an independent lot, but they have their weak points, just like everyone else. You saw them and talked to them the other night. They see me as their patron. I fund their creative efforts and most of all I make them feel special, unique, the chosen few standing at the leading edge of the art world."

"What were you getting in return?" Croft asked as he edged the metal upright several inches to one side. There was a faint clicking sound from behind the bookshelf. He shot a quick glance at Mercy who was crouched beside him.

"I had a rather interesting project developing, Falconer. A project that will now have to be temporarily terminated because of your interference. Thanks to my forethought this time around, however, it can soon be restarted in another location. It involved sending my proteges all over the world in search of artistic inspiration. They loved the travel, of course. It was a tremendous creative influence on them. And here and there in their travels they would make small side trips to see acquaintances of mine, fellow art patrons. Such side trips were favors to me. Paintings were often exchanged within this worldwide community of people who were involved with art."

"What were these traveling artists really transporting for you, Gladstone?" Croft took his hand away from the metal shelving and shook his head firmly at Mercy when she impatiently started to push against it. He lowered his voice to a whisper and said, "Not yet. If we open his escape hatch now Gladstone might get a signal telling him the security's been breached. Wait."

Mercy stifled a groan but obeyed.

"What do you think my artist friends were doing?" Gladstone sounded genially amused. "Take a guess, Falconer."

"Your connections in the Caribbean were drug related. It's your field of expertise. You might have changed your face and your name and the kind of books you collect, but there's no reason to think you've changed your way of doing business. You were a major link in the cocaine trade down in the Caribbean. Is that still your area of interest?"

"You seem to know me very well, Falconer. How can that be? Where did you learn so much about me?"

"I spent a lot of time researching you three years ago."

"I'm flattered. So, it was indeed you on the island that night."

"It was me." Croft leaned back against the wall of the vault, his arms folded across his chest. He looked bored but patient now, as if all he had to do was wait and everything would be settled to his satisfaction. "So was it drugs again this time, Graves?"

"Yes, Falconer. Drugs. Nothing so crass or commercial as heroin or cocaine, however. Those trades are already being monopolized by others and it would have been difficult to break in again without revealing my former identity. No, this time I was carving out a unique niche for myself in the more progressive drug market."

"The designer drug business. Wide open territory for new entrepreneurs. Was the stuff you used on me the other night an example of one of your new products?"

"Interesting stuff, wasn't it? It needs refining, but it's almost ready. Should be very popular with those who want to get very drunk without paying the price of a hangover the next day. When we used it on you we wanted you to become so drunk that you passed out when you fell into the pool."

"Making my death appear accidental."

"Precisely. The wonderful thing about these so-called designer drugs, as the media has labeled them, is that they're pure laboratory creations. One does not require land for growing the basic product or vast armies of peasants for harvesting. They are the creations of technicians working with the best lab equipment. They are also infinitely variable. The molecular structure of a particular creation can be altered readily and presto, a whole new product is created. That flexibility makes it almost impossible for the authorities to track down the source. As soon as they've identified one drug it disappears from the market and another takes its place. They can't even write laws fast enough to make the new product illegal."

Mercy stirred restlessly, wishing Gladstone would finish his gloating confrontation. She began prowling the vault again until she saw Croft eying her with faint disapproval.

"I heard some of my followers claiming to have seen a specter that night of the fire," Gladstone went on thoughtfully. "Several panicked, you know. Many of them ran into the flames in a stupid attempt to rescue me or die with me. Such fools. Most of them were so far gone on drugs and hysteria they didn't know what they were doing. But I heard them shouting about a figure who kept appearing and disappearing in the shadows. They said you signaled them to join you."

"Some of them did join me," Croft said.

"What did you do with them?"

"I sent them home."

"How noble and generous. Were you well paid for your work that night, Falconer? Just a businessman's curiosity, you understand. I find myself wondering what sort of compensation a man in your unusual profession receives. It has just occurred to me that I will need a new chief of security after tonight. Miss Ascanius has not proven very useful in the final analysis. I should have known better than to rely on a beautiful woman, but I was initially impressed by her array of talents. She had acquired a great many skills, you see, in an effort to prove herself something more than just a lovely face. But in the end I'm afraid that was all she was. A pretty face. I shall now have to look elsewhere."

"Believe me, Gladstone, you couldn't afford me."

"I was afraid you might take that attitude. Well, it was just a thought. One last question or two, Mr. Falconer, and then I really must be going. How did you find me this time?"

Croft didn't respond.

Mercy remembered the microfilm she had mailed to herself and started to mention it to Croft in a whisper, but Gladstone was speaking again.

"It was the book, wasn't it? Not many people could have traced me with only that damned book as a lead. Most people wouldn't have bothered to try because most people assumed I was dead. After three years who would have thought anyone would have noticed that book's reappearance? Or worried about the buyer who wanted to obtain it? I was sure it was safe to go after it. So very sure, and I wanted it badly."

"Why?" Croft asked quietly. "What's in that book that made you risk exposing your new identity?"

"The key to a great deal of power, Mr. Falconer. Without it, I would have had to spend far more money and time acquiring that power. Now I will have a shortcut. I find I can never get quite enough power. Isn't that strange? I have no trouble moderating my eating habits, drinking habits or my sexual needs. But when it comes to power I seem to be endlessly thirsty. Now that I have *Valley* back in my possession, I shall be able to try to satisfy that thirst."

"How did *Valley* escape the flames that night, Graves?"

"Believe me, I have given the matter a great deal of thought. I certainly had no time to get it from the library. I had my hands full saving my own neck. I imagine that one of my followers was not, after all, quite as naively enthralled with me as I had assumed. It must have been someone close to me, someone who suspected the importance of that particular book."

"You can't trust anyone these days, can you?" Croft murmured.

"Unfortunately, one must always have assistants when one

conducts business on a vast scale. One such individual must have kept his or her head long enough to grab *Valley* from the library the night everything fell apart on the island. He escaped with it. But once he had the book, he apparently could not figure out its secret and eventually it got sold. Ultimately it wound up in a trunk full of bargain books. Probably sold for a fraction of its value. And then Miss Pennington found it and advertised it. An amusing trick of fate, eh, Falconer?"

"There are no tricks of fate, only patterns that eventually form complete Circles."

"You are an interesting man, Falconer. I would like to have spent more time discussing your unique brand of philosophy. But I don't have that luxury. I believe enough time has been spent on this little question and answer session. I must be going. I trust the two of you will enjoy your lingering demise within the vault. It will take a bit longer that way, of course. The air conditioning system will filter out some of the smoke for a while before it is overwhelmed. But if you get impatient to get it over with more quickly, feel free to open the vault door and step outside."

"Where you or Isobel can put bullets in our brains?" Croft asked.

Gladstone chuckled, that rich, charming, charismatic laugh that never failed to captivate. "I've told you, Falconer, no bullets. No, I'm going to use the method you demonstrated so ably three years ago. See how much you enjoy being caught in the middle of a firestorm. It is a rare thrill, believe me. A man who has apparently made a career of living on the edge, as you have, might find it an interesting way to conclude that career."

"You're going to set fire to this place just to get rid of us?" Croft demanded. "Seems a little extreme."

"Not really. Not when you consider the implications. Last time you were working for someone, Falconer. You would have had no reason to come after me otherwise. You are, in effect, a mercenary. I have no option but to assume you are again working for someone. The government, perhaps. This is undoubtedly just another assignment for you. Getting rid of you will not get rid of whoever sent you. I must assume and plan for the worst possible case. I have done so. I must destroy everything once more in order to convince whoever sent you that the trail has once again come to a dead end. While we waited for your arrival tonight, Isobel and I packed some of my more valuable treasures. And I still have my bank account in Switzerland, of course. My labs around the world are still functioning and will go into a holding pattern until I contact them once more in a new guise. This time I am prepared for catastrophe, Falconer. I learned that from you."

Then there was silence. Croft watched the intercom closely for a minute as if he could detect Gladstone's presence or lack of it outside the vault. A few shuffling movements and a scratching noise came through the grill. Then there was a dull thud. After that there was more silence.

"I think he's gone," Croft said, moving away from the wall.

"What did he mean about the firestorm?" Mercy stopped her pacing and walked over to the movable shelf.

"He's probably got some system rigged up to totally destroy this place. He won't want to leave any evidence at all this time around."

"What was that awful thud we just heard?" Mercy asked anxiously.

A muffled explosion outside the vault prevented further inquiries. She spun around, staring at the solidly shut door. There was a second, smaller explosion seconds later. Then silence. "Croft, let's see if that shelving really is an exit. Now. Please."

He nodded and set his hand to the section of shelving.

Mercy glanced once more at the vault door. "Croft?"

"Hmm?" He was working quickly now.

"I think I just realized what that thud might have been."

"I was afraid of that," Croft muttered.

"It was Isobel, wasn't it?"

"Tell yourself it was just Graves being clumsy," Croft advised.

"We've got to see if she's out there," Mercy said urgently.

"Are you nuts? It sounds like World War III is starting out there."

"But, Croft—"

"Oh, hell. And here I was thinking we were on a roll." But Croft had risen and was already unbolting the vault. "Nothing's gone right in this operation so far, why should it get any better now?" Cautiously he pushed open the vault door. "One quick look and that's all."

A blast of heat and long banners of smoke were waiting on the other side of the vault. The tropical garden was a wall of flame. Mercy stared out through the narrow crack in the doorway.

"My God," she whispered in awe.

"Gladstone is a thorough man." Croft started to pull the heavy door shut again.

"Wait," Mercy yelped. "There she is on the floor. It's Isobel. I can see her."

Croft followed Mercy's gaze. "He said she hadn't proven especially useful. I'm inclined to agree."

"Wait, she might still be alive. We've got to check. It will only take a second. She's lying right outside the door." Mercy was trying to push past him.

"Mercy, we don't have time for doing Isobel any favors. She's probably dead."

"He wouldn't have shot her. He said no bullets, remember? He probably just knocked her out or something.

The thud we heard was her body falling. Open the door." Mercy shoved hard against the steel panel.

Croft hesitated briefly and then swore and opened the door a few inches. The heat was getting intense but Mercy knew it was the smoke that was most dangerous at this stage. She held the hem of her shirt over her nose and took one step outside the vault. She grabbed Isobel's leg and started to tug. Then Croft was beside her, effortlessly yanking the unconscious woman into the vault.

As soon as Isobel was inside, Croft slammed the door shut and quickly bent over Isobel. Mercy crouched beside him.

"Is she alive?" Mercy demanded.

"She's alive."

"Then we'll have to take her with us."

Croft sighed. "I know." He got to his feet. "Let's see what's on the other side of that shelving."

He slid the metal upright to one side. There was an oiled, mechanical sound behind the shelving and suddenly half the wall swung silently inward. A yawning black tunnel stretched out in front of them. Cold but clean smelling air was filtering through the tunnel into the vault.

"We won't be able to see a thing," Mercy said quietly. "Even your night vision can't be this good."

Croft went down on one knee beside Isobel and quickly searched the pockets of her jumpsuit. "Luckily for us, Isobel is ever the prepared pilot. She's got a small flashlight on her."

Isobel groaned at that moment and coughed. Croft scooped her up and tossed her over his shoulder.

"I'll carry her and go first. Stay right behind me, Mercy."

"Believe me, I'm not going to be dragging my feet."

"Good."

"Remind me to tell you about the microfilm when we get out of here."

"What microfilm?" He aimed the flashlight down the long, rocky tunnel.

At least there was something he hadn't already figured out, Mercy thought. "Croft, you don't know what a lift it gives me to catch you off balance occasionally."

"What do you mean occasionally? You seem to do it on a regular basis."

"I only do it for your own good," Mercy explained with deep sincerity.

Chapter
TWENTY

The trip through the upward sloping tunnel was uneventful. He had guessed right, Croft decided as he emerged on a hillside overlooking the estate. Gladstone had provided himself with a reliable escape route. There was always a certain satisfaction when the logical analysis of an opponent's actions proved correct.

The darkness that was waiting outside the tunnel was alive with the leaping flames of fire that were consuming Gladstone's mansion. The roar of the blaze filled the night.

"Good God," Mercy breathed as she emerged beside him and stood gazing down at the inferno that was destroying the house. "I can't believe we were trapped in there just a few minutes ago. How did the fire get so big so fast?"

Croft dumped Isobel carelessly down onto the ground. "He must have used explosives to start it. Did a good job of setting them, too. There won't be anything left in another few hours."

"The dogs," Mercy whispered, suddenly remembering the animals.

"I set them free hours ago."

Isobel stirred and opened her eyes. She coughed wretchedly, trying to clear her lungs of the smoke she had inhaled after Gladstone had left her to die. "I'm the one who did a good job setting the explosives."

Croft glanced at her. "Gladstone has a nice way of showing his appreciation."

Her dark eyes blazed with a bitter fury. "That bastard. He blamed it all on me. He was the one who insisted on getting the book back. If he hadn't been so eager to get hold of it, you would never have found us."

"Don't count on it." The sound of helicopter rotor blades whipping into life brought Croft's attention back to the scene below.

"He's getting away." Mercy was incensed. "He can't do that. We can't let him escape now. Not after everything we've been through because of him."

"He's not going anywhere," Croft said softly.

Isobel raised herself up on one elbow to stare down into the compound. "So that's why he insisted on having me give him flying lessons several months ago. He said it was for safety reasons. I should have known he didn't care about anyone's safety except his own."

"A typical drug trade employer," Croft remarked. "The attitude goes with the territory. Everything and everyone is expendable."

"He has the lives of a cat," Isobel whispered angrily. "He told me once he always survives. He was right."

"Not this time," Croft said quietly. He looked at Mercy. "Stay here with Isobel."

She looked up at him anxiously. "Where are you going?" Even as she asked the question Croft saw the realization dawn in her eyes. "No, wait, Croft. He'll be armed. You can't stop him alone. We'll find him again. He won't be able to hide from you."

He touched her dirt smudged cheek. "He's not going to get away. I'm going to finish it this time. Understand?"

She closed her eyes. When she opened them again her gaze was as clear as ever. "Yes."

"I love you, Mercy."

"I love you. Be careful."

"I will." He turned and moved quickly down the incline. The helicopter was just starting to lift off the ground. Gladstone hadn't seen Croft yet. He was concentrating on his flying.

Croft reached the compound wall and swung himself up onto the top of the stone barricade just as the copter rose a couple of feet, shuddered and suddenly settled back down onto the landing pad.

Gladstone must have just taken a look at the fuel gage and realized there was almost nothing left in the tank, Croft thought in satisfaction. Gladstone would know now that his first escape route had been cut off.

In that moment Gladstone looked through the glass bubble that surrounded him and saw Croft hunkering casually on the wall. The glare of the flames from the house revealed Falconer, who smiled like a dark ghost in silent, predatory anticipation.

Shock and stunned fury turned Gladstone's patrician face into a mask of hatred and fear. Croft dropped lightly down from the top of the wall. He broke into a run, heading for the crippled helicopter.

Gladstone scrambled frantically around inside the cockpit as the rotors whined to a halt. Then he found what he was seeking. He leaped out of the confines of the helicopter clutching a small pistol in both hands. The paper wrapped package containing *Valley* fell to the ground at his feet. He ignored it as he brought the nose of the gun up, aiming at Croft.

But it was too late. Croft was already too close. He put out a hand in an almost casual movement that was so fast Gladstone didn't have time to register it. The weapon went flying into the darkness.

"You goddamn bastard," Gladstone screamed. Instinctively he stepped back out of range. "Stay away from me, you son of a bitch. Stay away, damn it! What are you? Some kind of ghost? You're supposed to be dead."

The leaping flames of the fire were reflected in Croft's eyes as he moved toward his victim. He said nothing, closing in on Gladstone with a slow, relentless tread that had a temporarily mesmerizing effect on Gladstone. It was obvious Croft was in no hurry to finish this. This time he would be certain.

From her vantage point on the hillside, Mercy had a clear view of the action. The moment Gladstone had leaped from the helicopter with a gun in his hand she had instinctively started forward. But a broken cry from Isobel jerked her attention back to the other woman.

"It can't end like this," Isobel screamed. "I won't let it!" She was pelting forward down the hill, racing past Mercy and heading for the gate in the wall.

Mercy flew after her. She dashed through the gate a few steps behind Isobel and realized the woman was heading for the helicopter. Against the backdrop of roaring flames Croft and Gladstone were still playing out the deadly game of predator and prey. Both men were oblivious to the women.

Isobel reached into the helicopter and fumbled beneath the seat. Breathing quickly, her muscles propelled by a surge of adrenaline, Mercy reached the machine just in time to see Isobel scrambling back out of the cockpit with a gun in one hand. She had apparently kept it stashed under the pilot's seat.

Mercy's foot struck an object on the ground and she stumbled. As she caught herself she saw the package containing *Valley*. She knew that shape and size. She also remembered the weight of the book. Without stopping to think, aware only of the fact that she needed a weapon to counter Isobel's gun, Mercy reached down and grabbed the heavy package.

"I'll kill him," Isobel was yelling. "I'll kill both of them." She was ignoring Mercy, steadying herself for a shot at one of the two men who were moving slowly toward the wall of fire.

In that moment Mercy couldn't tell if Isobel was aiming at Gladstone or Croft. She couldn't take the chance that it might be Croft.

Mercy swung the book in a violent arc that connected with Isobel's gun arm.

Isobel yelled and the gun fell to the concrete pad. Mercy leaped for it.

"You little bitch!" Isobel was holding her injured arm, her fury and pain clearly revealed in the light of the fire. "I'll kill you. I'll kill—"

Gladstone's scream of rage and terror interrupted the threat, paralyzing both women for an instant. Both Mercy and Isobel swung around just in time to see Gladstone trapped between the fire and Croft. Croft was deliberately closing the gap, giving his victim a hellish choice of fates.

How could either man stand the heat of the flames? Mercy wondered. They were both so close to the fire. She kept the gun clutched tightly in her hand as she watched the awful ritual played out to its final conclusion.

Gladstone was screaming what sounded like gibberish as Croft closed in. But just as Croft was gliding into the final step that would bring Gladstone within reach, his victim succumbed to the hysterical panic that was obviously clawing at him.

"No! No, I won't let you do it. I won't let you do this to

me. You and all the others are trash. Stupid, blundering trash. You're not worthy ... There's always a way out. There must be a way out. . . ."

Gladstone turned and ran straight into the flames. Something heavy fell from the roof, an object that was alive with fire. It struck Gladstone just as he crossed the threshold of his once proud home.

Mercy saw Croft start to dart forward. "Croft, no! He's dead. You can't touch him now. It's over." She ran toward him, fearful that his need for vengeance and certainty would carry him forward into the flames.

Croft swung around at the sound of Mercy's voice as if halted by an invisible chain. He stared at her for an instant as she raced toward him. His body was silhouetted by the lethal glare and the heat was washing over him. Then something flickered in his gaze, an expression of longing and unutterable need.

"Mercy!"

"It's over, Croft. It's over." She threw herself into his arms and he caught her close in a savage embrace.

"I know," he whispered hoarsely. "I know." He led her quickly away from the intense heat.

Together they ran back toward the helicopter. Mercy glanced around in amazement.

"Isobel's gone!" she shouted.

"No loss. Let's get out of this compound."

Croft led her through the gate and back up the hillside. There in the cool darkness Croft stood watching for a while, fulfilling his need to be sure this time.

After a moment Mercy asked quietly, "What went wrong with the helicopter?"

"I drained the gas tanks last night before I entered the house. The Jeep doesn't work, either. I didn't want him to have any exits this time."

Mercy touched his hand. "Is it over now?"

He knew what she meant. "It's over. This time they'll find his body in the flames. This time I'll be sure. I saw him go down. He's dead." He paused and then he said quietly, "I think it's time."

"Time for what?"

"To call the authorities. That's what you've wanted to do all along, isn't it?"

"Finally! Shall we start with the sheriff?"

"I was thinking about the nearest fire station. There's so much cleared land around the compound that with any luck that blaze probably won't be able to spread very far. But there's no sense taking chances."

Mercy stared at him in disbelief. "No sense taking chances? It's a little late to start thinking about that, isn't it? But then, that's one of the things I've always admired about you, Croft. Your sense of timing."

But she was reaching out to catch hold of his hand, threading her fingers securely through his. Croft felt the reassuring energy of her love pouring into him and he drank it into all his senses. It revitalized him, nourished him, comforted him. He needed her, he realized, in ways he had never needed another human being. It was safe to need her because she would always be there for him.

"Are you all right, Croft?"

"Yes," he said. "I am now." Mercy was safe and the last of the screams left from three years before had faded away forever. The old Circle was closed and a new one lay before him.

"What about Isobel?" Mercy asked reluctantly. "She got away."

"I think she's smart enough to keep going." He saw the package containing *Valley* in her hand. "Don't tell me you managed to save that damn book."

Mercy glanced down. "It came in rather handy a few minutes ago. Isobel got a gun out of the helicopter. She was going to use it on either you or Gladstone or both. I couldn't tell which. I used *Valley* to knock it out of her hand. Worked like a charm."

"Whoever said," Croft observed thoughtfully, his eyes gleaming with relieved amusement, "that that kind of literature has no socially redeeming value?"

Mercy's shaky smile warmed the chilly night.

The first Doberman appeared out of the woods in front of them as they made their way back to where the Toyota was parked. The second dog was sitting beside the car, seemingly guarding it. Both animals went up to Croft, greeting him silently. Mercy watched the moment of silent animal-human communion and groaned.

"Why do I get the feeling I'm going to be buying a lot of dog food in the future?"

Mercy was exhausted by the time they reached Denver. Croft had driven straight through, stopping only to notify the authorities anonymously of the fire and to fill the Toyota's gas tank. When they finally pulled into a motel parking lot, all she wanted was a long hot shower before dinner.

"Do you think the motel clerk will mind us taking two Dobermans into the room?" she asked Croft as she glanced dubiously at the dogs in the back seat.

"I'll speak to the clerk," Croft said blandly. "I'm sure he'll understand."

Mercy wasn't particularly surprised when that proved true. Croft had a way of getting what he wanted.

"I wonder what will become of Isobel," Mercy said during dinner that evening. "That woman gave me the creeps. She is also a twit."

Croft's mouth lifted in genuine amusement. "You have a way of seeing some things in very simple terms, don't you? I think, at the bottom, you and I share a very similar philosophy of life. You're right. Isobel was a twit and Gladstone had a way of attracting twits. As he said, there are always plenty of people out there who are willing to surrender control of their lives to someone else in exchange for a feeling of being unique and important."

"So what do you think will happen to her?"

"I don't know and I don't particularly care." Croft shrugged. "As far as I'm concerned, she was just a nuisance. I was after Gladstone, not her. She knows that, which is why she'll disappear from our lives. I imagine she'll find another employer and become someone else's problem. Sooner or later she's going to wind up in jail or dead. It's inevitable. She's not quite as smart as she should be to have a successful career working for people like Gladstone. She doesn't know the fundamental rule for survival in that kind of job."

"Which is?"

"When to get out."

"Oh." Mercy shivered at the casual way he outlined Isobel's probable future. "You were right about Gladstone or Graves or whatever his name was, Croft. He was an evil, dangerous man."

He looked at her. "I should never have let you get close to him."

"Don't start in on that," Mercy advised. "I didn't give you much choice in the matter."

"If I had been sure from the start that Gladstone was really Graves I could have taken steps to prevent you from coming in contact with him."

Mercy glared at him warningly. "I don't like either the direction this conversation is taking or that look in your eyes."

He blinked owlishly. "What look in my eyes?"

"That one that says, 'I perceive that I may have failed to properly carry out my full and noble responsibility in this particular instance.' A sense of responsibility is all well and good, Croft, but you have a tendency to carry it too far.

What happened on that mountain was not your fault. You saved our lives and Isobel's, too."

"You saved our lives by discovering that tunnel in the vault."

Mercy felt suddenly pleased with herself. "That was clever of me, wasn't it?"

"Of course, you wouldn't have been in that vault in the first place if you had followed my orders." Croft slipped the point of his verbal shaft in smoothly while Mercy was still preening.

Mercy's sense of satisfaction evaporated in the heat of her ire. "You have some nerve to start lecturing me after all I've been through in the past few days."

"What do you think I went through when I saw you get out of the helicopter? You nearly ruined everything."

Mercy chewed on her lower lip, aware of a sudden, enormous weight that felt suspiciously like guilt. She sighed. "I'm sorry, Croft. When they told me you were a prisoner I didn't think I had any choice but to do as they said."

"I know," Croft surprised her by saying. "In your shoes I probably would have done the same."

"No, you wouldn't have done the same," Mercy declared morosely. "You would have thought of some brilliant way to infiltrate the household and rescue me. Which is exactly what you did."

"I think we can safely say that we rescued each other. Let's close the subject, Mercy. I can see that if I give you the lecture you deserve I'm going to have to watch you grovel while I listen to a lot of pathetic, tearful apologies."

Mercy hesitated for an instant, aware that he just might be teasing her. "I'll make a deal with you," she finally said. "No more groveling apologies from me if I don't have to listen to any more heroic claims of full responsibility for allowing me to get into danger in the first place. I can't stand to hear you talk about how you owe me and how you always pay your debts. Agreed?"

He looked at her for a long moment. "You don't want to bind me to you with a debt of honor," he said slowly.

"Is it necessary to hold you that way?" she asked gently.

"No. The truth is, there's nothing you could do to get rid of me."

Mercy smiled brilliantly. "Good." Then she looked at him intently. "Will you want to go back to the kind of work you were doing three years ago?"

"No. That was over long before I met you. It was time for it to be over. That's why I opened the self-defense schools. I knew I needed something else to do with my life. I had spent long enough exploring the side of me that responds to violence. I wanted more time for studying the part that finds pleasure in logic and philosophy and another kind of strength."

"You seem to know yourself so well."

He smiled. "Most of what I'm learning about myself lately I'm learning from you."

"It works both ways, I think. I've learned a few things from you, too." She glanced up. "Here comes the wine I ordered. Just what we need."

Croft watched the waiter pour the two glasses. When the man had left he picked up one glass and turned it slowly in the light, studying the clear red liquid. His eyes were thoughtful—too thoughtful.

Mercy's intuition told her what was going through his head. "You don't have to worry about it, you know," she said.

His gaze rose to meet hers. "Worry about what?"

"About ever getting really drunk again. You're not your father, Croft. You didn't drink too much the night of Gladstone's party; you were drugged. I doubt if you will ever get

genuinely drunk in your entire life, but if you do, one thing's
for sure."

"What's that?"

Mercy smiled as she picked up her own glass. "We know
now you're not a mean drunk like your father was. Lech-
erous and horny, yes, but not mean. Even when you were
high as a kite you were in full control of your dangerous
side."

"There are times, Mercy, when you can be a great comfort." His eyes were not at all remote as he looked at her
over the rim of his glass. They were filled with warmth and
love and a hint of laughter.

"To us," Mercy said, raising her glass to touch his.

"To us."

"Oh, by the way," Mercy began smugly, "I have something to tell you about some microfilm I found in the spine
of *Valley*. My cleverness is going to astound you."

Croft groaned. "I was afraid of that."

It was dawn when Mercy first stirred the next morning.
Without opening her eyes she edged her foot around under
the covers, feeling for Croft's solid presence. The bed was
empty beside her. Perhaps Croft had gone downstairs to take
the dogs out for a morning run. But when an inquiring,
damp nose nuzzled her palm, she knew the dogs were still in
the room.

Mercy finally lifted her lashes and sat up slowly, careful
not to make any undue noise. Croft was where she had
thought he would be at that time of day. He was sitting
cross-legged and motionless near the window, gazing out at
the mountains in the distance. He was wearing his jeans, but
nothing else.

Mercy was grateful Croft had the basic intelligence not to
risk sitting naked on a motel room carpet. There was no
telling what kind of dirt might be imbedded in the rug. The

man had a certain amount of common sense under that rigid code of behavior, after all.

She watched him for a moment, loving the strong, lean shape of him in the early light. Not at all ghostlike, she thought in amusement.

Quietly she got out of bed and reached for her travel robe. The Doberman that had been checking on her went back to settle down beside its companion in the corner. Mercy went into the bathroom without disturbing Croft. When she came back out a few minutes later she knew he was almost finished with his meditation. He hadn't moved, but she sensed the changed level of awareness in him. She was slowly growing accustomed to the subtle link that bound them.

"Good morning," she said quietly and went to stand in front of him.

His expression altered as he looked up at her. The detached quality disappeared, replaced by a direct warmth that sank into her very bones.

"Good morning," he said.

Mercy smiled and sat down across from him, tucking her legs under her in imitation of his own position. "I think it's time we talked."

He smiled slightly. "What about?"

"There are a couple of questions concerning our relationship that remain to be settled."

"Everything is settled, Mercy."

She knew he meant that. She stared at him wonderingly. "Is that right?"

"There will be a period of adjustment, but that's not important. The only important thing is that we're going to be together."

"Are we?" She felt slightly breathless.

"I love you. The Circle of my life wouldn't be complete without you, Mercy."

Glorious relief washed through her. "Oh, Croft, I feel the

same way. I don't know how it could have happened so quickly or so completely, but I know I want to be with you for the rest of my life. I know it in a way I can't fully explain, a way I've never known anything before in my life. But I'm absolutely sure of it. I love you."

"When the pattern is comprehended and accepted and the Circle is complete, everything is as clear and transparent as a watercolor painting. The truth glows with life when it's revealed." Croft reached out and took her hand in his.

He looked into Mercy's eyes as the full light of dawn blazed through the window. His love for her was abundantly clear in the depths of his hazel gaze. He was right, she realized. The truth glowed with life when it was revealed. She felt his fingers tighten around her and knew that the link between them was unshakable. In some way she would probably never be able to fully explain, they belonged together and they both accepted that fact.

The truth glowed between them. Two minds and two realities shimmered, blurred and finally meshed for a dazzling instant of time.

And then the moment of realization was past, locked forever in their hearts and minds.

"There are, naturally, one or two details to be ironed out," Croft said musingly.

Mercy was still feeling slightly dazed by the experience she had just been through. "Details?"

"I understand that you can't move to Oregon. You have to be near your business. That means I'll have to move to Ignatius Cove. That's no problem. I can run my business from anywhere along the coast. But we'll have to find a bigger place closer to the water. There are going to be three dogs, I'm afraid. I've got another one at home. A neighbor looks after him when I'm gone. They'll all need room to run and so do I."

"Well, I expect we'll be able to find something larger than

my apartment." Mercy was feeling very agreeable at the moment.

"I will require a meditation room in our new home, a place that's used for nothing else except contemplation. I'll teach you how to meditate properly. I'll also have to instruct you in the proper selection of tea. I can't be expected to exist on tea bags for the rest of my days. And you'll need painting lessons."

"Anything else?" Mercy asked sweetly.

"We'll probably have to get rid of your television," Croft said, thinking. "I dislike TV. I find the flickering screen disturbing, not to mention the junk that's on the flickering screen. And then there's the matter of your taste in interior design. I realize you like bright colors, but with a little instruction, I think you can be made to appreciate the subtle nuances of more refined shades."

Mercy eyed him dangerously. "Is that the end of the list of your, er, requirements?"

"There are probably some other things that will come to mind. I'll jot them down as I think of them."

"Wonderful. Tell me, what am I going to get out of this relationship?"

He smiled complacently. "You'll be getting a man who will be able to help you control that streak of recklessness in you. A man who will always know what's best for you and who will see to it that you get what you need, even if it's not always quite what you want. You will also be getting a dedicated sex slave who will be devoted to your personal pleasure. What more could a woman ask?"

That did it. Croft's newfound ability to tease her was getting out of hand. Mercy launched herself at him, pushing him backward onto the carpet. He went down easily, his eyes full of wicked laughter. She pinned his arms on either side of his head while she straddled his chest.

"That's enough out of you, sex slave."

"Are you going to assault me again?"

"Darn right, I am."

"Good. Then I suggest we get into a more comfortable position." He moved without any warning, rolling over and pinning her beneath him.

"Croft!" she sputtered, torn between laughter and mock outrage. "Let me up. You're mashing me."

"You're right. This position might be more comfortable for me, but I can see where it could be a little wearing on your sweet tail. This carpet isn't very thick, is it?" He got to his feet, taking her with him.

The room whirled briefly around Mercy and she clung to Croft to steady herself. When everything settled back down she found herself lying flat on the rumpled bed. Croft was already unfastening his jeans. When he stepped out of them she could see that he was fully aroused. The heavy weight of his manhood throbbed with anticipation. He shuddered as he came down beside her and gathered her into his arms. The teasing light vanished from his eyes and was replaced by a far more intense expression.

"I always seem to need you so much," he said in harsh wonder.

"I think I'm losing the initiative in this assault," Mercy whispered. She felt him, hard and impatient against her thigh.

"That's all right," he assured her thickly as he lowered his mouth to her breast. He kissed the budding crest with gentle adoration and then raised his head again. "I'll take care of everything."

"I had a feeling you would," she whispered dreamily. She put her arms around him, stroking the sleek, muscled contours of his back. "Croft, I love you so much."

"I know," he said, his eyes turning to molten gold. "I can sense it and see it every time I look at you or touch you. You can't begin to guess how good it feels to know you're there for me. It's like nothing else I've ever known."

"I can imagine exactly how it feels because I know you're there for me. A very unique feeling, isn't it?"

"An incredible feeling." He buried his face against her throat with a soft groan of desire. Mercy shivered delicately as he drew his palm down between her breasts and over the small curve of her stomach. When he stroked lower she murmured his name softly and lifted herself against his hand. Her hand slipped down to his thigh and she sank her fingers into his hard, muscled buttock.

"*Sweetheart.*"

"Oh, Croft." She trembled again when his touch became more intimate. His fingers probed with exquisite care, finding all the secret, hidden places and making them tingle with need. He touched her until she was wet and warm and aching with her need.

He stroked and caressed until Mercy was twisting in his arms. She touched him just as intimately, holding the heavy heat of him in her palm. When he said her name against her skin and urged her legs apart with his ankle, she clung to him.

"Take me inside you," Croft said in a hot whisper. "I need your warmth. I need to feel you all around me. Silky and smooth and strong. It feels so damn good when I'm inside you, honey."

She parted her thighs for him, pulling him to her with an urgency that matched his own. Carefully, fumbling a little, she guided him to her. He groaned and then he was there, seeking the intimate connection with her body. As always she reacted primitively to his bold, aggressive hardness. It was almost as if her body sought first to challenge and then to welcome and conquer the invader.

For an instant the delicate muscles at the opening of Mercy's soft, feminine sheath tightened in resistance. Croft pushed himself slowly forward, insisting on his right to enter and then, before the resistance could intensify, he withdrew. Her hips lifted immediately in a frantic attempt to retrieve what had been lost. Croft repeated the slow entry, opening the entrance more thoroughly until Mercy cried out at the deliciously exciting sensation. Then he once again withdrew.

The sensual teasing drove Mercy wild. She clutched at Croft, struggling to hold him to her. "Now," she gasped, her teeth at work on his ear. "I need you now."

"You couldn't need me as much as I need you."

Then he was driving slowly and completely into her and she was welcoming him, stretching to encompass him, closing around him, clinging to him. He was locked within her and he held her imprisoned in his arms.

The fierce, driving passion took them to a shatteringly intense climax that seemed to last for endless moments before leaving them adrift in a buoyant sea. Together they floated in each other's embrace as love and morning sunlight warmed them.

It was a long time before Mercy stirred and lifted herself on one elbow to smile down into Croft's eyes. "I think I know what you mean about closing the Circle."

"Do you?" He lifted his fingers to toy with her hair.

"We're a closed Circle, you and I, aren't we?"

"Yes," he said. He pulled her back down into his arms. "You know something? You might make a better student of philosophy than I would have guessed."

"I've been taking lessons from an expert."

"How good are you at walking dogs?"

A Doberman in the corner whined in anticipation as if he had understood Croft's question.

Two months after their return from Colorado, Mercy stood on a short ladder between two towering aisles of used books and waved a feather duster over the tops of the books. A bookseller's work was never done.

As she worked she mentally planned the evening ahead. Croft would be returning soon from the two-day visit to one of his schools in California. She wanted to have something special for him. Something besides the scandalously tiny set of see-through baby doll pajamas she had bought the previous month for their honeymoon.

Fresh shrimp might be nice. With a Caesar salad, perhaps. And a bottle of Chardonnay.

The plans for dinner were falling into place nicely when Mercy sensed she was no longer alone in the shop. The bell over the door hadn't rung, but her feather duster stilled on top of the shelf of books. Mercy smiled to herself.

Croft was back.

She turned her head and there he was, standing at the end of the aisle. Dark and lean and potentially dangerous, but never a threat to her. As usual, he had materialized without a sound, but she knew he was very, very real. He held a package in his hand.

"Croft! I wasn't expecting you for another couple of hours."

He smiled and opened his arms as she clambered down off the ladder and raced toward him with a smile of eager welcome. "I got away early." He kissed her thoroughly before pushing the package into her hands. "Here. This is for you."

"What is it?"

"A gift from Ray Chandler."

"Chandler?" She wrinkled her nose as memory returned. "Oh, yes, your friend. The man whose daughter you rescued from that island. How did you happen to see him?"

"I told you he worked for the government. Not being on overly familiar terms with the various and assorted government authorities, except for Ray, I decided to send him that strip of microfilm you found in *Valley*."

"I wondered what you'd done with it." Mercy was busily unwrapping her package. "But why would he send me a gift? He doesn't know me."

"No, but he's grateful for the gift you gave him."

"The film?" Mercy looked up. "What was on it?"

"A list of names. Some of them were powerful drug merchants with whom Gladstone did business in his earlier incarnation as Graves. The rest were the names of some interesting users."

"Users?"

"Very highly placed people in this country who apparently have a drug habit. It was more than just a list of names. It contained a variety of incriminating evidence against his business associates and the important buyers. Apparently Gladstone had developed the information while he was still known as Egan Graves and kept it as both an insurance policy and a potential source of blackmail. Most of the people on that slip of film are very powerful and virtually untouchable. But the information about them that Gladstone put together might make it possible for the various governmental authorities to identify and neutralize at least some of them."

"Gladstone was trying to rebuild his kingdom."

Croft nodded. "Having that list back would have given him a quick boost up to the status he had once enjoyed."

Mercy finished unwrapping the package. When the nearly perfect first edition copy of Mrs. Beeton's *Book of Household Management* appeared, she laughed aloud. "An appropriate wedding gift for the bride."

Croft frowned. "It's not exactly my field of interest, but I was told it was rare. Something that would attract a lot of interest in a catalog."

"Oh, it definitely will," Mercy said quickly, examining the title page. "It's a first edition, 1861, and it's still in its original cloth binding. Fine condition, too. It's a lovely item. I can't wait to thank your friend Mr. Chandler."

Croft relaxed, smiling indulgently. "He asked how he could thank you and I told him to find you a book you could use to restart your short-lived career as an antiquarian book dealer."

Mercy laughed. "Mr. Chandler must have some interesting resources available to him."

"He does." Croft glanced at his watch. "Ready to go home?"

"I'm ready. We'll have to stop at the store on the way. I want to pick up some fresh shrimp and we need more dog food."

He nodded. "Sounds fine. But then, everything sounds fine around you. Let's go."

"Here, you can lock up." Mercy clutched her new treasure carefully and handed him the keys to the shop. Then she retrieved her purse from behind the counter, opened the door and stepped out onto the sidewalk to wait for him. The bell tinkled cheerfully as the door closed behind her.

Croft looked at her through the glass as he finished checking the back door locks. He still couldn't get over the fact that she was his wife. It sent a wave of elation through him that couldn't be equaled by any other kind of knowledge.

When he finished checking the back door, he opened the front door and walked outside to join Mercy.

As usual, when Croft entered or exited the shop, the bell overhead didn't make a sound.

Croft turned back with a frown. Some old habits were hard to break. "Just a minute, Mercy."

He unlocked the door, went back inside the shop, closed the door and smiled at Mercy through the glass. Then he reopened the door and stepped outside again.

This time he made sure the bell chimed loudly.

"You don't have to prove anything to me, you know," Mercy told him with loving laughter in her eyes. "I never did believe you were a ghost. Just a little hard to pin down at times."

Croft grinned at her and threw an arm around her shoulders to pull her close to his side. Then the grin became a roar of full, masculine laughter that filled the street and Mercy's heart.